I climbed up on t[...]—walked up the entire [...] two-story boat between me and the sun, checking the guards, wards, and alarms as I went.

All were disarmed or disabled.

Not good! Sooner or later the Nasty Things were going to come calling again—I'd come to accept that.

I'd just figured on having a little more time before they found me.

I eased the mud-slimed Glock out of its holster at the small of my back, chambered the first round, and stepped onto the gangplank, finally able to stand erect.

A demon erupted from the doorway leading to the salon on the main deck.

The *New Moon* tilted towards me as the monster's mass doubled, quadrupled, octupled with its transformation into a spelunker's darkest nightmare.

It was vaguely man-shaped—emphasis on "vaguely" —standing somewhat erect upon tree-trunklike legs. Its arms bowed out on either side like a gorilla on steroids and long, sharp claws curved like scimitars from black, leathery fingers. Its thick, shaggy pelt rippled, revealing tectonic plates of muscle. The demon glared down at me with baleful eyes and opened its impossibly wide maw. To say its head looked like a bat's would be about as accurate as saying a Tyrannosaurus rex resembles a gecko.

It paused as it eyed me and then roared: "Where the hell have you been? We've been worried sick!"

Also by Wm. Mark Simmons:

DEAD
EASY

Wm. Mark Simmons

DEAD EASY

A Baen Books Original

Baen Publishing Enterprises
P.O. Box 1403
Riverdale, NY 10471
www.baen.com

ISBN 10: 1-4165-5604-4
ISBN 13: 978-1-4165-5604-6

Cover art by Clyde Caldwell

First Baen paperback printing, December 2008

Distributed by Simon & Schuster
1230 Avenue of the Americas
New York, NY 10020

Library of Congress Cataloging-in-Publication Data:
2007010170

Printed in the United States of America

10 9 8 7 6 5 4 3 2 1

Dead Easy was undertaken during a particularly tumultuous period of events that made the writing of this book far different than the experience I envisioned in the original synopsis and proposal. I'd like to thank the electronic *First Readers Club* whose feedback and supplemental input was most helpful during a period of extraordinary change and limited access to my familiar resources and support. Any errors, inconsistencies, and faults herein are my own.

Richard Acosta, J.J. Brannon, Kyle Carmichael, Benjamin Cock, Thomas Erickson, Erik Fischer, Tracy Fretwell, Tana Hamza, James Hayes, Jack Long, Lee Martindale, Robyn McNees, Greg Normington, Jr., William A. Oates, Porter Peaden, Sanjay Ramamurthy, Anthony D. Rhodes, Dawn Rodriguez, Roger Ross, Brad Sinor, Anthony Stasak, Lynn Stranathan, Jim Wagner

Thanks guys!

Special Thanks also to Clyde Caldwell and Christine Klingbiel for their part in bringing certain characters, past and present, to life.

Finally

This one's for Howard and Jules

You never know who's going to end up in your five.

Ride, Captain, ride upon your mystery ship
On your way to a world that others might have
    missed

> —Skip Konte/Frank
> Konte/Mike Pinira
> *Ride Captain Ride*

I'd like to be under the sea
In an octopus's garden in the shade
He'd let us in, knows where we've been
In his octopus's garden in the shade . . .

> —Ringo Starr
> *Octopus's Garden*

And you tell me over and over and over and over
    again my friend,
Ah, you don't believe we're on the eve of
    destruction.

> —Barry McGuire
> *Eve of Destruction*

And the sea gave up the dead which were in it . . .

> —Revelation 20:13

Chapter One

HERE'S A QUESTION.

Do people wear straightjackets because they're crazy?

Or do they go crazy because they're wearing straight-jackets?

Because I can tell you right now those long-sleeved, buckle-down, canvas kook-shirts are so uncomfortable that you *are* likely to go mad if you're stuck in one for any extended period of time.

I don't know how long I'd been stuck in mine but I'd probably be well on my way to foaming and raving and going absolutely starkers were it not for the drugs. They kept me calm. Relaxed. Even while my own voice was

1

screaming in the back of my head that I was in really deep doo-doo!

Doo-doo . . . ?

Given the normal vocabulary of my fight-or-flight responses, the fact that the voice shouting from my hind-brain was coming up with that word choice *had* to be another side effect of the drugs.

That *and* the inability to stay focused.

Or remember how I got here in the first place.

And: drugs were the only explanation as to why the babelicious Dr. Fand did not command my full attention while she was in the room for our latest session.

Well, more of a cell than a room, actually. With padded walls and recessed lighting and absolutely no windows to permit one to gauge the passing of time. Or weaken loony-town security by giving me something to bang my head against.

I had this warm, fuzzy sense of contentment that my well-being was *so* well looked after.

Or maybe that was the drugs, too. My attention had shifted from my psychiatrist to the cell décor and there was no other adequate explanation for that. Unless I really was as crazy as Dr. Fand professed.

"Not 'crazy,' Mr. Cséjthe . . ." She pronounced my name correctly—"Chay-tay"—but added some little foreign inflection that I couldn't quite attribute to any specific nationality.

". . . a 'psychotic break' is a coping mechanism," she continued. "Your mind was traumatized by the accident, by the deaths of your wife and daughter. You blame yourself because you were driving, because you survived and they didn't . . . "

Maybe the drugs weren't that effective: memories began to burn through my medicated haze like napalm strikes in a thick London fog. Two years had passed since I'd awakened in a morgue next to what was left of Jenny and Kirsten, yet the sudden flash of pain tied to that memory was brisk and sharp.

Like fresh stitches as the anesthesia wears off.

"Your subconscious wrestles with the unfairness of life, the injustices of fate," Dr. Fand went on. "With pain. With regret. It tries to make sense of what seems so senseless. Like a skinned knee, it tries to heal your memories by forming a false skin—a scab, if you will—to insulate the trauma from the rest of your mind. It builds a layer of false memories, creates more acceptable 'realities' for you to inhabit while dealing with your grief and rage."

"Like this one?" I growled, shrugging against the heavy canvas and leather garment that pinned my arms across my body.

"Really, Christopher . . . " She paused. "May I call you Chris?"

"You can call me anything you want; you're the doctor." And my keeper.

And something more that I couldn't quite put my finger on . . .

Perhaps the drugs . . .

"Coyote-ugly" stories are legion. Romantic trysts struck up at a bar with attractive strangers after an injudicious amount of alcohol, leading to sobering morning-after revelations. "Babes" or "studs" reverting to their pre-buzz, unenhanced appearances. And the hung-over temptation to gnaw one's own arm off, coyote-fashion, to facilitate escape without waking the stranger clinging to it like a steel trap.

I wondered if Dr. Fand would look any different after the drugs wore off. She was more of a babe than anyone sober would expect of a psychiatrist. In fact, Doctor F was more of a babe than anyone might produce without the benefits of an airbrush or the latest photo-editing software with all of the graphical plug-ins.

So . . . probably the drugs.

She had blonde hair, so white with silvery highlights that age might have been inferred had any lines begun to etch her flesh. Instead, the corona of platinum hair that was not precisely white and not precisely silver, gave her an ethereal appearance. Her tilted, lavender eyes added an exotic cast to her features. Small nose, wide mouth, skin like porcelain, kiln-fired with attar of rose. She wore a white blouse that seemed tailored to accentuate how her bosom stressed the crisp, not quite opaque fabric. Her abbreviated suit jacket looked more like a bolero vest with sleeves and her matching dark skirt was short enough to show the better parts of her thighs before she sat down on the folding chair she'd brought in for our latest session. If the gems that glittered at her throat and dangled from the peekaboo lobes of her ears were real, then head-shrinking was more likely avocation than primary paycheck. She had to be independently wealthy.

Of course, I might just be the one pro bono case in her life-files of the rich and insaneous. That . . . or it could just be the drugs.

"Let's talk about what's real, Chris."

I dragged my attention back to the conversation.

"Up until the accident you had no difficulty with separating fact and fiction, fable and reality. I imagine that you read fairy tales to your daughter when she was little. Maybe watched monster movies when you were younger. But you understood the difference between make-believe and reality. Until the car crash."

"So . . . you're suggesting brain damage?" I asked.

"Not in the manner of which you speak," she said, crossing her legs in a manner that threatened to re-distract me. "Not a physical injury but emotional trauma." It came to me that she wasn't wearing stockings or hose. "It is as if your mind has drawn upon fable and fairy tale to construct a psychic hedge-maze, a place to wander about, insulated from the harsh realities of a cruel and apparently senseless world."

"So you're saying I've like rearranged my perceptions of reality to . . . to . . . "

Trying to follow a coherent line of thought was like trying to tune in a distant radio station on bad batteries.

". . . um . . . like . . . create an alternate world . . . inside my head . . . "

I needed to keep my responses short. I only had so many functional brain cells. When I wasn't diverting half of them to assist my speech center, I could actually feel my mind starting to clear.

". . . where I can hide from my own pain and loss?" I finished weakly.

She clapped her small, perfect hands in a similitude of delight. "Very good, Chris! I believe that we are starting to make some progress here."

"Progress," I repeated.

"Yes, the first steps toward recovery are anchored in recognizing that one is ill. Denial is counterproductive to therapy and recovery."

"Therapy," I said. "Recovery."

"Yes," she said. "As pleasant as it may be to live in a fantasy, isn't it better to build the sort of a life that we want in the real world?" She looked at me and waited. "Isn't it, Chris?"

My lips were dry and I licked them. "I'm thinking . . ." Not very well yet but enough to know that something was terribly wrong.

Wrong beyond occupying a rubber room with no time sense or idea of how I got here in the first place . . .

"Well," she said, "whether or not we think we're ready to take on all the aspects of a fully actualized personality, we still have responsibilities whether we're ready to acknowledge them or not." She looked at me expectantly.

"As . . . for example . . . ?" was my eventual response.

"Your son."

I groped around in my mental fog for a minute or so. "Will?"

She leaned forward. More distraction: she wasn't wearing a bra, either. "Is that what you've decided to call him?"

Named him? What would she say if I told her we'd actually met during my little trip to New York six months ago? And bonded while cleaning out a Nazi fortress in the Rocky Mountains shortly thereafter? When it came to father and unborn son camping trips, nobody had more merit badges than the Cséjthe clan.

That is not, however, the sort of family business one shares with one's shrink. Particularly when sporting the me-so-crazy line of active wear. I pulled helplessly at the buckled sleeves anchored behind my back. "How long have I been here? Is he born yet?"

She nodded slowly. "Yes. An hour ago. His mother died in childbirth."

I wasn't prepared. "Lupé?" More napalm spattered across my mind, the fog recoiling from its fiery remembrances. "Oh my God!" I choked on a sob but tears would not come. The drugs oozed back and forth in my skull, attempting to quench the flames.

"The important thing is that your son is alive, Chris. He's alive and must be looked after. I have some papers for you to sign so that he *can* be taken care of. You realize that you are in no shape to do that right now. And he would be better off in a foster home than a state orphanage. Don't you agree?" She held up a piece of paper.

The drugs sizzled across the overheated parts of my brain like the tarry sludge of boiled-down coffee at the bottom of the pot. The paper looked more like parchment than an eight-and-a-half by eleven sheet of twenty-pound white bond.

"My son," I whispered.

"And you want what's best for him, of course."

"What's best for him," I murmured.

"But right now you cannot be there for him. He's your responsibility. But you are not well enough, right now, to be responsible." She held up the parchment. "The only responsible thing you can do, right now, is sign over your parental rights to a foster agency so that they can place him with a loving, normal family. At least until you're well enough to return to a normal life for yourself."

I looked down at the floor, my stomach twisting viciously. "You're saying that I cannot take care of my own son."

"Mr. Cséjthe"—it was no longer Chris now—"you are still suffering from a psychotic break. You think that you are a vampire . . ."

My head bobbed up. "I am *not* a vampire!"

"But you said—"

"I am infected with *one* of the two viruses," I continued, locking my eyes on hers, "that combine to create the undead condition. But. I. Am. Not. A. Vampire."

Not yet, anyway.

The suddenness and intensity of my response had startled her. The parchment dropped to the floor and settled near my feet as she held her hands up before her. "All right, Mr. Cséjthe. I apologize for misquoting you. But don't you see? Vampire or half vampire, it all comes down to a similar disconnect."

She picked up another sheet of paper—this one more in line with your typical, office-supply standards. "I've distilled the notes from our previous sessions. Let's revisit your perception of events around and following the accident that killed your wife and daughter." The sheet she consulted looked more like a typewritten report than the slightly curled parchment at my feet.

Perhaps it was the difference in the fonts.

"You say that you passed out while driving because you had been forced to give a blood transfusion to Count Dracula . . ."

"Prince."

She looked up. "I'm sorry, what?"

"Prince," I corrected, "not 'count.' Now you're the one confusing monster movies with reality. Vlad Dracul the Fifth of the Bassarab line was never a count. Back during the fifteenth century he was the prince of Walachia. Some of the more popular sources identify him as Vlad III: there's a bit of historical confusion over the Bassarab Vlads II through V—which was 'Tepes' and which was 'Tsepesh'; Daddy 'Drakul' and progeny '-ula.' In terms of his own position in the family line, he invokes 'the fifth.' But, whatever the number, he was a prince. And I can assure you that he takes umbrage whenever the popular entertainments demote him."

Umbrage. They were getting sloppy with the pharmaceuticals: the medication was definitely wearing off.

Her smile was small and sad. "Again, Mr. Cséjthe, take a mental step back and try to consider your own words from anyone else's perspective." Her eyes flicked down to the transcript of our previous session. "You say that the virus that turns the living into the undead is actually a—" she stumbled a little here "—combinant supervirus. That this supervirus is made up of two lesser viruses."

I nodded. "One resides in the blood of a vampire, the other in the saliva. Each has its own effects on the human host. Stoker chronicled some of the effects on those victims who were initially bitten but not immediately drained or killed. He did not, however—nor did anyone else that I know of—document the effects of the blood-borne virus without the combinant effect of the salivary pathogens. We know that a vampire makes another like himself by infecting his victim with both viruses through the bite *and* the commingling of blood."

She shook her head. "Bram Stoker wrote novels. Fiction. Entertainments. Though I must say, Mr. Cséjthe, your imagination would serve you very well if you turned it to inventing stories for readers of a certain bent. Alas, it does not serve you by redrawing your own perceptions of reality, it only does you harm.

"But—" she held up her hand as I opened my mouth again "—let me continue. You believe that, as a result of this transfusion, your blood is now infected with *one* of the two viruses and this makes you allergic to sunlight and garlic but gives you increased strength and speed and the ability to heal faster than normal people." She looked up. "Did you notice your own words, here? *Normal* people. You acknowledge that what you are describing falls outside of the boundaries of normalcy. Of reality."

My inner English major joined hands with my stubborn streak. "The words 'normal' and 'real' are not interchangeable, Doctor. Something can be real without being normal."

"You have no fangs," she continued, ignoring me. "You claim to have met other creatures of myth and fable since the accident. You believe that your lover, the mother of your newborn son, is a werewolf. That a three-thousand-year-old Egyptian sorcerer resurrected the bodies of your deceased wife and daughter and possessed them with demonic spirits. That the four-hundred-year-old countess—" she glanced up to see if I would correct her use of titles "—Elizabeth Báthory, tried to bind the spirits of the voodoo gods and bring about the end of the world."

"Actually," I corrected, "it was the demoness Lilith, masquerading as Erzsébet Báthory. And the *voudon* spirits are properly referred to as *loa*, not gods."

She made a little noise and returned to her reading. "You now believe that you can talk to the dead. That your blood is now further infected with mummy serum—"

"Tanna leaf extract . . ."

"Mmm hmm. And, in addition to human blood you say you've tasted the blood of a werewolf, an angel, and a demon—"

"Actually, it was the blood of a human host who was possessed by a demon at that particular moment and I'll just stop talking now," I said as she gave me a look over the top of her printout.

"—and that the infamous Nazi doctor, Josef Mengele," she continued, "or his clones—injected you with thousands of tiny machines called nane—nun—"

"Nanites. And we're probably talking millions, now."

"—microscopic machines that infect your preternatural flesh in new, mysterious and unknown ways. That you have died and lived as a ghost for a couple of days. That you are able to bloodwalk—" She looked up. "How does that work, again?"

"The Wendigo taught me how to enter another vessel through a chakra-point and possess their body for a time."

She nodded. "The Wendigo. I see. How about a demonstration, then? Prove it by possessing me." She smiled another sad smile. "Go ahead."

I exhaled and shook my head. "The chakra entry only works on lower forms of animal life. Well, I've only used the chakra technique with a wolf, actually. To possess a higher life-form, I have to enter the host through their blood. That's why it's called bloodwalking."

Her smile grew sadder. "Mr. Cséjthe, if you think I'm going to injure myself to provide blood for your delusional claims, you are sadly mistaken." She returned to the paper. "You count among your friends, some zombies that live—" she glanced up but I didn't say anything, "—in the graveyard next to your former residence, a fortune-teller whom you claim to be the 'real deal,' another woman who now runs the detective agency that you started up a year or so back. Which would sound normal except that you claim that her dead nephew also works for the both of you. Then there's an ancient, Central American bat-headed demon—"

"Camazotz," I said, nodding. "Though I wouldn't call him a friend, exactly. More of a stalker/would-be disciple."

"I suppose that would be difficult: maintaining a friendship with a demon *and* an angel," she said archly.

"Who? Mikey? To tell the truth, I'm not sure whose team he plays for or whether he's a free agent. Most days I suspect it doesn't really matter."

Apparently Dr. Fand didn't think it mattered, either. "And a two-headed woman," she finished as if I hadn't spoken at all.

I cleared my throat. "You left out Billy Bob Montrose and J.D."

"Another vampire and the ghost of yet another one." She sighed. "What would be the point?"

"Just trying to keep the record as accurate as possible. So, I guess I should also point out that Deirdre isn't technically a two-headed woman. She is a woman who has temporarily acquired a second head."

Dr. Fand's eyes widened but retained a weary cast as she asked, "And the distinction being?"

I shrugged beneath the confines of my straightjacket. "A 'two-headed' woman implies that both heads are actually hers to begin with."

Dr. Fand tossed the sheet of paper aside and it, too, wafted down to the floor. The second page still looked like paper while the first page still looked like parchment. Maybe it wasn't the drugs, after all.

"I had hoped that the antipsychotics that we've administered would give you some moments of clarity. Can you not see how ridiculous your version of the past two years sounds? Vampires, zombies, demons, cloned Nazis? No judge is going to grant you custody of a child that you have no legal claims to. You had not cohabited with Ms. Garou even long enough to meet the definitions of a common-law union." She got up and reached down for the parchment on the floor near my feet. "So, do what's best for your son, Mr. Cséjthe. Sign the papers that will ensure a good foster home for your son. Don't send him off to a state orphanage."

I twitched my right foot as she picked up the form in question and she was back and out of reach in the blink of an eye.

"Why do you care, Doctor?" I asked slowly. "What is my son to you?"

"I'm human," she answered. "Is it so strange that I should care as to what happens to an innocent child? And you are my patient. I don't think that we can properly start your treatment and recovery while you are tied to outside problems and presumed obligations. So, let's get you back on the road to sanity, Mr. Cséjthe. Sign the paper."

I smiled a crooked grin. " 'Sign, sign, sign!' they said. 'Sign, King John, or resign instead!' "

Her hand fluttered to her chest. "I beg your pardon?"

"Look, Doc—may I call you 'Doc'?—I realize that a crazy person isn't going to think too rationally, especially when loaded up on drugs that turn one's head into a Chia planter. So, it's no wonder that I'm having trouble figuring a couple of things out, here. Maybe, if you could help me sort them out, it would make sense to do your Magna Carta thing."

"Well—"

"First of all, you say I'm having a psychotic break, designed to substitute a kinder, gentler reality for the big, bad, real world. If true, wouldn't I come up with something more pleasant than being infected with a necrotic virus that is slowly turning me into a monster?"

"Well, I—"

"And wouldn't I construct better fates for my family than to have their bodies desecrated and possessed by the dark sorceries?"

"That—well—"

"You see, I just don't understand how this 'coping mechanism,' as you describe it, would set me up with a perceived reality, populated with monsters and such, when *that* is far worse than what you say is the normal reality. In this so-called protective fantasy, my wife and daughter are still dead, I'm a monster, and the world is a far worse place than I ever imagined before. So, I have to wonder, Dr. Fand. Where did you get your training? 'Psychiatry for Dummies'?"

Her violet eyes flashed fire and she drew herself up to a height that did not seem possible for her diminutive frame. "There's no need to insult my intelligence!"

"Why not? You're insulting mine!"

"The science of the human mind is not a simple matter and I hardly expect you to understand the complexities of your own case in a few short sessions, Mr. Cséjthe!"

"In other words, you're the doctor so shut up and do as you say." I shook my head. "Are you a lawyer, too, Doc? See, the other thing that bothers me is how you're so keen for me to sign over my son. Never mind the fact that you've raised the threat of state orphanages—an institution rendered extinct by family services and the foster care system nearly a century ago. No, you see, the signing of a paper presupposes some sort of transfer of rights—yet you've just told me that I have no legal claim on my son. If no judge will recognize my relationship with my son's mother, how will signing a paper serve any purpose? Especially by a guy who's not in his right mind. I believe the phrase is *non compos mentis* and we're not talking the 'Freshmaker mints' here." My eyes flicked from hers to the parchment in her clenched fingers. "So what is the point of paperwork if we're operating outside of the courts? And I gotta ask myself: why would a shrink traffic in black market babies?"

She stared back at me, her face colorless. "You must realize that you are quite mad."

"Mad? Lady, I'm so pissed it's going to take years of anger management sessions to dial me back down to moderately hostile! The drugs were pretty effective at first but my metabolism has had time to adjust. I've been able to think a little more clearly of late. And—while I wish to God the past two years really were a delusion or a dream—your *One Flew Over the Cuckoo's Nest* performance just doesn't convince."

"You question my credentials? You're not a psychiatrist!"

"No. I'm an English teacher." *Was an English teacher.* Who gave exams. *And time for her to take one of mine . . .*

"American and World Lit," I babbled on. "Not so much a scholar of Jung and Maslow. More a scholar of Shakespeare. A very savvy shrink, the Bard. Wrote this little treatise called *Hamlet*. Now I know what you're going to say: When B.F. Skinner talks, people listen. But if you listen to the depressed Dane, brooding around Elsinore castle, he comes up with some very effective self-therapy."

"I don't know what you're babbling about!" she said irritably.

I sat back and stared at her. "Time's up. Put down your pencil and close your booklet."

"What?"

"The test's over. You flunk."

She arched a wispy eyebrow but I could tell her temper was starting to fray badly. Even if she'd had the training, she would have lacked the discipline. "I don't think you're qualified to administer state psychiatric boards, Mr. Cséjthe."

I arched right back at her. "Bet I could fake it better than you, though."

Her smile showed more teeth than tolerance. "What would be the point of such a bet?"

I leaned forward. "How about this bet? I'm betting the sum total of your credentials as a Freudian are a couple of wet dreams and a soggy cigar."

Her face went white. The crumpling parchment in her fist looked positively ethnic in contrast. "Churl!" Her hair began to stand away from her head like a static cloud. "You dare to speak vulgarities—"

I had her, now. Just another little push or two . . .

"Wanna hear my analysis, Doc? If I *should* call you 'Doc.' I think you're some kind of schizo-ceramic. That's shrink terminology for 'crackpot.' "

The parchment in her hand suddenly burst into flame and her violet eyes began to glow with an unearthly light.

"Um," I said, feeling the overheated parts of my brain go cold, "I was betting on you being FBI. Maybe Homeland Security. Guess I was wrong. Wasn't last year's tax audit after all, huh?"

"If you will not give me what I want, then I shall simply take it when I will!" She floated up off the floor, a nimbus of lavender light flickering around her. "Then you will come to us, begging to do our will!"

I got up, too, though a little less elegantly and a lot less otherworldly. "Why wait?" I growled. "Let's negotiate now!" I ran at her and head-butted her into the padded door. Which flew open and the two of us continued our momentum across the hall and into a less-yielding wall.

She appeared to be doubly surprised: first, that I *would* do such a thing and second, that I *could* do such a thing. That she could appear surprised at all and not totally unconscious from the dent she made in the wall was not a good thing. Women who levitate and glow and cause things to spontaneously combust are not to be messed with. You take them down and out immediately or the amount of living-to-regret-it may be short-time and intense.

She threw out her hand in a gesture and uttered something in an unintelligible language. There was no misinterpreting the echo-chamber quality in her voice, though. A wind sprang up and I felt tingly all over.

Other than that, nothing.

And that seemed to surprise her all the more.

In any kind of a fight it's those half-second hesitations that can make all of the difference. I pushed up against her and grabbed her ear with my teeth. "Any chance you watched *The Silence of the Lambs* for your homework, Doc?" I mumbled around and into her ear. "Unless you want me to go all Hannibal Lector, I suggest you start unbuckling me!"

Then I noticed something as she squirmed against me . . .

No, not that.

Not those, either.

I'd gotten my incisors through her tresses and latched onto the upper crest of her ear. I eased my tongue out to verify the configuration as she bellowed: "Setanta!"

Crap! Assuming the other side was a match, she had *pointed ears*!

"Setanta!" she shrieked. The next shriek was less intelligible as she twisted and my tongue slipped, giving her a full-bore wet willie.

I broke my "hold" and we exchanged looks of horror.

A huge guy wearing leather and a baroque, oversized mullet appeared at one end of the hall. He took one look and started to run toward us.

I whirled and ran in the same direction—away from him, that is.

I wasn't going to get very far. Major Mullet had longer legs and the thews of an Olympic decathlete. ("Thews"? *Had* to be the drugs . . .) I, on the other hand, had no clue regarding the layout. And the faster I tried to run while wearing a straightjacket, the more likely I was going to end up body-surfing on a waxed floor.

And again, there was the handicap of the drugs.

But I was short on options so I ran . . .

Sheet-rocked corridors gave way to flag-stoned floors and rock-faced tunnels. Glowing patches of lichen and phosphorescent fungi replaced fluorescent tubes. I had to slow my pace as the hallway became an earthen tunnel with odd bits of root and stone projecting out into my path.

Okay. I was underground.

Add in pyrokinesis, pointed ears, and levitating ladies and it wasn't a total leap to figure I was inside a faerie mound. Except: one, I had no idea what the inside of a faerie mound was supposed to look like. And: two, there were no such things as faeries.

Or vampires or werewolves, right?

A human woman could still have exotic, upturned eyes and even pointed ears—if the genetic mutations parsed just right. But levitation, psychokinesis, and creating purple glows out of thin air? Too bad I was a total white belt in the dojo of elf-defense.

I staggered against a wall, spun around the bend, and fell to my knees. Except my knees never quite touched the ground. The Mullet had me by one of the leather straps across the back of my laughing jacket.

"The time grows too short for such nonsense," he hissed, jerking me back so that I slammed into the brick wall. The leather-clad brick wall that was his chest, that is. He spun me around and seized my throat, lifting me off the ground.

My lungs immediately went into overdrive but there was no more air coming *or* going. And not a lot of blood, either. My eyes went into screen-saver mode and my brain began the shutdown sequence to hard-drive hibernation. I tried kicking but my legs seemed weak and unresponsive. My arms and hands spasmed painfully and, far away, I heard a distant oath.

And felt the floor.

Against my face.

My vision blurred back from reddish black enough to see the goon "Doctor" Fand had sicced on me. He was standing a few steps back and looking back at me with a frown that was two parts speculation and one part consternation.

I pushed myself up from the floor. It would have been nice to lie there a little longer—just until the tidal wave of nausea washed back out to sea—but this Setanta guy didn't look like the type to give extended time-outs. I flattened my hands like blades of flesh and struck a tai chi pose hoping my opponent had seen just enough kung fu flicks to be intimidated.

He was intimidated, all right. "How?" he asked. "How did you do that?"

I wasn't about to tell him the Glenwood Community Health Center offered evening classes in Tai Chi or Eastern Meditation Techniques. And then I suddenly understood why he was so impressed.

My arms were free.

The closed sleeves were torn open at the ends and the leather straps that buckled behind my back were shredded and hanging in tatters.

No wonder he had backed up. Hell, even I was impressed!

"You—you're not human!" He took another step back.

"Oh, I get it," I said, "*she's* the brains and *you're* the brawn. It's all so *clear* now."

"Nobody tells me anything!" he groused.

"Maybe if you didn't have this whole *Dog the Bounty Hunter* vibe going on, people would take you a little more seriously."

He stopped backing up. He tilted his head and fixed me with a look I can only describe as "distant." Ditto the voice: "What did you call me?"

He didn't look offended. He seemed . . . thoughtful.

His face lacked the tilted-eye exoticism that set Fand apart from ninety-eight percent of the human race. Likewise, the retro-hippie headband that tamed his reddish blonde Jheri curl 'do, revealed ears that were rounded in such a way to eliminate elven DNA from the suspect list. Never mind the fact that he was a foot taller than me and a hundred pounds heavier—all muscle: if he was human I should be able to take him. Laying aside the issue of my virally-enhanced strength, a single scratch would be sufficient to initiate a bloodwalk and go riding around inside his brain pan. Then he would be my bitch and we'd see about discouraging any future kidnapping plans involving me or my family.

That which does not kill me makes me angrier.

But then The Mullet screamed two words: "Your *eyes!*" And, whirling about, ran back the way he'd come.

Well, that worked, too, I guess.

"Heh," I said, watching him go. "What a maroon!" I reached behind me and started working on the remaining buckles and straps, singing under my breath: "Vampire-man, vampire-man; friendly, neighborhood, vampire-man, / Is he strong? Listen, bud: he's got necrophage-mutant blood! / Look out! Here comes—"

My musical improvisation came to a screeching halt as I got a good look at my hands. My fingernails had suddenly turned into inch-long talons!

Razor-sharp, inch-long talons!

Silvery, shiny, razor-sharp, inch-long talons!

I reached out and tentatively scratched at a piece of stone embedded in the tunnel wall.

The rock flaked and crumbled like badly cast Styrofoam.

I double-checked, just to make sure. Yep: limestone substrate and harder than any chunk of premium 4400 concrete you were likely to find.

I looked back down at my undamaged, stone-cutting, extendable talons. "Grandma," I murmured, "what big claws you have."

No wonder The Mullet had stopped chasing me: I'd just pulled a double Freddy Krueger and without any gloves!

Then I remembered: it wasn't my hands that had made him scream and flee in terror . . .

It was my eyes.

        ᴧᴧ   ᴧᴧ   ᴧᴧ

I didn't know much about faerie mounds in the theoretical sense (and nothing at all from the practical). I did
remember enough poetry and fable from undergraduate
coursework in Medieval and Romantic Lit to recall that
they sometimes housed entire armies, if not cities.

Not exactly the case here.

Wandering back along the now-deserted corridor I
discovered that I had been incarcerated in the underground equivalent of a Winnebago. All I had seen, up
until my escape, was the inside of a padded cell. I had
never actually observed anyone but Fand and the guy
sporting the achy-breaky coiffure during my confinement. At least not that I remembered. And, all in all,
there were maybe three more rooms—one of them
sleeping quarters for two.

Everything had the look of a cot and bare walls, temporary setup for short-term occupancy. Which explained
how they were able to evacuate so fast and leave nothing
of apparent value behind.

Except the rest of my clothing and personal effects.

By the time I found these, my mystery-alloy, press-on
nails had disappeared. This made buckling on my fanny
holster so much easier. But, as I checked the magazine
and seated my Glock 20 under my shirttail, I was faced
with a minor dilemma. I wasn't sure which was more
disturbing: that ten incredibly hard and sharp metallic
knives had sprung out of my fingertips without explanation or warning—or that they had disappeared again
without rhyme or reason.

A more thorough search of the premises was out of
the question as my captors might be on their way back

with reinforcements. The more distance I put between this place and me, the soonest, the bestest. With or without Swiss army digits, an automatic handgun loaded with silver-tipped dumdums has its limitations.

And such were no damn good against sunlight, which my newly retrieved watch said was on its way in a few hours.

I found an exit and emerged from a hillock in back bayou country.

It was dark. Not that I didn't expect darkness but it was the kind you only find far from human habitation and the electrical grid. The moon was high in the sky and the color of blood. Its uncertain light lent a dim tint of dread to the shadows that seemed to writhe just beyond the edge of my vision.

I took a moment to do a three-sixty scan of my surroundings. Then did another turn, running a check in the infrared spectrum. No heat signatures. The entire area appeared to be devoid of life. Which was both reassuring and discomforting.

I pulled out my cell phone, a long shot at best as it hadn't seen a charger in—how long? Yup: dead as a doornail. These past two years I'd learned that "dead" has all sorts of relative meanings when it comes to biological organisms. But you could always count on the steadfastness of technology dependent on batteries: dead really does mean dead.

I tucked it back away and took another look 'round at the horizon. Without knowing where I was, directions—north, south, east, west—were meaningless. Better to find indications of human habitation—city, town, farm, road—and head toward that.

As I said, it was dark and far removed from the artificial lights of human influence. So far removed that there were no lights visible in any direction from where I stood, even on the distant horizon.

And, of course, no signs on the ground around me of anyone's comings or goings.

Great.

In old movie serials and pulp thrillers the classic death-trap usually comes equipped with all sorts of technology: sliding doors, lasers, conveyer belts, spike-lined pits, vats of acid. Where's the menace in a long walk home?

In the past two years a three-thousand-year-old Egyptian necromancer, an ancient Babylonian demon, cloned Nazis, cybernetic monsters, vampire assassins, and a female dhampir had tried to do me some ultimate harm. Their best efforts had failed. But if I didn't get home before dawn it would make little difference. My sensitivity to solar radiation had increased over the past six months. Since I was only "half-undead" it would probably take me twice as long to burn to a pile of ashes as a full-fledged vampire.

But the end result would be the same.

Just more painful.

I started with a slow steady jog, hoping I was headed toward rather than away from civilization and negotiable transportation. And something to drink.

I was very, very *thirsty*.

Chapter Two

AS I CROSSED over the Ouachita River riding shotgun in a Ford pickup truck, the sun was just minutes away from marking me as "target acquired." We made an illegal turn and, after a series of unnerving switchbacks, found the unmarked exit and skidded onto a gravel service road.

"You're going to have to drive a little faster," I told Dennis, a heavy-set young man wearing a "Ducks Unlimited" camo cap.

"I don't know where I'm going," he answered pleasantly. "I hit a rut or take a curve wrong, we'll roll." He didn't sound too worried.

"Maybe," I told him. "But if the sun arrives before we do, no amount of detailing is going to salvage the inside of your cab. Trust me."

"I trust you," he said, his voice still disconnectedly pleasant and detached from such trivial concerns as massive blunt force trauma and fiery immolation. His foot pressed down on the accelerator.

I had miscalculated the time and distance factors, discarding the alternate options of going-to-ground before going home. After three months of captivity I wasn't too keen on going all snoozy and vulnerable without allies around me. I needed to know the truth about Lupé. And whether Will, Jenny, and Kirsten had been born yet.

I shook my head: I needed to focus on the immediate problem at hand. Doing the orange-barrel polka on a twenty-mile stretch of bad road had put us seriously behind my original ETA. And I needed to stay focused on my driver in order to keep him focused on his driving.

The trick with vampiric mind control is to sufficiently bend the subject to your will while leaving them enough autonomy to perform the more sophisticated tasks. Maybe it served some plot point in the old fright flicks to have some mindless drone shuffle around the castle croaking "Yes, master." And doubtless there are fanged pervs who get off on doing the whole control freak on some long-necked honey down in their crypt even today. But when it comes to racing the sun down back roads and across not-so-open fields? Trust me: it's better to let the driver make most of the judgment calls.

I was clutching my shoulder harness, the dashboard, the door grip, and bracing against the cab's ceiling in alternating patterns like frenetic genuflections of religious frenzy as we bounced and spun and revisited iconic moments from all seven seasons of *The Dukes of Hazzard*.

At least it was keeping my mind off of the cramping hunger pains that kept drawing my eyes to his neck.

Just get home . . . just get home . . . , my mind chanted.

I periodically called out directions while he smiled and executed hair-raising stunt maneuvers. All the while continuing to chatter about the Book of Revelations and how all the signs pointing to the "End Times" were nearly in place.

I let him chatter. If he ended up going either too fast *or* too slow, it would definitely be the end times for one Christopher L. Cséjthe. And, as I said, it's best to keep 'em pointed in the direction you want and give 'em their head.

Forget the old *Dracula* Univérsal Pictures' black-and-whites or Hammer/Seven Arts colorfests. Unless the necrophagic virus that transforms the living into the undead has done a tour of *your* frontal lobes, this whole mental domination thing probably sounds a lot simpler than it really is.

For example, after hiking through miles of underbrush—not to mention a significant amount of overbrush—I finally did make it to a dirt road. And eventually flagged down a ride. You think it's easy getting someone to stop and pick up a stranger on a back road at three am? Not even Bela Lugosi, standing out in the middle of the road, doing the bulgy-eyed, hand-wavey thing, could have managed that.

Especially Bela Lugosi, standing out in the middle of the road, doing the bulgy-eyed, hand-wavey thing.

No, this guy stopped because he was a decent, God-fearing, Good Samaritan.

Who seemed to think that the recent spate of earth-quakes around the world, flu pandemics, volcanic erup-tions, wars and rumors of wars—not to mention a blood-red moon for the past couple of weeks—indicated that Yahweh was texting a very special visit in His celestial BlackBerry.

I guess my chauffeur figured it couldn't hurt to squeeze in a few, last-minute good deeds on the way to the Rapture. I refrained from asking whether he was an adherent of the pre-Trib, mid-Trib, or post-Trib doc-trinal flight plan. He seemed a little busy as we spun off of the road and across a series of fields for the final lap.

We made it with just moments to spare.

The golden fingers of dawn were groping through the trees across the river as we skidded to a stop next to a low stone wall. A cemetery lay just beyond. I jumped out and turned to my driver. "Thanks, Dennis. I really appreciate the ride." I tossed a couple of twenties on the seat. "Hey, man; look at my eyes . . ."

He did. He was very accommodating—had been nothing but since stopping to pick me up.

"You're going to turn around now, drive back to the highway, head for home, and crawl into bed. When you clock back in to your job this evening, you'll be able to tell all your buddies how you stopped to help a van full of cheerleaders with engine trouble and got distracted. Very distracted." I intensified the look I was giving him, pouring my will into his head through his eyes. "That's *all* you will remember. *I* do not exist. This *place* does not exist. Do you understand?"

He nodded, smiling. "Cheerleaders! Did I get lucky?"

"What?" The windshield was beginning to reflect a broken orange thread limning the tree line. "Oh. Yeah. Sure. Why not? You got lucky."

His smile grew. "How lucky?"

I didn't have time for this. Neither did he if Judgment Day was, indeed, just around the corner. "PG-Thirteen lucky. And if you ask any more questions they won't be cheerleaders, they'll be nuns. Elderly nuns. Buh-bye." I slammed the door and hopped the low stone wall that marked the boundary of the old graveyard. Beams of golden death began to slice through the distant woods. I heard the truck take off as I stumbled and wove between tumbled tombstones and mossy monuments. I vaulted another low wall on the far side.

And then I was running past the remains of my house.

⋀⋀⋀   ⋀⋀⋀   ⋀⋀⋀

No banking institution in Northeast Louisiana will touch me when it comes to a home loan. I can't get homeowner's insurance for love or money. I can hardly blame them. I mean, who else moves into two different houses and utterly destroys each within the first year?

Rock stars excluded, that is.

In my own defense, how many other homeowners have fanged enforcers, cybernetic juggernauts, paramilitary black-ops squads, lycanthropic lynch mobs, and undead assassins dropping by to collect the reward for the mortgage holder's untimely passing?

Add fire elementals to that list, I thought, as I ran around the scorched cinder pit that once was my basement. Someone had taken the game to a whole new level a couple of months back and sent something very ancient and other-worldly after me. Not that vampires aren't other-worldly, you understand. But, while the undead inhabit a different zip code than the rest of humanity, fire elementals dwell in a separate time/space continuum. At least they do until one shows up on your front porch one night and tries to wrap you in its fiery embrace. Then it's all Elvis Karaoke Hour with multiple refrains of "hunk-a hunk-a burning love."

But that's another story.

A patch of sunlight fell upon my shirt and I felt my chest grow warm. I had maybe thirty seconds before I was on my way to matching the ash and charred stubble décor of my former domicile. Putting on a burst of speed, I reached the end of the front yard, passed the stairs leading down to the dock some thirty feet below and just jumped off the edge of the bluff.

I had counted on my altered physiology to keep me from breaking my legs on the landing.

I hadn't counted on the mud to cushion the impact.

Or sink me in up to my knees at the water's edge.

The wooded bluffs on the far side of the river put this stretch of the bank into enough shadow that I had a few extra minutes before the sun found me. I looked up and over at my new residence, moored at the dock just some forty feet away.

The *New Moon* was an eighty-four-foot-long, double-decker houseboat.

I'd thought that living aboard a boat would be confining but, so far, it had proven just the opposite.

I had plenty of room.

For now.

Lupé was hiding out down in New Orleans until our son was born. After that? Well, the last time she deigned to speak to me she made it clear that she wouldn't be coming back anytime soon.

And maybe never if Fand was to be believed.

I pushed that thought away immediately. I'd been deceived and lied to on so many levels that there was no point in borrowing trouble until I got the facts. Focus on the known problems: if—*when*—she returned, we'd need nursery space for three. Mengele had cloned my dead wife and daughter and I'd managed to retrieve their cryogenically suspended fetuses before his compound and labs were destroyed. Now they were incubating away in surrogate wombs and would have a second chance at life. In fact, stepmother, half sister, and Will were due to be delivered within a week to ten days of each other.

I could never mock *The Jerry Springer Show* again.

Deirdre was down in New Orleans until the Theresa Kellerman situation was resolved. She also claimed that she was providing security for Lupé and "the kids." I suspected she wanted a front-row seat on whether or not my ex-fiancée and I would reconcile. Suki had returned to Seattle.

The house had ended up being too big for me and Zotz before the fire elemental showed up and performed the ultimate house warming. Rebuilding with an eye toward permanence seemed an exercise in futility as long as all of the wrong people knew where I lived.

Still, the boat was just a temporary fix. Once my son—and my formerly dead wife and daughter—were born, I was going to have to revisit the real estate market.

Or, to quote the insightful and prescient Chief Brody: we were going to need a bigger boat.

I was hopeful, anyway.

But I refused to dwell on the intermediate future right now. Thoughts like that could wait until I was emotionally insulated with antidepressants—my own prescriptions, not potluck from the faerie pharmacy. Bigger boats and hopeful reconciliations could wait. Right now, here in the immediate future, I needed a rope and a tow as I struggled to free myself from the knee-deep muck.

Preternatural strength was of little help: there was nothing to pull or push against. I had no leverage. Working one leg half out of the muck forced the other in more deeply.

And a guillotine blade of sunlight was easing down the face of the cliff behind me with every passing minute.

I flopped backward, spreading my weight across the surface of the mud and tried backstroking my way out. It was slow and ungainly but it provided some traction and my legs eventually popped free with wet, sucking sounds.

The sun was now high enough that I could no longer stand without doing my sulfur match-head impression. I rolled over and began to creep, on hands and knees, toward my floating sanctuary.

A couple of months ago I probably wouldn't have tried so hard.

All those crappy vampire novels make the fanged nightlife seem romantic and exotic—a real panacea for the mundane, nine-to-five, dronelike existence that plagues so many of the still-warms. Well, here's a news flash for all the blunt-toothed wannabes: the reason ninety percent of the undead don't survive their first year and master vampires rarely attain age spans of a century or more?

Suicide.

Those that don't go rogue and get hunted down by their own kind usually end up making some kind of dumb-shit mistake with death-wish underpinnings. That or engage in a deliberately willful act of self-sabotage.

Fearless vampire hunters, stakes, holy water, cloves of garlic, crossbows, and crucifixes—much further down the list on the undead actuary tables.

Why is cheating death such a downer you ask?

Well, first of all, no one actually ever cheats Death. It's not logistically possible. Death owns the poker table and the deck, marks the cards, and has been dealing multiple hands since before your ancestors crawled out of the primordial oceans and climbed up into the trees to begin with. You know all that nonsense about knowing "when to hold 'em and when to fold 'em"? The house odds are unbeatable and inescapable. The only workable strategy to shortcut Death is dying. As long as you're alive Death can screw with you. Semi-alive, undead—Death gets that much more time and opportunity to toy with you and on a much more cosmic scale. Drs. Mooncloud and Burton, even Mama Samm, say it's the combination of my meds and the depression talkin' here. But I'm tellin' ya: forget all the attractive come-ons of the Goth lifestyle. All you have to look forward to is the unrelieved horror of a cold eternity. Without love. Without warmth. Without light. Killing to live. Living without purpose except to kill.

Undead is a sucky existence.

Thirty feet.

I was luckier than most, I suppose. I was still half human. Perhaps I still had half a soul. I wasn't totally dependent on blood. Yet. And having money and owning a blood bank meant that I didn't victimize anyone. Directly. With the exception of those occasional little "accidents" . . .

Twenty feet and I had to drop and crawl on my belly another ten to reach the New Moon's shadow.

But my wife and my daughter were dead because of me. My lover had left me. I could practically count on my fingers all of the people who *didn't* want to kill me or turn me into some science-project-of-the-damned . . .

So I had taken to popping Prozac and Paxil like Skittles (. . . taste the rainbow . . .) and had numbed down to the point where I was just playing a waiting game. Either Lupé and I were going to get back together and this half-life I had cobbled together would start to feel like it was worth all the bother again . . .

Or not.

And then we'd see which would catch up to me first: my enemies or the consequences of not seeming to care too much.

About anything.

Apparently my not-so-normal metabolism made me resistant to the beneficial as well as the detrimental effects of drugs and pharmaceuticals. Hell, if it hadn't been for this brand new threat to my soon-to-be-born son, I'd probably still be sitting on a rock about fifty miles back, humming "Here comes the sun, little darlin' . . . "

But however worthless I felt my own twilight existence, fatherhood involves obligations—even in the womb. Literally or figuratively, now was not the time to be a deadbeat dad.

I climbed up on the walkway to the pier and duck-walked up the entire span to keep the silhouette of my two-story boat between me and the sun, checking the guards, wards, and alarms as I went.

All were disarmed or disabled.

Not good! Not surprising, either. Sooner or later the Nasty Things were going to come calling again—I'd come to accept that. Even anticipate it.

I'd just figured on having a little more time before they found me.

I eased the mud-slimed Glock out of its holster at the small of my back, chambered the first round, and stepped onto the gangplank, finally able to stand erect.

A demon erupted from the doorway leading to the salon on the main deck.

For the briefest of moments it appeared to be human but, as it left the confines of the man-sized hatchway, it expanded to inhuman size and proportions. The *New Moon* tilted towards me as the monster's mass doubled, quadrupled, octupled with its transformation into a spelunker's darkest nightmare.

It was vaguely man-shaped—emphasis on "vaguely"—standing somewhat erect upon tree-trunklike legs. And I say "somewhat" because its massive head bumped up against the overhang from the bridge deck forcing it to hunch forward, Quasimodo-style. Its arms bowed out on either side like a gorilla on steroids and long, sharp claws curved like scimitars from black, leathery fingers. Its thick, shaggy pelt rippled, revealing tectonic plates of muscle. The demon glared down at me with baleful, lamplike eyes and opened its mouth. The impossibly wide maw looked like a diorama of Carlsbad Caverns: a dense forest of stalactites and stalagmites in place of dentition. To say its head looked like a bat's would be about as accurate as saying a Tyrannosaurus rex resembles a gecko.

It paused as it eyed my Creature-from-the-La-Brea-Tar-Pits outerwear and then roared: "Where the hell have you been? We've been worried sick!"

　　　　　　　🦇　　　🦇　　　🦇

The muddy runoff from yours truly had the shower drain backed up before the hot water ran out. I stepped out of the stall just as it turned into a sludge-lined wading pool. As I grabbed a towel and dried off in the master bedroom, I could hear the susurrus of voices through the cabin door. It was way past my bedtime but the forward salon was full of people. Apparently there had been search parties and strategy sessions going on for the past three weeks so it would be rude to blow them all off with a quick "good morning and good night."

I pulled on a pair of old, worn jeans, all the while looking longingly at my neatly made bunk. I was still trying to wrap my mind around the time differential when there was a knock at the door.

"Are you decent?" asked a muffled voice. It sounded like Olive.

"No," I answered, slipping into a paint-spattered work shirt. "But I am presentable." I began buttoning. "More or less. Come in."

Olive Purdue was a slender black woman who looked to be on the shy side of thirty when she was professionally attired in one of her color-coordinated pantsuits. Wearing jeans and a T-shirt, as she was now, made her look even younger. In point of fact, my former secretary was closing in on forty and liked to do *The New York Times* crossword puzzle in ink. Once I had figured out that I lacked the temperament and the organizational skills to run a detective agency I had found a better use for her talents. Now she ran it for me as my partner.

And it clearly irked her that she hadn't been able to track me down during the three weeks I'd gone missing.

"Three weeks?" I asked again as she entered and offered me a steaming mug. "I've only been gone for three weeks?"

"Obviously your . . . captors . . . wanted you to think it was three months," she said as I took it and tried to judge the color of its contents.

The shades were drawn and anchored. The only artificial light angled in from the bathroom. (Excuse me. "Head." Nobody warns you that owning a boat will involve learning a foreign language.) I tried sniffing: there was still mud up my nose. "What's this? Coffee?"

She shook her head. "O-Neg. I warmed it up for you."

"Thanks." I took a sip. Even warmed-over, plastic-stored hemoglobin had it all over caffeine.

The trick was to stay away from that potent ambrosia that bubbled straight from the vein. . . .

I had almost given into The Hunger on the ride home. The only thing that had kept me off of the driver's neck on the long drive back was the knowledge it probably would have gotten me home ten minutes too late.

That and the fact that I didn't have any fangs. Not any real ones, anyway.

And then it came to me that the motivation for my restraint was practical. Not moral. The forward momentum in my transformation from man to monster had not abated.

"It would appear that the plan was to get you to sign over your parental rights," Olive continued. "It would be easier to twist your arm if you believed your child to be already born and the mother dead."

"Yeah? Well, they screwed up," I growled.

"What tipped you off?"

I didn't want to have this conversation three times. I didn't want to talk, at all. But, get the social obligations out of the way, all at once and with everyone present. "'Twas the Bard of Avon, milady," I said, opening the door and stepping into the corridor barefoot. A little meet-and-greet and then head for bed. Suspended animato, Mr. Roboto.

"But why?" I couldn't help asking as we moved forward, past the open galley and entered the salon that took up more than a third of the main deck. "Why *my* son? Who isn't even born yet? And why act like they need my permission to kidnap him?"

Camazotz Chamalcan, ancient Mesoamerican bat-demon, was sitting on one end of the sofa on the port side. He wasn't all big and batty, now, having collapsed down and into the avatar of a small, nattily-dressed black man. "This is why I keep saying we need to go back!" he was saying.

"But even if we knew where this place was," a newcomer argued from a chair near the helm, "you won't find anything. They'll be long gone."

The new guy was big. Tall rather than bulky, with a lean muscularity that indicated an extremely athletic lifestyle and a tan that suggested that he pursued it outdoors—no gyms and barbells for nature boy, here. His shaggy brown hair was streaked with natural blond highlights and fell past his shoulders in thick, tangled locks. He wore a black leather biker's vest with matching pants and no shirt. He didn't have chest hair so much as a pelt with brief glimpses of bronzed skin here and there. Olive had introduced him as "Fenris" and—even without the no-last-name, Norse affectation—there was little doubt that our guest was a werewolf.

Likewise his companion, sitting cross-legged on the floor and leaning up against the sliding glass doors that led out onto the fore deck.

Volpea's tan was so dark she made Fenris look pasty in comparison. She had more hair, too—also thick, also brown, also streaked from the sun—all gathered to her scalp and falling to the small of her back. She wore cut-off jean shorts and a khaki shirt tied midriff style to reveal an eight-pack of killer abs. Daisy Duke does Pilates.

Between the two of them they radiated so much health and energy that I felt like I needed a doctor. Maybe I would. They were probably enforcers. The questions were: from which demesne and why were they here?

"What other options do we have at the moment?" the deconstructed bat-demon countered. "First, captives would provide us with hostages—negotiating materials, should the need arise. Second, it reduces their ranks, reducing their threat. Third, one or more captives provide us with information, answers to questions like the one the Bloodwalker just asked."

I winced. "Don't call me that."

"A waste of time," Volpea disputed in a husky voice. "Even if you acquired a prisoner, they'd as like tell you nothing."

Zotz shook his head. "They would tell me . . . *everything*."

I don't know which creeped me out more. His voice, his words, his inhuman smile that never quite touched his eyes. Or maybe it was the eyes, themselves: eyes that looked like nothing so much as the deep dark holes that had spawned his kind.

The ancient Quiché Mayans had believed that the Afterlife—or the "Underworld" as most Mesoamerican cultures weren't big on the concept of "Heaven"—could be directly accessed through consecrated gateways called cenotés. Cenotés are essentially deep caves with sunroofs—great water-filled sinkholes that could serve as a cistern for an entire civilization or a sacrificial pit for thousands of human sacrifices.

The ancient ruins of Chichen Itza have two such sinkholes: the smaller Cenoté *Xtoloc* which served as the city's water supply, and the large and fearsome Well of Sacrifices where young girls were drowned as sacrifices to Chac, Mayan rain god and cosmic monster. When your hands and feet were bound and your body was weighed down with sacrificial jewelry and ornaments, the whole "gateway to the Afterlife" was more than a religious euphemism. A little push by the priests and, if the fall didn't kill you, your drowning was sure to be accomplished swiftly.

"And then what?" I asked. It should have been a rhetorical question—the kind you don't even ask out loud.

Certainly not of an ancient, bloodthirsty bat-demon. "Turn them over to the authorities? I don't know about The Mullet but I doubt that a woman who can levitate and start fires with her bare hands is going to stay locked up in a conventional jail for very long." My only defense was that I was too tired to think clearly.

He snorted. "Why would we turn your enemies over to those who have no hope of restraining them? After they yield up all the information that we require, we should slay them so that they cease to be a threat."

Mama Samm D'Arbonne, palm reader, fortune-teller, and honest-to-God juju woman, was sitting on the other two thirds of the couch that Zotz occupied. She lazily lifted an oversized hand and suddenly bitch-slapped him upside the head like a stroke of black lightning.

Despite the fact that Mama Samm was immense and Zotz was single-serving sized, she was still human. Zotz only looked it for the moment. I would have feared for all of us had I not seen her do it a half dozen times before. Even a couple of times when he was still all supersized and demony.

"Now what do I be tellin' you about wastin' Mr. Chris' time?" she scolded, her ever-present white turban leaning forward aggressively. "He gots too much to worry 'bout wit'out some raggedy-ass monster always fallin' off the wagon . . ."

"What did I say?" he whined, flinching back as her hand came back up.

"You show up 'bout six month ago, all 'help me find the higher path, please, sir.' But you ain't learned nothin' in all this time. Now here you be talkin' 'bout torturing an' killin' folk. Next thing you know you be cravin' the sacrifices, again."

"But they aren't people," he argued. "They're creatures of earth and sea and air! Not human."

"Faeries," I muttered, closing my eyes and wondering how I could even contemplate a rational discussion of the subject matter. "I think the point that Mama Samm is trying to make, Zotz, is about you, not them. If you continue to set your feet to the path of violence, you harm yourself. It's about what happens to *your* heart, *your* soul—how your thinking is shaped and hardened, when you see every encounter as nonnegotiable."

Fenris and Volpea exchanged looks. Zotz muttered something under his breath. The only words I could make out were: " . . . see you negotiate . . . warrior-thane . . . "

I sat down at the table on the starboard side of the salon—a bit heavily if anyone was paying close attention. I had been running on pure adrenaline for more hours than I could remember and thought I might need something solid to hold onto before we were done. The warmed-over blood helped. I still needed some serious sack time in order to get my head rebooted and back in the game. But my unborn son's life was in danger and I had a boatful of people who had spent the better part of a month trying to find me. Not only did I owe them the basic amenities but there was also the matter of the two lycanthropes. Enforcers or freelance, it wasn't a good idea to show weakness or vulnerability until I knew more about whom—or what—they represented.

"Okay," I announced over the conversations being murmured around me, "I very much appreciate all of your efforts to find me during this little interlude. The question is where do we go from here?"

"As I was saying," Zotz began.

"They're gone, Bats. Let's move on." I turned to Mama Samm. "They want my son. I want to know why."

Mama Samm and Olive exchanged looks across the room.

"What?" I said.

"The world's been a little—busier—in your absence," Olive offered cautiously.

Like it was my fault? "Define 'busier,'" I said, not liking the hesitation in her tone.

"Well, there were a couple of big quakes in Mexico and Central America, some major volcanic activity out in the Pacific Rim . . ."

I shook my head. "That was before I got shanghaied to Elvesville."

She shook her head back. "And since. Grand total of quakes in the past month, five. Two small islands reported sinking this past week. An undersea volcano growing in the southwest, bringing the grand total of spewing geological formations to four at present. Two major tsunamis, one minor. And the reason why people are looking up at the moon and using astrology and astronomy in the same breath."

"Atmospheric debris," I observed. "Filtering reflected light. Turns the moon's albedo the color of Ocean Spray CranApple juice."

"Maybe." Olive laid a hand on my arm. "But, for a lot of people, this falls into the Signs and Portents Department."

"The question is," Zotz growled, "does it juice the elves in a similar direction?"

"What do you mean?"

"Come on, Cséjthe, think. Some faerie tries to trick you into signing over your son . . . "

The look on my face must have been a little blank.

"Who's about to be born in the midst of end-of-the-world signage?"

"First of all," I said, "a lot of babies are about to be born in the next eight or nine weeks. And I don't consider three or four temblors, some heavy seas, and a handful of eruptions in the notorious Ring of Fire to be irrefutable evidence of the Last Days. You want end-of-the-world theories you should've been around for World War II or the great flu pandemic of 1918."

Zotz gave me a Mona Lisa smile. "I was."

Oh yeah.

"And, signs and portents aside," he continued, "none of the other babies being born at this point in history have your son's unique pedigree. Put 'em together?"

It was food for thought. "Okay," I allowed, "maybe there is a connection. Maybe the elves are all Seventh Day Adventists and this is their come-to-Jesus moment on the wheel of time. Whatever. Priority number one is making sure that security is airtight and in place, starting right now. Today."

Mama Samm D'Arbonne folded her immense hands in her immense—er—lack of a lap. "Now don' you be worryin', Mister Chris. I speaks with Miss Lupé every day since you ups and disappears. She be fine an' Miss Marie be seein' that she have plenty of protection while she a guest of Orleans Parish."

I gave her a glancing scowl: she knew I hated her Aunt Jemima act. It worked for the rubes who knew her as a mild-mannered fortune-teller—reading palms, cards, tea leaves, whatever the customer would fork over the most cash for. But that was all shuck-and-jive, sleight-of-hand costuming for her true gifts. And she wasn't so mild-mannered with her backroom clientele.

"I want to see for myself. I want to see Lupé."

Fenris started to rise but Volpea yanked him back down as Mama Samm shook her immense head. "Now, Mister Chris, you knows that won't do! She don' want to see you and New Orleans is our friends as long as you stays north. You try an' go down there and there be nothin' but trouble!"

Volpea fixed her gold-brown gaze on me and tried a smile. It almost touched her eyes. "You know the agreement, Mr. Cséjthe. You must understand why Marie Laveau cannot allow you to enter her domain."

"Yet you can freely enter mine," I growled back at her. "Right?" I turned back to the fortune-teller. "I need to know that she's safe! I need to know that our unborn child will be safe! That Jenny and Kirsten—" I broke off; saying entirely too much in front of Laveau's eyes and ears.

"That is why they are here," Mama Samm answered, her gesture taking in the two weres. "I was preparing to visit New Orleans when you disappeared. Now that you are back, I can go."

I cocked an eyebrow and gave her The Look. I didn't need to say anything. It was well known that she was no fan of Marie Laveau. Once upon a time the Voodoo

Queen of New Orleans might have been a sister prac-
titioner but, more than a hundred years before Mama
Samm was even born, Marie had been turned by a vampire and was said to have lost her way on the Invisible
Path.

I guess I was too tired to do The Look properly. She
returned my gaze with a calm expression and said:
"Madam Laveau has been preparing a solution to Deirdre's problem and needs my assistance. I will have the
opportunity to look in on Lupé and Dr. Mooncloud personally as your surrogate. So, if there's anything you want
to send them, have it ready by tomorrow morning and
I'll take it with me."

"The only thing you won't be sending," Fenris rumbled, giving me a little less of a neutral expression, "is
yourself. That's why we're here."

And there it was.

It wasn't just my physical presence the other enclaves
feared. It was the fact that I could bloodwalk—project
my consciousness from body to body, possessing others
and wrecking havoc on small populations if I so chose.

As in New York, six months ago.

And beyond that, there was the danger that *any*
enclave permitting my freedom within their borders
would risk the appearance of an alliance with the Bloodwalker. Any suggested alliance and they, too, might
become anathema within the undead communities, risking censure, war, annihilation from all of the other
demesnes.

So Laveau and Pantera had sent a couple of enforcers
to make sure that Mama Samm traveled light when she

came to visit. No smuggling rogue semi-vampire shades inside her own head when she came a-callin'.

Bugger.

I held up my hands. "Okay. We'll keep it long distance. For now. As long as I'm satisfied that they're safe and happy. Otherwise all bets are off."

Fenris didn't like it and started to say so. Rather than give his protests any further attention, I asked our fortune-teller: "How come you didn't foresee my abduction or the location where I was being held?"

"No one ever expects the Elvish Inquisition," Mama Samm answered placidly.

I barely had time to get my eyebrow back up before Zotz chimed in. "Time does not pass in the same manner within a faerie mound. This suggests a distortion of the time/space continuum and could explain why the juju woman could not scry your location."

I was very tired and had run out of expressions so I took another sip of the cooling O-Neg in my mug. It was starting to coagulate. Like my brains. I really needed to wrap this up and crawl between the sheets. "Okay," I said, "aside from the Elfsteinian Clock Paradox, what else do we know?"

"Perhaps your nanobots have activated," Olive offered. She held up a small, steaming pitcher. "Freshen your drink?"

I blinked. "What?"

Mama Samm nodded, causing the great, white turban atop her head to wobble like a bobble-head mummy. "Think about it. At any time were you glamoured? Bespelled? Under any form of enchantment?"

I shrugged. "If I was, how would I know? Besides, they kept me drugged."

"And what would be the point of that if their majicks were not for naught?" the fortune-teller elaborated.

"Not for what?"

"Neutralized," Olive translated, pouring more sanguinary snackage into my mug before I could stop her.

"Elven magic defeated by nanotechnology?" I sighed. "It's about time that crap those Nazi boojums injected into me did something worthwhile." The nanobots that swarmed through my bloodstream and crawled through my tissues had yet to activate in any meaningful way. Beyond setting off the security scanners at the airport, that is.

Zotz nodded sagely. "The magic of the Sidhe is nullified by cold iron."

I started to take another drink but stopped. "Whoa, Bats! When did you become an expert on the Fey Folk?" The ancient demon's preferred method of information gathering and research was watching television. Lots and lots of television. It was only in the past month that I had been able to get him a library card and out the door to a more literary form of inquiry and examination.

"Lately I find that it is not enough to learn the ways of this time and culture," he said. "I think it wise to understand the ways of those tribes and forms which exist outside of natural law and perception."

"So you're deep in the stacks, dusting off tomes that pull back the veil on the unseen kingdoms?" I tried a sip of my now "freshened" drink. Too hot now. And the older contents had curdled a bit and risen to the top. No wonder jugulars were still the carafe of choice for the fanged crowd.

He shook his head. "I use the library's computers to surf the internet. Did you know that 'fairy' also means homosexual?"

I started to choke. Olive reached over and laid a manicured hand on his shoulder. "When Mister Chris is able to talk I'm sure he'll want to tell you how unreliable the internet can be as a research tool."

Zotz considered and nodded. "That would explain the librarians' consternation over some of the source materials that I have accessed."

"Consternation?" I repeated weakly.

"They seemed quite distressed."

Fenris cleared his throat after half a beat. "What are nanobots?" he asked.

Glances were exchanged. Perhaps too much personal intel already had been.

"We have some personal business to discuss . . ." Mama Samm said with a slight nod of her head.

". . . and, rather than bore our guests," Olive added diplomatically, "why don't you take them up topside, Jamal? Where they can enjoy the sun."

We all turned and looked at Olive's nephew. He had tucked himself down against the wall, next to the corner fireplace, across from the helm. The shadows and his dark skin had provided camouflage up till now. Twin qualities of stillness and silence conjoined to chameleon him out of sight and mind. The gangly teenager unfolded slowly, standing up, still not uttering a word.

Jamal had been quite loquacious for the first seventeen years of his life. Perhaps I should rephrase that: Jamal was quite the chatterbox for the *entire* seventeen years of his life. Which had ended last year in the destruction of the BioWeb laboratories. Now he just sat or stood very quietly until asked to move. He performed simple tasks with an economy of movement. He never slept. Instead he would gaze straight ahead, his cloudy eyes unfocused, and seem to listen to distant music no one else could hear. He never spoke unless spoken to. And never answered in more than one or two syllables.

I could never decide which I felt the most guilt over: that running errands for me had put him in harm's way and, eventually, brought about his murder?

Or that, in bringing him back to the land of the semi-living with an infusion of my own tainted blood, I may have done more harm than good?

Fenris got up and stood near Jamal. "No need to keep us occupied out of earshot," he said. "We can get in a little run, pick up some supplies, pack, make preparations for tomorrow's return trip." He looked over at Mama Samm. "Unless you'd like to leave later today?"

"Honey, I gots to sleep before I makes a long drive down to Nawlins. I's an old womans." The serious voice was gone and the old shuck-and-jive mask was back, firmly in place.

Volpea stood a bit reluctantly, I thought. Both enforcers were probably under orders to bring back as much intelligence as they could gather. So whatever we didn't want to discuss in front of them was surely eaves-drop-worthy.

"Jamal will see you to shore, then," Olive said.

Jamal didn't require a direct order. He seemed to pro-cess well enough most of the time though you'd be hard pressed to find anyone more close-mouthed about it. But he made no further movement toward the door.

"Jamal?" Olive asked.

Her nephew's lips moved. A sound of sorts emerged. "What is it, baby?"

"Tu-lu," he finally muttered.

"What?" I'm not sure who asked that question. Maybe we all did.

"*Ph'nglui mglw'nafh Tulu*," Jamal rasped, "*R'lyeh wgah'nagl ftagn . . .*"

We all sat there for a minute, stunned. Was it that Jamal had spoken in multiple syllables? Or that the words coming out of his mouth were pure gibberish? Or that the gibberish sounded like some actual, foreign language?

Some terrible, unspeakable language?

Perhaps it was the effect of strange sounds emerging from the vocal apparatus of a dead man.

And then Jamal raised his hand and gestured toward me with a drooping, clawlike hand. "He's coming, Mister Chris! He will wake and the world will fall into dreams of madness!"

And then he started to scream.

Chapter Three

IF THIS WAS one of those "dreams of madness," it didn't start out so bad.

I was eight years old again along with Scotty Steadman. Cecil Rosewood was barely seven but acted nine.

As the school system didn't offer "accelerated alternatives," they had declared Rosewood an honorary eight-year-old and bumped him up to Mrs. Standhart's third-grade classroom.

It wasn't an immediate fit. Rosey was smaller than the rest of us. Worse, he was smarter than the rest of us. Since Steadman and I were less intimidated by either factor, he ended up under our social tutelage, running with the two of us even when school was out: evenings, weekends, summers yet to come . . .

We had just spent another Friday night in Scotty's tree house, and then slipped next door, down into the family room in my parent's basement: the Saturday morning ritual of cartoons and breakfast.

It was already warm out and Steadman was totally at home in his Underoos—both fashion statement and practical choice as the sleeping bags had turned us all sweaty and disheveled. The Steadmeister held the opinion that pajamas were too babyish for such mature eight-year-olds as ourselves. Easy enough to say when your underwear approximates Batman's crime-fighting costume. It lent an air of daring to the skinny, freckled kid—something that would otherwise elude him into his all-too-brief adulthood.

Scott Steadman would die in an automobile accident at the age of twenty-three.

Cecil Rosewood, whom the rest of our classmates called "Poindexter," went the sartorial opposite. He wore jammies with feet. Perhaps his mother made them: Sears & Roebuck had phased out pj's with enclosed footwear back when I was graduating toilet training. If it hadn't been for the mashed potatoes, we would have ragged him unmercifully. Rosey had made the groundbreaking discovery that—properly stuffed with mashed potatoes—pajama booties approximated the low-g effects of a moonwalk for a third-grader playing astronaut.

Poindexter was a pioneer.

As for me? Since my mother was of the opinion that underwear—even the sort designed for the Bat-cave—was inadequate for warding off the effects of pneumonia, the best compromise I could affect was shorts and a T-shirt. Neither super-heroish nor outfitted for out-of-this-world EVAs.

Neither one thing nor the other.

It was a condition I would come to know much more intensely many years after Scotty Steadman's bones were moldering in Hattonville Cemetery and Faith Rosewood miscarried Cecil's only son after three healthy daughters.

That's the problem with dreams: you know too much and understand too little.

Like the debate the three of us were presently engaged in.

"He's a fairy," Scotty insisted, watching Winky Dink cavort across the TV screen with his cartoon dog, Woofer.

A local independent station had unearthed the ancient, black-and-white cartoon series as an alternative to the networks' Technicolor toon franchises. It had to be cheap: my parents talked about watching it when they were kids. As far as I knew, no one watched it now. *Winky Dink and Me* was just time filler and background ambience until *Transformers* came on. Only occasional bursts of noise and action penetrated our sugar-driven, breakfast-cereal buzz as we argued and debated the greater mysteries of life. This morning it had started with the philosophical question of whether Superman was really Clark Kent or whether Clark Kent was really Superman.

"I don't get it," Rosey had kept protesting. "They're the same guy. It depends on which clothes he's wearing."

In search of a more debatable topic we stumbled onto religion.

"Hey, Poindexter," Scotty had challenged, "can God do *anything*?"

"Yeah, sure." Rosewood's family, name notwithstanding, were devout Catholics. Then, sensing a trap: "Anything He *wants*, that is."

"Can He create a rock that's so big that even He can't lift it?" Scotty beamed, inordinately pleased to have poised such an airtight conundrum.

I expected Rosey to laugh it off after a moment—Catholics, in my eight-year-old estimations always had that theological Get Out of Jail Free card. Nuns and priests on TV and in the movies were always invoking it.

But Rosewood wasn't defaulting to the old "It's a mystery" line. The emotions flickering across his puffy features were moving from confusion to consternation. He was taking Scotty's challenge seriously.

And therein lay a path to madness.

"Not to worry, Poindexter," I said, poking him with my elbow, "I got this one." I turned to Scotty. "The answer is yes."

Steadman's eyebrows fairly danced. "So, you're saying that God could create a rock that's so big, even He, Himself, couldn't lift it?"

I nodded. "That's right."

Steadman let out a laugh like the bray of a jackass. "So, if this rock is too big for God to lift, then I guess it's not true. If you said that God could do anything— that's one thing He couldn't do! He couldn't lift the rock!"

I'd actually asked my father this one a while back. Grownups are supposed to know all about stuff like this.

Unfortunately my dad must have missed the handout on this one. His answer was basically "why would God want to do something like that?" Obviously, He wouldn't. End of story.

My father would never understand the rules of debate with the Scotty Steadmans of the world.

I, however, got a crash course every week. I shook my head and smiled. "Not true. He *could* lift it because He's God. God can do anything."

Scotty's smile slipped a little. "Wait a minute. You don't understand," he said. And laid it all out again like I was some sort of feeb.

I nodded again. "God can do anything," I repeated. "He is so powerful that He can create a rock too big for Him to pick up."

Scotty's smile was back. "So, if He can't pick it up—"

"Oh no," I interrupted. "He *can* pick it up. He's God: He can do anything." My smile, on the way up, passed his, on the way down.

"But—but—wait—"

I waved my hand dismissively. "Don't worry, I got it. God can create this rock that's soooo big that even He can't pick it up."

"He can't . . ."

"But since God can do anything, He *can* pick it up because He's God." I grinned at Rosewood who seemed to be warming up to my philosophical take on kindergarten cosmology.

The Scottster, however, was starting to look a little pissed. He knew I could keep this up all day and the only way to beat me at this game was to—well—beat *on* me. Friendship is, at times, a veritable balancing act and the scars of failure can be more than metaphors.

"I got a question," Rosey piped up, defusing the moment. "What's Winky Dink supposed to be?"

That was a very good question.

We turned and paid a little more attention to the star-headed cartoon currently trekking across Marshall McLuhan's post-cultural apocalyptic wasteland.

Whereas most animated characters have heads too large for their bodies, Winky Dink had a balloonlike cranium that made the other toons look like pinheads by comparison. Crowning his hydrocephalic head was a five-pointed hairstyle that looked like he was wearing someone's Christmas tree star for a beanie. Add in lousy art direction, crude animation, and facial features that resembled those of a rabid squirrel on crack (not that we had a clue regarding any of the pharmacopoeia of recreational substances as of yet) and you had the makings of a forgettable cartoon.

Except for a rather unique premise . . .

Each week The Dink (as Scotty liked to call him) embarked on a new adventure and encountered a series of obstacles in his two-dimensional world. At several points in each story, the program host—a real, live human being—would interrupt and ask the audience for help. None of that "make a wish" or "think really hard" or "clap your hands" baby crap to keep-Tinkerbell-from-dying nonsense. The Dink needed his audience to use "magic crayons" to draw a bridge or a ladder or something of practical value to help him get out of a jam. Long before interactive television or home video games, the Dinkster required active audience participation.

"I think he's a star," Cecil argued. "Like a star person. Or a star that's alive."

"That's his hair, Dorkbrain. It just looks like a star because it has five points and it's yellow." That last statement was more of a guess on Scotty's part as the black-and-white spectrum had translated its true color to a faint suggestion of gray.

The concept of artistic intervention sounded simple but wasn't. For one thing you were supposed to use the "magic" crayons that came with a kit you had to send away for. And there was a piece of clear plastic you were supposed to put over the TV screen before you started drawing. This came with a "magic" erasing cloth.

Not only did the Dink think it was important to use the magic "Winky Window" on our TV screens but our parents did too. Apparently Georgie Peterson had ruined his parent's brand new, six-hundred-dollar color television when he tried to assist ole star-head without using a Winky Window, first. There were differing versions of the story—one involving magic markers—but they all ended up pretty much the same. My guess was *Winky Dink and Me* would be replaced by something *less* interactive before the summer was up.

Just as well; we were *Transformers* fans, instead.

"Stars aren't alive, Poindexter," Steadman was still rolling his eyes at Rosewood as Winky Dink disappeared and some equally ancient, black-and-white commercial came on.

"Sez who?" Rosewood retorted.

"Odd Og, Odd Og," the commercial jingle singsonged, *"half turtle and half frog . . . "*

"There's nothing alive in outer space! There's no air to breathe!"

"Maybe he don't need air."

"Dork! Anything that's alive needs air."

". . . don't you laugh at him at all!" some kid in the commercial was declaiming. "Odd Og plays ball!"

"Maybe there's aliens that don't breathe air," Cecil argued.

"Course they breathe air. They wear spacesuits, don't they?"

"Not space monsters. Space monsters don't wear spacesuits."

"That's because they don't fly on spaceships. They stay on their planets and kill Earth people who come there."

The plastic monstrosity in the TV commercial was sucking up a succession of toy balls and spitting them back out of its oversized mouth like one of those machines in the batting practice cages over at Henderson Park.

"Maybe the Dink's half fairy and half star," I suggested, taking my cue from the mildly disturbing commercial.

Scotty shot me a look of half amusement and half disgust.

"Well, we don't even know if it's a he or a she or an it," I added lamely.

"I'm all three," Winky Dink announced from the TV screen. "I'm what you would call an asexual being."

The commercial was apparently over but I wasn't so sure the show was back on. The Dink looked different—like somebody else was drawing him now. His voice was different, too. Less human—which was really saying something in contrast to its typical, chipmunk-on-helium quality.

Steadman's mouth dropped open. "Did the Dink just say a dirty word?" he asked me.

"Poindexter," the not-so-Dink said, turning as if he could see Cecil sprawled across the hassock in my living room, "I need a submarine. Or, rather, your buddy Chris is going to need one. Think you can draw us up one?"

Cecil stared back at the screen, open-mouthed. "Asexual" had shot past him without even ruffling his hair. He was still playing catch-up. "Huh?" is all that he could finally manage.

"Hurry, my little bipedal tadpole!" the Dink insisted in a lower, older voice. Older in an ancient sense. "Make haste before the next commercial! The Dragon is coming and we must catch him while he still dreams!"

Cecil continued to stare, his eyes taking on a glazed and confused aspect. "Dragon?"

Scotty whirled on me, his own eyes alive with excitement and perhaps more than a little fear. "Quick! Where's your crayons?"

"Don't have any," I mumbled around suddenly numb lips.

Actually, I did have crayons. Just not the "magic" variety. Nor did I have the special, protective Winky Window to put on the TV screen. Scotty knew this: he had pronounced drawing along with Winky Dink to be as babyish as wearing pajamas to a sleepover.

"Plastic wrap," he said, turning and running for stairs leading up toward the kitchen. "Where does your mom keep it?"

How would I know? Aside from the refrigerator and the cookie jar, kitchens are unmapped territories to eight-year-old boys.

There was a sound of drawers being rifled and then Scotty Steadman was thumping back down, taking two steps at a time, and running back toward me, trailing a cellophane tail of Saran Wrap.

"Are you a star person?" Cecil finally managed to ask the cartoon character on the screen.

"**We come from beyond the stars**," the thing pretending to be Winky Dink said. "**Hurry, child of Earth! The constellations are nearly aligned and the Old Ones grow restless. Even before he appears, there will be others. . . .**"

Another advertisement started as Scotty tried to get the cellophane to adhere to the front of the television. There was something even more wrong with this commercial than there was with the not-so-Dink. I couldn't tell, at first, because Steadman was in the way and the picture had gone bad.

Winky Dink Land was nothing but a series of striated bands of differing grays in the background most times but now the screen was filled with swirling grays and patches of leprous white. There were some colors, too, but they weren't colors I could name. They weren't colors I had ever seen before. They gave me a headache and the half-digested cereal began to curdle in my stomach.

"Do not attempt to adjust your television set," Rosewood intoned, trying to lower his voice to sound like the Control Voice on *The Outer Limits*. "We control the horizontal. We control the vertical . . ."

Steadman chuckled as he wrestled with the clinging plastic. "You may be a dork, Ceec, but you're our kind of dork."

Whatever was wrong with the video portion of the signal, the audio was unaffected. The commercial singers had started in again but now the words were slightly different: *"Yog-Soth, Yog-Soth; half demon and half god . . ."*

The thing that oozed onto the flickering television screen bore no resemblance to the plastic, half turtle and half frog of a few moments before. Both could be described as unnatural juxtapositions of disparate taxonomies—but that was where all similarities ended. This thing was larger—but its true size was impossible to map against the amorphous grays at the back of the small picture tube. There was simply nothing to lend it perspective but itself. And what there was to see did not appear to be all of it . . .

Plus, it did not appear to be a battery-operated piece of plastic. *It was alive.*

The . . . thing . . . appeared to be a seething mass of tentacles—but little like an octopus and less like a squid. The writhing, squirming mass seemed both gelatinous and chitinous in its various parts—like a festering knot of centipedes, feasting on a large and agitated spider. And the appendages were covered with additional appurtenances—eyes, mouths, cilia, claws. All of them alive with their own, separate intelligences!

Cecil was standing now, his mouth slack and open, his eyes wide and almost frantic but for their stillness. He had the better angle: Scott continued to block my view of the writhing horror as he struggled to fit the plastic wrap in place. Even as I was largely spared the full impact of the monstrous apparition, Scotty was too close and too distracted to focus on the hideousness just inches away in a seething sea of phosphors.

And then I smelled it: the sharp, acrid, ammonia stench. By now I could count my nightmares in the hundreds but this was the first time one had come in Smello-vision.

Steadman smelled it, too. "Aw, jeezely cripes!" He glanced back at me and then looked at Cecil. Looked again. Turned back to me. "Poindexter's pissing himself!" he said in a horrified whisper.

I had already seen the dark stain expanding outward from the crotch of Cecil's pj's like a mindless amoeba. All I could do was nod. And raise a leaden arm to try and point.

I couldn't even find my voice to say "look out" or "run"—even as Cecil began to shriek like a tugboat whistle, emitting short, sharp blasts of ear-numbing sound. My arm was still on its way up as the tentacles came out of the swampy gray radiance of the TV tube and grasped Scotty by the neck and one arm.

He was too surprised to scream, at first. Or offer much resistance. By the time a half dozen fleshy ropes had emerged to secure him and drag him into the foggy maelstrom inside the set, the screaming was pretty much over and I was waking up.

It was only a dream.

So . . .

Any minute now . . .

Some sense of relief would rush in to replace this overwhelming dread that had followed me into the world of the waking.

Any time now . . .

But the closest I could come to a happy thought was the sense of relief that Scott Steadman was still dead in the real world. The twisted, burning, metal pyre that eviscerated him years later on Interstate 44, just outside of Oklahoma City, seemed a far kinder fate than the horror waiting just outside this fragile reality.

Dreams of madness . . .

No wonder I felt little relief in waking up. A trio of third-graders shrieking in terror over something that never really happened didn't hold a candle to the more gruesome memory of Jamal's screams from earlier this morning. Horrific ululations of terror that went on and on.

And, more appalling: ended abruptly.

Olive's nephew hadn't calmed down or tired out. He had just . . . stopped. As if he was a piece of equipment—an organic relay for data from some hellish dimension—and a switch was thrown, a circuit breaker was finally tripped.

Then Jamal's eyes had turned black. Even the whites. His eyes sat in his sockets like ebony marbles, staring like the emptiness of the cold void between the stars. He simply stopped screaming, his eyes went dark, and he had stood there like an ancient pillar, the sole remains of a ruined ebony temple, a remnant from long eons past.

I shook my head as I sat on the edge of the bed. The event was bad enough: no need to embellish the creepiness with my own macabre mood. Mama Samm or Olive would report back to me once they knew more. In the meantime I had more pressing issues.

Like the safety of my unborn son. CNN was turning into a clone of CBN and the 700 Club, reporting hourly that the world was going to hell—capitalization optional. It wasn't just the seismological and climatological phenomena. It was the parade of atrocities on the hourly newscasts that suggested we were well past the "two-minute warning" and humanity was running the clock out in "sudden death overtime."

School shootings were a weekly occurrence now. More often than not, teachers and principals were shooting back. Parents were murdering their children at unprecedented rates. Adolescents increasingly divided into two parallel tribes—those who saw suicide as preferable to pointless years of meaningless existence and those who felt that if each of us was "owed a death" then two, three, half a dozen or more, were even better.

Birds fell from the skies like viral bombs, their carcasses incubating new generations of plagues. Four-legged animals went berserk and savaged anything that came within reach before spinning in endless circles, mad farandoles that ceased only when their frantically beating hearts burst.

Churches preached intolerance. Mosques sermonized jihad. Philosophies mentored nihilism. Politicians abandoned statesmanship to practice mindless partisanship, making war against each other while real enemies made lists in the shadows of their national monuments. The culture of cynicism that had grown up over generations had taught us to mock heroes and scorn sacrifice.

In the end it was greed and selfishness and vanity that out-Zenned the Buddhists on mankind's path to ultimate Nirvana. Somewhere along the line we had decided it was safer to believe in nothing. Nothing can betray you; nothing will disappoint. And, seemingly close to the end, nothing was what we were left with.

Ultimate Nirvana.

Sunyata.

Emptiness.

Oblivion.

Extinction.

As for me? My personal path to the Nirvanic state was more of a Kurt Cobain thing—minus the mumbling and really bad fashion sense. I was feeling, more and more, like a clockwork puppet, rapidly winding down to entropic oblivion. It was only those little surges of horror, here and there, acting like momentary jump starts to keep me going.

As usual, my metabolism was messing with my meds. The antidepressants made me too numb to think, the dread I felt for my unborn family clouded any residual judgment. More than ever, I needed to see Lupé, to know that she was all right. Up until now I had taken the advice that she just needed "time" and that we just needed "distance" and that, eventually, she'd "come around."

Well, screw that.

If the world was going to Hell in a FedEx hand basket, we needed to talk. Soonest. How would I ever have a chance of fixing things between us if she never took my phone calls and all of my letters continued to go unanswered? Absence rarely makes the heart grow fonder. More often it makes the commitment go wander.

Perhaps it wasn't her.

Other individuals, groups, species had a vested interest in keeping us apart, in maintaining the status quo. I knew most of the weres wouldn't be happy but the idea of a baby sharing wampyri and lycan/were heritages was enough to make the real power brokers, the vampires stain their undies crimson.

So why was Marie Laveau taking Lupé under her wing?

Pagelovitch lending natal support through Dr. Mooncloud was his way of keeping his finger on the pulse of change. When I had first turned up as an anomaly in the scheme of things his first reaction had been to find a way to exploit me as a resource. Other Domans would have exterminated me and maintained the status quo. He still had hopes of convincing me to return to Seattle. My son was probably just his latest bargaining chip.

Or a better addition to his preternatural petting zoo.

But Marie Laveau was half-mad and her unpredictability made her all the more dangerous. I really needed to get down to the Big Easy before unseen and unfathomable machinations closed any more doors between Lupé and myself. And I didn't have time for any distractions like Twilight Zone podcasts from the zombie help.

But I did have to pee.

The blackout curtains on my cabin windows admitted no light but I instinctively knew it was late afternoon even before rolling over to check the bedside clock.

I groaned out of bed and attended to business without turning on the light in the head. Some things take time getting used to: pissing red instead of yellow was one I hadn't managed, yet.

Finishing up I realized that I was thirsty, as well.

Bad enough dealing with fey foes who abduct you, menace your family, and threaten violence. But when they screw up your sleep cycle a definite line has been crossed. . . .

Since I had crawled between the sheets without undressing there was no need to fumble for my robe. I did, however, fumble into my shoulder rig. I checked the freshly cleaned and oiled Glock before sliding it into the holster. (Thanks, Olive.) If you think wearing a gun to raid the refrigerator is silly then you haven't been paying attention. If anything, I still wasn't taking my own "Wanted" status seriously enough.

I padded into the galley and pulled another blood pack from the refrigerator. *Cold or warm?* There's very little difference between refrigerated and reheated hemoglobin once it's been stored for any length of time—in terms of sustenance, that is. Taste is an entirely different matter. Too bad microwaving breaks down the cellular elements and renders blood both unappetizing and non-nutritional.

I wandered through the salon while tiny blue fingers of propane flame caressed the saucepan on the stovetop.

There had been a precipitous drop in The Hunger after my little sojourn in Colorado. Was it the result of the out-of-body experience I had when I "died"? (A second time?) Or, more likely, a side effect of the nanites Dr. Mengele's clones had injected into my body? Before Jamal had gone all Edgar Cayce on us this morning, Olive had suggested that the microscopic machines in my bloodstream had finally "activated." There was sufficient evidence that they had been performing rudimentary activities all along—replicating, performing cellular repairs, even some tissue augmentation. My lowered dependence on blood made sense as a byproduct of my microbiological makeover.

So what did Olive mean by "finally" activated? And why was I suddenly looking to scarf the same amount of hemoglobin that usually sustained me over the course of an entire week in less than twelve hours? Stress? Yeah, that always amped up the Bloodthirst. Being subjected to a little faerie B & D, doped up and probably starved in the process, running from the sun, and learning that my unborn son had attracted the attention of "people" who were not known for their humanitarian virtues . . .

Or maybe the time differential had had a hand in reprogramming my body's electromagnetic fields—a little jet lag from the time-zone difference between the realm of the faerie and my own personal reality show.

And then there was that presumed blast of elven mojo . . .

I shook my head. *This was just plain nuts.* The more I thought about it, the more Dr. Fand's version of reality made sense.

I peeked through the forward curtains. One of the New Orleans enforcers was just outside, on the prow.

If Volpea was "standing watch," this was a novel approach.

She was stretched out on a lounge chair wearing a great deal of cocoa butter and very little swimsuit. From this angle I couldn't tell if she was alert or dozing. She wore sunglasses and her face was turned toward the water. I had no desire to be caught staring so the wise thing to do was to back away.

Right now.

Just take a step back.

Any minute now . . .

What's the harm in looking? asked that lately all-too-familiar voice inside my head.

I closed my eyes: I was *not* going to have this conversation again. At least not so soon after the last one. And the topic seemed to arise with increasing frequency these days.

It's just looking . . . the silent voice repeated.

The loyal heart knows no distractions, I rebutted. Yeah, like I'm having a conversation with a completely different person.

Loyalty? To whom? Your ex-fiancée who can't stand for you to touch her? Who refuses to see you or speak to you? Or Deirdre, who's got her own medical problems? And is totally out of the picture unless Marie Laveau can figure out what to do with that malignant growth on her shoulder?

That's just the problem with relationships these days, I volleyed back. Too many people ready to abandon ship on the first patch of rough water.

Whereas you're so ready to go down with the ship that you won't even "man the pumps." No wonder you're in a funk: you haven't gotten any for the better part of a year!

I'm not depressed because I'm celibate.

Celibate! Celibate! Dance to the music! the other voice singsonged to an old Three Dog Night tune.

Clearly channeling one's sex drive into any kind of serious conversation was problematical when one's neurotransmitters were out of whack.

Yeah, so contemplate the bikini-clad babe that's practically in your lap, dog!

Lapdog? She's one of Laveau's enforcers. She's practically the enemy.

So? First rule of strategy: know your enemy.

It was obvious that "the enemy" was in shape. All sorts of delightful shapes laid out and on display. The muscles in her arms and legs had better size and definition in repose than a reasonably fit female athlete would display while flexing. Her abdomen was knurled with knobs and striations of muscle. A topaz-colored gem in a silver setting dangled from a ring piercing the deep whorl of her navel. She retained just enough body fat to soften the angles and edges toward a more feminine ideal. In fact, the twin triangles of her swimsuit top bulged sufficiently to suggest artificial enhancement but I knew that lycanthropes and implants don't mix.

If I have to explain that to you, you might as well look elsewhere for stories less challenging to your—ahem—intellect.

Too bad you can't go out there and offer to rub some more lotion on her b—

She started to stir and I finally found the will power to back away from the sliding glass door.

The water on the stove was starting to hiss and steam so I dropped in the blood pack to begin the warming process. Perhaps I should have skipped the culinary hassles and tried it cold: I was feeling a bit overheated, myself, at the moment.

It's not lust; it's the predatory programming of the necrophagic virus . . .

Keep telling yourself that.

Shut up.

I turned the burner down to the barest flicker of flame and opted to let the bag steep for a while. If Volpea was sunning herself out on the bow, then Zotz had to be around somewhere. He'd never leave me alone on the boat while I was sleeping and certainly not with Crescent City muscle on board.

I found him at the other end of the boat, also outside, which meant he was in a more trusting mood than usual. I joined him on the aft deck, under an awning that provided enough shade for the both of us. As long as I kept my visit short, that is. Even with direct cover, peripheral sunlight is a bitch over time and cumulative. But this little tableau was too choice to take in at a distance.

The human-looking Zotz had ensconced himself in a deck chair next to a plastic cooler. He had fired up a stogie, popped the tab on a can of beer, and was flicking a fishing line over the side as I arrived. I sat on the plastic cooler and took in this bucolic scene. "When did this start?"

He took a drag on his cigar, a pull on his can of beer, and let out a little line on his reel. It was awkward, almost suspenseful, and oddly fascinating to watch: inhuman reflexes multitasked processes that were clearly unfamiliar to him and yet carefully studied and practiced at the same time.

Plus he only had two hands to manage three objects.

"The juju woman believes that I should not hunt," he answered, juggling the fishing pole, aluminum can, and cigar. "That it is counterintuitive to my quest for redemption."

"Really?" I asked. "She said hunting was counterintuitive?"

"In so many words," he said. "So. Many. Words. Punctuated with bouts of punching and slapping." Another puff, another pull. "But she didn't say anything about fishing."

"Fishing," I said.

"Your Bible has Jesus saying: 'Follow me and I will make you fishers of men.'"

"You *told* her that?"

"Of course not. I have no wish to be pummeled further, even if it doesn't really hurt. Physically, anyway." He pulled the line in a bit. "But fishing is enough like hunting to . . . " he considered, " . . . satisfy certain urges. And it teaches me a little more about being human."

"Really?" I gee-whizzed. "Tell me more!"

"I am still learning. It is touted as a sport but it is really a religion, no? I have observed other congregants on the river and upon the so-called television sports shows. There are some variations but the similarities are greater than the differences." He waved his cigar. "The burning of incense." Sloshed the beer in his can. "The sacramental wine." He reeled his line back in. "And, of course, the meditative trance. One might achieve the Zen-like state of *samadhi* were it not for the occasional interruptions of the fish." He checked his hook. Impaled upon the barbed, J-shaped metal was a disintegrating squiggle still identifiable as a Gummi worm.

"Catch much?" I asked, keeping my voice even.

He shook his head. "The problem may be my bait. Or, as the sportsmen refer to it, the 'lure.'"

"Ya think?"

He waggled the tab key off of his beer can and knotted it onto the line just above the hook. "Maybe I can find a feather or two tomorrow along the shore. It will be about time to change worms by then." He flicked the rod with a surprising amount of grace, sending the line back out into the river's flow.

We sat in silence awhile.

"Any word on Jamal?" I asked.

He gave me a look that said: *you know I would have told you if there was any news at all.*

"Any new thoughts on what the message means?"

He repeated The Look.

"Me neither," I said.

"Why are you up?"

"I got thirsty."

Zotz gestured with the rod. "Blood in the fridge."

"Heating some up. But I'm not so sure it's a good idea to be upping my intake right now."

"Why not? It's what vampires do."

"I'm not a vampire! At least, not yet. And increasing my intake may be messing with my head right now."

He smiled, white teeth gleaming sharply in the shade. "Fishing is good for thinking. But it can be good not to think overmuch. Perhaps you should try a six-pack of mood enhancement."

"I've got enough crap in my body," I growled, "without adding to my biochemical imbalances."

"And, of course, you wouldn't want to relinquish any personal control."

"Oh yeah," I said bitterly. "Because staying in control is so important. Look how well it's working for me, so far."

"You're alive," he countered mildly, taking a puff on his cigar. "You've outwitted and survived enemies that have been the scourge of cities, of nations, for generations." Another puff. "Vampires fear you, the dead revere you." Puff. "And, personally, I think you're a helluva guy." Puff. "Not that you don't irritate like a pernicious rash sometimes." Puff.

I blinked. Ran through a number of responses in my head. In the end I just grunted. Depression and exhaustion: the two great levelers of social conversation.

Zotz took a long meditative draw on his stogie. "Did she really say 'churl'?"

I nodded, staring off into the deadly glare twixt sky and water. "Yep. Just goes to show, you can take the girl out of the fifteenth century but you can't take the fifteenth century out of the girl."

"Was that the moment you knew she was a ringer?"

"No. Just before that. I brought Shakespeare into the conversation—"

"Don't tell me, let me guess," he said, flicking the line back out into the river. "You did some fishing of your own with the old 'Madness in Hamlet' conundrum."

I nodded slowly. "How did you know?"

"Are you kidding? It's a classic! Depressed, tormented Dane runs around a dark, drafty castle ranting like a madman and committing murders in the first and third person. But the big myst is whether Hams is really bonkers or just holding onto the horizon effect of his sanity by acting out."

I rolled my head trying to loosen the kink that a month's worth of straightjacket-wear had strapped across my neck. "Yeah, I figured if she was a legitimate shrink, she'd recognize a simple, first-year-psych-student talking point." I held up a finger. "First, ghost or no ghost, he comes to the conclusion that dear old dad was murdered." I held up a second finger. "Then he figures out that Uncle Claudius did the dirty deed." Third finger. "And that mommy dearest helped 'off' dad so she could 'boff' Claude . . ."

"Talk about putting the 'fun' in 'dys*fun*ctional,'" Zotz interjected, "vice is nice but incest is best."

I thought about pointing out that Gertrude hadn't actually committed incest by strict definition but I had a final point to make: I held up my fourth finger. "And, as the prince can add two plus two, it's becoming increasingly clear that the new king can subtract one from three and Hamlet's likely to inherit his late father's medical condition."

"You mean *dead*ical condition."

"Precisely."

Zotz took a pull on his beer and set the can aside to play with his line a little more. "So, back to the famous madness in Hamlet problem: which side of the debate do you fall on? Genuine psychosis? Or faking it?"

I shrugged. Without the straightjacket it was nice, almost pleasurable. I resolved to do it more often. "I always favored the 'crazy like a fox' viewpoint."

Zotz nodded. "Good cover. Kept the king from ordering Rosencrantz and Guildenstern to go all *Pulp Fiction* prematurely."

I shook my head. "Yeah, but it was more than that. It's the concept that Hamlet had to *act* crazy to keep from *going* crazy. The crazier he acted, the saner he became."

The demon eyed me. "That would explain a great deal."

"You think?"

"In terms of *your* coping mechanisms, that is."

"Thanks a lot, Bats."

"Don't mention it, Half'n'half. You're a prince, too—but you're reading the wrong play."

"What do you recommend? *Macbeth*?"

He flicked the line out over the river again. He was getting pretty good at it. Of course he was getting a lot of practice since he couldn't really be catching anything with Gummi worms and aluminum can pull-tabs. "*A Midsummer Night's Dream.*"

I made a noise down deep in my throat. A little deeper and it would have been an actual growl. "Elves. Faeries. Sprites. Pixies." I sighed. "Pink elephants on parade . . . "

"Don't worry, Dumbo," he said, "now that we have a couple of names and an idea of the general nomenclature, I can narrow the focus of my research."

I stood back up. "Good to know you'll be doing more than checking out online porn at the library."

"We also serve who sit and surf."

The tip of Zotz's fishing pole suddenly made like a dowsing rod: it dipped once, twice, three times. "Looks like I've finally caught something."

"I don't believe it." I stared at the line gone taut, angling off into the gray-green waters of the river. "It's got to be a snag."

"It's pulling on the line."

I shook my head. "Maybe it's a tire . . . an old boot. A snapping turtle?"

He got up and walked to the edge of the deck as he reeled in the line. "Grab that net, would you?"

I picked up the landing net next to the cooler and joined him at the deck's edge. There was just enough peripheral shade to keep me safe if I didn't lean way out. "What are you going to do? Cook it or eat it raw?"

He shook his head as the line decreased its angle and approached the side of the boat. "Catch and release. The thrill of the hunt is enough."

Given the mercury and PCB levels hereabouts that was probably not such a bad idea. I knelt down to assist in the final stage of capture.

The fishing pole bowed down as if Zotz had hooked a serious game fish. A channel cat? Suddenly the pressure slacked off for a second and he leaned over to see if he had lost his fish. The pressure returned with a vengeance just a moment later and a sharp tug caught him by surprise. He was overbalanced and tumbled into the turgid waters.

"Zotz?" I gingerly knelt down and gauged my closeness to the deck's edge. While his batlike form might seem inimical to an afternoon plunge, he had lived at the bottom of a sunless pool for more than a thousand years. Maybe that's why he'd made little splash and less sound going in. A few minutes in a freshwater river wasn't going to inconvenience him any.

Vampires, on the other hand, don't fare well in watery environments—hence the old "don't cross running water" proscription. Which was why living on a houseboat made a certain kind of twisted sense when undead assassins made occasional house calls.

Of course, I wasn't too keen on falling in as my own buoyancy issues were seriously impaired these days. So, living on top of a floaty moat: a mixed blessing, at best.

I reversed the net and extended the handle as an improvised handhold, expecting Zotz to break the surface any moment.

I had to wait.

The eyes that came up and peered at me from just below the surface looked like his. At first.

Inhuman. Large. Glowy, even.

But where Camazotz's demon eyes were fiery lanterns lit with red flames from a hell of coals and brimstone, these orbs were lit from a colder realm, a cool luminescence that knew neither warmth nor passion.

A head broke the surface of the Ouachita River. And then another: fish-heads.

Fish-heads?

Roly-poly fish-heads!

Bigger than bowling balls and disturbingly humanoid in appearance!

An arm came out of the water. It was gray-green and mottled in the manner of something amphibian. The hand that grasped the edge of the deck was clawed and webbed, looking more like a mitten fabricated out of neoprene and fishhooks than a human appendage.

I duck-walked backwards as the Creature from the Black Lagoon's second cousin, twice-removed, started to haul itself up out of the water and onto the deck of my boat. No "request permission to come aboard" or "may I have a moment of your time to share the good news of Neptune's gospel?" Just up and over and slither on board as I stood up and unsnapped the safety strap on my shoulder holster. The second fish-man followed right behind the first.

They hunched over like a pair of aquatic Quasimodos, seemingly unsure as to whether to stand erect or scuttle about on all fours. Rows of gill-like openings pulsed along the sides of their scaly necks and their gaping, lipless mouths revealed rows of tiny sharp teeth.

I pulled out the Glock and backed up a little more, wondering what was keeping my giant Mesoamerican, water-spawned bat-demon down so long.

I wasn't too keen on the most likely explanation.

Fish-face number one looked from me to the tackle box and back again. Fish-face number two looked past my shoulder, trying for the old fake-out, there's-something-behind-you look.

I wasn't falling for any of that. "So," I said, pointing the automatic at one and then the other, "can I offer you fellows anything? Gummi worms? Silver wad-cutters?"

Something hit me from behind and I stumbled, dropping the gun. Instinctively, I ducked and, as I felt something scrape the back of my head, I threw an elbow back. I heard something snap—it felt more like cartilage than bone.

One fish, two fish; black and blue fish!

Did I mention my preternatural strength and reflexes? "Sorry, Charlie," I smirked.

Did I mention my underdeveloped prioritization skills?

That gave the two in front of me time to wade in. One on one, I might have gone all Captain Ahab on someone's finny ass. Two on one changed the dynamics and I found myself forced back across the deck. And number three wasn't down for the count. In short order they swarmed me and we all went over the side.

A half second of free fall through direct sunlight and then I smashed into the water with a trio of amphibian airbags to help cushion the impact.

I remembered to grab a lungful of oxygen on the way in.

Unfortunately a clawed hand tore five bloody furrows in my side and made me gasp as we hit: I expelled air and swallowed river water. *Not good!* A little preparatory hyperventilation and I might be able to hold my breath for three minutes. This was assuming I wasn't engaged in some strenuous activity like fighting for my life against the sushi squad, here. Sucking water on my way down had seriously cut into my onboard reserves.

And while ten . . . now fifteen . . . now twenty feet of water helped filter the killing rays of the sun, it also obscured reference points beyond a couple of yards in any direction. My only chance of getting out of here without drowning was to *walk* out. Quickly. Swimming was out of the question: vampires can't.

And there's no such thing as the *un*dead man's float.

As soon as my feet touched bottom, I began to move. Even if I didn't know which direction I was going, standing still was going to get me nowhere.

And then the fight recommenced.

Well, not so much a fight now as a clumsy dance routine in slow motion. Arm thrusts and jabs were the rule—not swinging fisticuffs—and the best I could do was keep two of them off me at a time. They had claws, I didn't. They had sharp, pointy teeth; mine were blunt, dull, and I would only drown that much quicker if I opened my mouth.

A giant vise started screwing shut against my chest and I knew that I was already down to my last minute or so of cognitive functionalism: the remainder of my life would be metered out with a stopwatch, not a calendar. Escape options were fading off the table.

Face it, Cséjthe: the best you can hope for is to make someone sorry they've picked this particular fight.

Unfortunately, these things were in their element, now, and I wasn't. They had all the time in the world. All they had to do was keep me under, stop me from moving toward shore, and let the water do its work. But they continued to nip and scratch and lunge as if mere drowning wasn't enough. My blood hazed the already murky water and I realized something with a shock: *there was a part of me that seemed almost glad of it!*

Well, why not? As Shakespeare once penned: "All that lives must die, / Passing through nature to eternity."

Of course, that line belonged to Hamlet's "mommy dearest" so maybe she wasn't the best refuge for moral gravitas.

Everyone around me had been yammering about clinical depression for the past six months. Was I really so far down in the emotional depths that I was ready for the ultimate analgesic? Tennyson understood that grief was not necessarily a bad thing. He wrote: "Let love clasp grief lest both be drowned . . ." *Drowned . . . right, now there's a fitting analogy . . .* "Let darkness keep her raven gloss. / Oh, better to be drunk with loss, / To dance with death, to beat the ground . . ."

Well, one last dance and let's be honest: I was more invested in payback than survival, now. Too bad either motivation was going to go unfulfilled.

My chest was on fire and my limbs were gone all leaden now. And then one of the fish folk flickered in and clamped razored teeth deep into my upper thigh. I grimaced and choked involuntarily on a lungful of water. It was like taking a sledgehammer to the chest and my skull burst like a bubble under deep, dark waters.

Chapter Four

IT WASN'T LIKE going into a tunnel of light . . .

It was like going into a swank and pricey restaurant with my ex-fiancée on my arm.

I hadn't seen the wine list, yet, but the starfish was wearing a tuxedo.

"Ah, Monsieur Cséjthe, Mademoiselle Garou!" it exclaimed. "Welcome to Club Palmyra! Will you be dining with the captain this evening?"

More than a few neurologists are of the opinion that the whole "life after life" phenomenon is nothing more than oxygen-deprived brain cells firing off random memories—a free-association meltdown as consciousness gutters out like a dying candle flame.

I looked across the restaurant with the oceanic décor and ship motifs. A tiger was seated at a table on an elevated dais in a clamshell-shaped alcove. It was too far away to see if it was dining on a bowl of breakfast cereal.

Such theories might vaguely explain my watery death segueing into a watery night out on the town and a trip to a weird theme restaurant.

The tiger waved a furry paw in our direction.

Perhaps vague *was too strong a term . . .*

I looked at my ex. When they say that pregnant women glow, I don't think it means that they actually shed light. Lupé, however, was giving off enough illumination to pass as a giant nightlight. Her thick brown hair was piled on top of her head and the expanse of décolletage and back revealed by her scalloped evening dress had lightened up considerably from its customary coffee-and-cream complexion. I raised a hand to shield my eyes as she amped up the "glow" another hundred candlepower. "What do you think, dear?"

She patted her swollen belly as hair started to sprout across her face. "Is it safe for the baby, Patrick?" she asked, as if the maître d' were an old friend. "You know how important he is to the Old Ones."

"You mean the elves, right?" I asked.

The starfish adjusted the small towel draped over an armlike appendage. "Do not worry, Mademoiselle; Prince Dakkar has restricted his diet to seafood these past one hundred and fifty years."

I was suddenly hungry. Actually, I felt as though I'd been starving for weeks and had just now noticed it. "Seafood," I said. "Do you have clam chowder?"

The starfish bowed slightly. "Of course, sir. Though we restrict our menu to the New England recipe. Manhattan style, if you'll forgive my impertinence, is an abomination and we do not countenance it here."

"Er, okay," I said, noticing that the floor was very wet.

"This way, please," our pentagrammic maître d' announced.

I looked at Lupé who linked her arm in mine. She had accessorized with a fur stole and it was hard to tell where the stole ended and her arm began. Her face was completely furry now and beginning to elongate into a pronounced snout. The proliferation of hair was eclipsing her pearly radiance and the effect was much like the moon slipping behind a darkening cloud. I was so distracted I didn't notice that the water was actually rising until it was above our ankles.

"Isn't this taking the whole marine-ambience thing a bit to excess?" I asked.

Lupé, seemingly oblivious to the dark waters now swirling up to her knees, tapped our echinodermic attendant on the—er—shoulder. "I'm not that big on fish," she said. "What would you recommend?"

"Maybe a little less surf and a little more turf," I grumped as the water wicked up my pants legs.

Our escort leaned back and whispered conspiratorially: "I'm not supposed to espouse menu favorites but the Krabby Patties are to die for."

"You don't say?" I refrained from asking if there was a SpongeBob Happy Meal.

It was slow going, now, as the water had reached my waist and Lupé was getting ready to dog-paddle. "You know," I said, "as brain death hallucinations go, I could've drawn a lot worse from the deck of my life—especially the last couple of years. But I'm drowning in a freshwater tributary, not a saltwater ecosystem. And I'm totally not gettin' the Tony the Tiger/Guess Who's Coming to Dinner vibe . . ."

The starfish stopped and turned to me as the lights in the restaurant flickered and went out. Lupé lost form and became a beam of light, cutting through murky waters that had risen above our heads. The light put the five-limbed creature in silhouette and it changed subtly.

"Time is short, small one." His voice echoed strangely, as if from a great distance. More than that, it seemed weighted with the age of untold centuries. Millennia . . .

"Your son must be sacrificed before the sleeping god wakes or your race will come to a terrible end."

"What?" I felt as if an electric shock had just exploded throughout my body leaving me numbed, burned, and dazed. "What are you saying?"

"In the end you must sacrifice him. If not for humanity's sake, then for his own. You would not want him to live in such a world as would be ruled by the Dread Master of R'lyeh!"

I didn't have a clue as to who this so-called dead master of really something or other was but he was in for a real ass-kicking if he posed a threat to my unborn son. Likewise anybody even hinting at bad karma for Chris Cséjthe's pride and joy.

"Free will is but a human delusion, a cosmic self-deception for your infant race," he continued and his voice began to diminish, as if he were starting to move away from me and picking up speed. "**I tell you this one last thing. Ignore it at your peril and the doom of your entire species!**"

Great, a seafood restaurant with a waiter who doubled as a fortune cookie. "I'm all ears, Garçon." I growled.

"**You cannot order the calamari**," it rasped in nearly inhuman tones, "**it orders you . . .**"

A fishy face suddenly swam into view, its buggy luminous eyes staring at me above an expression of gape-mouthed surprise.

I reached out with my hand, trying to grab its neck but it pulled back. Neither of us was fast enough: I couldn't get my fingers behind its head and it couldn't totally evade my hand. I ripped its throat out, instead.

A cloud of blackish blood erupted from its torn flesh and it sank out of sight. Either this particular water bogie was made of papier-mâché or . . . I looked at my hand: small clumps of sushi still clung to my razor-tipped fingers!

My razor-edged, straightjacket-shredding talons had reappeared like ten spring-loaded switchblades!

Another froggy foe darted in and it was time to focus on matters directly at hand. All I had time to register was someone had shoved a scuba mouthpiece halfway down my throat and that the murky water had brightened considerably. I could see the other two more clearly, now, and prepare for their attacks.

And this time the flipper was on the other foot. As the second fish-man darted in, I threw up an arm block across his throat to keep his teeth from my face. The back of my hand and forearm had snagged a piece of silvery kelp, a ribbonlike leaf that stood out edgewise from my skin. When fish-face pushed up against the edge there was a burst of bubbles and blackish blood.

Its, not mine.

Of course this could still be part of the brain-death dream rave.

Which would account for the disposition of my third finny foe: he seemed to be occupied.

A bright light cut through the water illuminating a series of tableaus beyond. In the distance I could make out a large, batty form going all Maytag agitation cycle on a cluster of froggy folk. Apparently he merited more attention than half-monster me. Other silhouettes, however, were bottom-walking past him and in my direction, the light at their backs. If I didn't finish my third assailant quickly, they'd be upon me before I could find a way to climb back out of the river.

But my third assailant had an assailant of its own. An arm was wrapped across its scaly torso while another clutched at its goggle-eyed head. That arm snapped back and the fish-man's head twisted past the point of spinal cohesion. I could hear its neck snap even underwater. Then I got a glimpse of my foe's foe.

It looked like a woman.

A human woman.

Or, maybe, not-so-human as she bore a strong resemblance to Suki, one of Stefan Pagelovitch's vampire enforcers.

Her eyes looked dead.

Then the light went out.

Most of it, anyway.

There was still enough ambient light filtering down from above to reveal my immediate surroundings. But the creature that had saved me, and the other figures beyond, were now in murk and darkness, as if a great underwater searchlight had been switched off.

I looked up again and saw the keel of the *New Moon* about twenty feet above me and over a ways.

Vampires don't swim, they sink like a rock. Once in, they don't come back out. But I reached up and pushed down with cupped hands, kicking off the riverbed as if I still had a modicum of buoyancy.

And I began to rise!

I swam to the surface and then splashed my way to shore. I reached up to pull the breathing apparatus from my mouth but it was gone. By the time I had stumbled back up the gangplank and onto the boat, a large, batlike monster was wading ashore as well.

I climbed up onto the roof and scanned the waters from the secondary wheelhouse. All looked quiet. But, as Zotz joined me, shrunk down to human form and suddenly dry, I thought I could see something out in the main channel of the Ouachita River.

"I thought you couldn't swim," he said, offering me a towel.

"I thought you knew how to fish," I answered, taking it.

Something was moving under the surface of the river. Something big where the channel was deepest. A greater shadow shaped like a giant manta ray . . .

It moved away, angling upstream. Within a few minutes I couldn't tell if it had gone away or gone deeper to bide its time. I raised a hand to shade my eyes against the glare of ten thousand diamonds as the waters fractured the sunlight and reflected it back up at me.

"Hey!"

I turned and saw that Volpea had finally stirred from her lounge chair at the front of the boat. She was standing atop the ladder, one foot on the top deck, holding a saucepan stinking of burned blood and plastic. She pulled off her sunglasses for a better look.

"I thought they called you Bloodwalker!" she said, her mouth imitating our fishy visitors of just minutes before.

"Yeah? So?" Out of the corner of my eye I noticed that Zotz was doing a similar fish-face impression.

"Maybe they should call you Daytripper, now," he rumbled, still in demon voice.

That's when I finally realized that I was standing out in broad daylight, getting a double dose of solar spectra, without turning into Cséjthe flambé!

∗∗∗   ∗∗∗   ∗∗∗

Volpea called New Orleans.

Zotz called Mama Samm.

While Mama Samm called the Gator-man I wrote up a makeshift list and sent Zotz into town. He scanned my notes as he opened the door and headed for the gangplank. "Some of this may be a little hard to come by," he said.

I smiled and felt my face grow tight. We were adding spear guns to our on-board armory. Also, redundant fishfinder gear until I could get my hands on more state-of-the-art sonar equipment. "Improvise," I suggested.

"How about some Cajun fishing tackle? I know a couple of construction sites."

I shook my head. "It's illegal to even store dynamite, much less use it, without a permit."

Zotz sighed and looked down. "Hoss, I'd venture a guess that permits are about to be the least of your worries for the near future." He looked back up at me. "Wouldn't it be simpler to just cast off and move downriver?"

I looked back. "Like all the way down to New Orleans?"

He shrugged. "You know you're going."

I glanced over at Volpea who was across the salon and engaged in a conversation of her own. "Yes. But the moment the *New Moon* reaches Natchez, New Orleans will go to DefCon One."

"My offer still stands."

I sighed. "I am *not* climbing inside a demon's head."

"Better a willing Trojan Horse than an unwilling one," he argued. "Besides, the classification 'demon' may not be technically accurate."

"It's close enough, Hoss."

Camazotz Chamalcan believed that he was formed out of the essence of ten thousand tormented souls—human sacrifices to appease a concept that had no external reality. Up until the moment the pain and fear of those victims coalesced into a corporeal manifestation of mass horror, that is. Their essence became the abomination they were originally sacrificed to appease. Perhaps a little DNA of the prehistoric *Desmodus draculae*, the gigantic ancestor of the modern vampire bat, *Desmodus rotundus,* got into the mix, somehow—a civilization's need to believe in darkness given form, created it out of their own.

He and I had spent many a long night discussing Plato's shadow creation concepts and the question of whether form follows function or function follows form.

I dreaded the day we segued into Calvinistic concepts of predestination.

Like any newborn infant, his overriding impulse upon first awakening was to feed. But achieving sentience centuries after the Mayans had vanished and the sacrifices had ceased, the Death-eater found it necessary to leave his watery womb and go out into the world in search of sustenance.

Which he found in overwhelming abundance.

Death was everywhere, to abbreviate Shelley.

And not just death but suffering . . .

Pain . . . horror . . .

More than the bread of wickedness and the wine of violence, it was a moveable feast with pogroms here and genocides there and more wars than rumors of war.

Until, at last, gorged beyond surfeit, he had stumbled back to his birthplace in the green oblivion of the timeless jungles, filled with tens of millions of deaths and sick with sins of a thousand civilizations. He tried to sleep, sought solace in the depths of the dark waters, but found that he could no longer rest, no longer find peace in the dreamless sleep of centuries. Others' deaths were now manifestly his Death. Others' sufferings were now his Suffering. The hopelessness of millions had become his own.

You *are*, as they say, *what* you eat.

How and why he had come to me was something that still didn't make much sense. Except that we were both unique and one of a kind as far as monsters go.

And neither of us wanted to be monsters any more.

So, I guess he thought he might learn from me. I don't know what he'd learned so far.

I, in turn, had learned from him these past six months and it was all I could do to keep from returning to Chichen Itza and do a Greg Louganis into the Well of Sacrifices. Anything to still the voices and memories inside my own head.

"Dr. Mooncloud is throwing two cases of medical gear into the back of an SUV even as we speak," Volpea announced as Zotz grumped his way off the boat. "She said she'll be here in five hours."

"She'll be here in four," I said, picking up my own cell phone.

"It's a five-hour drive—"

"Did you tell her I was sprouting stainless-steel manicures and walking around in broad daylight?"

She looked a little nonplussed. "Well . . . yes . . . "

I nodded. "She'll be here in less than four. Where's your other half?"

She looked even more uncomfortable. Maybe it was because she was wearing nothing more than a teeny-weeny bikini and the air conditioner was on. "I'm calling him now."

"Not exactly a direct answer to the question. Maybe you can do better after he reports in." I turned my back on her and called Seattle.

Stefan Pagelovitch would sleep until sunset—which was two time zones later than here. As a master vampire, he could be roused during the day for emergencies but I wasn't about to strain our relationship any more than it already was.

So I spoke to Ancho.

The *vivani* was a member of the Seattle enclave that Pagelovitch ruled but wasn't a vampire, himself. He had once referred to himself as a "dusky elf"—something I hadn't taken seriously at the time because I was still freshly traumatized by my initial exposure to the other Things-that-go-bump-in-the-night. Besides, a *vivani* didn't look anything like those cutesy books of Tinkerbell clones they sell in quaint little bookshoppes, Renfaires, and scifi conventions.

Ancho looked like a big, hairy man with long, sharp fingernails.

He had claimed that the taxonomy of elvenkind was split along three branches: dark, light, and dusky. We didn't get much deeper than that back then as I was still doing my basic research on neck biters. It had taken a major leap of—what? Faith? Credulity? To accept that mutagenic viruses could reprogram human DNA and sufficiently mutate the biological processes to actually create the undead condition. Okay, I was able to move vampirism out of the realm of superstition and into the realm of science.

Werewolves were a little more troubling.

Issues of displaced mass got into a level of physics that was way beyond my comfort level. Still, there was enough medical and zoological data to make some actual sense of what I saw and experienced. And living with a lycanthrope tends to help you over the hump of skepticism.

Ghosts?

The phantasmagorical appearances of my dead wife had not entirely convinced me that she was more than a side effect of the necrophagic virus playing havoc with the perceptual centers of my brain. In other words, I had chalked Jenny's post mortem appearances up to occipital delusions.

But my own little out-of-the-body experience with the shade of former vampire J.D. acting as tour guide had proved pretty convincing. I could now believe in the unseen.

Within limits.

But elves weren't anywhere close to my limits; they were well across the county line and into the next state. Viruses and mutations and quantifiable paranormal phenomena are one thing, ancient magical races are quite another.

Still, that little trip out west with the Wendigo had blurred a few more lines between what was possible and what seemed not . . .

And now that I needed the faerie four-one-one? It probably wasn't the best idea to rely too heavily on a certain smut-surfing bat-demon with public library access to the internet.

And there was another reason to call Seattle, as well . . .

"Is good to hear your voice, my friend!" Ancho's voice boomed at sufficient volume to make my cell phone buzz as though set to *vibrate*. "How are you doing now?"

"Fine, Big Guy. How about yourself?"

"Ah! My Basa-Andrée is big with child again! I hear you are soon to be proud papa, too! Too bad you cannot come for visit, anymore . . . "

I shook my head trying to clear the disturbing image of a pregnant *aguane*. Ancho was married to a water elemental, possessed of an ethereal beauty when sporting about in rivers, lakes, and fountains. Out and about on dry land, however, she was about the ugliest woman I could ever imagine.

And the past couple of years had put my imagination on steroids.

"Yeah, well right now I'm Mr. Persona-non-grata up your way but maybe things will relax down the road," I offered. "I was hoping you wouldn't mind sharing a little information in the meantime."

"Well, you are only prohibited from coming here in person," he said thoughtfully. "As long as you are not asking wrong kinds of questions."

"Fair enough," I allowed. "Ancho, you once told me something about faeries—about how there are three different kinds . . ."

"Are many different kinds," he corrected, "but, yah, three different realms."

"Right. You said: light, dark, and dusky . . ."

"Yah, different kinds in each realm."

"With different powers and purposes?"

"Among different kinds, yah. And everybody different like humans are different, too. Realms not having anything to do with powers or—how you say—purpose. Good or evil?" I could almost see him waggle his hand. "Not to do with realms. There are bad light elves and good dark elves. All mix up, just like humans."

"Which is the kind that steals children, Ancho?"

There was a pregnant pause. "Steal children? *Human* children?" His voice betrayed a note of alarm. "Is not done so much anymore! The world has changed!"

"What do you mean 'changed'?"

"More humans, now. Live together closely. Ten generations ago, sun go down and all was darkness. Much woods and fields and many hidden places. When cloudy or new moon, our world strong beyond feeble glow of lantern or candle. Now is little night and much steel and concrete. You have lamps that flash like sun over great distances and no shadow, no dark or hidden place is safe . . . " His voice had gone soft and sad but suddenly snapped back with a tone of barely controlled disgust. "So, is not done so much anymore."

"But why?" I asked. "Then or now, why do the faerie kidnap children?"

"Most do not. Did not even when humans were cattle and huddled in the great dark. But for those who did? Are different reasons like different kinds. One—individual or tribe—loses a child of its own and cannot conceive. They adopt from the race of Men because they are too ancient to renew themselves with pure lineage."

"Hmmm," I said. "Sort of like the House of Windsor . . . "

"Sometimes a human child is seen to be abused or neglected. The Folk take that lost one out of mercy or kindness."

So, sort of a Fey Folk Family Services . . .

"And once, every generation or so, there is a Telling."

"A Telling?"

"When a babe is foretold. Is anointed . . . gifted. Child is taken to help fulfill special destiny or . . . " He paused. "Are you asking about a specific child?"

My hand was gripping the cell phone so tightly I was in danger of crushing it. "Or what, Ancho? Prevent its destiny from being fulfilled?

"Christopher, are we talking about *your* child?"

"My son hasn't been born, yet."

"But something has happened. What can I do?"

"If I describe an elf and her human servitor, do you think you could identify them?"

"I do not know. But for you I will try."

So I described Fand and Setanta as best I could. Answered the dusky elf's questions about their clothing and jewelry.

It wasn't enough.

"But their names," Ancho said, "seem familiar. I will ask around."

"Thanks, buddy," I said, forcing the tension back out of my voice. "I really appreciate it."

"Is there anything else I can do?"

I hesitated. Time for that other thing. "Yeah, would you ask Suki to give me a call when she rises?"

There was a long pause. "Is not a funny joke, my friend."

"Joke?"

"The Doman was angry enough about your threat to the other demesnes. He forgave you for Deirdre; her making was largely your doing. But he feels Suki and the others were betrayals."

"Um, Ancho, this isn't a joke. I really want to talk—"

"Tell her," he continued, "that if she ever leaves your protection, he will make an example of her to the rest of the Northwest demesne."

"Ancho—"

"Goodbye, my friend. Be careful and guard your son."

The connection clicked off and I was left holding a silent lump of plastic to my ear.

᪻᪻᪻   ᪻᪻᪻   ᪻᪻᪻

"Your eyes . . ."

It eventually occurred to me that I was the only other person aboard the *New Moon* at the moment. I turned from the upper deck railing and looked at Volpea. "What?"

She had thrown on a white shirt but hadn't bothered to button it. The material billowed out behind her as the wind angled up off the river. With her bronzed skin and articulated musculature, she looked like some caped crusader from the comic books. *It is I, Bikini-woman!*

She stepped a little closer, reducing the quantity, if not the quality, of distraction. "Um," she said, "you know the old saying about how the eyes are mirrors of the soul?"

"Windows," I said. "The eyes are the windows of the soul. Not mirrors. Thomas Phaer, 1510 to 1560."

She stared at me.

"Falsely attributed to Aristotle and Shakespeare."

"Now you're scaring me."

I shrugged. "Just saying . . ."

"Well," she brushed some hair from her face and took another step, "yours are more like mirrors than windows. At this rate your reflective moods will soon be more literal than metaphorical."

"Great," I muttered. "Maybe I can get a temp job, working for Galactus."

She was back to staring at me.

"Galactus?" I repeated. "You know . . . the Silver Surf—?" I sighed. "Oh, never mind." I turned back to the railing and gazed out at the tree-lined bluffs across the green undulations of water.

Looking up at the bleached turquoise sky, I realized, again, just how much I had missed the sun. Not that I didn't look out of a shaded window from time to time. It wasn't even that long ago that I had still been able to slather on enough SPF 1000 sun block for very short excursions outside. Longer on those days that were heavily overcast. But to stand fearlessly out in the open, enjoying the view up close and the warmth of sun on my back? The need might diminish over time but it would never completely fade away.

And it wasn't just me.

Rumor had it that, of all the vampires caught out in the open and immolated by the rising sun, fewer were caught by accident than previously supposed.

Even transformed, we are not emotionally designed for immortality.

I, myself, wasn't suicidal. Yet. Just clinically depressed, according to Drs. Mooncloud and Burton.

And Mama Samm.

And Camazotz Chamalcan.

And even The Kid, though he hadn't been around to haunt my new digs for a while. Apparently ghosts don't have an affinity for water unless they drowned there to begin with. Since J.D. had been a vampire—with the attendant hydro phobias before he kicked it for the second time—his visitations were rare and usually involved an event of some significance.

Apparently my abduction and return weren't significant enough.

"Tell me about Lupé Garou," Volpea said.

Oh yeah: still had company. Not suicidal but depressed enough to be dangerously distracted. And no longer as averse to risk as I once had been. Not a good sign. I had to keep my head in the game—if not for me then for my son. And, although two werewolf enforcers from New Orleans were more likely to be allies than enemies, I couldn't simply trust in others' better natures. To paraphrase the Tao of the Tomb: shit happens.

In my case it happens a lot.

Over and over.

Like preternatural laxative.

"You probably know more than I do, by now," I growled. "I'm up here. She's down there. You can visit. I can't. I should be asking you that question."

She came to stand beside me at the railing. "Is it true that you were lovers? That the child she carries is yours?"

"Is this any of your business?" I turned back to the view across the river but that wasn't what I was seeing anymore.

"It is the business of the Pack," she said gently. "For, if it is true, it tears at the Covenant. Fang and Fur may be sundered."

"Ask me if I care."

"You have a reputation as Warlock, as Oath-breaker. You are anathema to our traditions."

I snorted. "Whose traditions? The vampires who rule the weres? Or the weres who have been subjugated by the undead for a thousand years, now? Half of it's a lie, you know."

"And what half is that?" There was no shock or consternation in her voice. Either I was preaching to the choir or she wasn't about to take anything I said seriously.

"About it being death or some sort of folderol for a vampire to drink a werewolf's blood," I told her. "How do you think a Doman acquires their powers, after all?"

Her breathing quickened. She wasn't as fully briefed as she'd thought. "And what," she asked carefully, "happens when a lycanthrope drinks the blood of a fanged master?"

I shrugged. "Ask Lupé. Although I'm not sure that I would count as I'm not—" *Dammit: saying more than I should . . .* "You realize, of course, that even though we are no longer together, I have published a fatwa, promising to destroy anyone who harms her or the child. And then utterly destroy their bloodline as well."

I saw Volpea nod out of the corner of my eye. "Of course. It is why she is still alive despite the breaking of The Covenant." I felt her gaze slide across me. "At least as long as you live, that is."

"Doing fine so far."

She shrugged. "People die."

I nodded. "Yes. Yes, they do. In fact a whole lotta people have died over the past year because they haven't learned to leave us the hell alone. You want covens and packs and enclaves that are socially dysfunctional and obsessed about miscegenation? Fine! Keep your clubhouses and secret handshakes and have your silly little rules and rituals. But don't be pulling any pointy sheets over my head and telling me that I have to sign up for your nonsense! I've got my own clubhouse, thank you very much, and I and my people will do our own family planning!"

"Then why," she asked after a long silence, "is your lover and the mother of your child taking refuge in New Orleans instead of staying up here in your . . . um . . . clubhouse?"

"Why don't you ask her?" was all I could come up with after a slightly shorter pause. "Why do you care?"

"Because I'm curious. Because you are not what I expected. Because I do not know if you are the greatest threat that the New Orleans' demesne has ever faced . . . or its last, best chance for salvation," she said, turning toward me. "And I cannot make that decision without knowing you better." She pushed herself against me. "I think I *want* to know you better . . ."

I reached down, grasped her upper arm, and moved her back. At least I tried to move her back. She was strong and solid and not ready to move. And I couldn't budge her. Well, my leverage was all wrong . . .

I didn't want to step back because predators always recognize a retreat as a sign of weakness. I had learned that early on. I just hadn't learned how to deal in situations precisely like this.

"One of the reasons Lupé is not here is that she walked in on a conversation very much like this one and got the wrong idea," I said. I did not speak softly, I spoke quietly. There is a marked difference.

"Well," Volpea said, reaching up to finger my shirt, "she's down there . . . we're up here . . . so she can't walk in and get the wrong idea this time . . ."

"How about Fenris? Suppose he gets the wrong idea—"

Her index finger came to rest on my lips. "I told Fenny to stay away for a couple of hours. I told him I had a better chance of getting information out of you if we were alone."

"What kind of information?" I mumbled around her finger.

"Some of us want to know where your sympathies lie . . . " The finger left my lips and trailed down my chin.

"Sympathies?"

"The conflict between Lupin and Wampyri. If you had to choose sides . . . " The finger ghosted my throat and made a lazy tour of my chest.

"I thought it was a matter of public record that I've always taken my own side," I answered.

"You, yourself, have said repeatedly that you are not a vampire." The finger trickled lower.

"Not yet, anyway."

"You resist the Embrace . . . " Lower. "You are still potent . . . " Uncomfortably low. "And we have questions regarding your plans for . . . expansion . . . "

I grabbed her hand and brought it back up. Lucky for me she didn't resist.

Even luckier, I didn't squeak when I said: "Expansion?"

"Your demesne. At least what you claim as your own gathering of allies and were-lieged."

I finally took that step back and released her wrist. "And why should I tell Marie Laveau all of my plans? We already have a mutually agreeable arrangement."

I had released her wrist but Volpea had performed a smooth reverse and now had mine. "Because, as much as she and the other fanged masters would like to know how you fit into their plans, it is the Lupin who ask. And, depending upon your answers, they may be the key to your supremacy over all other demesnes."

I stared at her.

"Do you understand?"

Well, yes and . . . "Not really. No."

A moment before she was looking at me like I was a seven-course meal in a five-star restaurant. Now she wore the expression of someone whose tuna casserole was a little overdone and was thinking about ordering pizza delivery instead.

"Look," I said, "it's not that I don't see where you're trying to go with this. It's just that it doesn't make any sense. If the Lupin want to rise up and throw off the shackles of vampire oppression, you've got my blessing. I won't get in the way. But if you're talking about the weres all signing up to be members of my demesne? Well, what is that? Trading a bunch of undead masters for another? Uh-uh. I can barely manage my own affairs much less anyone else's. And the whole point of seceding from the demesne system would be to free yourselves from anyone's domination. So, best of luck to you. Hope it all works out. And drop me a postcard from time to time."

"It's not that simple," she said.

It was for me. It had to be. I had complications enough without getting involved in additional hostilities. On the other hand, no sense in pissing off another werewolf. Much less a whole new clan or pack or furry activist coalition. *Tread carefully, Cséjthe . . .*

"Tell me about bloodwalking."

"What?" Tread carefully *and pay more attention!* "Why? So you'll know what to look for if I try anything?" I grumped.

The seductive look was back in place. "Because maybe I'd like to know what I'm getting myself into should I decide to invite you in."

"Invite me in?" I echoed stupidly.

Now I'll be among the first to admit that there are times that I can be, well, obtuse. A little slow on the uptake, at the very least. Occasionally. Not often, mind you, but . . . sometimes. More rare than common—

The point is, I find it helpful to feign confusion at times in order to get people to volunteer more information. Such as when their motivations are obviously suspect.

Like now.

"I need you to consider our cause," she elaborated. "You might be more inclined to do so if I were able to smuggle you in to see your . . . people . . . under Marie Laveau's nose."

I stared down at her. It wasn't that great a distance as she was tall. "You're talking about giving me a ride inside your head," I murmured.

"Maybe. It would depend on a number of things."

"Like what?" I asked, already knowing the negotiations would likely involve some sort of compromise on my part.

"I would need to know what kind of a man I would be sharing my body with. And would my mind be violated? Or is it possible for my thoughts to remain private if I so wish it?"

I didn't like it. You don't give intel to the enemy. Or, at the very least, to strangers. Especially when you have so little, yourself. But if Volpea was even halfway serious, it would be my best and possibly only chance for slipping through the Voodoo Queen's cordons and seeing Lupé.

Explaining my mode of transportation to Lupé could be a big problem but this was not the time to look a gift wolf in the mouth.

So I explained what I did know from my surprisingly limited experience in invading other people's bodies. I told her that I had never tried being the "passenger" aboard a willing host. That all of my experiences in blood-walking had involved taking control of the body of an unprepared host and relying on shock and surprise to help keep their consciousness suppressed while I sat in the "driver's seat," as it were. And that the only time I had actually delved past anyone's surface thoughts while visiting was to fish a security pass code out of a panicked guard's memory—which he surrendered as soon as I asked the question. That's all.

I promised to be a gentleman, if that helped any.

Her response, after a long pause, was that her only formal acquaintance with any "gentlemen" was at "gentlemen's clubs."

It was at that point that something *else* that had been bothering me—along with all of the other things that had been bothering me—suddenly jumped the queue and rushed to the front of the line. I looked down at the discolored patch of skin on Volpea's wrist where I had grasped it a moment before. I could still see remnants of my handprint.

I looked at her hand now firmly enclosed about my own wrist. "Doesn't that hurt?" I asked.

Her lips quirked into a smile. "Define 'hurt.'"

Fenris and Volpea had been briefed, of course, about the silver deposits in my body. A couple of silver bullets from January's assassination attempt had dissolved in my bloodstream before they could be removed. As a result, my touch was more than a little uncomfortable to silver-sensitive creatures like lycanthropes. Lupé had found my embrace unbearable and my lips on her forehead had produced blisters. Just another of the several causes for our present separation.

"There is a very thin line, at times, between pleasure and pain, Domo Cséjthe," Volpea said breathily, moving my hand to her side and holding it to the curve of her waist. "There are those who season their food with dabs of catsup while others prefer quantities of Tabasco." She moved my hand so that my fingers trailed across her belly, leaving reddish streaks across her bronzed skin. "And there are ways, for those who choose them," she said as my fingers brushed her belly ring, "to build our tolerance— even our enjoyment—of intense stimulation."

I took a closer look at reddened interception of flesh and jewelry. "So you're saying this isn't the standard stainless steel setting?"

She shook her head with a sly smile. "Silver alloy. As is this . . . " She pulled her top open, exposing her right breast. A more elaborate ring spiraled about and trans- fixed her engorged nipple with a ruby clasp.

She stepped back and tugged on my hand. The red streaks across her finely muscled abdomen were already beginning to fade. "Let's go back to your cabin and I'll show you the others . . . "

Others?

As in more than one others?

I started to do a mental inventory as she pulled me toward the steps leading down to the deck below.

Compromises, I told myself; *you knew this would likely involve compromises. Everything has a price.*

The question was, was the price too high?

Chapter Five

THE QUESTION OF PRICE got postponed before we reached the cash register.

Mama Samm and the Gator-man arrived just as I was starting to resist Volpea on the public side of my cabin door.

At least I'm pretty sure I was starting to resist.

I did end up losing my clothes and getting a thorough going-over. Just not the one I had been promised a few minutes earlier. In fact, Volpea departed early in the process with a look that said we had unfinished business.

I spent the better part of the next two hours out in the salon getting poked and prodded and asking when I could get dressed again.

The Gator-man was a Cajun *traiteur*—a backwoods "treater"—who had performed preternatural surgery on Lupé and myself when we had been shot six months back. Since Lupé was a werewolf and I was—what? Growing less human every month? We couldn't very well present ourselves to the local ER. Imagine trying to join an HMO and having to list preexisting conditions. So my health-care options were severely limited. The arcane properties of my necrophagic virus kept me away from traditional doctors and these untold millions of microscopic machines in my bloodstream screwed up any hoodoopathic alternatives.

Even the preternatural options available via the demesne system were severely constrained. I was lucky to have worked out an arrangement between Pagelovitch and Laveau for the use of Dr. Mooncloud's services but I couldn't actually visit any existing clinics, myself.

Staying healthy was going to be a very iffy proposition from here on out.

The Gator-man couldn't "read" any conjure marks on me from my stay at the underhill Hilton. "But I do not know if these Hillfolk are kin to the mound dwellers that I know, me," the old Cajun said.

"How about the silver load levels, Alphonse?"

He shook his head and his ivory moustache bristled as he pursed his lips. "You got more, you. Should be less but metal is not leaving your bones."

"Wait a minute," I said. "How can I have more silver now than I did when the bullets first dissolved in my body? I think I'd know if somebody shot me again."

"Obviously his body is hoarding all of its Ag atoms so it can create defensive weapons when he's under attack," Mama Samm mused. "Could these tiny machines be building Ag atoms out of junk protons and electrons?"

"Have you touched or handled anything silver, you?" Alphonse asked me. "Maybe you be absorbing silver molecules through skin contact."

"What? The nanos are sucking silver out of my pocket change and off of my grandmother's flatware?"

The *traiteur* lifted my arm to show me. "Look, you: skin is more dark, yet shiny. And eyes . . . "

I sighed. "Yeah, yeah, I know. Mirrored sunglasses would be redundant. But what does it mean?"

The outer door flew open and Camazotz stood in the entryway with an armload of containers. "It means," he announced in a shockingly girlish voice, "that his nanobots have kicked into high gear and are now running new programming and subroutines!" He stepped into the salon and then we could see that it was Dr. Taj Mooncloud, standing behind him, who was speaking. "And, if we don't find a way to reverse the process, he'll develop a full-blown case of Argyria!"

🦇 🦇 🦇

It was like tag-team medicine in sudden death overtime now. Taj and Alphonse were both short, round, and brown. She was both a shaman and a medical doctor with long black hair, a heritage from her Amerindian father and East Indian mother. He was a Cajun homeopath whose coloring hinted of exotic Creole bloodlines that dramatically set off his white bristle of a moustache and shock of ivory hair. Between the two of them they poked and prodded, consulted and argued while mutually lecturing me on aspects of depression, latent death wishes, and self-destructive tendencies.

Argyria, I learned, was a condition where silver compounds deposited in body tissues reached critical levels. One of the side effects was a transformation in skin pigmentation to blue or bluish gray.

No wonder I was feeling a little "blue" of late.

Except: "I'm not turning blue, I'm turning brown," I protested.

"Once you go 'black,' " Mama Samm called from the galley, "you won't want to go back!"

"Black and shiny," Zotz commented, passing through with a spool of wire, "super-fly!"

"No one says 'fly' anymore," I grumped. "And Ron O'Neal would roll in his grave."

Mooncloud chuckled. "I'd say the nanites are augmenting his melanin to provide extra protection—if not invulnerability—to solar radiation. I wouldn't be surprised if they figured out a way to turn his skin green if it meant saving his life."

I groaned.

During this time Fenris arrived and left again, taking Volpea with him. Zotz made multiple trips around the boat, trying to install the transducers for the fish-finders without damaging the hull. More than once he tracked bilge water across the carpet and gave me a look daring me to say anything about it. In the end, he picked up the phone and bribed someone from the marina to come out in the morning and do a professional install.

He wasn't off the hook. Shortly after getting the new gear stowed, the spear guns cached, additional weapons cleaned and checked, and a quick rinse in the semi-operational shower, he was pressed into mess duty under Mama Samm's watchful eye. By the time I was allowed to put my clothes back on, the sun was down, and Zotz was getting instruction on how to properly clean fish in the galley. Regular fish, that is; not the giant mutant bipeds we tussled with earlier.

"How's he coming along?" I asked as Mama Samm came toward me, wiping her hands.

She sighed. "All too well. Apparently 'skinning' and 'disemboweling' are second nature to demons." She turned her attention to Dr. Mooncloud's latest row of colorful concoctions in the test tube rack on the table. "How about him?"

"There's not a whole lot I can tell without an electron microscope or an x-ray machine," Taj answered. She stared at the latest color change wrought by reagents in a small flask bubbling over a portable Bunsen burner. "But there's little doubt that the nanobots have activated in his body."

"They weren't wholly dormant before," I pointed out.

"True, but there's a vast difference between tissue repair, silver reprocessing on a passive, background level and then jumping up the process to redistributing mineral and bone deposits—perhaps even migrating, replicating, and daisy-chaining in sufficient quantities—to create projective claws and arm blades."

"But not out of silver," I argued. "Whatever popped out of my fingertips was hard enough to slice through limestone substrate. Silver's too soft."

"I'm sure your nanites are working with a number of different molecular source materials, producing alloys to

fit whatever tasks they deem necessary," Mooncloud
mused.

Now that was creepy on more than one level. "At
this point we've entered the comic book realm," I said,
repressing a shiver.

"The preferred term is graphic novel," Zotz called
from the galley.

"A rose by any other name and no way I'm gonna wear
spandex," I growled.

"And you never found any scuba gear that would
account for your underwater revival?" she continued,
ignoring that last comment.

I shook my head. "But someone was helping me down
there. Someone who looked a lot like Suki."

"One mystery at a time," she said. It was the third
time she had changed the subject when I had invoked
the Asian vampire's name. Apparently when the Doman
of Seattle says that someone is "dead to him," he not
only means personally but everyone who works for him,
as well.

"For now, I want you to consider another theory,"
she continued.

"I'm not going to like it, am I." It wasn't really a
question.

"The blood and tissue samples we took just after your
return from Colorado—before all the Domans agreed to
place you on joint quarantine status—showed evidence
of an evolutionary trend in your nanite technology. There
were several different types of nanomachines found in
your samples. Yet, they fell into two functional classifica-
tions. Those that repaired damaged tissues on the cellular level. And those that repaired and replicated the
other machines.

"Over the course of time we observed that some of the nanites evolved into machines with different functions as the tissue samples aged and withered. The very nature of their purpose was challenged as a piece of tissue removed from its larger component no longer functions the same—if at all. The machines seemed to adjust their programming to deal with changes in environment, oxygen levels, hormonal flux—"

"You're saying that these itty-bitty bots built me some kind of breathing apparatus? An artificial gill? In a matter of minutes? That's nuts!"

"I dare say," she replied calmly, "along with vampires, werewolves, demons, and fish people."

"But how do they know—?"

"You want a wild guess? Or should I dress it up fancy and offer it as a theory? Maybe these things are programmed as a collective consciousness, a sort of hive-mind. And their cybernetic imperative seems to be to sustain life. Even to proactive extremes, it would appear. When you were threatened with physical violence, they improved your abilities to defend yourself. When you were denied oxygen, they found another way for you to extract it from your changed environment. In fact I'd be surprised if they're not already working on two fronts: separating oxygen molecules from your CO_2 and recycling. They're adjusting your parameters so you can evolve as your circumstances change."

The thought of a million microscopic machines inside me made my skin crawl. Sadly, that was probably more than just a metaphor. "So what are they doing now?"

She shrugged.

"What got them activated? How do I turn them off?"

"As to the first question, has anything happened to you that falls outside of your normal routine, recently?" she asked.

I considered my recent stay at the Fairyfield Inn and the weird tingle from Fand's miscast spell. "Maybe," I allowed. "How about 'I've got you under my skin, part deux'?"

"Turning them off?" She looked nonplussed. "Why would you want to? Mengele obviously programmed these microscopic machines to keep their host hale, healthy, and hearty under the most extreme conditions—in other words, *your* typical operating environment. Why look a gift horse in the mouth?"

She had a point. And I knew that my reaction was largely emotional rather than rational. "But these things have been practically dormant for the better part of a year," I argued. "One little run-in with Tinkerbell's big sis and suddenly I'm Christopus of Borg—I will be assimilated! Every six months or so I run up against something far more scary than a faerie faux shrink! Tell me this isn't going to go somewhere dark or disgusting down the road."

She just sat there and stared at me impassively. Perhaps not the most descriptive of terms as there was something at the back of Mooncloud's eyes that was anything but passive. "What do you think I can do? All of the medical facilities best equipped to diagnose these latest changes to your physiology are now off-limits. Why? Because you've pissed off every Doman in the known demesne system." The impassive look became a glare. "Do you realize they may not let me back into the New Orleans enclave because I have had contact with you?"

"Not to worry," I answered as Fenris and Volpea made a return entrance. "The Wonder Were-twins are here to make sure all returnees are Cséjthe-free ere they depart."

"And we depart tonight," Fenris announced abruptly. "We've been recalled." He turned to Mama Samm. "You must be ready to leave with us within the hour if you still wish to visit New Orleans with Laveau's blessing."

Mama Samm looked at me. "Olive will need help with Jamal while I'm gone."

I nodded. "Don't dawdle and I'll baby-sit nights." I turned to Zotz. "Think you can manage the day shift?"

He nodded solemnly. "I do not sleep. And the boy is better company than some. . . ." He cast a meaningful glance back at his nemesis.

"Fine," Mama Samm said, ignoring him. "Then I am ready to go, now. My bags have been packed for days and are out in the car."

Fenris turned to Dr. Mooncloud. "You must depart, as well, Doctor. How long before you are ready?"

Taj considered the sprawl of equipment. "Ten . . . fifteen minutes, tops."

"Please begin packing up. It is imperative that we return as soon as possible." He turned to me. "Domo Cséjthe. No disrespect to you is intended but we have our orders. We must ensure that you have no opportunity to infect any of our charges. I must ask that you return to your cabin and remain there until we depart."

I flexed my hands, my fingers, willing my battle claws to pop out. Just as well they didn't: taking him down wouldn't have accomplished anything beyond scratching an itch.

And New Orleans' security would just ramp up to impossible levels.

᙭   ᙭   ᙭

With apologies to E.A. Poe, suddenly there came a tapping—as if someone gently rapping. But not upon my chamber door.

I crossed my cabin and peeked behind the blackout blinds covering the window (I refuse to call something that isn't completely round a "porthole") over my bed.

Volpea stood on the narrow side deck running the outer length of the boat. She put a finger to her lips and gestured for me to open the window.

"Still want to go?" she whispered as I knelt on the bed and slid the glass aside.

I hesitated then nodded. The catch on the window was easy; the catch on this deal might be a lot more difficult . . .

"If I give you access to my body, do you promise to leave me in control and respect the privacy of my own thoughts?" she asked.

The "access to my body" phrase started to trigger that other voice in the back of my head but I told it to shut up and let me think.

I don't like to make promises I can't keep. So I generally avoid making them to people I don't know who have motives I don't fully fathom. Volpea took a half step back when I didn't answer: my window of opportunity was narrower than the physical casement I had just opened. And it was going to close in another moment.

"I promise," I said too quickly to sound anything like sincere.

She gave me a searching look. "I'll have to trust you. And hope that you will not betray me."

Ditto, I thought as she stepped forward and reached through the small window. Cupping her hand behind my head, she leaned in and kissed me. Deeply. Hell, she tried to tickle my tonsils with her tongue! Which—big surprise—seemed to have a piercing of its own.

And then I tasted blood.

She had bitten her own tongue to give me my opening.

I closed my eyes and concentrated on the "gateway."

Leaving my own body and entering another's through their blood is always a bit disorienting. A little more so this time, as I hadn't had time to prepare. I suddenly found myself holding on to my own body!

We had a hold of *me* by the collar.

Slowly, we lowered my body onto the mattress. I don't know if the solicitude was for my unconscious comfort or an attempt to prevent the thump of a collapsing body from alerting Fenris. I did know that somebody needed to cut back on the doughnuts. In any event, my carcass ended up sprawled on its side, looking less asleep than passed out at the end of a three-day drunk. A certified Kodak moment.

Unexpectedly, I began to snore.

Lovely.

✠✠   ✠✠   ✠✠

The next ten minutes were a blur as Volpea hurried back around to finish loading Dr. Mooncloud's medical supplies and keep Fenris distracted from the sounds of a slow-motion buzz saw originating from my bedroom.

I was working very hard on not doing anything.

It's very disorienting to find yourself in a whole new body.

Even more so when your arms and legs are moving and engaged in tasks that you have nothing to do with. Imagine your own reaction if your body suddenly took off of its own volition and began doing things without your say so. It's sort of like having a very organized seizure: the urge to take back control of your limbs is overwhelming.

But I'd promised Volpea I'd stay in the passenger seat. And the last thing I needed was for an alpha-male werewolf to be treated to the sight of his partner flopping around on the floor because her body couldn't figure out who was running the show.

So I worked very hard at not doing anything. I was even concerned that too much thinking might distract my host at a critical moment. Instead, I concentrated on the sensations of a change of flesh.

My previous sojourns in female bodies were fleeting—with the one exception of a headless corpse, so that didn't really count. Everybody is different and, in like manner, every *body* is different, so gender differences aren't necessarily as obvious as one might first imagine. Obviously there were changes in the plumbing. And such physical alterations as height, lower center of gravity, and having bosoms meant posture and locomotion were slightly different, now. Hopefully, I wouldn't have to run for my life without a little practice, first.

And a good sports bra.

As for the endocrine system, it was a little too early to compare hormones.

Though there were these little tingly spots that I'd never encountered in other people's flesh and rarely in my ow, ow, ow-*holy crap, I now knew the locations of all of Volpea's silver piercings!*

My limited experience with body-swapping was pretty much limited to humans and the undead. Vampires, as a rule, are inhumanly strong. But their strength is cold and machinelike. If Volpea was any example, lycanthropes were vigorous, powerhouses of raw energy, surging and thrumming just beneath their skin. In a cage match, I might bet on the vampires but it wouldn't necessarily be a sure thing in every instance.

Other than the fact that she could probably kick *my* ass.

Her hearing was very sharp, too. More acute, apparently, than her male counterpart's. Volpea's ears were picking up my snoozy noises just fine. Even Camazotz Chamalcan kept throwing suspicious glances at my cabin door.

<Ask him to help you with something outside,> I told Volpea. <He's going to say or do something unfortunate if we don't tell him. And he needs to know since he'll be babysitting for two, now.>

It was almost too easy.

Fenris went outside to perform a final check on both vehicles and Volpea gave the demon a quick sketch of how things stood.

Then it was time to go.

Nice, easy, uneventful, and we were on the road five minutes later with no one apparently the wiser.

ᮭᮭ   ᮭᮭ   ᮭᮭ

Dr. Mooncloud had driven up in one of those trucks badly disguised to look like a car. Mama Samm rode shotgun with her. The werewolves had arrived a few days earlier in a '68 AMC Gold Rambler Rebel. Yee haw. I spent the first few minutes wondering how they got the parts to keep this antique running. Then Fenris spoke.

"Did you have another opportunity to press our cause with the Bloodwalker?" he asked.

"Yes. In spite of too many interruptions," my own ride answered from the passenger seat.

"And would you say he was . . . receptive?"

"Receptive might be just the word to describe the progress of our present stage of negotiations," she said.

Tall, dark, and hirsute nodded and hunched over the steering wheel. No more words were exchanged which left sufficient silence for me to take up the conversation.

<Hey. I thought I was pretty clear back at the boat: *not* interested in joining any overthrows right now. Especially when my friends and family are smack dab in the middle of the Boston Commons!>

>The Boston Commons?< she queried, confused over the real estate reference.

<Tiananmen Square, then, and tanks for your concern. The only deal on the table is *you* take me to see my people and *I* respect the privacy of your thoughts.>

>Well, if you want the plan to go smoothly, I'll need to say whatever it takes to keep certain people happy and unsuspicious. Or would you rather I default to complete honesty and let the chips fall where they may?<

I started to raise mental hands in surrender but stopped as soon as I felt Volpea's hands twitch. <Okay. I overreacted. Sorry.>

"What's the matter?"

We both looked over at the driver. "What?"

"You look like you're in pain," he said.

"I have a headache."

<Nice.>

>Should I mention it seems to be heading south?<

< >

"I need to stop for gas. I'll grab coffee and aspirin, too," he offered.

"Thanks."

Maybe I had misjudged Mr. Grumpy-fur. He was a real gentleman. Gassed up the car, bought two coffees, three different kinds of analgesics, and snagged extra creams, sugars, and napkins whilst V and I were in the ladies room.

This was a new experience for me. I'd never hung around long enough to try out any of the pages in the owner's manual. And you'd think a lady would be kind of shy about company in the can. But I guess it couldn't get any more intimate than we already were—at least not without a little mind mingling. So I did my best to "look" the other way while the essentials were taken care of. I am, after all, a gentleman.

Just not a "perfect" gentleman.

Back in the car, back on the road, it was obvious that we had taken a detour.

"What about Mooncloud? And the juju woman?" Volpea asked between sips of lousy truck-stop coffee.

"Mooncloud didn't require an escort to get here," Fenris answered. "Our job was to make sure the Blood-walker wasn't inside anyone's head who returned." He turned and looked at us. "They're clean, aren't they?"

We swallowed. And almost gagged. *Bad! Bad coffee! Down, boy, down!*

"Of course," she choked over the last swallow. "I checked on him, myself."

"Sorry." He turned his attention back to the road.

"What?"

"About the coffee. It's pretty bad." He gestured with his own cup. "But we need something to keep us awake until we get home. Cream and sugar help kill the worst of the taste."

"What's the hurry?" she asked. "We could have caught a few hours sleep; returned in the morning."

Fenris shook his head. "The call came from Pantera. She's hearing the Voices, again."

"That's not good."

"It gets worse. She's built another altar."

"And?"

"He wouldn't say. But it sounds very bad. Worse than any of the other times. He wants us back tonight!"

To say the conversation waned after that would be an understatement. Silence fell in the car like a cold, hard vacuum from the ass end of the universe. It was even still and quiet inside Volpea's head.

<Marie Laveau is building altars?> I nudged.

>It has been forbidden,< she answered slowly.

<Why?>

>Because it always leads to something dark and terri-ble happening.<

<And who has forbidden it? Pantera?>
>Marie, herself. When she is sane . . . <
I thought about that.

A hundred and fifty years ago, before she had been turned by a vampire, Marie Laveau had been a Voudon priestess of great renown and power. So much so that when her daughter took up the practice of Santeria, it was widely believed that she was the original Marie Laveau, immortalized by the loa, themselves. Mother and daughter did share a common interest in voodoo but, the original Marie found that her powers were now limited: she could no longer go about in the day and the "right-hand" path had begun to close as her vampiric nature became ascendant.

According to Mama Samm, the elder Laveau was wise enough to back away at that point, lest the darker, "left-hand" path consume and destroy her. She was content to stay in the shadows, offering advice and tutelage to her offspring so that her daughter eventually surpassed her in power and knowledge.

But not longevity.

The mother did not share the Dark Gift with her daughter. She was still sane enough to recognize that immortality carried too great a price. So Marie II lived a full life and passed away, full of years and, she hoped, went into the Light at the end of her days.

But wisdom does not always grow when it marches in an endless parade of days. As the years then decades then generations passed, Marie I would make occasional attempts to reinvoke the powers and blessing of the loa. Time and again, Mama Samm once told me, the former voodoo priestess had to relearn that the Dark Gift had forever distorted the pathways.

Bad things happened.

Marie Laveau retreated into solitude to nurse her disappointments. And, it was rumored, fight off the madness that whispered from the shadows and haunted her dreams.

New Orleans became an "open demesne" where individuals and gangs vied for turf and, occasionally, supremacy. Marie had her cotillion of undead sycophants and servitors but had not taken a serious interest in power plays for over a century. As far as the other undead factions were concerned, she was a myth, a legend, a boogeyman story the older vamps trotted out to keep the young fangs in line when they got a little too ambitious. But being undead wasn't enough. Unseen and unheard over time pretty much added up to unimportant for the latest generation.

Until she took a consort a few years back.

That's when everything had gone to hell in South Louisiana for a time. Or so I've been told. This was before my time, back when I had a family and went to sleep at night, blissfully unaware that there really were things that went "bump in the night."

The gossip about her new "Latin lover" was sparse and contradictory. The parts that did agree had the Pantera family coming up from some remote place in Central or South America—the stories varied on the finer details—and doing the tourist thing in New Orleans. It was around the changing of the millennium, during one of the Mardi Gras.

The thing about tourists is they don't know safe territory from the hunting grounds. And they don't know at what hour the boundary lines move and the territories shift. The Panteras had found themselves too close to the wrong alleyway on the wrong street at the wrong hour of the night.

Worse, what preyed upon them was not a pickpocket or a mugger or anything human.

Jorge Pantera lost his wife and son that night. And his own mortality. Only his daughter emerged unscathed—though there are quiet disputations about that, too. Conjecture and supposition; it's all gossip, come out of a city that elevates gossip to a high art form. What was known is that Marie Laveau avenged his family's murders and took father and daughter under her personal protection.

Then it got complicated.

Once upon a time, Marie Laveau had been the "Queen of New Orleans." The return of her libido coincided with her return to that throne. That, in and of itself, would have ruffled a few feathers. She opted for maximum political turmoil by elevating a stranger—a foreigner—who had no experience, no wealth, no power—worse, no history—to rule the Crescent City at her side. To say that this arrangement did not sit well with many would be a vast political understatement.

Much closer to the statistical truth to say it didn't sit well with *any*.

Still, the survivors of the internecine wars that erupted soon thereafter learned to accept it. Those who didn't, well . . . didn't.

Survive, that is.

Even Sammathea D'Arbonne, who doesn't take crap from anybody, shows the Queen due respect. She doesn't like her or trust her, but neither is she dismissive or careless.

Me? I'm a lot shakier in the "care" and "respect" departments but Laveau and Pantera were giving shelter to my people so I was more inclined to mind my manners.

Right now I needed to mind the scenery: I turned my attention to looking at the passing landscape through Volpea's eyes. I hadn't been carsick since I was a kid but the creeping nausea in my gut suggested that I'd spent too much time on inner contemplation. The key to avoiding motion sickness, I remembered belatedly, was to go with the flow.

Unfortunately, we were off the main road and down some rural back road where there weren't enough lights to show any scenery: looking out the window did little to placate the pit vipers of nausea coiling and uncoiling in the pit of our stomach.

And now our head was starting to pound while feeling curiously light and airy at the same time.

"I don't feel so good," Volpea croaked.

It was true, she really didn't. I didn't feel so hot, myself, for that matter.

"What's wrong?" Fenris asked.

"I don't know. I feel nauseous . . ."

"Carsick?" he asked. "Are you going to hurl?" The turn signal went on. Fenris had to be an import: Louisiana drivers don't use turn signals—I suspect they don't even know what that stick on the steering column is supposed to do. "Crank your window down! You're not

blowing chunks all over the interior!" We decelerated
and drifted over onto the shoulder. "Do you feel like
you're going to pass out?" We rolled to a stop and he
opened the driver's door and jumped out.

"Don't be silly," V was muttering as he came around
and opened the passenger door. "You don't pass out from
carsickness." She dropped the coffee cup from her
nerveless fingers. "Uh, oops . . ."

I followed her eyes down to the floor. There wasn't
enough liquid left in the paper cup to make much of a
spill. <Uh, Volpea—>

"Come on," Fenris said, extending his hand. "Get out.
I'll hold your hair."

We just sat there. "Um," my muddled host said after
a moment, "my legs don't seem to be working . . ."

<Oh crap! We've been had!>

"Are you sure?" Fenris leaned in to take a closer look
at our eyes.

"Um, yep; nothing's moving . . ."

<V! The coffee! It—>

Fenris shifted his stance, brought his other hand out
of his pocket. "Sorry. I gotta make sure." The device in
his hand looked like an old garage door opener. Except
it made a stuttering, clicking sound and suddenly there
were little arcs of blue electricity dancing between two
metal prongs on the end.

He pressed the prongs into our side.

*Correction: someone swung a sledgehammer into our
side!*

*And the car flipped over and over and over and over
and down into darkness.*

▬▬   ▬▬   ▬▬

<Hello?>

> <

<Anyone there?>

> <

It was dark. And hot. And I hurt like hell!

I'd say "we" hurt like hell but Volpea didn't seem to be in the same room.

Maybe there wasn't room for the both of us: it was tight and I was turned on my side, my arms cuffed behind me and my knees tucked up against my—um—tits. So, I had at least one point of reference for "where" *I* was.

I tried listening for additional clues. From the ringing in my ears I'd have to guess the bell tower of Notre Dame cathedral.

There was some kind of vibration, though I could only feel rather than hear it.

I tried fumbling behind me but my hands were numb from lack of circulation. Lucky them! The rest of me wished it could be. I was one, medium-sized, pretzeled bruise. My ribs felt like they were snapped where the stun gun had made contact. And my muscles were either stony lumps of petrified tissue or semiliquefied residue that puddled here and there under my sandpapered skin. Speaking of puddles, V had lost control of her bladder during her encounter with Ole Sparky. I didn't know what the big bad wolf had dosed the coffee with but stun guns are the next best thing to whoop-ass in a canister—talking 55-gallon drums, here, not 16-ounce pop-tops. The sensations were akin to being run over with a car or beaten by a highly motivated chain gang.

At least we weren't dead.

But, considering the way I was feeling, it was a small blessing, at best.

Gradually I became aware of the floor beneath my body. It sagged. Beneath the thin support of carpeted pressboard I could feel the circular hump of a spare tire. We were cuffed and gagged and bound in the car's trunk.

So where were we going?

It was at least another hour before I got the answer to that question. In the meantime, I was on my own: Volpea remained unconscious and blissfully ignorant of how much she was going to hurt when she woke up. Maybe that was best. It wasn't my body and I could disconnect a bit from the pain. And what I was about to do was probably going to hurt like a sonofabitch. With apologies to my lycanthropic host.

It did hurt.

A lot!

Even if Volpea was flexible enough to pull it off under normal circumstances, her body was now a Gordian knot of bruises, contusions, and still twitching nerves and muscles. Even bent double, I had to dislocate a shoulder in order to scrape ass over cuffed wrists and bring our arms back up in front of us. It wasn't as difficult as you might think. From what I've observed, lycanthrope physiology is one step away from being naturally double-jointed: all those bones, sockets, muscles, sinews dislocate, migrate, relocate every time a were transforms from human to animal and back to human again. Of course it hurts like hell and the transformation unleashes a huge flood of endorphins to attempt to counterbalance the agony of each shift. Dislocating a shoulder while retaining human form: less easy and far more painful. By the time I was able to pop our shoulder back in place and pull the gag out of our mouth, it was practically chewed in half, anyway. Still, a stroll in the park compared to attempting the same contortions with a human-normal physique.

The blindfold came next, partially dislodging the earplugs, and suddenly I could see and hear. Not a lot to see: light leakage from the back of the taillights gave dim illumination to the car trunk's interior. And the sound of tires on old and poorly maintained pavement, told me we were off the main highway.

The handcuffs were tricky. Maybe Volpea could shape-shift and slip them off but something told me that Fenris had already anticipated that: there was a reason she was still out while I was all alert now and "enjoying" the tingly aftermath of 900,000 volts. If it wasn't for the miniscule amperage, Fenris would be transporting tailgate barbecue instead of a slightly singed hostage.

I tested the tensile strength of the anodized steel chain connecting the metal bracelets. Nope. Short of a hacksaw, key, or lock pick, my wrists were going to be treated to an extended period of propinquity.

My ankles and knees were a different matter. If Fenris had used professional leg restraints or even plastic "ties," I might've had a problem. Rope, even in a cramped, awkward space, was easier to work with and our legs were free in a matter of minutes.

Now what? Try to pop the trunk lid and signal for help? Jump out of a moving car? Possibly into oncoming traffic? And if someone did stop to help, would they be equipped to deal with a werewolf enforcer who had already taken down his preternaturally powerful partner?

I didn't like the odds. But then I couldn't think of one thing I had liked so far.

As I shifted position for the thirty-seventh time, I felt the thin flooring over the spare shift with me.

Perhaps there was another way to "retire" from this situation. . . .

᪥᪥   ᪥᪥   ᪥᪥

By the time the car reached its destination, I was ready.

There was plenty of warning. First, we left the main road and went some distance on a gravel surface. Then another turn onto a dirt road. And, eventually, the ride turned so rough I had to assume we were off-road entirely. Given that a '68 Rambler Rebel is not an all-terrain vehicle, I knew that it wouldn't be long so I assumed the position.

I was right: we came to a stop in just under two minutes and the engine was turned off. The car resettled itself as the driver got out and slammed the door. I braced myself, waiting.

I waited a lot longer than I expected.

Eventually there were footsteps and voices approaching the trunk.

"You're sure she's completely neutralized?" a new voice was asking.

"She's been dosed with enough aconite to knock her out for forty-eight hours, Gordon," Fenris growled. "Even if she did wake up, she won't be able to shape-shift for at least a week and she's under restraint."

"Wolfsbane?" The new voice sounded horrified. "How did you calculate the dose for her?"

"You're missing the point," my oh-so-ex partner snapped. "She knew there would be risks. She volunteered anyway."

"For *her* version of the plan," the other argued, "not yours. But this new twist—"

"—is a simple practicality," Fenris interrupted. "If the Bloodwalker will not assist us in overthrowing the madwoman and that blasphemy she has set to rule over us, then we must turn this opportunity to our advantage. By destroying the Bloodwalker, we gain Laveau's trust and favor. Hell! We earn the gratitude of every bloodsucking Doman in the country!"

"But we are still slaves to the vampires."

"Perhaps. For a bit longer. But Laveau becomes less suspicious of our motives and loyalties. We earn better opportunities to rise up, strike back, and free ourselves from the fanged oppressors!"

"And do you think the other enclaves will sit idly by and allow one demesne's werewolves to overthrow the masters? They will have to crush us as an example to their own packs of shape-shifting servitors!"

"Perhaps they will be too intimidated," Fenris replied.

"Intimidated?"

"They have tried to kill the Bloodwalker many times and he only grows more powerful. I think they would hesitate to challenge those who accomplished what they, themselves, could not. And then there *are* the other packs. They should be more than willing to rise up and challenge their own masters once they have witnessed our success."

"It is a bold and dangerous risk that you propose, Fenris. The council must decide whether we are prepared to gamble on such high stakes. And I cannot help but wonder if Volpea would feel the risks were justified."

There was the sound of a key being inserted into the trunk lock.

"She was willing to risk her life in defying our vampire masters to join this rebellion. She was willing to risk her life to try and seduce the Bloodwalker into joining us. To even offer up her body and her mind, distasteful as it might be, so that he might hear our offer."

"Somehow I do not think he will be very receptive to anything you have to say after what you have put him through. And I doubt Volpea will ever trust you again, for that matter."

"She is a soldier. She will either understand that some things must be done or she is not worthy of the cause. Frankly, I do not believe that we can trust this creature, this half-vampire, to help us in any way even if he did want to. He is a liability at best and now, possibly, a threat to our existence just because of the little that he does know. No, the council can deliberate but Volpea and I are directly exposed and every *were* in Louisiana will be suspect if he is allowed to live."

"I see your point. This has not gone according to the original plan and, although your hand is heavy in its changing, she bears some responsibility, as well. Perhaps Volpea will vote to sacrifice herself given that there seems to be no way back. But she would know the mind of the Bloodwalker better than any if he resides within her. She should have a seat at the council and be given a say as well as a vote."

"There is no time for that! We are already missed and must return to the city or everything we've worked for will be undone!" The trunk lid came up and I got a glimpse of two figures: Fenris and a shorter, older, bearded man. "We must act tonight and Volpea won't be able to speak or vote, as you say, for another day or two!"

As I rose to my knees and cocked both arms back over my left shoulder, both turned to look down at where I was supposed to be, curled up and unconscious. By the time it was registering that something was very wrong, I was whipping the heavy tire iron around to smash into the side of my captor's head.

"Voting by proxy," I snarled as Fenris dropped like a sandbag from a scaffold, "Volpea signifies in the 'nay' category!"

I turned on the other guy who was starting to back up. "Don't move!" I bellowed.

He stopped.

"Keys! Check his pockets."

The beard looked down at Fenris and hesitated.

"Now!"

He bent and started riffling though the unconscious man's clothing. "This is all a big misunderstanding . . . " the guy called Gordon began.

"Yeah, yeah, I heard. Seduce the Bloodwalker. Try to convert him to the cause. Oh wait: here's a better plan. Let's kill him for the street cred. Too bad about Volpea. I'm sure she'd agree to sacrifice herself if we'd gotten around to mentioning it."

"This was Fenris' idea."

"Sounded like you were getting ready to sign on." I gestured with the tire iron. "That's the trouble with lots of exposition. Unless it's meaningless jabber designed to distract your opponent, it'll just come back and bite you in the ass before the end."

He produced a set of car keys. There was a handcuff key on the ring. "It isn't up to me," he protested. "It's a committee decision."

"Well," I said, "too bad they're not here."

He looked around. So I had to, too.

The poet Francis William Bourdillon wrote that "the night has a thousand eyes."

The songwriting team of Weisman, Wayne, and Garrett grabbed the line and turned it into a hit for Bobby Vee.

No one was likely to write poetry or top-40 hits about tonight's ocular statistics.

Perhaps thirty feet away, reflecting the pale glow of the automobile's trunk light, were two rings of eyes. There were maybe two dozen in all; a semicircle that might account for standing, human watchers and another that suggested the audience was crouching—though in what form I could only guess.

"Great," I said. "Let me guess. A quorum?"

"I'm sorry, Volpea. I know this wasn't part of the original plan but what Fenris proposed does make a certain amount of sense . . ."

"Volpea isn't in, right now," I announced. "You'll be negotiating with the guy who trashed the New York demesne."

Apparently everyone was still playing mental catch-up. I didn't know much more about my bloodwalking ability than everybody else but I had discovered one little advantage while staggering around Mengele's fortress: I could take control of a dead body. So, not so much of a leap from a corpse to an unconscious corpus.

"The keys, Gordo."

He looked at me. And then back at the glowy eyes of our unseen and, so far, reticent audience.

I waggled the tire iron at him. "Uh uh uh! Here's how it works, Gordy. You do anything but hand me those keys within the next fifteen seconds, and I toss this thing. At you. Not hard enough to cripple you. Just hard enough to draw blood. Which opens the door and rolls out the welcome mat, if you get my drift? Then I don't need Volpea's body because you'll be my new bitch. At least until your committee, here, decides to kill *you* to get to *me*." I looked back at them. "Of course, anybody who gets within smacking distance runs the same risks . . ." And looked back at Gordon. "That's ten seconds, now, G: only five left. Four. Three."

He started to toss them to me.

"Uh uh uh. *Hand*. Not *toss*. You toss?" I waggled the tire iron again. "I toss."

He stepped toward me, the keys held out like they had a sputtering fuse protruding from the ring fob.

Stepping out of the trunk without falling on my face was a major accomplishment. My—our—hell, Volpea was still unconscious so they were mine for now-*my* legs were numb and wooden from hours of confinement. And trying to hold a tire iron while your wrists are handcuffed doesn't permit much support work while extricating one's self from a car trunk and taking keys from the enemy while surrounded by a couple dozen more.

Fortunately, the element of surprise had not only served me well, but I was able to ride it into an additional two minutes of overtime.

"Now here's how we're gonna play this," I announced as I fumbled the handcuff key into the evasively tiny lock entry. "I'm no big fan of Marie Laveau but, for the moment, she has something that I want and I have no reason to upset her. Hopefully that will all be done, soon, and, as far as I'm concerned, what happens in the Crescent City, stays in the Crescent City." The cuffs dropped from my left wrist. "And since I have familial bonds with one of the furry folk, I can't help but see you all as family." The other cuff unlocked and my metal bonds dropped to the ground. "A somewhat dysfunctional and difficult-to-get-along-with family." I turned to Gordon. "Get in the trunk."

"Wh-what?"

"Get. In. The. Trunk." I waved the tire iron emphatically. Much simpler when your wrists are free to pursue separate trajectories. "I just want a little travel insurance." I turned back to the committee. "So, Volpea and I are going down to the Big Easy where I will check on things that are important to me. Mentioning peripheral issues like werewolf coups will not be important unless somebody decides to make it a matter of concern *do you GET MY DRIFT!*"

I heard murmurs that could have been interpreted as growing consent. Gordon was nodding his head. "Why," I asked him, "are you not in the trunk, yet?"

"I—I—"

"Look, I'm a reasonable guy," I said, lightly smacking his upper arm with the tire iron. "Maybe you don't have any experience in dealing with reasonable guys." I whacked him a little harder. "I'm not going to tie you up or gag you or knock you unconscious." *Whap.* "I'm just going to drive down the road a little ways and, once I see that I'm not being followed, I'll release you." *Smack.* "Okay?"

"I guess—"

"Now get in the damn trunk before I stop being reasonable!" I yelled, whacking him across the rear. The look in his eyes said I'd be sorry for that particular humiliation but, honestly, there's only so much crap I'll put up with in a single evening.

And there was a good chance that my borrowed body was PMSing.

Chapter Six

I PULLED OVER and let Gordon out about thirty minutes later.

And reiterated my little warning about how any further messing with me would activate my whistleblower instincts.

And that any werewolf revolutions ought to be postponed until late fall or early winter—anytime *after* my son was born and my people were elsewhere.

He seemed a little pouty about how this whole seduce-and-use-the-Bloodwalker subplot had turned out so I scratched his cheek and repeated my demands while jogging around the inside of his skull. By the time I was back out and reinvested in Volpea's body, he had adopted a more cooperative attitude.

How long that attitude might last was another matter. The long walk he faced in getting to a payphone might alter his new spirit of rapprochement. If so, I'd deal later. Right now I had people to do, things to see. I drove away, leaving him bloodied by the red wash of the Rambler's taillights and headed back to the not-so-main road.

Fenris had diverted us to the back roads. Between that and the hostage-management pit stops, I was unlikely to make New Orleans before sunrise. Fine with me. Laveau and Pantera would be doing the coffin snooze along with just about every other vampire in the Big Easy. That just left their human servants and the weres—more than a little tricky; less than downright impossible.

The changes in the landscape were less noticeable in the dark as I drove south, only the more obvious details popped at the periphery of the headlights. Pines and deciduous hardwoods gradually give way to softwoods and a growing number of palms. Waterways and bayous become more abundant. Cinderblock outbuildings and bait shops were secretly mating and begat more shacks and temporary structures. Fewer structures stood on concrete pads, more and more were raised on brick and rusting iron pier foundations. Depending on their proximity to the water, some buildings were raised high enough to sit under. Others you could park a car under. Some, a couple of tractor-trailer rigs.

More than a few actually were.

I stopped for gas at a little off-road island of bait, groceries, and knickknack shacks offering such delicacies as alligator-on-a-stick and fried nutria. This bathroom break was all up to me and proved to be educational. I wasn't sure how the knowledge gained would come in handy but I figured the sooner I was back to working with directional plumbing, the better.

I splashed a little water in Volpea's face and got back in the car. A mile down the road the headlight on the driver's side blinkered out. Now I was tunneling through the darkness on an unlit secondary road with one dim headlight canting off to illuminate more gravel shoulder than asphalt lane. I missed my infravision. If Volpea was able to shift her eyes into the infrared spectrum, I was unable to trip the appropriate wetware switch.

A lot of moody piffle has been penned about "The Witching Hour" but I find the early morning hours more disquieting than midnight. Maybe once upon a time the line of demarcation between the old day's demise and the new day's birth had some mystical connotations but today's kids stay out too late clubbing and bar-hopping. Things don't really get quiet and lonely and deserted till around three in the am. A perfect time to feel the atmospheric pressure increase as I drove south.

The personification of history—in the North, in the East, in other regions of the country—generally exists as a series of shrines or preserved sites. Call 'em monuments or historic registers or sacred spaces, these "places" coexist with present day life and landscapes but stand as separate, static patches of real estate—sort of like windup clocks run down to silence on a shelf of electric chronometers.

History is different in the South.

Down here you steep in it like a teabag gone soft and soggy in ancient waters. Southern history is like Einstein's clock paradox, simultaneously existing in the past, present, and all conceivable futures, spanning transdimensional vertices and theoretical probabilities. Time travel is a science fiction fantasy anywhere else. In the South it is a common state of mind. An addendum to daily unraveling of the ticktock of moment-to-moment existence. Here, this moment in time is all times and all times may be found in this moment and in this place.

Especially in Louisiana where land and water mix in uncertain quantities and configurations. The farther south you go, the less terra firma you enjoy. Boundaries drift. The world shifts. Elsewhere you gaze upon this patch of history or that. Here, history in its vast, unknown entirety, gazes upon you—watching with ancient, unblinking, reptilian eyes.

And, sometimes, very late at night—or very, very early in the morning and deep in swamps and bayous—it feels *hungry*, as well.

Night driving used to sooth me. By the time I reached the causeway across Lake Pontchartrain, I was ready for any kind of distraction. Even though the sunrise was still moments away, I fished Volpea's cell phone out of her purse and thumbed in Mama Samm's number.

" 'Bout time you call," she answered before I could even hear the first ring. "You have any trouble?"

"Um," I said, "do you know who this is?"

"Should I put this number on my speed dial list or are you gonna be abandoning that foxy lady for some other poor fool's body in the next couple of hours?"

I blinked. *Was everybody in on my spur-of-the-moment ploy to infiltrate Laveau's demesne?*

"No," she said, as if reading my thoughts, "Doctor M thinks you be all tucked in, back home. Nobody else suspects. So far. Think you can keep a low profile? For a change?"

"Depends on the wolf pack." I gave her a quick sketch of the night's events.

"Boy, you come down here and it gonna hit de fan, fo' sho!" she scolded. "You jes' turn around and go back home. You gots other fish to fry."

"Not until I talk to Lupé."

"I'll take her my cell phone and see that you have your talk."

"In person," I insisted.

"Well now how that gonna happen wi' your body back on the *New Moon* and you all dressed up 'Dude look like a lady' style? I think explanations are gonna take more time than you got."

I ground Volpea's teeth. She had a valid point. But I couldn't go home without seeing Lupé and looking in on the others. "I'll figure something out."

There was a longer pause at the other end of the line. "I have an idea," Mama Samm finally said, the regional patois suddenly absent from her voice again. "Meet me at the Place d'Arms Hotel."

ᴧᴧ   ᴧᴧ   ᴧᴧ

The Place d'Arms is the only hotel located on Jackson Square—the St. Louis Cathedral, Café du Monde, and French Quarter are only steps away. Nevertheless, I repeated the address over and over as I drove, hoping that the litany would distract me until I made landfall, again.

I had reached the midpoint of the Pontchartrain Causeway, connecting Mandeville and Metairie. At that location on the twenty-four-mile span, neither shore of the second largest salt water lake in the U.S. was visible—just mile upon mile of open water in all directions. Beautiful and more than a little creepy: it was as if I were suspended over an endless ocean on a fragile ribbon of concrete and steel, dissolving into nothingness at both ends.

I've felt that unease, that dreadful vulnerability of insignificance when out on the ocean in a boat of any size. Canned like Spam in a car, trundling over a narrow conduit—like a tightrope act where you cannot see the ends of an uncertain cord—awakens something more in me, each time I make the trip. Something more and more like dread.

· This time it was worse.

It was every childhood fear I'd ever had of the water and more. It felt as if there were unseen things squirming beneath the inky waters—along with something that ate sea monsters and submarines for breakfast.

And the creeping impression that the axis of the world was subtly shifting, preparing to tilt reality over on its side and me into the nightmare beneath the surface of a barely sane world.

By the time I reached the southern shore of the lake and headed into Metairie, I was drenched in sweat and practically singing the address over and over. Not at the top of our lungs, of course.

But loud enough to keep the windows rolled up.

Making landfall didn't ease my unease all that much. "Dry land" is a subjective term south of the estuary. Reading that New Orleans is largely built inside a bowl of levees and situated below sea level was an abstract concept until a little trip down for a convention a few years back. I was walking along a levee abutting the Mississippi River and looked up to see a freighter sailing majestically past.

Some thirty feet above my head!

Don't get me wrong, I like waterfront locations. Especially the kind where I can look down and out over the vista of a lake or river or ocean.

Not so fond of the water being high enough to look down and out over me.

So, Marie Laveau could relax. I had no desire to pick up real estate on her home turf. New Orleans is a nice enough place to visit, but an extended stay in an inside-out fishbowl doesn't appeal to my long-term peace of mind. The Big Easy makes me uneasy.

I have a similar antipathy toward Southern California—don't blame me, that's San Andreas' fault . . .

As I angled into the glare of the sunrise, I pulled down the car visor to shield my eyes. There was a vanity mirror clipped to the visor.

And in the darkness behind me a pair of ancient, yellowed eyes swam into view!

I shrieked a little.

My reflexes or Volpea's?

"Damn, Jefe!" exclaimed a familiar voice. "Dat you in dere? You one fine lookin' woman!"

I tilted the mirror to be sure. Yep. Black top hat. White ceremonial paint forming a skull-like pattern over a midnight-dark face.

The Baron. Loa of the Dead.

Probably still pissed that some of his homeboys preferred my company to his.

"Samedi. What a delightful surprise." My tone suggested just the opposite.

All of my dealings with the Voudon Avatar of the Grave had been strained to this point. Aside from our vast theological differences, I had inadvertently "taken over his territory" while he and the other loa were bound and imprisoned by Elizabeth Báthory. And even though I was still sending him referrals on every animated corpse that shambled across my path, it would be just like him to rat me out to Laveau.

He chuckled. "Oh man—can I say 'oh man'? You is so busted! Tryin' to sneak yo' lily white ass into the Queen's territory!"

I shook my head. "Oh, this is so bad," I moaned.

"Yes, it is," he agreed.

"So bad . . . that the great Baron Samedi has been reduced to running errands for Marie Laveau," I continued.

He stopped chuckling. "What?"

"I mean, it's just sad and embarrassing."

"What you talkin' 'bout?"

"And she's even got you up pulling guard duty past cock's crow." I shook my head. "The least she could do is give you a badge or some kind of uniform. Like a rent-a-cop or something . . ."

He was suddenly up front and sitting next to me on the passenger side. "The Baron works for no one!" he hissed through clenched teeth. "I am here to warn you!"

"Warn me of what? That you're about to run and tattle on me to your boss lady?"

He reached out and clutched Volpea's arm. The coldness of the tomb slid through muscle and sinew like

winter ice down a canted roof. "Shut up and listen!" he
hissed. "It's on account o' dat crazy-ass bitch I been
searchin' the length of this state for yo aura since moonrise! Dere be things I gots to tell you!"

"Do tell?" I said mildly. "Well, I would pull over and
give you my full attention but I'm kind of on a compressed timetable, Mister Graves."

"What you should be doing, Protestant Boy, is turning
this hunk-a-junk around and skedaddling north as fast as
you can. But since I know that you won't, I'm here to
warn you. I only have a few minutes before de spell is
used up an' I go back to de groun'."

"How sad," I said, still failing to articulate any tone
of sincerity. "Feel free to fast forward past the social
pleasantries and cut to the chase. What's up, Papa Doc?"

The thing that looked like an emaciated black man,
daubed with white paint and wearing a top hat and rag-
gedy old tuxedo, stared out the window at the rising
sun—a view that had to be even rarer for him than it
had become for me.

"First thing. Marie Laveau be crazy. She smart enough
not to show too much of what really goin' on inside her
head but she be well on de way to bat-shit insane!"

I could've said "It takes one to know one" or "Isn't
that a case of the pot calling the kettle black" but, if he
was really on a limited timetable it was best to get on
with it. "You're wasting your mojo, Topper: tell me something I don't know."

The Baron shook his head back at me and I could hear
the dry rasp of bone on bone beneath his parchment
husk. "Jus' 'cause she crazy don't mean she not dangerous! She know most of what she doin' so dat's what make
her crazy fo' sho."

"That and the voices," I offered.

"Dat's jus' it," he said, his yellowed, sunken eyes taking on a haunted look. "De voices is real! She not hearing voices 'cause she crazy—she crazy 'cause she hearing voices!"

With a start I realized that the cocky Loa of the Dead was afraid. He had seemed remarkably self-possessed last year when set free from Lilith's imprisonment. But now fear was oozing from him like a sponge leaking vinegar.

"Whose voices?" I asked, noting an edge of unease had suddenly crept into my own voice, as well.

A variety of expressions crossed the loa's face as he struggled to answer. "There are things . . . ancient things . . . that dwell in the dark places . . . "

"What?" I asked. "Like vampires and voodoo gods?"

His head snapped around and he glared at me, at once angry and terrified. "It began *here*! Back in the *very* beginning! *Before* the first vampire made landfall! *Before* slaves from the West Indies arrived to practice the True Faith!"

"Yeah, yeah, leave me a religious tract. You were saying about these voices? Something's really whispering in her ear?"

"Some things! *Ancient* things! And a Great Old One!"

"A great, old what?"

"It be known by de many masks it has worn, in de many places it has gathered foul congregations." The Baron was whispering, now, glancing about as if we might be under some arcane surveillance. "It is the Black Man, worshipped by witches in England; the Faceless God and the Black Pharaoh, celebrated in Egyptian cults;

feared as the Black Wind in Kenya and the Floating Horror in Haiti; the Dark One here in Louisiana; the Dweller in Darkness to the North, Mr. Skin to the West, and the Howler in the Night, Lord of the Desert, the Haunter of the Dark, and the Crawling Mist . . . " His voice trailed off. "I am starting to fade! I must tell you—"

"A lot of fancy titles," I groused. "Any chance of get-ting a name and address?"

"*Nyarlathotep,*" the Baron answered in a creepy, new voice.

It was deeper, older, and more terrible than anything I had ever heard come out of a human-shaped mouth before—and I've heard enough terrible things coming out of human mouths to give the Hell's Angels night-mares for the rest of their lives.

"*Pleased to meet you,*" he grinned, "*hoped you'd guess my name . . .*" His mouth didn't seem to match the words I was hearing. Furthermore, his lips and teeth were black: the Baron's physical form had undergone a subtle shift.

In fact, his mouth no longer seemed to match his face except in coloration.

"Sooo," I said, trying to steer for an exit ramp before the drive got any wiggier, "I guess I'm getting the whole ancient dude vibe: anyone quoting early Stones lyr—"

He/it giggled like a lunatic Smurf. "*Do you want to see something* really *scary?*"

"Actually, I'd like to finish the conversation with Baron Samedi which you so rudely interrupted." I was looking for a place to pull over and park. "So take a number and we can socialize when it's your turn."

The thing wearing Baron Samedi's avatar turned its face away, saying, "... *really*, really *scary* ... ?" and I went from looking for a parking place to scouting for a place to abandon the car while it was still rolling.

The "Baron" turned back around and his face was gone.

The cold, rubbery tentacle snaked over my right arm before I could make any sense of what I was seeing.

But there was no sense.

A red, monstrous pseudopod was writhing toward me and it came from the center of the dark ovoid that had replaced the Baron's head. It was growing from the empty space where his face should have been! Except there was nothing but a dark portal leading to some deep, secret darkness at the hind end of the universe!

And as a blood-red tentacle—totally unlike anything octopoid or cephalopodan—came squirming out of the ancient dark, my mind began to gibber like a thorn tree filled with monkeys. It wasn't just horror that paralyzed me, thrilled me into a new level of shocked insensibility—it was the inability of my brain to reconcile what I was seeing with any reference point, biological, historical, mythical! My foot pushed the brake pedal to the floor only because my legs had gone rigid with shock. And I stared as the red serpentine rope of unnatural flesh slithered over our arm and brushed across my/Volpea's breasts!

A second, minor shock buzzed through me and my left arm came up involuntarily. My left hand reached down and flung the tentacle aside so that it smacked against the windshield. "Watch the tits, Romeo!" Volpea's sleepy voice muttered from our slack lips. The tentacle slid down the inner surface of the windshield glass, leaving a streaky trail of mucus before rearing up like an offended cobra.

In the meantime I was trying to open the driver's side door to beat a hasty retreat. The problem was I was trying to do it with my left arm which my host had just appropriated to fend off the monster with the cop-a-feel face.

<V! Open the door!>

> . . . kinda girl . . . think I am . . . ?<

<Open the damn door! Now!>

> . . . <

Somewhere inside our skull something started buzzing.

<Volpea!>

> . . . <

She was snoring!

I tried to turn and use my right arm but the seatbelt caught me in midturn. Now I couldn't reach the door handle with my right or fend off snake-face with my left! And, so not helping, the sun began to angle through the windshield so I was half blinded, as well.

"*Wgah'nagl ftagn!*" whispered the ancient voice as the crimson rope circled our neck, probing our right ear.

Reaching up, I grabbed at the cable of tightening flesh but only succeeded in having our fingers trapped against our throat. The interior of the car seemed to dim and I coughed against the mounting pressure. "Yeah?" I choked, "Well *ftagn* you!"

The pressure suddenly disappeared.

As did the rope-faced monstrosity that had possessed the Baron.

The spell permitting the Loa of the Dead to appear past cock's crow had finally expired.

History.

Samedi had said something about "it" beginning here—whatever "it" was that he was trying to warn me about . . .

Before the vampires.

Before the voodoo.

Which meant *early* history.

So I thought about that after I recovered and resumed my drive toward St. Ann Street.

You don't spend too many years living in Louisiana without learning something about its history. I was no expert but I did have a salient grasp of the basics.

The Mississippi River was first—or should I say "officially"—discovered back in 1541 by the Spanish explorer, Hernando de Soto. Like so many things in history, however, it's not who got there first but who developed the real estate.

One hundred and forty-one years later a Frenchman by the name of Robert de La Salle sailed down the Big Muddy for the first time and erected a cross somewhere near the city's present location, claiming the entire Louisiana territory for his boss, King Louis XIV. Both explorers would later be immortalized by having early motor cars named after them. Since the king didn't get around so much he would have to settle for lending his name to a line of furniture.

The juxtaposition of river and seaport was too good to pass up forever—just another thirty-six years as the swamps were somewhat problematical. So the first French settlements on the Gulf Coast were established at Biloxi. Finally, in 1718, Jean Baptiste Le Moyne, Sieur de Bienville, established a settlement on the lower Mississippi which he dubbed "New" Orleans. Three years later the French Quarter was laid out behind levees erected by the engineer Adrien de Pauger. The city began to prosper, Le Moyne probably heard fewer "Baptiste" jokes, and in 1723 the capital of the French colony was moved from Biloxi to New Orleans.

Neither Le Moyne nor de Pauger has had an automobile named in their honor.

Despite the legendary French fondness for eating frogs and snails, life in the early colony was neither easy nor consistently successful. We are, after all, talking about living in the middle of a swamp. A very big swamp. Surrounded by many other swamps. The climate was subtropical with all of the disadvantages of weather, temperature, humidity, rot, insects, protozoa, wildlife.

And the natives were usually restless.

Guerrilla warfare is grim enough when the aborigines have had a century or more to adapt to the contested landscape. When that landscape is thousands of miles of swamps, bogs, sloughs, mires, and fens, the only workable strategy is to huddle together and keep building earthen walls, hoping they keep the darkness and the Others out as well as the water. When the stories began to circulate that not all of those Others might be human, it was not entirely the typical Eurocentric racism of its day.

There were things in the swamps that even the natives feared and loathed.

Chalk it up to the superstitions of unenlightened times but then, once upon a time I would have laughed at the idea of elves or fish people or Mesoamerican bat-demons.

Not laughing so much these days.

And lest we still trust the larger part of American folklore to weak-minded simpletons, there's an old pioneer saying: "The cowards never started and the weak died along the way." The first French colonists certainly weren't sissies so you can't chalk up three hundred years of superstitious gossip to Gallic timidity in a strange land.

Following a pattern that would later be subsumed by the Botany Bay enterprise on the other side of the globe, the population was bolstered by deported criminals and prostitutes. This solved the overcrowded French penal system and added to certain colonists' incentives when the first eighty-eight women arrived from Gay Paree. The fact that their previous address—*La Salpêtrière*—was a Paris "house of correction" may have enhanced their status rather than diminishing it.

Six years later another boatload of women arrived. These were the Ursuline Sisters, a Dominican order, who established convents—the second of which is still standing and may be toured even today (though it is no longer used according to its original purposes). The original *Salpêtrière* "sisters" doubtless established some devotional houses of their own—The House of the Rising Sun is still celebrated in story and song—though it is unlikely that any of the original structures still exist. Still, "congregants" continue to be served in a wide variety of locations and formats even today.

The Big Easy began to hit its stride in the mid 1700s as it finally found a way to deal with French restrictions on trade with England, Spain, Mexico, Florida, and the

West Indies. It decided to ignore the rules. Trade grew as a result. The once pristine Mississippi River was choked with traffic carrying goods in and out of the city as well as its growing seaport. Too bad the French were about to lose their lease.

The Seven Years War was a dust-up between all of the major European powers that ended in 1763 when Louis the XV—also known for a line of settees and bric-a-brac furnishings—signed the Treaty of Paris. This seemed to end France's ambitions in the New World and Louis, no slouch in the assets management department, slipped the Louisiana deeds under the table to his cousin, Charles III.

What seemed like a good idea at the management level didn't go over so well with the tenants, however. Chuck was the king of Spain and the French colonists weren't so keen on having a new landlord even if he was considered "family." The new governor for the colony was turned around and sent packing upon his arrival. The success of this rebellion was short-lived, however, as Spanish General Alexander O'Reilly (really!) showed up with twenty-four warships, two thousand troops, fifty pieces of artillery, and a big ole can of whupass. Executing the six ringleaders of the insurgence, he guaranteed the haunting of the future U.S. Mint and total establishment of Spanish rule.

For three more decades.

Say what you will about the Spanish, at least they had a better grasp on the concept of a free-market economy. They relaxed trade restrictions with other countries which caused the average businessman to prosper and the black marketeers to consider signing up for career change seminars back in Sicily.

A lot of people chalked up what happened next to an accident. Maybe. But you've got to wonder how a single fire can burn down more than 850 buildings in a swamp, surrounded by water on three sides and more swamp on the fourth. If the Good Friday fire of 1788 wasn't the result of covert urban planning, it had the same result. Not only were most of the French-style structures lost, the Spanish rulers enacted zoning laws mandating that all future buildings of more than one story would have to be constructed of brick. This led to a decided "Mediterranean" period for the architecture of the region.

The next decade was a veritable explosion of trade and commerce. And multiculturalism as slaves, goods, and colonists poured in from Saint Domingue. And that introduced Voudon, better known as voodoo after Saint Domingue became better known as Haiti.

Which meant whatever the Baron was alluding to had happened earlier.

But how much earlier? That question remained unanswered as I parked and walked into the courtyard of the Place d'Arms Hotel.

ʌ•ʌ   ʌ•ʌ   ʌ•ʌ

There might have been some irony in Mama Samm taking a room in a hotel with several well-documented hauntings. Except for the fact that it's getting harder to find a hotel in New Orleans that doesn't have a ghost or two. And if you doubt me, just sign up for some of the "Haunted Tours" that service the tourists on a nightly basis.

I can't speak for the authenticity of the ghosts but don't buy into any of the vampire sites in the Garden District. The real bloodsuckers relocated to Faubourg-Marigny back in the eighties. Only the poseurs show up for the tourists.

The Place d'Arms is actually eighty-three rooms distributed throughout eight renovated, historic townhouses framing the courtyard. So finding the right room was a little trickier than knowing the floor and number. Mama Samm found me before I found her.

She shushed my attempts to update her on my most recent encounters on the way to her room. "Plenty of time to talk once I Spock you up," she said, unlocking her door and hanging out the do not disturb sign before closing it behind us.

She had already arranged her room for the ceremony. There were candles everywhere. Which she set about lighting. The bed had been moved away from the walls and a pattern of white powder circled it on the carpeted floor.

I eyed a stack of emptied Sweet'N'Low packets overflowing the top of the dresser. "I thought you had to use salt."

She looked at me like I was an idiot. "That's for zombies."

Oh. Well. Of course. No point in mentioning the recent studies suggesting links between artificial sweeteners and brain seizures.

"Now lie down with me," she ordered, arranging herself on the king-sized bed so as to allow a narrow strip of leftover space.

"What? No candy or flowers, first? Aren't you even going to try to chat me up?"

"Lie down," she insisted, "we haven't got a lot of time!"

"Seriously," I said, sitting on the edge of the mattress. "We do need to talk. Something just happened—"

"We'll talk once the spell is complete."

It was dimly registering somewhere that she wasn't affecting her "street" voice which meant she was deadly serious and focused. But I was still unsettled by recent events. And one other thing.

"I still don't understand," I continued, refusing to lie down. "I proposed this once before . . ."

Mama Samm sat back up and shook her head. "I wasn't ready back then. Too dangerous to let you go rattling around in here," she tapped her temple with a sausage-sized finger, "all lóose and wild."

I shrugged. "Volpea didn't have any complaints."

She gave me one of her looks that explained the "Mama" part of her surname. "There's a great deal of difference between what's going on in that vixen's head and what you'd have access to in mine."

I felt my face grow a little warm. "It's not like that. It's . . . it's . . . been very platonic."

The fortune-teller's eye widened. "Platonic, huh?" She started to chuckle. "Oh. I should think so." She turned and started lighting the candles and incense on her side of the bed.

"You don't believe me?"

"Oh, I believe you, baby."

"Then what's so funny?"

She shook her head. "Nothing, child, nothing. You inside her head, sharing her body. All those nerve endings. Only be funny if you still didn't know Volpea be particular to the company of others of her kind."

"What? Werewolves? Of course I know all about the whole furry/yiffy predilection; Lupé and I are an anomaly."

She shook her head again, the chuckles escalating into giggles and moisture starting to twinkle at the corners of her eyes. "Oh, Chris honey! She's not a were*wolf*. And, anyways, it's not a *species* thing I'm talking about—it's a *gender* thing."

"Gender thing?" I echoed.

"As in preference."

Preference?

Oh.

"Oh!" I said. Then: "So it was an act . . . "

Mama Samm pushed me back down on the mattress. "I thought Fenris and Gordon had pretty much enlightened you as to a plot?"

"Well . . . yeah . . . "

"But maybe you were hoping it wasn't a total act?" She nodded sympathetically. "Oh, baby, maybe you right. We get you over to see Miss Lupé right away. It been too long." She lay back down next to me. "Now close your eyes and count backwards from one hundred and seventeen."

I closed my eyes. More in embarrassment than obedience. Well, this was awkward. Not that I actually had been seduced, you understand . . . I never would have allowed an actual seduction to transpire if such had been the case. But I had been taken in by her apparent sincerity. Which meant that I was slipping. Or that she was very, very good!

And that I couldn't trust her!

I opened my eyes to ask Mama Samm what we were going to do with Volpea after I was out—but someone had pulled the shades, turned off the lights, and blown out the candles.

<Mama Samm?>

>It is done, child. Relax a moment and allow the realignment to settle.<

<This isn't the same. It feels totally different.>

>It is. I have created a zone where you may exist and observe without actually interacting—<

<You've put me in a box!>

I felt her nod, though the sensation was different. Distant.

>Something between a safety deposit box and hanging a privacy curtain. Just relax and enjoy the ride . . . <

She opened her eyes and sat up. There was a little disorientation as the room swung around and I tried to focus through a different set of foci. Sharing Volpea's body, I saw everything pretty much the way she saw. Peering out of Mama Samm's specially prepared "zone" was more like trying to function while looking through a weak pair of binoculars.

I was still adjusting to my sudden farsightedness when Volpea sat straight up and grinned at us.

"*Od'glf hajf vfa'nafh,*" she said through blackening lips. The voice was very familiar but it wasn't hers any more than it had been Samedi's scarcely an hour before. "*Fhtagn Azathoth ph'ghaan Cth'tu—*"

Mama Samm's fist was the size of a small ham and it smacked into Volpea's darkening face like an ancient battering ram taking out the gates of a small castle. V's head snapped back, her eyes rolled up and she dropped back on the bed like a collapsing Jenga stack.

<Wh-what was that?> I asked as the immense juju woman heaved herself up and off of the bed.

"That was jus' bad manners!" she muttered aloud as she stomped around the hotel room, blowing out candles and stuffing a small arsenal of religious artifacts and apothecarial vials and tins into her shopping-bag-sized purse. "He may fancy hisself an elder god but there's no excuse for bad manners! The Crawling Chaos has sumptin important enough to say to me, he can damn well come in person to say it!" And with that, she shouldered her handbag-of-many-items and we were on our way out the door.

Chapter Seven

I WAITED UNTIL Mama Samm had situated her bulk in the back of a cab and directed the driver to an address on University Place before starting up.

<What the hell is a "Nyarlathotep" and how does he make other people's faces grow tentacles? What about Volpea? Is it safe to just go off and leave her like that? What if the maid comes in to clean? What if Mr. Dark 'n' Scary attempts another hostile takeover? And are you serious about this elder god crap? You called it the Crawling Chaos like it was some sort of name! So does that make ole octopus-nose "Mr. Chaos" to casual acquaintances and "Crawly" to his close friends?>

>Are you finished, yet?<

<Finished? I'm just getting started! Since this doesn't appear to be totally off the map for you, I'd really appreciate a little more disclosure on your part! I mean I've got the Pisces Patrol making houseboat calls, Nazi nanobots turning me into a cross between Lee Majors and Hugh Jackman, lesbian werewolves pretending to seduce me—>

>*Stop babbling!*<

I stopped.

>There was only one.<

<What?>

>Lesbian. Singular. Not plural. And she isn't a were-wolf. The only harm there is to your pride. Given her preferences, you could choose to see her deception as a compliment.<

I scowled at her. Being on the inside of her head, the expression was probably lost on her. <The more salient point is there's some genuinely scary shit going down, here!>

>Yes. Yes, there is. I wasn't sure until now that we were dealing with his kind—<

<His *kind*? You mean there's more than one of him?>

>You're getting hysterical, again. I won't be discussing this with you if you get all excited. It opens ancient path-ways in the mind that should stay closed and forgotten. And it draws their attention.<

<I'd say it's a little late for that, already.>

>What? The Deep Ones?< I caught a mental image of my fishy foes reflected from her thoughts. >They are mere flesh and blood, the mortal detritus of those who

opened their minds and their flesh to the madness generations before.<

<So, these Deep Dudes—*not* the Big Bad you're talk-
ing about here?>

>Mister Chris, do you know your Bible? Do you know
the story of Sodom and Gomorrah? Of Lot's wife?<

<Pretty much.>

>Sodom and Gomorrah were bad places. Evil places.
Abraham tried to bargain with God. Made the Lord
promise to spare the cities if he could find fifty good
people living there.<

<Yeah, I remember. He couldn't find fifty decent folk
in the whole city.>

She nodded. It was an interesting sensation. >Then
he negotiated down to forty-five. Then thirty. Then
twenty. Ten. Couldn't do it. In the end only Abe's
nephew Lot and his family could be evacuated. God told
'em: '*Don't* none of you look back! This place is too evil
to stand!'

>The Bible says evil can enter in through the eyes
when it beholds that which is sinful. When Lot's wife
disobeyed God and looked back while He was a-destroy-
ing all that evil, she was destroyed, too. Turned into a
pillar of salt. A lot of them man preachers like to say she
was punished for disobeying her husband and disobeying
God. Like God going to take time outta scrubbing the
toilet to hose a crumb off the back porch. No, I think
Lot's wife looked back while the power was pouring
down on all that evil and some of that evil entered by
way of her eyes—just like the Bible says. And the power
that was chasing right on its nasty-ass tail followed right

on in and destroyed that woman just as it turned two whole cities into dust and ashes.<

<So, what's your point here?>

>That, just as you're supposed to avert your eyes from evil lest it enter in, you must turn your mind away from madness, or it will enter you and have its way within, as well. What I am trying to do here, Mister Chris, is stop you from turning your attention to things that don't bear thinking about. Because if you turn your attention to Them, They will eventually turn Their attention to you!

>There are things that you have seen that would give most people nightmares for the rest of their lives. But they are still the things of this earth, this Creation. But there are things that dwell in the darkness between this Creation and others—awful, empty, evil places—Places of Madness! Things that don't belong here. Shouldn't be able find Their way here. But They *want* to come! They hunger! And sometimes They find ways! Terrible ways! Unthinkable ways! And They don't even have to actually be here! Just by whispering through the keyholes of the universe, just by casting Their shadows over the line between our reality and Theirs, They infect places. And the people who get caught there for very long get infected, too!<

<So this Crawling Chaos is only a shadow?>

>You *have* only met the shadow of Nyarlathotep, though he alone walks the earth at this time. One *other* sleeps on this side of the gate. The rest—Azathoth, Shub-Niggurath, Yog-Sothoth, the rest of the Great Old Ones, the Outer Gods—are exiled outside of this universe and cannot, *must* not, *ever* return or Creation will unravel and the stars will gutter into eternal darkness!<

<Then maybe we should go back and you punch Mister Chaos some more until he yells "Uncle".>

>It don't work like that, child. What you saw and heard was just a shadow, not the real thing. If the real Nyarlathotep had showed up in person you'd be dead or forever insane. Besides, he been walkin' this earth for a long time, makin' trouble here and there. As for the rest? As long as Their great priest sleeps, They ain't comin' nowhere. Now, I don't talk about these things because the best way to let sleeping gods lie is to not wake them up. Think about Them too much and They begin to dream. You don't want Them dreamin' about you. Their dreams . . . *leak* . . . <

<But—>

>But nothin'. I told you, this is something that is way out of your league. You may be all badass and bluff when it comes to bad peoples and vampires and shapeshifters. But you ain't no astral physicist: the Great Old Ones should be left alone. To sleep. You can't do nothin' but quicken Their dreams. *And I will kill you myself if I ever get the idea that you might disturb the eternal slumber of the Master of R'yleh!*<

There was that weird title again. I would have asked for an explanation but after a long explanation about not explaining certain things, the last was thought with such vehemence that I was shocked into mental silence.

>But enough of this,< she continued. >I have said too much already and we will speak of it no more. All things have an ending, even this world and this Creation. But when it comes—whether next week or a thousand years hence—it will be as Yahweh, God of this Creation ordains it. Not mad abominations from Outside in the

Great Dark. Our work is to deal with the evils of *this* world, of *this* Creation. We do not—we cannot—concern ourselves with the Endless Oblivion Outside and Beyond! Right now you are about to see the mother of your unborn son. And your . . . (ahem) . . . colleagues. You need to focus. I'm risking enough carrying you around this city without you going all Busby Berserkly inside my head now that we're on our way to Marie Laveau's inner sanctum!<

< >

>What's that? I didn't hear you!<

<Yes, ma'am,> I said politely.

At which point we had arrived at the Orpheum Theater.

Located in the central business district, the Orpheum has had its share of past lives. The Beaux Arts terra-cotta theater opened in 1918 as a part of the vaudeville circuit. It saw its heyday, however, as a movie theater—one of the crown jewels of the RKO chains. Even after they reclaimed a section of the first balcony for a projection booth, the "O" could still seat an audience of 1660 people, spreading them around a main floor, two separate balconies, and a number of private boxes. Back in the Jim Crow days of the previous century, the audience was segregated. "Colored" seating was restricted to the second balcony and that could only be accessed by stairways from the outside alleys on either side.

That was then, this is now. We walked up to the front doors of the building that was now home to the Louisiana Philharmonic Orchestra and knocked.

A crash bar boomed two doors over and we were admitted by a young Latina girl wearing jeans and a T-shirt. The T had a picture of a crawfish and some message about "sucking heads and pinching tails." She did not look happy.

"Sammathea D'Arbonne?" she asked, looking us up and down.

Mama Samm nodded. "I thought you were off at school, doing summer studies."

"I am. Oceanography. I'm assigned to crew the *Spindrift*, which is in port for a few days so I wrangled leave for the weekend."

The big fortune-teller leaned toward the girl to peer at her more closely. "Oceanography, huh? How you likin' all dat water?"

The girl smiled like Alice's Cheshire Cat. "It's full of all kinds of fascinating fish. Follow me, please." She turned and led us through the small lobby and into the orchestra foyer.

<So, I'm guessing she's not a member of the early morning cleaning crew. . . . > I observed, noting that the tightness of her jeans did little to impede the wiggle of her posterior as she walked ahead of us. A pendulum of black hair fell to the small of her back and swished in counterpoint to the ticktock of her budding hips. It was a reflexive notation; I was still a bit shell-shocked from recent events and Mama Samm's outburst.

Or would that more accurately be referred to as an "inburst"?

Mama Samm harrumphed inside our head. >This is Jorge Pantera's daughter, Irena, so behave yourself.<

<I am behaving myself!> I protested. <She's too young, anyway.>

>And probably a lesbian,< Mama Samm added wryly.

<Oh, now cut that out!>

"When we are done here, I must ask you a favor," Iréna Pantera said as she led us down and then back up and onto the stage. "It's about my stepmother . . ."

It took me an extra moment to realize that she was talking about Marie Laveau.

"We'll talk after my visit," Mama Samm told her. "I'll require some privacy, you understand. But we'll meet afterwards and you can tell me all about it, then."

Irena nodded, her chocolate eyes narrowing as if to squeeze her agitation down to a more manageable compactness.

She led us off into the wings and down a corkscrew spiral of metal stairs to a chamber under the stage. Across this room was another door that required a key. Past that door was a narrow bricked alcove with stairs leading down into darkness. She flipped a switch, illuminating a string of bare bulbs tracing the descent, and we eventually found ourselves in a metal-sheathed room that resembled a modern elevator façade. A ten-key number pad replaced the binary up/down configuration.

Irena punched in a code, shielding the keypad with her body so we couldn't learn the access number. The door slid open to the left and we entered another metal-walled room that was, unmistakably, an airlock.

"We're below the water table now," Irena explained. "This egress doubles as security and protection against flooding."

That made sense. New Orleans was notoriously short on any kind of subterranean construction. You don't put buildings with basements in a swamp. And, between vast bodies of water that make periodic attempts to overrun the levees and an aggressive groundwater table that seeks to rise to the level of the Gulf of Mexico, the Mississippi River, and Lake Pontchartrain, even the dead get aboveground housing. The limestone and marble crypts that fill Cypress Grove, Greenwood, Metairie, Lafayette, and all three St. Louis cemeteries like so much tract housing protect the corpses from the decompositional effects of ground water.

Perhaps more importantly, they protect the ground water from becoming corpse consommé, as well.

The real problem is not the abundance of water so much as the illusion of land. The lower portion of what the maps identify as Louisiana is a geological illusion. You don't have to go back more than a few million years—an hour or two on Earth's curriculae vitea—to find ocean here. Ocean going all the back to the very Beginning. Beginning with a capital B. The primary engines responsible for the subsequent landfill were rivers and tributaries that moved dirt in a migratory course to the South, building thousands of miles of new coastline one quarter of an inch at a time.

The trouble is, mankind showed up and moved in too soon on the geologic calendar. Not only moved in too soon but shut down the remaining landfill engines, building dams and locks and levees, choking off the silt and sand migrations that had fed the delta regions for the past hundred million years. The one remaining engine—the "hemi" of the northern half of this hemisphere—is still

called the Big Muddy. But the earthen cargo for which
it is named no longer spills out into the Gulf of Mexico
to continue its millennial task of shoring up the shore,
growing the ground, and deepening the dirt. We've managed to dredge and divert and choke the Mississippi
River to where it's both dammed and damned. And, as
a result, the process has reversed itself: every year more
land is lost. The sea is returning to claim its ancient and
rightful territory. Louisiana loses the equivalent of two
football fields to the ocean every day.

Don't believe me? Look it up.

Still don't believe it? That's because the concept is
unthinkable.

And that's why it continues. You can't motivate people
to combat something they can't wrap their minds around.

Let's face facts: it takes a certain amount of denial to
live in a swamp, below sea level, surrounded by vast
amounts of water held back by flimsy walls of earth and
ancient cement.

Maybe I just have a better imagination. Or a clarity of
perspective since I live in the solid, northern end of the
state. Whichever, I couldn't help flinching when the
inner door of the airlock opened. By all rights there
shouldn't have been anything on the other side but water
and/or compressed silt and muck.

Instead, there was a dry and spacious corridor.

Of stone!

For a fleeting moment I felt the first quiverings of a
fresh, full-blown panic.

Then I saw that the floor, walls, and ceiling were nothing like the stone-flagged, earthen tunnels in the Faerie
Mound. Here the construction was tightly-fitted stone

blocks of gigantic dimensions. The passageway itself would have allowed four of us to walk abreast with plenty of room on both sides. Instead, there were only two of us, fleshwise, and Mama Samm and I had to follow our diminutive guide, feeling uncharacteristically tiny amid such cyclopean architecture.

The floor beneath our feet felt pebbly and uneven and the nearest wall seemed to contain some three-dimensional motif or decoration.

<Wander a little closer to the right and let me get a closer look at the wall's surface.>

>Yo mama, Cséjthe?<

If I'd had my own eyes I would have blinked. <What about my mama?>

>What kind of manners did yo mama teach you, boy?<

Oh.

<Please?>

>Very well.< She steered over and turned her eyes toward the dressed stone to our right. >Just remember I ain't no taxicab and you ain't no high-tipping fare.<

<Yes, ma'am.>

The surface of each ten-by-fourteen-foot block was adorned like a prehistoric diorama of aquatic life. Trilobites, brachiopods, gastropods, bryozoans, cephalopods, crinoids, tabulate and rugose corals, pelecypods, littered the walls, the floor, and, presumably, the ceiling which was illuminated here and there by another bare bulb on a naked string of wires every twelve feet or so.

<Uh, I'm looking at Paleozoic fossils, here!>

Irena turned back and saw us touching the knobby protrusions of petrified flora and fauna. "Oh," she said, "I see you've noticed one of our great mysteries."

"Mmm-hmm," Mama Samm agreed. "Giant blocks of dressed stone dating back to the dinosaurs . . . "

"Oh, much older than the dinosaurs. Most of these," Irena indicated the scattering of ancient forms, "date from the Devonian and Mississippian Ages of the Paleozoic Era—between 380 and 420 million years ago."

"Well, honey, I may not know the exact numbers, but I do know my sequences."

<Sequences?>

"Sequences?" Irena echoed.

Mama Samm nodded. "I mean you got more than a bunch of pretty rocks stuck in your old stone walls." She ran a large finger along one of the tight seams where a calcified crinoid had lodged around four hundred thousand centuries ago. "Seems these fossils showed up here *after* this stone was cut, *after* this place was built. Which means whoever built it was really, really old. Older than the dinosaurs! Certainly older than humans! Our ancestors didn't show up until about six million years ago. And they didn't get around to doing anything like this until like ten seconds ago in geological time. So, who built this place?"

"The Krell," Irena answered.

ᴀᴛᴀ   ᴀᴛᴀ   ᴀᴛᴀ

Actually, she was pulling our leg. No one in the New Orleans demesne had a clue but neither was anyone inclined to look a 400-million-year-old gift horse in the mouth.

All that Irena knew was that Marie Laveau had led her "people" down into the underspaces of the Orpheum back when it was first being built at the turn of the last century. The Voices told her where to dig, and she enlisted the bodies of dozens—and eventually hundreds—of thralls to excavate the miles of prehistoric stone corridors and chambers choked with mud, ranging from packed sediment all the way to fossilized strata. As the decades passed above, a succession of airlocks were constructed, openings were sealed, collapsed rooms and hallways walled off, and foot by foot, yard by yard, sections were cleared and areas were made habitable.

The ancient underground city was not reclaimed by archeologists but by monsters. Led by a monster who was hearing voices even back then. So the best clues as to the identities of the ancient builders were excavated along with the tons of mud, sand, silt, and petrified sediments, and dumped in ditches, canals, trash heaps, the river—wherever the equally disposable thralls could dispose of hundreds of thousands of cubic feet of earthen debris one bucket at a time—without attracting undue notice. It took decades just to carve out sufficient space for Marie and a staff and guest list approaching seventy. But what was time to creatures that might be immortal. Especially in preparing the perfect shelter to retreat to when threatened? Laveau might be crazy but she wasn't stupid.

<Except for the fact she's set up housekeeping in a temple of the Great Old Ones,> I mused.

>What? This was never a temple. And it wasn't built *by* or *for* any Great Old Ones, Mister Chris. Don't you be talking or thinking no nonsense about which you know nothing about!<

<Elder Gods, then. You said something about Elder Gods.>

>I said "Outer Gods" not "Elder Gods." The Elder Gods oppose the Outer Gods!<

<Then—um—logically—this place did belong to the Elder Gods.>

>Excuse me?<

<Well, if the Great Old Ones are also the Outer Gods and this place belonged to the big ancient scary types that weren't their friends, one would assume—>

>I never actually said that the architects of this place were the enemies of the Great Old Ones.<

<Your tone implied it.>

>My tone—look! This is part of an ancient complex built by the Elder Things!<

<I thought you called them Elder Gods. And said they weren't the contractors.>

>Elder Gods are *different* than Elder Things! Elder *Things* were an alien race!<

<Well, this is all very confusing. . . . >

>And I told you we are *not* going to discuss this. The Elder Things came here a thousand million years ago! The Great Old Ones hated and feared them! The Elder Things waged war against the Mi-go, the Great Race of Yith, and the Star Spawn—<

<So, these Elder Aliens are, like, the good guys? I think I'm gonna need a scorecard, here.>

>They're *gone*, Mister Chris! Wiped out! Extinct. Between their wars without and the rebellion of their dreaded shoggoths within, the last remnants escaped to the stars eons before the first hominid climbed down from the trees!<

<Okay, I'm going to stop now. Not just because I have no idea of what you're talking about but because I got

you to use the word "hominid." That, alone, is worthy of silent contemplation . . . >

Plus we both needed to focus on the remainder of Irena's account. She was telling us about rooms, still being excavated, where great murals adorned the walls. Scenes of fantastic tableaus featuring an incredible array of creatures unlike anything Irena had come across in her biology or zoology texts. Murals which were defaced and destroyed at Marie Laveau's command. Presumably the Voices told her to do so, and so these Voices—presumably—were no friends to the original architects of this place.

Which continued to beg the question.

Unfortunately someone was being a big ole party poop on *that* subject.

The one thing Irena could tell us about these Voices is that they had spoken to the Vampire Queen of New Orleans again, early this morning. Laveau had staggered out just an hour or so before sunrise, muttering that she had to obtain "The Russian Key" before it was gone.

"And for all I know, she's just ashes on the morning winds, now," the young woman finished, visibly upset.

While my host and I were both of the opinion that this wouldn't necessarily be such a bad thing, we both realized that Marie had saved the lives of this girl and her father. That she probably cared for them in her own way and that they had come to care for her, too.

So Mama Samm promised to do what she could to find out what had happened to Irena Pantera's oh-so-wicked stepmother once she (we) had looked in on her (my) people.

The clinic wasn't anything like the medical facilities for the Seattle demesne.

Of course, the medical needs of the undead and their lycanthropic servitors were pretty simple. Whatever didn't outright kill them seemed to have little lasting effect. As for those exceptions—Laveau's management style was more of a hands-off, live-and-let-die approach. I was guessing that the better equipment in the treatment area was on loan from Stefan Pagelovitch. With all the blather about how I posed such a threat to the other enclaves, I found such little signs of détente encouraging.

The chambers were uniformly large, so the patients were clustered together and given the dubious privacy of individual prefab cubicles and curtains. Big surprise: even undead health care sucks . . .

Dr. Mooncloud was already on duty and came bustling up with a stack of clipboards.

"Any problems? I was starting to worry."

Though I didn't have the same access to Mama Samm's nerve endings as I did when Bloodwalking in other bodies, I got the general sense of her planting her massive fists on her Gibraltar-like hips as she gazed down at Taj. "I used to live in this city, Doctor, and I know my way around better than most. If there is a reason I do not live here now, it is largely because of Marie Laveau. But she has invited me and so what have I to fear?"

Mooncloud shrugged. "You've visited before. Even dropped in back when she was headquartered at the Lalaurie House. But not down here." She crossed her arms across her chest and seemed to repress a small shudder. "*This* place isn't right. You know the old digs were haunted. But this place is . . . I don't know . . . fundamentally wrong on so many levels that I just don't know where to begin . . . " She shook her head. "And we may have another problem."

"What kind of a problem?" Mama Samm asked.

"You know how the coastal demesnes have been losing vampires of late? Well, it's happening here, too. And now we're starting to miss some weres, as well."

"That's not been a problem elsewhere. The defections were limited to the undead," Mama Samm mused.

"Well, Volpea and Fenris seem to have gone missing. A few of Laveau's other wolves have disappeared, as well. I don't know if it's connected but the good news is I spoke to Pagelovitch a couple of hours ago. I think I've finally convinced him that Cséjthe's not playing Harriet Tubman for the disaffected members of the Seattle enclave."

"I suppose that's something," my host mused, "but I doubt our boy'll be chomping at the bit to visit him any time soon."

"Nor would he be encouraged to do so. That little stunt he pulled in New York has all the demesnes and domans rattled." Mooncloud looked back over her shoulder. "In the meantime, I've got cranky patients right here."

Mama Samm turned our gaze from Taj to the curtained beds, then over to Irena Pantera lounging against the far wall, then back to the doctor. "I will need to speak with them in private, Doctor. If you would be so good as to keep Jorge's daughter occupied?"

Mooncloud nodded enthusiastically. "Oh, *my* pleasure! Believe me! Anything to get away for a while!"

She turned to corral Pantera, muttering something about hormones, and we moved to the first curtained alcove.

A woman lay upon a bed surrounded by a sophisticated array of medical monitoring equipment. Despite the tape holding her eyelids shut and the respirator covering the lower half of her face, it was obvious that she was a stranger. Mama Samm, however, lingered at the entryway.

<Hello? Not one of ours. And a little rude to stand and stare.>

>It would only be rude if there was someone here,< she admonished. >This bed is empty.<

<Doesn't look empty to . . . > Oh.

The vital signs monitors were eloquent in their own way: the mountain range redux of P-wave, QRS complex, T-wave, over and over, measuring the depolarization/repolarization of the human heart. ECG, NIBP, SPO2, all registering the mimicry of life. But the EEG told a completely different story. The alpha, beta, theta, and delta readouts should have rippled like wavelets from four different rivers. Instead the sine waves unspooled like a four-lane highway across the great salt flats of Utah. And, like that level wasteland, what inhabited that hospital bed was potent with mirages but sterile and lifeless, all the same. Once upon a time a person had inhabited that flesh, those bones. Whatever the essence of personhood—personality, memory, thought, reason, emotion—was gone now. All that remained was what we linguistically recognize as such . . .

The remains. .

Turn off the respirator, disconnect the machinery and remove the personalized care that kept those remains fed, cleansed, and maintained within certain tolerances and the natural process would take hold. Rot. Decay. Putrescence. Dissolution. A final breakdown to the building block components of Biblical construction: ashes to ashes, dust to dust.

But not yet.

For now the remains . . . remained. Science had some purpose yet unfulfilled.

And I had a pretty good idea what that was.

Another curtained alcove. Another bed. Another carefully maintained husk. Another possibility. Another choice.

And another in the third cubicle.

The fourth held more. Much more. A ghost in the shell. Two ghosts, actually: a very pregnant Lupé Garou half-lay, half-crouched in the hospital bed, looking up at us with weary, wary eyes.

"Well," she snarled, "what's his excuse this time? Grateful *Dead* concert? *Monster* truck rally? Breaking in a new *body*guard?"

"I heard that!" piped another familiar voice. It came from beyond the next curtained screen.

Mama Samm dragged a pair of chairs over, next to Lupé's bed and settled her ample derriere across their twinned surface. "You don't take his phone calls, you don't answer his letters . . ."

"What phone calls? What letters?"

"If you didn't get them, it's not because he didn't call or write. Did you try to call or write him?"

Lupé shook her head, confusion replacing the fury in her eyes. "I was waiting for him. If he didn't hear from me he should have come in person."

"You think it's easy for him to come to you?" she asked softly. "You keep runnin' away, what's a man supposed to think?"

"I'm carrying his baby!" Lupe protested.

"Keep your voice down," Mama Samm admonished. "Too many peoples already knows your bidness. You think his stayin' away is all about pride? You been a monster so long, lived with monsters so long, you can't understand how he feels about being a monster, hisself. Other werewolves, other vampires, seek the societies of their own kind. He has no kind. And chasing someone who flees from him just makes him feel more monstrous."

"I didn't think—"

"That's right, you didn't think. You all just pregnant hormones and bent out of shape because your man is the demiurge on the cusp o' time. Well, it bad enough that there be things and groups of things that want to do him harm. How much do it help when the mother of his child goes running off to enemy territories, endangering herself, her child, and the man she claim to love?"

"I—I'm not in danger here," she protested.

"Yeah. You so safe you can't leave even if you wanted to."

"Why would I want to?"

"Have you tried?"

Lupe had no immediate answer to that.

"I know you cannot go back to your family or your pack. They would destroy your child as an abomination. And you along wit' it, just to please their vampire masters."

"So I choose to stay here where it's safe," she reasoned.

"You are *kept* here," Mama Samm corrected, "because you are a political asset. You are a bargaining chip that keeps the Bloodwalker out of Marie Laveau's territory and impresses the other enclaves that she has something to hold over him. Once the child is born, she will have two bargaining chips. Do you understand how that works? Two chips mean you can play—or dispose of—one without losing the bargaining power of the other."

"Particularly," Lupe puzzled out slowly, "if I am the one she uses and holds our baby back in reserve . . . "

"So you see," the big fortune-teller continued, "your safety is temporary at best and ephemeral in the long term."

<Ephemeral?> I repeated. <Since when did you start using words like "ephemeral" and "hominid"?>

>*Reader's Digest.*< Mama Samm mindwhispered. >"It Pays To Increase Your Word Power." You should subscribe. I'm particularly fond of "Life In These United States."<

"What do you suggest I do?" Lupé asked quietly, looking about as if to gauge our present level of privacy.

"You can start by talking to the one person who cares about you beyond your political value as a hostage or a science project. You can stop punishing the man for something you imagined he did and find out what really happened."

"She knows what really happened," chirped Deirdre's voice from the other side of the curtain. "She's just not finished running her tests."

<Tests?> I echoed as Mama Samm wrenched herself up and out of her dual chair arrangement.

Three long strides and the curtain was swept aside to reveal two faces leaning forward to eavesdrop.

Every face to face (to face) encounter with Deirdre and Theresa since our return from Dr. Mengele's Rocky Mountain fortress was a fresh shock to my sensibilities. The fact that I hadn't seen her/them for nearly six months didn't help. Neither did repeated viewings of *The Hitchhiker's Guide to the Galaxy*—the Mark Wing-Davey 1981 incarnation of Zaphod Beeblebrox, not the Sam Rockwell performance from '05, that is. There's something about a pair of heads sharing a single body that is just so wrong on so many levels. And that's before we even get to the aesthetics. Trust me on this one, the old saw is wrong: two heads are *not* better than one!

Deirdre looked suitably embarrassed, her face blushed scarlet, nearly matching the arterial red of her hair. Theresa's face was pale in marked contrast to her coal-black locks. Her present pallor had nothing to do with surprise or fright, however. Chalk it up to a prior Goth lifestyle and a more recent condition as a headless corpse. Or a corpseless head. In any event, she wasn't embarrassed. The only thing I'd ever known to embarrass this bad-news brunette was her failure to achieve full-blown monster status during the "Lilith Affair." Not—I thought as I considered the place where Theresa's neck was fused to Deirdre's shoulder—that she was entirely out of the running now.

"You *ladies*," Mama Samm said, pronouncing the word as if she wasn't completely sure of it, "need to go lie back down and let peoples have their private talks. Your turn will be coming."

"Don't blame me," Theresa whined with a contradictory smile, "I'm just along for the ride."

"You look tired," the juju woman said abruptly. "Why don't you take a nap?"

Theresa's head suddenly dropped forward, her chin falling on Deirdre's chest. Her mouth lost its subtle sneer and began to emit gentle snoring sounds.

"Thanks," Deirdre said. "You don't know how much—"

"You need a nap, too," Mama Samm interrupted. "But I'll give you another ten seconds to get back into bed, first."

Deirdre turned and fled. Mama Samm reclosed the curtains. Turned back to Lupé. "What you think you testin' for, child? To see how much rejection your man can take? By the time you have your answer, you'll be alone and he'll be that much further away. Is that what you want?"

Lupé started to speak, then stopped and closed her eyes and shook her head.

The fortune-teller turned couples counselor repositioned the two chairs closer to the bed and repositioned herself upon them. "Then *talk* to him," she said, settling back. "I'm tired. I think I'll take a little nap, myself."

Her eyes stayed open but I had the sudden impression that I had been left alone in the cubicle with the mother of my unborn son.

"Lupé . . . " I tried through thicker, wider lips.

Her ears pricked forward. It seemed impossible that human ears could move in such a manner but the impression was unmistakable. "What . . . ?"

"It's me."

"It's you?"

"Chris. I'm . . . inside. Riding shotgun inside Mama Samm's head."

She stared at me, her eyes widening.

"I bloodwalked." Well, technically Mama Samm pulled some kind of juju move but this was confusing enough without getting into specific details.

"Chris?" she whispered. She glanced around as if expecting an undead Ashton Kutcher to appear.

I tried nodding the fortune-teller's head. The result was a perilous wobble.

Lupé crept out of bed cradling her swollen belly. "What are you doing here?"

"I've come to see you. You won't take my phone calls, answer my letters. Marie Laveau has forbidden me to come in person. What was I supposed to do?"

"I don't know. I didn't know. Someone must have interfered—" She crouched down to look in our eyes. "Are you really in there? She let you inside her head?"

"Yeah. She made up a guest room and everything."

She frowned. "How do I know it's really you?"

I tried shrugging Mama Samm's shoulders. All around, these days, I really sucked at shrugging. "I guess we should have agreed on a code word or phrase," I said, "just before you ran away. Too bad I left my wallet in my other pants."

"Well, you certainly do sound like him." Her mouth was hardening into a straight line.

"How about telling you something only I would know? Like that sound you make when we—"

"All right! All right!" she said, covering my mouth with one hand and awkwardly embracing me with her other arm. "You're him. You. Chris."

"I'd better be the only one who knows the sound you make when we—" The hand went over my mouth again.

"Do you want us to take you out of here?" I asked when the hand was removed a second time. "Say the word and Mama Samm and I will lean on Mooncloud and we'll pack your bags right now."

Lupé glanced at the screens on either side of her cubicle—toward the bed containing the body on life support, then toward the alcove where Deirdre and Theresa were sawing twin logs. "Not yet . . ."

"Why not . . . yet?"

My once-and-hopefully-future fiancée leaned closer and murmured: "She's working on a process to neutralize the silver in your body." She reached out and touched Mama Samm's face. "Your other body. How can we ever . . . be together . . . until you're clean again? Laveau needs more time. And she has promised Theresa her new flesh tonight. If I leave before then she might renege on her promise and hold her and Deirdre as hostages. If we take them with us now—" She shook her head. "I don't think Deirdre can stand it much longer."

I stared back at her through Mama Samm's eyes. "And you say she's ready to move Kellerman's head to her new body tonight?"

"She's already prepared redundant donor bodies. All she lacks is some kind of powerful artifact or key ingredient. I think she went out to fetch it early this morning."

Since that seemed to jibe with Irena Pantera's account of her stepmother's disappearance, it looked like we might be closing in on some closure with Theresa Kellerman, at last.

"All right," I said. "I'll give it another twenty-four hours. Then we blow this fallout shelter and head back to West Monroe with or without Pete'n'Repeat."

Lupé shook her head. "You wouldn't seriously consider leaving them here."

"I wouldn't want to but family comes first," I said, feeling sick at the thought of leaving Deirdre behind.

"Yes," she said, taking Mama Samm's hands and tugging us to our feet, "yes, it does." She led us back to the divider and pushed the curtain aside. "I know you fear for our son as much, if not more, than you fear for me. But you have your unborn wife and daughter to think about, as well . . . "

I looked through the parted curtains because Lupé clearly wanted me to see something. But all that was immediately evident was the hospital bed and nightstand that served as spartan furnishings for Deirdre's and Theresa's cubicle. And Deirdre and Theresa, of course: sprawled across the rumpled bed in careless repose where Mama Samm had just sent them for their conjoined naps.

Then I saw what I had not noticed before: the strained pajamas across the convex curve of their mutual belly. Third trimester well begun!

"Oh, what fresh hell is this!" I groaned.

Mama Samm's mind roused, flared in the darkness adjacent to my own. She took in the same tableau and processed the evidence more swiftly than I.

>The plan was always to provide surrogate wombs for the cloned embryos of your late wife and daughter, Christopher.<

<But this?>

>Why not Deirdre? Would you rather a stranger—?<

<I wouldn't want Kellerman in the same obstetrics wing with a fetus, much less sharing any kind of a mind/body connection!> I fumed.

The curtain on the other side of the cubicle was swept aside. Mooncloud and Pantera stared at me. "Is there a problem?"

The two-headed surrogate stirred in their sleep and rubbed their belly with their left hand. "Mommy take . . . good care . . . you . . . " Theresa murmured dreamily through a sly smile.

<Oh, bloody hell!>

Chapter Eight

IRENE PANTERA SEEMED particularly desperate that her stepmother be found before her father awakened at sunset. Whether it was out of concern for him or for herself, I could not tell. Even those familial bonds that survive a "turning" are never really quite the same. How can they be when the person turned loses their humanity? Whichever her motivation—dutiful daughter or daddy's little thrall—it was the leverage Mama Samm needed to get us admitted to the "holy of holies."

<So where do we look, first?> I asked as we were let into Marie Laveau's chambers.

My physical host loosed a mental snort. >You s'posed to own a detective agency. So, start detectin'.<

<But you're the one who knows her. Has had steady communications with her these past few months. Maybe we should—>

"Please do not disturb anything," Irena said as she turned a switch on an external lighting circuit. "My stepmother would be very angry if she thought I had come in here. I don't know what she would do if she discovered that I had brought outsiders into her peristyle." Bare bulbs nursed reddish sparks to fully whitened glows, illuminating the cavernous room.

Tapestries softened the harshness of the stone-block walls but couldn't diminish the effect of the room's vast dimensions. Laveau's furniture would have been ornate in the parlors of old New Orleans' historical houses. Down here in this echoing, warehouse setting they took on the appearance of cheap, dollhouse furnishings.

There was a bed—no need for the comforting confines of a coffin so far underground—and a row of armoires, some containing clothing, others serving as organizers for relics and apothecarial supplies. Being limited to the use of Mama Samm's eyes, it was hard to examine much in the way of evidence when her head kept swinging this way and that.

<If you want me to detect, you need to slow down!>

"There's an altar," she announced abruptly. Irena stared at her. I would have, too, if there had been any way to take a couple of steps back. For all of their history, Marie Laveau and Sammathea D'Arbonne had never met anywhere but on neutral ground. "Somewhere near by!"

She cast about like a dog attempting to pick up a scent.

And we saw it together: large tapestries covered the walls to our left and right as we came through the door. But the wall on the opposite side was a curtain, not a tapestry.

Mama Samm approached it with her arms out, hands extended, and palms forward.

<I've got a bad feeling about this . . . >

>Oh, hush up! You sound jus' like them bad movies you always watchin'.<

<Those "bad" movies, as you call them, are actually educational. You can learn all sorts of things from them.>

>Like what?<

<Like—the killer is never really dead. No matter how many times you dispatch him. Or when you find a dead body don't split up and go out alone in the dark to look for clues. . . . >

>Mmm-hmm. And, of course, don't get naked to take showers or have sex in creepy old houses, or wear nighties with high heels in case you have to start running.<

<Good advice, wouldn't you say?>

She shook her head as she reached out to touch the heavy, dark curtain. >First of all, Cséjthe, there ain't much chance that *we* are going to split up. Second, I ain't taking no shower nor wearing no nightie and I sure as hell ain't running—in high heels or anything else, for that matter.<

<Well, we haven't discussed the more fundamental rules,> I argued, as she pulled the edge of the drape aside. <Like the one about the monster always being on the other side of the door.>

>This is a curtain, not a door,< she snapped, as she pulled the split open wider.

The monster was on the other side of the curtain.

᭟᭟᭟   ᭟᭟᭟   ᭟᭟᭟

Call it a Sigourney Weaver moment.

Or maybe not.

The actress who inhabited the role of Lieutenant Ellen Ripley in the first four *Alien* movies was mercifully absent in the fifth, *Alien vs. Predator* installment. In other words, she wasn't around—cinematically speaking—to see the intergalactic trophy hunters take on the face-hugging, chest-bursting, acid-blooded, extendible-double-dentifriced denizens of LV-426.

So, lacking the reference points for those particular close-encounters-of-the-third kinds, she certainly wouldn't/couldn't imagine the flipside.

I'm talking about the *other* kind of "close encounter."

Despite the unlikely biological gestalt, my first impression in looking at the thing that reared up on the other side of Laveau's false wall, was that at least one "Alien" and one "Predator" had eschewed the polemics of their peers and slapped "make love, not war" bumper stickers on their respective spacecraft. More than that, they had made the two-backed star beast.

Performed personal docking maneuvers.

Linked life support, engaged thrusters, ejected a payload or two—spawning the thing that lurked on the other side of Laveau's curtained divider.

Bad enough either species might have the bad taste to reproduce. The thought that they might cross-pollinate and produce a love child twice as hideous? Well, a

single glance at Junior here was enough to guarantee the
passage of any extraterrestrial miscegenation laws that
the rest of the universe might want to legislate.

In theory, that is, because our particular monster was
a statue.

Fortunately.

Because nothing that hideous—that appalling—could
actually exist outside of a seriously twisted imagination.

Except . . .

<Okay. I know who this is.>

>Ah . . . < There was a moaning sound far back in
the depths of Mama Samm's mind. >I was afraid of
this . . . <

<It's Gnarly.>

I felt the double take without her actually moving her
head. >What?<

<Whatsisname. Nyarlathotep. Ole tentacle puss.>

I mean it was pretty simple to figure out. Laveau was
hardly the type to go in for movie collectibles. And this
thing didn't quite match up to the aforementioned creature features. The first glaring dichotomy was that someone had replaced this thing's head with a mutant octopus.
After that anomaly, other bits—like the scaly body and
the long, narrow wings that emerged from its shoulders
like an ill-fitting Burberry trencher—were evidence that
Moby Squid, here, had nothing to do with either Hollywood franchise. In fact, the prodigious claws on its hind
and fore feet seemed almost quaint after taking in the
tentacled face for the third or fourth time.

And, while I'd never laid eyes on such a diverse collection of grotesqueries in a single critter, there could be
only one pseudopod Pinnochio on the suspect list . . .

Except . . . >This is *not* a graven image of Nyarlathotep, Cséjthe.<

<It isn't?>

>No.<

<Oh. Well then. Who? Or what . . . is it?>

>Don't you know?<

<Doctor Octopus?> I ventured.

>What? No!<

<Dr. Zoidberg?>

> <

<Billy the Squid?>

>I do not know why I even asked.<

<I don't know why you asked, either. Obviously you
know; I don't. So, tell me.>

>I was testing to see if a link had been established.<

<Meaning?>

> <

<Davy Jones? From *Pirates of the Caribbean*—not
The Monkees, of course.>

>Stop making up these ridiculous guesses!<

<Then *tell* me what I want to know!>

"What is it?" Pantera asked.

<Yeah, what is it?>

"Child . . . " Mama Samm turned away from the grotesque carving in green stone and stared blindly back at
the door on the far side of the room. " . . . we gots to
find Marie Laveau soon as possible! Her life is in great
danger!"

<It is?>

>Yes,< she answered me with uncharacteristic grim-
ness. >We got to kill the Vampire Queen of New Orleans
before she can bring about the end of the world!<

᠊ᴧᴧ᠊   ᠊ᴧᴧ᠊   ᠊ᴧᴧ᠊

Irena went to work searching for any clues that might help us locate her stepmother, totally unaware that Mama Samm was plotting Laveau's murder. While the stepdaughter combed through her personal effects, the juju woman concentrated on Laveau's tools of the trade. Me? I was just along for the ride.

The statue stood upon a crude altar against the stone wall just ten feet beyond. By now I had seen a few voodoo shrines and altars but the collection of trinkets, offerings, and spell components weren't like anything I had run across in illustrated books much less up close and personal. But then I doubted Marie Laveau would practice any form of Voudon like anyone else.

Above the arcane workspace—above the statue that reared over us as we approached—cryptic symbols were scratched and clawed, like a mad etching from some meaningless alphabet:

La Mayyitan Ma Qadirun Yatabaqqa Sarmadi

<It doesn't look like French,> I observed. <Maybe Yoruba. If it's a clue, we should copy it down. Perhaps one of the voodoo shops has African connect—>

"That is not dead which can eternal lie," Mama Samm intoned, staring at the eerie inscription. "And, with strange eons, even death may die!"

<Well . . . *that's* disturbing . . . >

"What does it mean?" Irena asked.

"They are the words of the Mad Arab."

<"Osama bin Laden?"> Irena and I asked together.

"What? No! I speak of Abdul Alhazred, the madman! He who brought forth *Al Azif* from the Nameless City in the wastes below Irem and in his final days in the cursed sector of Damascus, during fell days of the eighth century!"

I stole a glance at Irena, out of the corner of Mama Samm's eye. Clearly we were simpatico: she was as baffled as I.

"So that would be a big 'no' to my second guess," she reasoned aloud; "Jafar from Disney's *Aladdin*, as well?"

I was starting to like this girl.

My hostess, however, turned her attention back to the altar with disgruntled musings on the inadequacies of today's educational system.

Since I had to look where she looked, we contemplated the shimmery topography of Laveau's voodoo workstation.

What first appeared to be a riot of color, shape, and purpose slowly emerged to the patient eye as an ever-shifting pattern of geometric shapes, like an ever-evolving equation in three dimensions. Beads of various hues, sizes, and configurations flowed in cacophonous strands over and under and around and about everything: strands of pearls and gems, Mardi Gras leis and rosary chains—the latter ritually defaced and changed into something foul and fell. The chromatic rainbows of droplets seemed to be in constant motion, appearing and disappearing in the shimmering landscape like herds of tiny chameleons, transforming and redefining their relationships with their surroundings.

Two books were immediately visible in the roiling collage. They were positioned side by side with uncharacteristic precision. Mama Samm picked up the one to the left and looked at the title: *L'Île Mystérieuse*. A quick perusal of the book's interior revealed two things: that the text was in French and a portion of one line had been highlighted: *34°57′ S 150°30′ W*. Repeatedly fanning the pages revealed no other markings or notes but the author's name gave us some additional context. We were holding an old French edition of Jules Verne's *The Mysterious Island*.

The other book was in English and of more recent vintage: *And The Sea Will Tell* by Vincent Bugliosi. A quick perusal of the contents yielded another highlighted set of coordinates: *5°52′ N 162°6′ W*.

>What do these numbers mean?< Mama Samm asked me.

<They're geographical coordinates. Longitude and latitude—>

>I *know* that. You're the boat person. Where are they? What do they have in common?<

<What do I look like, a world atlas? I need charts. Though I'm pretty sure of two things. Both locations would be somewhere in the Pacific Ocean. And both probably refer to islands.>

>Anything else?<

I shrugged. Or tried, anyway. Not having my own body or having it while wearing a straightjacket—pretty much the same end result. <One's from a book by a French science fiction author back in the 1870s and the other's from a book by the guy who prosecuted Charlie Manson back in the 1970s.>

Mama Samm flipped to the front. >Says 1991 here.<

I tried shrugging again. <Different case. Try digging around and see if Laveau's got *Helter Skelter* tucked away in there.>

Mama Samm plunged her hands into the shimmering sea of beads, bowls, and offerings and pulled another book to its chroma-keyed surface. It seemed to resist her efforts to extract it but, with a mighty heave, it finally pulled free.

It was an old, leather-bound tome, heavy with thick, parchment-like pages. Mama Samm examined the fine, golden-brown binding, marred only by a stippled, circular impression near the outer corner. <What's that?> I asked as she held the book a little further away.

>A nipple.<

<A . . . nipple . . . ? Like as in . . . ?>

>Yes, Cséjthe, this accursed thing is bound in human skin.<

Well.

Okay.

I mean, *yuck*, but it's not like this sort of thing is totally unheard of.

The practice of binding books in human skin was not completely uncommon in centuries past: some of our country's finest libraries have such books in their collections.

Put your library card back in your pocket, psycho nerd: they're not out on the public shelves.

A lot of said volumes are medical texts where the doctor/author had access to skin from amputated parts, patients' bodies that went unclaimed, executed criminals, medical school cadavers, and the very poor—who never had much say over their own lives while still breathing and even less after they had stopped.

A 1568 anatomy text by the Belgian surgeon, Andreas Vesalius, resides in Brown University's John Hays

Library. The College of Physicians of Philadelphia has several volumes bound by Dr. John Stockton Hough, who diagnosed the city's first case of trichinosis. He used some of that patient's skin to provide covers for three of his tomes.

And while some physicians were credited with the practice as a means of honoring some patients and/or providing an educational tie-in to informative works, other books have a decidedly unsavory hint of marketing attached. Two nineteenth century editions of *The Dance of Death*—a medieval morality tale on the theme of how death prevails over all, rich and poor—are bound in human skin.

An 1837 copy of George Walton's memoirs was bound in his own skin. Walton, a highwayman of some repute, bequeathed his own hide-bound book to one of his victims. No doubt with some "pound of flesh" joke invoked at some point in the process.

The Cleveland Public Library has a Quran that may have been bound in the skin of its previous owner, an Arab tribal leader. I shudder to think what the Vatican may have tucked away in its secret archives.

<So . . . what sort of book would Marie Laveau have on her altar, bound in human—it is human—?>

>Yes.<

<—human skin, that could contribute to the kind of sympathetic magic that would bring about the end of the world?> The skeptic in me was uncomfortable with voodoo having any kind of influence outside of the tourist industries for New Orleans and Haiti. Of course, the skeptic in me was uncomfortable with the concept of

vampires and werewolves and demons and elves when you get right down to it.

She opened the book and gasped.

Actually, there was no sharp intake of breath. A "gasp" is the closest analog I have to my host's reaction to the spiked script that slashed across the pages in crabbed lines. The inside of her head seemed to grow dark as if all of the light in the room had dimmed and a simultaneous eclipse of the sun had commenced outside. The darkness seemed to roil with menace and inaudible voices that gibbered and whispered just beyond the range of human hearing.

Irena did gasp, though. "Is it the *Necronomicon*?"

<*Necronomicon*? What's that? The Phonebook of the Dead?>

Mama Samm ignored me and rounded on Laveau's stepdaughter. "What do *you* know of such things, little girl? A Latin or Greek translation of that monstrous work would be an abomination beyond telling! But *this!*" she hissed, shoving it toward Irena like a weapon, "this, is far worse! It is one of the *Al Azif*—the original Arabic texts of Abdul Alhazred the Mad! No original copy of the source material has been known to have survived the first millennium!"

Until now apparently.

<And yet like a long overdue library book—> I mused.

>That's it! I need to be getting you outta my head and finding you another ride back home, *now.*<

<What? No way. Not without my peeps! And you can use my help—>

>You are a distraction and you are using up conjure memory that I am likely to—<

She had opened the book and was turning the pages as if each piece of parchment had been dipped in excrement. Dozens of handwritten notes had been scribbled in the margins—in a variety of handwriting styles and inks. Two notations seemed to jump off the page with unnerving vitality.

Additional coordinates: *47°9′ S 126°43′ W* and *49°51′ S 128°34′ W*.

Without setting the book down Mama Samm fished through her valise-sized purse and landed her cell phone.

"Um," Irena said, "cell phones don't work down here. You can't get a signal."

"Can't, huh?" Mama Samm touched the phone to her forehead and whispered something that even I couldn't hear. Then she hit number six on her speed dial and within two rings Zotz was on the other end of the connection.

"Everything all right?" my erstwhile caretaker asked.

"Didn't anyone ever tell you the proper way to answer the phone is to say 'hello'?" Her voice lacked its accustomed snap.

"Caller ID," he answered. "I knew it was you."

"I got an assignment for you."

"Oh goody. My existence has no meaning when I'm not steppin' and fetchin' for your beneficent consideration and past kindnesses."

"This is for Mister Chris," she said sourly.

"That's different; I actually am in his debt."

"I need you to do some research for us—him. Can you go online without getting distracted by all the nasty stuff?"

He sniffed. "The fact that my studies of the human condition include research on human sexuality—a major factor in human motivation to both create and destroy—does not mean that I am a porn addict, madam. I merely seek clarity."

"Yeah? Well, I got some numbers for you to clarify. You got a pencil?"

"Gimme a moment."

While Zotz rummaged for a writing implement, I whispered in her—um—"ear" to ask after our own, personal homeland security.

"Ready whenever you are, S.D."

"Before we continue I need to ask you a question," she said, shooting a sidelong glance at Laveau's stepdaughter.

"What? Like Truth or Dare?"

"No. Like how's the fishing up your way? I hear it's so good the fish are just climbing out of the river and into your boat. Are they still biting?"

"Uh, that's a big negatory there, Big Mama. But we are taking no chances. I've got spear guns and firearms stashed everywhere, the weapons lockers are unlocked, and I've rigged a dozen homemade depth charges. The fish-finders are alarmed and running night and day. No one's sticking their feet in the water and anything sticks its head out, I'm taking it off."

"Good to know. I'm gonna give you four sets of numbers, now. They're geographical coordinates in latitude and longitude. Do you know what that—"

"I know what longitude and latitude are; just give me the damn numbers. And tell me if 'his nibs' is all okay."

"He is. That's all I can say at the moment."

"Got company, huh?"

"You're smarter than you look. Of course, you'd have to be just to walk erect."

"Yeah, I love you, too. Gimme the numbers: Olive's coming over shortly to see if her nephew needs changin'. I'll make a run to the library then."

She repeated the four sets of coordinates, they exchanged a couple more unpleasantries and she refolded her phone and dropped it back into her bag.

"Um, Miss Sammathea?" Irena tugged on our arm. "I know there's no love lost between you and my stepmother. And this . . . book . . . means that she's probably crossed a line that—well—there's probably no uncrossing. But if saving the world could coincide with saving Marie Laveau from herself?" She looked up at us with large, liquid brown eyes. "Well, that wouldn't be such a bad thing, would it?"

Mama Samm gazed back down at her and smiled. I think the smile was meant to be reassuring. I know that it took all kinds of effort. "Where is she, child? Do you know where she's gone?"

Irena nodded. "I think so."

"Tell me."

"Better than that, I'll drive you."

Now it was the juju woman's turn to lay her hand on the young girl's arm. "It would be better if I went alone. Just tell me."

ᴧᴧ   ᴧᴧ   ᴧᴧ

My host fumed all the way to the New Orleans' Museum of Art.

>Another five minutes and I would have figured it out on my own!<

<Sure.>

>The newspaper was lying right there! Opened right to the Arts & Culture section for gods' sakes!<

<Not to mention the clippings taped to the wall above the altar,> I agreed.

>What? Where?<

<I guess that Necri-whatsis book had you sorta distracted.>

>It's hard to concentrate with a babbling fool carryin' on inside your head. Bad enough babysitting one. Now I'm babysitting two!<

"You alright back there?" Irena asked from the front seat. "You haven't said two sentences since we crossed Esplanade Avenue."

"I'm thinking, child." Mama Samm lifted the newspaper from her lap and skimmed the trio of grainy photos accompanying the article on the NOMA exhibition. "Marie Laveau said something about a Russian key. This exhibit contains hundreds of religious icons and artifacts from Russia and it closes tomorrow. The odds are, we're too late to prevent her from taking what she needs for her sorceries . . ."

"But, if we can figure out what she's taken," Pantera's daughter extrapolated, "it might give you a clue as to what sort of a spell she was working on and how to counter it?"

Tap.

Mama Samm nodded but I just folded my nonexistent arms and glowered at the back of Irena's head. <How about she didn't have enough pre-daylight to get into the museum, find her key, get back out, and reach alternate

shelter before sunrise? I'm betting she's still holed up inside, somewhere.>

Tap tap.

Mama Samm nodded again, this time for my benefit. >Which is why I didn't want her tagging along. The next time I see Marie Laveau, it won't be a "come, let us reason together" kind of moment.<

Tap-a tap tap.

<Well, at least she's pinned down until dark and sunset's still hours away.>

Tap tap-a tap tap tap-a tapita . . . .

"Listen, I'm going to drop you off by the front door," Irena said, putting on her turn signal, "because my umbrella's pretty small and I don't see any parking places under the one-hundred-yard dash."

Thunder boomed in the distance and the tapping of random drops of rain on the car roof moved from background noise to a roar of sound that essentially drowned out any further conversation.

Oncoming traffic switched their headlights on.

Between the back door of Irena's car and the front entrance of the New Orleans Museum of Art, I learned how to curse in Haitian, Yoruba, and some humming-clicking dialect that the old juju woman refused to identify for me.

Maybe it was a passing squall. Rain in Southern Louisiana and the Crescent City, in particular, was both common and transitory, sometimes occurring two to three times a day with hours of sunshine sandwiched in between. This might last twenty minutes, pass on, and we'd have a few more hours of daylight to keep Marie at bay while we searched the museum for her handiwork.

That would be a typical weather scenario.

Unfortunately, typical had gone out the window with tentacle-faced beings from other dimensions and dreamcasts from Deep Space Malign.

<Now what?> I asked, as she snatched up a brochure and began studying the list of exhibition areas.

>We split up and begin searching,< Mama Samm growled. I actually felt the vibrations.

<Hardy har,> I intoned as the thunder outside made an ear-splitting, tearing sound. It stopped "raining." Instead, water fell out of the sky as if some cosmic reservoir had, indeed, been ripped asunder.

>Irena and I split up,< she clarified. As Irena came slamming though the main entrance, looking like a drowned—well—certainly not a "drowned rat" as the saying typically goes. Her long, dark hair was plastered to her head, shoulders, and back so that the tips of her ears poked out like little kitty-cat triangles. Similarly, her shirt was now reapplied to the sweet curves of her upper body like a second coat of paint, semitransparent where the swell of bosom stressed the wet fabric, and leaving little to the imagination. Her jeans drooped on her hips from the weight of waterlogged denim, exposing a two-inch strip of bare, brown belly. Unlike Volpea's, the shadowed whorl of her navel was still empty and virginal.

>Will you keep your mind on the business at hand?< Mama Samm snapped, giving me a sharp mental elbow. >What would Miss Lupé think?<

<She already thinks the worst, so what should I care? Besides, I'm not really interested because—among so many other things—she is too young.>

>Not to mention, a lesbian.<

<Will you stop?>

She turned to Irena. "Baby, we can cover more ground if we split up. Why don't you take—"

Pantera's daughter shook her head, creating a small rainstorm of her own. "I'm sticking with you. If you find my stepmother first, I need to be there!" It was clear to both of us that arguing the issue would just waste more time.

Mama Samm sighed. "All right, let's go."

We headed for the main gallery with Irena trailing slightly behind, making squishy sounds in her wet sneakers.

‸‸   ‸‸   ‸‸

The overall theme for the exhibition was "Windows on Russia" but most of the collections on display were religious icons and relics ranging from the eleventh to the fifteenth centuries.

<So what are we looking for?> I asked. Irena voiced the same question just a half second later.

"I'm afraid this is more of an 'I'll know it when I see it' situation," she replied. >I hope.<

As we walked, she explained how icons were usually painted upon a wooden base or icon board which, in turn, was composed of several parts bound together and backed by planks. The picture is painted in the "ark," a shallow, rectangular groove or depression that has been primed with a covering of fabric, glue, and chalk and then covered with an initial coating of dark, red-brown or greenish paint. Ochre or whiting was applied, depending on the subject to be portrayed. After the portrait of saint or savior was accomplished, additional touch-ups were applied in gold, called "assist." While these were initially radial lines associated only with images of the Christ, they eventually ended up gilding everything by the fifteenth century. And, if gold wasn't enough, precious gems were included in some icons, and holy relics were embedded in more than a few.

Since the icons were at the centers of not only the churches and the church services but the very religious practices of many communities—which meant they spent a lot of time being kissed, touched, carried, incensed, holy watered, and hanging about in close proximity to generations of beeswax candles—they were further layered in ornate frames called "oklads," which were more like metal covers with cutouts designed to display the faces, hands, feet, or key elements of the icon enclosed within. These oklads were often made of silver or gold with elaborate workmanship and additional jewels, gems, and engravings and, in some cases, were capable of holding multiple icons and were called iconostases.

The question was, which would Marie Laveau deem most suitable for her dark purposes?

And how would the former voodoo queen handle such a sacred object now that she was of the undead persuasion?

As we slowly made our way to the eleventh and twelfth century galleries, we worked out a process where I would scan the even-numbered icons and their accompanying cards while Mama Samm took in the odd-numbered displays immediately adjacent. Irena made several attempts to find out what Mama Samm intended to do when they found her stepmother, as she worked the other side of the room. The conversation was rather choppy as other patrons occasionally drifted within earshot. Mama Samm tried to use these occasions to end the conversation but it was clear that Irena wasn't ready to shut up. Mama Samm's attempts to stonewall her only seemed to make her that much more determined to keep the conversation going.

And when she saw the old fortune-teller wasn't about to respond to any further lines of inquiry regarding Marie Laveau, Irena did the next best thing. As we moved into the gallery displaying the Pre-Mongol Period icons, she changed the subject.

"Tell me about the vampire demon you serve," she said. "Tell me about Domo Cséjthe!"

<S'cuse me?>

Mama Samm didn't bat an eye. "What do you want to know, child?"

"I've heard so many stories about him!" Irena continued. "Most of them are so unbelievable yet there must be something to them or my own stepmother would not fear him so. Is it true that he has already slain twenty wampyri lords as well as the Domans' Dracula and Báthory?"

<Gee, how Tolkienesque,> I observed. <The tale grows with the telling.>

"No, Miss Irena, these kinds of stories inevitably get the facts wrong," my host explained. "The count of slain vampire alphas is closer to forty, by now, with numerous attached lines wiped out in the bargain . . ." she continued.

<Actually more of a surrogate accomplishment,> I mused. <I didn't actually get my hands dirty. Or bloody. Much . . . >

". . . the Countess Báthory was actually a demon in disguise, bringing the number of hellspawn destroyed to four . . ."

<Four? Including Kadeth Bey and that fire elemental, I only count three! How do you figure four?>

". . . and Dracula lives but as Domo Cséjthe's thrall."

<*Thrall?*> I couldn't believe my ears! Come to think of it, I couldn't believe *her* ears! <You're making Vlad Dracul Bassarab V my *thrall*? Oh great! Once he hears that there won't be a hole deep enough! He's gonna be really pissed!>

"Is he tall, dark, and handsome?" Irena wanted to know.

"Tall? Yes."

<Go on. You're on a roll. Tell her I'm nine feet tall and eat lightning and crap thunder.>

>You full o'crap, all right,< she thought back at me. To Irena: "And dark. But handsome? I don't think 'good-looking' would be one of the terms to come to mind for anyone setting eyes on him for the first time."

<Well, finally back onto the main road, are we? Let's just stick to the truth from here on out. Wait, here's a better idea: let's just change the subject altogether!>

"Domo Cséjthe exudes a dark charisma that is irresistible over time," she continued. "It is how he draws others to his cause without using mind control or domination."

<What? Wait—>

"Oh yes," Irena breathed. "I understand he has taken many concubines!"

"I can't begin to keep count," Mama Samm answered.

<*Now* who's full of crap?>

"Is it true that the vampire lords are jealous and fear that he will sire a generation like himself through the wombs of the wampyri?" Irena continued. "That many of their females will turn to him for his potency after centuries of barrenness?"

"Word do get around," Mama Samm replied with a smile.

<*What* are you doing?>

"And that he is equipped—" Irena hesitated and her face turned a color to match the background ochre in half a dozen of the nearest icons. "—well, do they really call it 'The Stake'?"

<Oh. My. God. She thinks I'm some kind of undead porn star!>

>A star is born,< she agreed.

<Well, we've got to nip this in the bud! Tell her the truth! And find out where she heard this nonsense so we can . . . we can . . . >

>Oh, settle down! Ain't you learned nothin' from riding your big, bad, not-so-true reputation these past couple of years?< she scolded. >Your enemies will always seek to exploit the weaknesses and the motivations of the Christopher Cséjthe they know, not the one that you actually are. As long as those two peoples ain't the same, you've got some maneuvering room. Once you start feeding them the facts instead of fiction, your cover is lost and you is way too outnumbered to play fair wit' them odds. 'Sides, do you really want me to tell this lovely young thing dat the real Mister Chris is this pathetic, lonely man whose closest encounter with the opposite sex these past six months, has been with a gay shapeshifter who was only pretending to be interested

so she could trick him into getting trapped inside her flesh for purposes other than pleasure or procreation?<

<Gee,> I answered, <when you put it that way, I don't know why I even bother to carry my privates around with me, these days. Maybe I should put them in a little bitty coffin and bury them in my back yard. Oh, wait, I live on a boat: I don't have a back yard, anymore.>

>Oh, calm down, Mister Chris. At least you still have yours wit' you. Nobody chopped 'em off and put 'em on display in a museum halfway around the world like they did to this po' fool . . . <

I followed the nod of her head and saw that we had arrived at the entrance to a side room. Inside, the displays were confined to the artifacts and items relating to the last of the tsars: Nicholas and the royal family.

And not just the end of the Russian Romanov dynasty, but a unique tribute to the man who directly and indirectly brought doom down upon them: Grigori Yefimovich Rasputin.

The Mad Monk.

As I stared into the room beyond, it took a moment for me to realize what the fortune-teller meant by her last comment. Then I saw it: one of the track lights was focused like a baby spot on a glass cylinder that sat upon an elevated dais. The liquid within seemed to glow with a blue-white radiance of its own accord. The placard beside it proclaimed the contents within to be Rasputin's . . . er . . . genitalia.

Yikes!

And *yuck* for the second time within the past hour.

* * *

Albert Einstein's body was cremated after his death in 1955. His brain, however, was preserved in a jar for

many years thereafter. Today its remnants reside in a
number of jars: the consequence(s) of medical research.
Just one of many precedences, I suppose . . .

But pickled privates?

It's true that in another age the organs of certain
famous men were kept as—well—trophies. Scientific
curiosities. After they had passed on and had no earthly
use for them.

Napoleon's "package" was a famous example. And just
as Albert Einstein's *mental* prowess was legendary, so,
too, was the would-be emperor when it came to con-
quests between the sheets. If he'd been half the genius
in the field that he was in the bedroom, Bonaparte would
have conquered most of the Eastern Hemisphere.

Rasputin's sexual appetites were even more prodigious
according to legend. Small wonder that the
Russians—who mummified Stalin and Lenin, keeping
the latter on display even today in the Red
Square—would hang on to a piece of the guy who may
have done more for the rise of socialism than Stalin,
Lenin, and Trotsky all put together.

As we walked closer, we could see the placard attrib-
uted the temporary donation of "Rasputin Junior" to Igor
Knyazkin, Chief of the Prostate Research Center at the
Russian Academy of Natural Science in St. Petersburg.

Nudge, nudge; wink, wink . . .

According to the placard, the organ in question measured a full thirty centimeters in length—which might go
a long way toward explaining this unwashed barbarian's
popularity with the ladies of the Russian aristocracy. I
mean, being a so-called holy man will only get you so far

when you have the table manners of a pig and the body odor to match.

So, given the prodigious dimensions promised by the legend next to the display, it was impossible to *not* look. We all looked. Stared into the depths of the preservative medium that filled the small "aquarium" on the pedestal.

"I have to say," Irena said after a long, thoughtful pause, "eleven-point-eight inches isn't what it used to be."

Other than the slightly milky liquid, the tank was empty.

Mama Samm didn't say anything but I could tell that she was upset. I doubted it was from disappointment at missing out on hundred-year-old pickled privates.

"Maybe they took it out for—um—cleaning," Irena offered. Then shrugged, straightened up, and prepared to continue the search for a missing icon.

"*She* took it," Mama Samm said finally. "*This* is what she came for. This is what she meant by the Russian *key*."

<What? Are you saying Rasputin had some kind of a magic johnson? What can she do with—with—something like that?> If this was a "key" I didn't even want to think about what kind of a lock it was supposed to open.

>I do not know, yet. I must think. Be still for a while . . . <

While Irena was wandering around in the next gallery, we lingered and studied the abbreviated history of the Mad Monk of St. Petersburg, looking for clues and all the while wondering: what became of the monk, the monk, the monk, the monk. . . .

Chapter Nine

THE PHRASE "MAD MONK" is both alliterative and colorful but not wholly accurate as Rasputin was never a priest or a monk but a *staretz*—a religious pilgrim. In fact, he had little formal education or training in the Russian Orthodox faith. He was, instead, a self-styled faith healer and so-called psychic. If the czar and czarina had ordered a background check on their "spiritual advisor," his formative years surely would have given them pause.

As a young man growing up in a peasant village in Siberia, ole Greg was well known as a troublemaker. He had a taste for liquor, thievery, and women—and not necessarily in that order. Rumors of debauched and endless sexual appetites began early. He was barely into puberty when he had already developed the reputation of a rake.

At the same time, this Siberian seducer was quite the "holy" roller—when he wasn't off for a roll in the hay or a roll between the sheets. Some sources had him preaching the "word of God" since the age of eleven. Presumably he followed the dualistic path of most religious hypocrites: pious by day, priapic by night. Then, at the age of eighteen, he had a unique and most profound conversion experience.

It happened over the course of a few weeks while he was staying at the Verkhoturye Monastery. There he discovered the renegade Khlysty sect. The Khlysty philosophy taught that the only way to reach God was through sinful actions. Of course it wasn't that simple. Once the sin was committed and confessed, the penitent could achieve forgiveness. In other words, the central concept of the Khlysty was to "sin in order to drive out sin."

Sort of transcendence-through-the-12–step-process approach.

Rasputin had found a religious philosophy that embraced his hedonism and allowed him to exploit it in the name of God. Shortly thereafter he adopted the robes of a monk, developed his own self-gratifying doctrines, traveled the country as a *staretz* and elevated sinning to a new level of sacred self-indulgence.

By the time he'd reached his early thirties, Brother Lust's Traveling Salvation Show had journeyed all the way to the Holy Land and back, picking up a load of converts, including a surprising number of clergy from his homeland. And by the time he made a "pilgrimage" to St. Petersburg in 1902, many of the country's religious leaders were beginning to take notice.

The turn of the century saw a number of holy men, conjurers, psychics, healers, diviners, and unusual characters milling about the capital city, sniffing for opportunities as the royal family was in a state of turmoil. After the unexpected death of Tsar Alexander III, the young and totally unprepared Tsarevich Nicholas Alexandrovich had ascended to the throne and the situation was ripe for exploitation.

The young heir had already ticked off most of his family's royal connections in Europe on his way to courting and eventually marrying the princess who came to be known as Alexandra Feodorovna. Then he proceeded to burn his bridges with his own countrymen by holing up in the palace in Tsarskoe Selo. Seclusion is great for a couple of nobodies, madly in love with each other. Not so much for heads of state overseeing the largest land mass with its populous range of ethnicities and microcultures. Rasputin had a heavy hand in their unpopularity toward the end but the seeds of their destruction were sown early on.

The young Tsarina's primary duty was to produce the next male heir so it didn't help her popularity when she produced only daughters for four successive births. The palace doors were opened, at this point to a veritable parade of mystics and self-styled holy men. When all of that intense prayer and mystic ritualism coincided with a fifth pregnancy resulting in a boy, the stage was set for the appearance and disproportionate influence of some-one like the wily *staretz*.

Rasputin's "in" with the royal court turned out to be a little gift from Queen Victoria to the infant Tsarevich: Alexis had inherited his great-grandmother's hemophilia.

When the royal physicians were unable to control the episodes of bleeding, this bearded, wild-eyed man in monk's robes could perform seeming miracles! Skeptics would later say he used some kind of hypnotherapy.

Maybe . . . Gotta say, if I've learned anything over the last couple of years of living in the Valley of the Shadow, it's that there's more to blood than plasma and platelets, that genetics don't cover everything, and that vampires aren't the whole Neighborhood of the Weird. Forget heaven and earth, Horatio; there're more things in the Devil's Medicine Cabinet . . .

The stories about Rasputin are legion. Many are exaggerated or pure fiction. But even the most skeptical, rational-minded critic is broken, time and again, on two major issues. First, that, time and again, the *staretz* was able to stop Alexis' bleeding when the finest physicians in all of Europe and Russia were medically impotent.

And then there was the little matter of his presumed death back in December 1916 . . .

ᴧᴧ   ᴧᴧ   ᴧᴧ

<Wait a minute,> I said, as Sammathea D'Arbonne studied a loose wire on an "unauthorized exit" door.

>Don't got a minute, Mister Chris. Irena probably no more than a couple a dozen yards into the next gallery and goin' to beat feet right back here in another minute.< She gently depressed the crash bar and slipped into a back hallway.

<Yeah, well, I know the paul harvey . . . >

>The what?< she muttered as she lumbered down the "Authorized Personnel Only" corridor.

<The *rest* of the story. How Rasputin continued to piss off all of the other Romanovs, not to mention most of the military for meddling in affairs of state. And, once Russia was pulled into World War I, how his disastrous policy-making and political appointments were viewed as acts of treason. Talking Nicholas II into going to the Front to take personal command of the troops—no wonder the generals wanted to hang him! Which, in turn, left Alexandra in charge of the country back home. *Which*, in turn, left her increasingly reliant on her trusted *staretz*, advisor, and puppet master. The Romanovs couldn't put an end to him quickly enough.>

>And they didn't, Cséjthe, which is why we're here.<

That caught me up short.

According to history they'd killed him pretty dead. First the conspirators, led by Prince Felix Youssoupov, plied their victim with drugged wine and pastries laced with enough cyanide to kill four men. It didn't kill him, though. At least not fast enough. So they came downstairs and shot him in the back. The bullet wandered around his guts before lodging in his liver.

That should have killed him.

So they wrapped him in chains and carried him outside to dump the body in the river. They didn't get far before the "corpse" began to struggle again. So they dropped him and proceeded to administer a beating that would have killed an ordinary man. But, of course, this was no ordinary man so they had to shoot him again. In the chest at point-blank range. At the same time another bullet—a high-caliber slug—was fired from the bushes into Rasputin's head. Lieutenant Oswald Rayner, attached to the Secret Intelligence Service, had been dispatched by the Brits with his own license to kill. After an additional beating with a two-pound dumbbell, the body was dropped into the freezing waters of the Moika Canal on the Neva River.

But the autopsy determined that Rasputin was still alive and struggling even as he drowned under the ice. (Admittedly, this was superhuman resistance to a series of attacks—any one of which should have been fatal by itself.) But the key words to remember at the end: *autopsy*; *drowned*. In the end, Death doth make beggars of us all . . .

>Anastasia, Cséjthe.<

<What? That silly little Disney movie? Or Alexandra's fourth daughter who really died in the palace basement with the rest of her family?>

>Do you remember the woman who turned up back in the 1920s claiming to be the Grand Duchess Anastasia?<

<Oh please! And which one? Anna Anderson or Eugenia Smith? There were about ten different claimants, as I recall, though Anderson and Smith were the most compelling pretenders. Anderson even had the Romanov heirs and survivors in a lather for years.>

>Well, she knew things—family memories, secrets—that only Anastasia or another member of the family would know.<

<They both did—Smith and Anderson. And, even if Anastasia had survived her wounds and the family's mass

execution, she couldn't have been both Smith *and* Anderson!>

>One might think not.<

<And I seem to recall that there was some DNA testing, post mortem—>

>DNA only proves origins of the flesh. It means nothing in terms of a person's true identity if they are a Bloodwalker.<

It was like mental whiplash. <Whoa! Anastasia was a Bloodwalker?>

>Not a Bloodwalker, Cséjthe, but something like. And *not* Anastasia, but someone who knew the family intimately. Knew their secrets. Wouldn't die easily. And might inhabit a succession of hosts pretending to be royalty rather than presenting its own peasant origins.<

<Holy crap! Rasputin? What are we dealing with here?>

>Back when he was still a man, Grigori Yefimovich Rasputin was an acolyte of Nyarlathotep. What? You thought a simple peasant acquired the power of life and death over millions of Russians by mere happenstance?<

<Others have: Lenin, Stalin . . . >

>Pol Pot, Idi Amin . . . < she continued. >Nyarlathotep has many acolytes. And he sets them upon many thrones. But returning to the question of what we are dealing with now? I do not know the specifics. Only that Laveau is attempting to do something very bad!<

<Hey, I can play connect-the-dots well enough to guess that Laveau grabbing Rasputin's—uh—remains— means she's going to invoke the old monk's mojo in some way. But some specifics might help me know what I'm

supposed to do when we catch up with *la belle dame sans sanity.*>

>"Sanity" is not a French word.<

<There is no French word for sanity. Ironic, huh?>

>There's nothing you can do even if we do catch her in time. You're a passenger,< Mama Samm continued. >And I don't know how to explain the parts that I do understand. She's been preparing a summoning spell. Except *what* she's summoning never really departed—though its host bodies have died over the course of time. And she plans on opening a gate—although that gate is already partially open or Nyarlathotep couldn't bind Baron Samedi and manifest through his avatar as he did in your car.<

<Opening a 'gate'? Why do I get the feeling that this is only the warm-up to the "very bad thing" that Laveau is working toward?>

>Hush now! I've got to think! Where would that bitch go to work her spell?<

Somewhere dry and out of the rain, I thought to myself.

>No. She called up this storm. It's more than just a barrier that shields her from the sun. It's an energy vortex that she's set up to power the next part of her spell! And to tap into it she will have to be outside when the time comes. . . . <

<That certainly narrows our search parameters.> Note to self: sarcasm is difficult enough without the tool-box of inflection.

>She'll seek the highest ground possible.<

<Are we talking ground literally or metaphorically?> There was no high "ground" in New Orleans.

>She'll go, to the roof of the tallest building she can find,< Mama Samm answered, throwing her weight against a locked exit door. It gave way with only the briefest of hesitations and we were stumbling through the rain toward the parking lot at the front of the museum.

<That would be Place St. Charles—the old Bank One Center on St. Charles Avenue.>

>'Fraid not, Cséjthe. My money's on One Shell Square.<

<Bank One's got fifty-three stories. One Shell's only stacked to fifty-one.>

>Maybe so, but the Shell's fifty-two feet taller and it's got a big, flat roof to work wit'.<

<Laveau's casting a spell, not organizing a soccer match. How much room does she need?>

>Depend on de size of whatever she's bringing t'rough de gate.<

This was so not good!

Even worse, Mama Samm's conversation was starting to devolve into the Haitian-flavored patois she affected whenever the ectoplasm was about to hit the fan. It was her linguistic equivalent to suiting up in cape and tights before battling supernatural supervillains . . .

>What's that?<

<What?> I looked around and, of course, saw nothing.

>Did I just catch a flash of you imaginin' me in my underwear?<

<Um . . . >

A car slid alongside throwing a sheet of water over our already soaked carcass. Irena opened the passenger door from the driver's side. "Wherever you're going," she accused, "you'll get there a lot faster by not ditching me!"

Mama Samm wasn't done with me. >Don't you be lettin' your mind wander where it's got no bidness wanderin',< she sent as she slid onto the front seat. "One Shell Square," she told Laveau's stepdaughter. "And we're running out of time." >And none of us have time for engaging in fantasy lingerie daydreams right now!<

<It wasn't lingerie. It was more like long underwear.>
>'Specially *kinky* fantasy daydreams!<
Ow!

Baby got backhand!

ᴀᴛᴀ　　ᴀᴛᴀ　　ᴀᴛᴀ

One Shell Square was a monolith of white Italian limestone. A gridwork pattern of bronzed glass windows were arranged in rows of eighteen per floor on the wide sides and thirteen on the narrows. Fortunately, I wasn't very superstitious.

Very.

Maybe Laveau sensed us coming.

Or maybe it was just dumb luck that a freak lightning strike took all of the elevators off-line while the lights in every room on every floor continued to shine with undiminished luminosity in the storm's artificial night. There was no choice for it but to exit the lobby and take the emergency stairs up.

Irena Pantera and Sammathea D'Arbonne debated the definition of a "flight" of stairs as we ascended the first twenty floors. Irena held the opinion that the run of stairs from one floor to the landing between levels constituted "one" flight and that the reversed run rising from the landing to the next floor was another flight—thus totaling "two flights" between each floor, adding up to a total of one hundred and two flights to reach the top. Mama Samm insisted that landings and reversals didn't change the essentials and that the complete set of stairs between one floor and the next constituted a single flight and, therefore, there were only fifty-one flights to negotiate to the top.

It didn't make any difference in the total number of steps. And, while fifty-one seemed less daunting than one hundred and two, it was still discouraging enough to draw my attention away from the argument and contemplate my role in the approaching showdown.

Without a body to command I was just a useless spectator. Worse, I might prove to be a fatal distraction when Mama Samm needed to keep her wits about her most. Already the mountainous juju woman was tiring and Irena surged past her to take the lead on the stairs. As her pert derrière undulated with each step taken, my attention was drawn to an assessment of her slender frame.

Irena could be a mature sixteen or a late-blooming twenty-something. Her curves were understated and her frame was slight: I doubted she weighed more than ninety pounds soaking wet. Still any body was potentially better than none and the muscles that slid and flexed in her tanned, taut arms suggested youthful vitality and toned fitness. That might offer some advantage to a bloodwalker if I borrowed her flesh in the coming melee. The problem was, such an incursion, uninvited, was tantamount to rape. It was one thing to bump brains with some inhuman foe and take possession in the name of survival and good versus evil. Quite another to commandeer an innocent bystander and chalk it up to the necessities of war.

Your son is in danger.

Yeah, but if I didn't start drawing lines somewhere, I would quickly become one of the things I waged war against.

So, you've finally dropped your noncombatant status and admit to being at war.

Shut up, I told myself. I'll do what I have to when I have to but not before.

Still, I couldn't help assessing Pantera's compact form and thinking of ways to use it if push came to shove.

ᘏ·ᴥ·ᘏ   ᘏ·ᴥ·ᘏ   ᘏ·ᴥ·ᘏ

Push and Shove were waiting for us on the next landing.

As vampires go, neither was particularly imposing. Skinny to the point of emaciation, they looked like meth addicts who had recently been turned, Marie Laveau improvising a rear guard on the fly.

"Dinner has arrived," the tall black one announced to the short white one.

Irena stopped. The hair on her arms, her head, rose up as if the handrail she gripped was charged with static electricity.

Mama Samm never broke stride and kept climbing, mounting step after step like a clockwork automaton.

"Dibbs on the Big Gulp!" yelled the short, white one. And leaped on us.

Well, actually he was aiming for Mama Samm, who was too big to miss. He came sailing down over a half dozen stairs, arms and fangs extended, ready to rip and feed on contact. Mama Samm never broke stride but brought a massive left arm up and around like a windshield wiper, intercepting him like a bug in flight and tossing him aside. He tumbled over the railing before I could figure out how to get a psychic hold for a bloodwalk. About five floors down he began screaming as the realization sank in that this was an express trip to the first floor without any stops in between.

Then the lights went out.

Mama Samm never stopped climbing stairs.

Irena screamed.

"You okay, baby?" Mama Samm asked without stopping.

There was a low-pitched growling sound. And another scream. The second scream didn't sound like a girl's. But then, it didn't sound so much like a man's, either.

The smell of blood burst in the dark but I couldn't orientate on a specific target to bloodwalk.

Mama Samm kept climbing.

In the near silence between our footfalls I thought I could hear a stealthy, padding sound. And a quiet *chuffing*, as if something were moving ahead of us in the darkness. I opened my noncorporeal mouth to ask a question and then intuitively closed it. Tried to listen, instead.

Fourteen floors later I felt us slip a little.

Mama Samm took a steadier grip on the railing and slowed her climb, feeling the step ahead before planting her foot. Two floors above we encountered speed bumps.

Soft, squishy, fabric-enclosed speed bumps leaking fluids. Littered over two landings and a dozen stairs. Past those we picked up the pace, again.

<What about Irena?> I asked.

>Don't you worry about Miss Irena. You just worry about whether I'm too late to save the res' of the world. And don' distract me till I'm done!<

I lost count of the steps.

I couldn't tell if Mama Samm was counting or not: our massive mojo mama was like a machine, clumping up stairs without regard to fatigue, pain, or the myriad of obstacles placed in our way.

She only stumbled once.

A concussive blast—I don't know any equivalent word for the feeling that pulsed down the stairwell, shook the building, and scrambled our minds like two eggs in a frying pan—seemed to vibrate everything down to the cellular level. And maybe beyond. For a moment I saw shadow places, vast caverns and deep abysses. There were memories of ancient books and recent battles, a life divided by threes and mirrored doors between worlds. A line of Russian nesting dolls stretching off into a light . . .

>*Get out of my mind!*<

It was more than brute force lifting me up and tossing me out. I was momentarily mingled with memories: I was threshed, sifted, and blown back to a dark corner in the box in Sammathea D'Arbonne's head. I huddled there, dazed and disoriented from the kabalistic kaleidoscope of images and impressions that had shot through the nebula of my consciousness like a laser light show.

<Sorry,> I finally offered as she began to stagger up the stairs, once more. <I didn't mean to pry into any of your personal secrets.>

>It's not my privacy that's at issue here,< she answered back, >but your own safety. There are places

in my mind—and places where my mind could take you—that you would not survive!< She sent a couple of images, glimpses actually: in one I was vacant-eyed and drooling like a thirty-something newborn; in the other my flesh had burned to a crispy husk starting from the inside out. I scrunched a little deeper back into the corner of the mental box she was keeping me in.

>Now hush up and don't distract me! Laveau has unleashed a massive amount of power up there. I may be too late but it feels like she's not finished so I'm gonna have to go with that!<

And with that, she mounted the top of the stairs and threw herself against the access door to the roof.

There was a blue flash and we were back outside, in the open.

Some of the darkness from the stairwell followed us and swirled beside our legs. The fog may "come in on little cat feet" but there was nothing small or dainty about the feline paws that shadowed Mama Samm's stride.

A black panther seemed to coalesce out of the shadows. It regarded us with wide, golden eyes before turning and slipping past into more darkness around the two-tiered base of the roof.

No time to speculate on puss sans boots: Marie Laveau stood above us on the elevated, second level.

At least I assumed it was the former Queen of New Orleans: who else would be up here? But all of the accounts concerning Marie pegged her as a great beauty while this creature looked like a child's stick-figure drawing or a scarecrow.

Mama Samm seemed to recognize her, but she wasn't wasting time on long, lingering looks. She had turned her gaze upward and, of course, I could look nowhere else.

There was an opening in the clouds above One Shell Square.

Somewhere up there, above the upside-down purple mountain majesties of cumulonimbus incus, the sun was still shining. At least that was my assumption based on the time of day and the continuance of the laws of physics. However, the sickly green glow that leaked from the center of the collar formation over the roof looked more like leprous moonlight or a toxic waste spill from beyond the stars.

Even as we watched, a wraith of cloud material began turning in the opposite direction of the collar's lazy rotation, forming a hollow nub of blue-gray mist shot with lightning. It was pointed, like a gigantic, snub-nosed .38, back down at the exact spot on the roof where the scarecrow woman stood over a smoldering mound of flesh and hair.

Mama Samm took a step forward and the scarecrow whirled, brandishing an elongated, floppy object in her left hand.

<Whoa! Tell me her magic wand isn't what I think it is. . . . >

My hostess ignored me, reaching into her purse and producing a fistful of rosaries. With a couple of smooth, practiced motions, she pulled the loops apart and scattered the beads like a sower sowing seeds round about.

The scarecrow made a series of complicated gestures and the wind from the storm carried snatches of fevered mutterings to our ears. Sparks erupted all around us, snapping and rolling as the beads carried kinetic energies in all directions. Mama Samm's hand was back in her giant purse and emerging with some sort of crucifix.

There was more to it than that . . . a pair of hands, either folded in prayer or open in something like supplication . . . a ring . . . I couldn't be sure for, while I was using Mama Samm's eyes, I was focusing beyond her hands at the tableau on the elevated part of the roof.

Where the bundle of hair and skin was standing up.

And up!

Grigori Yefimovich Rasputin was six foot five back when he was alive. Death had done nothing to make him look shorter. And, at the moment, he was totally naked so he wasn't wearing platforms to achieve the effect. The inches (or centimeters) he was missing were to the horizontal rather than the vertical so, still "Mr. Big" in the public sense if not the private for now.

"What are you doing, Marie?" Mama Samm called into the wind.

"You know what I am doing," came the reply. The voice was ancient, screechy, like a rusted antique hinge. "You have read the book!"

" 'Loathsome Cthulhu rose then from the deeps and raged with exceeding great fury against the Earth Guardians,' " Mama Samm quoted from black memory. " 'And They bound his venomous claws with potent spells and sealed him up within the City of R'lyeh, wherein beneath the waves he shall sleep death's dream until the end of the Aeon.' "

"Don't stop," Laveau taunted. "Finish the prophecy! 'Beyond the Gate dwell now the Old Ones; not in the spaces known unto men but in the angles betwixt them. Outside Earth's plane They linger and ever awaite the time of Their return; for the Earth has known Them and shall know Them in time yet to come.' "

"The ravings of a madman!"

Marie Laveau nodded and grinned like an idiot child. "The Mad Arab, Abdul Alhazred! By his writings, through the holy *Al Azif* do we know our destiny!"

"Yeah? Well, here's my destiny . . ." Mama Samm gripped her odd relic in her right hand as she rolled up her sleeve with her left. " . . . I'm here to see you ain't be opening up any more gates and I'll just be punching the snooze alarm for any Old Ones who've gotten a little leaky of late."

"Old Ones?" the scarecrow echoed. "Oh, I have no intention of opening any more gates or doors or paths for any of the Star Spawn . . . "

As fascinating as it was to witness thaumaturgic trash talk between two hoodoo mamas, I was still keeping my eye on Mr. Monk. And that almost caused me to miss the overhead show.

Up in the clouds, the collar formation had become a vortex, spinning counterclockwise to the nub, which was elongating into a funnel of darkness. It groped toward the roof like a tentacle, the pseudopodia of a living, sentient thing. The *staretz* was standing, his arms raised, stretching toward the funnel as if trying to grasp a kite string . . .

. . . or take hold of the leash of a wild animal.

" . . . He Who Lies Dreaming," Laveau continued, "He Who Will Rise Again, already dwells on this side of the Gate. His Dreams slough away and His time draws near! The Deep Ones have returned and attend Him. They prepare the way for His return! As I prepare a new palace and throne where He will awaken and rule and summon those He deems necessary to restore the Old Ways! The Ancient Ways!"

"Honey, you ain't preparing shit!" Mama Samm shot back. "Your mojo is gone! Used up! It's plain to see you've got nothin' left!"

<The storm!> I interrupted. <Quit monologuing and look at the storm!>

"My work is done!" Laveau cackled as Mama Samm finally looked up. "I have done all that I have been commanded! This world will pass away and He will usher in a new kingdom! A new heaven and a new earth!"

And for a moment I caught a glimpse of a nightmare.

A vision . . . a proto-memory . . . a searing peek at the hell dimension that had been this earth—and many others—aeons before the coming of the dinosaurs. When then-ancient beings that fancied themselves gods, fell from the skies—fell upon the earth as predators fall upon their prey. Creatures of such immense scale and grotesque distortion that nothing in recorded Terran taxonomy provides perspective or adequate reference point for comprehension or understanding. Sanity is challenged, troubled, perhaps even impaired by exposure to the very imagery of these things. Their existence . . .

And their *hungers* . . .

Whatever rift was opened, whatever allowed this brief sidewise glance at the unspeakable horrors that once were and sought to be again: it blinked. And I reached out with noncorporeal hands to grasp that cosmic eyelid for another searing look.

For my son.

I could not allow such things back into the world where my son would be born!

And I saw the remains of a great city, smashed into rubble and kindling. In a hazed, gray-green twilight, a great army of deep dwellers moved among the ruins gathering corpses and stacking skulls. Reptilian work gangs constructed edifices of bone and a great cyclopean throne, preparing it to receive a god. A god who would rule a world of eternal night. Where love and virtue were unknown, alien concepts. Where all life was cattle and human life prized only for its greater capacity for fear and suffering. The Great Old Ones would return and rebuild the slaughterhouses they esteemed as temples.

But, to prepare the City . . .

. . . and the Throne Room nestled among the crushed spires of the St. Louis Cathedral . . .

. . . there had to be the Perfect Storm . . .

Holy shit!

Marie Laveau was going to flatten New Orleans!

Mama Samm's reaction was more practical. >Now that I know exactly what she's about, I have a better idea what to do about it.<

<Like what?>

Her only answer was to plant herself, massive, tree-trunk legs apart, and spread her arms like twin battering rams. >She's used up all of her mojo. She's got nothin' left.< And then she began to chant in some unknown, arcane tongue with lots of clicks and tongue clacks thrown in.

Almost immediately the howl of the storm overhead began to lessen. As it did, Laveau began to howl the more. I fancied I could see the rotating ring of clouds slowing and the funnel already looked shorter.

Rasputin-reconstituted redoubled his efforts at what-ever he was doing and the winds began to freshen. Light-ning cracked, thunder boomed, and the turbine of purple-black clouds kick-started a renewed power cycle. Maybe Marie Laveau was running low on batteries but her Russian proxy still had plenty of juice, it seemed.

Mama Samm tried some variations in the chants she was using—that was as much as I could discern from the gibberish above the rising sound of the storm. And I noticed two new things as I fumed in my own, helpless impotence. One: the big, black shadow shaped like a kitty cat had circled around the roof and was creeping up behind the giant, bearded, Russian eunuch. And, two: while seemingly undiminished in power, now, the whirl-wind formation had moved off center—was actually still moving—and the "eye" was now staring blindly down over the intersection of Poydras and St. Charles.

Given enough time, we might have managed a more fortuitous outcome. Timetables and fate, however, rarely accommodate one another. This was no exception.

Laveau screeched, produced a knife, and rushed at us. The panther, stalking the *staretz*, might have intervened but seemed totally focused on the mad monk. If Mama Samm broke the spell to defend herself, she might lose the opportunity to regain mastery later. Assuming she could adequately defend herself, in the meantime.

There was just enough time for me to process this and for her to say >Goodbye, Mister Chris . . . <

Then the world, the entire universe, was shattered by an explosion—a blast that tore us apart and sent my shredded consciousness hurtling through the darkness

.
.
.
.
.
.
.
.
.
.
.
.
.
.
.
.
.

and back into numbed solidity.

There was an awful familiarity to the waking/
reconnecting sensations that mingled mind with matter,
animus and anima, body and soul. I was home! Back in
my own flesh!

Tied to a chair.

Correction: *chained* to a chair!

It was immediately obvious that no slice-and-dice fin-
gernail action was going to be helpful here. Assuming I

could even produce my monstrous manicure for a third time.

Bad enough.

Worse: The Mullet was sitting watch over me. In the forward salon of my own houseboat.

So much for the sanctity of home and I was definitely gonna have to rethink the security angle of being surrounded by running water.

Questions about Mama Samm's survival and whether she had been successful in disrupting the storm would have to take a back seat to escape.

Looked like my best hope would be a rescue from Cama—

ZZZZZzzzzzZZZZZzzz

I turned my head and looked at Camazotz who was slumped over in human form in the chair next to me. Unfortunately, sawing logs wasn't the same as sawing through the heavy chains that bound his small but wiry frame to the chair back. And even if he were to awaken I doubted that the metal links were the only restraining factors in play here.

Unless I missed my guess, the "Doctor" was *in*.

Chapter Ten

THE BIG GUY Fand had called "Setanta" had made himself at home. In *my* home.

He was draped across the sofa with his size 14 boots crossed over an armrest. The smoke detectors had either died from the overload or had their batteries pulled because his cigar had created a nimbostratus layer of blue haze throughout the gallery. The overhead lights were visibly dimmer and bluer.

He was busily engaged with a wireless Playstation 2 controller and coordinated acts of mayhem on the plasma, flat-panel monitor on the far wall. Oblivious to my newly awakened status, he was urging his on-screen

Raiders from the "Land of Oak" and making oral suppli-
cations to the great deity Madden for victory.

"Setanta!"

Even though the voice was filtered by the reinforced-
steel, load-bearing ceiling of the main cabin, Fand's bel-
low was like an ice pick thrust to the brain. Even Zotz'
snoring faltered as The Mullet erupted from the couch.

"Is he still out of his head?" she yelled from somewhere above.

My chin was back on my chest and my eyes closed
before he could turn and look. Still, I felt his eyes all
over me as he clomped around the salon.

"Aye!" he bellowed back.

"Then get up here! We seem to have attracted some
attention!"

There was the sound of the aft door opening and closing, then heavy footsteps on the spiral ladder to the
third deck.

After a moment's silence I raised my head and turned
to see Zotz wide awake and looking back at me.

"Welcome back," he said quietly.

"Hell of a homecoming," I answered, keeping my
voice equally low.

He shrugged sheepishly. "They came prepared. Fey
Folk . . . what're you gonna do?" he asked rhetorically.

"We'll get to that in a moment. I'll need some intel.
Like how many there are?"

"Two for sure," he admitted reluctantly. "Maybe a
couple of others, coming and going, that I haven't seen.
But I did get a callback from your buddy Ancho before
Blondie and her boy-toy arrived. I can give you a little
background on them."

"Anything helpful?"

He leaned in. "Your vivani said you're messin' with royalty. One of the faerie queens, to be more specific. And while these girls all got reputations for playing the field, ole dandelion head, upstairs, has been down the road and around the bend a bit."

"Do tell." I glanced at the aft corridor. "And quickly."

"Seems she was once married to the Celtic sea god Manannan . . . "

"Was? Once? Widowed or divorced?"

"Divorced. With extreme prejudice from what I understand."

I nodded. "*I* certainly can."

"Anyway, after hubby dumped her she got herself in bit of a fix going up against some kind of warriors— 'Fomorians,' Ancho called 'em—for control of the Irish Sea."

"Sounds like she likes to pick fights."

"That would be my guess. Only she bit off more than she could chew, it seems. She had to recruit this Irish hero, Koochy-koo or sumptin'—"

"Irish? Sounds like Cuchulainn," I said. "Sort of the Celtic version of Hercules with berserker tendencies."

"Maybe it was fate. Maybe it was serendipity, seeing as how they sound like such perfect soul mates," the demon mused. "By all accounts she would have been 'canned Fand' if she hadn't recruited him to her cause. Problem was, Cuch wouldn't get on board unless quee-nie would marry him."

"Lotta street cred," I mused, "even for the great Cuchulainn: mortal marrying an elf. And royalty at that."

"Not to mention she's a hell of a good lookin' dame."

"Looks only go so far," I fumed. "And the key word in your previous sentence: 'hell.' "

Zotz shrugged and the chains clinked a bit. "Well, she agreed to his terms and, surprise, according to reliable sources, she fell hard for the big lug."

"Yeah, I bet they *all* lived happily ever after."

Zotz grinned. "Yeah. Well, things *didn't* work out as Emer—this was Cuchulainn's wife—was the jealous type and even Manannan wasn't crazy about his ex's new-found happiness."

"That's just so typical."

"Actually, more practical than petty," Zotz elaborated. "There was some sort of prophecy. Apparently the union between Fand and Cuchulainn would have eventually destroyed the Faerie and brought about the end of the world. *They* didn't care though, they were just two crazy kids in love."

"Any minute now you're going to tell me why this is important."

"So the elves got together and held a council of war."

"One Tolkien over the line, sweet Jesus?"

He eyed me. "You feelin' all right?"

"A little light-headed," I admitted.

"Not surprising seeing as how you've had nothing to eat while you were—uh—gone."

Right. Step one: escape. Step two: grab blood from the fridge on the way out. Step three . . .

"But in the end, it was her ex-husband, the sea god Manannan—"

I threw myself against the chains. "Is this in any way helpful to us, here and now?" I grunted. "I have got to get down to New Orleans! I don't have time for this!"

"Hey, you're the one who's always quoting the 'know thy enemy' stratagems. You want intel? I'm intellin' ya what I know."

I strained against the chains again. No acetylene torches popped out of my shoulders to help cut me loose. "Okay! Okay. I just can't be sitting here right now! Something really bad is going down right now and I really need to get back to New—" I shook my head. Mama Samm was in her element. I needed to think a little more clearly about my own circumstances. I took a deep breath. "Keep talking. Tell me everything Ancho said."

Zotz looked at me suspiciously. "Is the D'Arbonne woman all right?"

"Now who's changing the subject?"

He blinked first. "The sea god did some mumbo jumbo with drawing his magic cloak between Fand and this Cuchulainn while they slept together. The upshot? They never could meet again nor remember each other. Sweet, huh?"

"Yeah. Sweet. Think of all the plot lines you could tie up on *Desperate Housewives*. Did Ancho offer any *practical* advice?" I asked meaningfully.

"Oh yeah. He said, too bad you didn't meet up with her sister, instead. Seems she's a goddess of health and earthly pleasures. They used to call her the 'Pearl of Beauty.' This Liban is supposed to be a real sweetie."

"Um, yeah. That's. Real. Helpful." I sighed. "So what about this Setanta character? Do we know anything about him? He doesn't have the pointy ears so, unless he fell into a mechanical rice picker at an early age, I'm guessing he ain't one of the Fey Folk."

Zotz gave me another one of his "oh yeah" looks. "Sorry. Got sidetracked, I guess. I don't know if this is important or not but it sure got your vivani's panties in a wad. He said to tell you that Setanta is his real name. His birth name."

"And this is significant . . . why?"

"He said to tell you that Setanta *is* the Hound of Ulster."

It took another moment to sink in. Then: "Holy crap!" I said. "That means—"

But what it meant was lost in the next moment as the sliding glass door at the front of the salon opened and my heart stopped.

᠅᠅   ᠅᠅   ᠅᠅

I died, of course.

Anytime your heart stops, it naturally follows that you die. Of that you can be sure.

What you can't be sure of is where you will go next—though I've known more than a few smug SOBs who thought they had it all figured out.

In this case, however, I went to Heaven.

No dinking around on the Ethereal Plane like the last time. Just the heavenly glow of golden sunset light pouring in through the opened doorway, framing the unearthly beauty of an angel coming to take me into Eternity.

The Bible says something poetic about being "gathered unto the bosom of Abraham" but there was nothing patriarchal about the bosom that stressed her orange wetsuit. The neoprene top was unzipped and gaped wide. Multiple strands of pearls, puka shells, and antique gold draped from her neck and provided a modicum of modesty. She glided toward me until she was close enough for me to count the copper flecks in her sea-green eyes. We both stared, studying each other like two completely alien species meeting for the first time. She leaned closer, her perfect lips the color of coral parted and—

"Liban!" bellowed Fand's voice from the aft passage-way, "Get away from the prisoners!"

My angel gently turned to face my once and current warden. Which left me to figure out that I was still alive and still chained to a chair on my houseboat.

"He's too dangerous!" the platinum-blonde-haired fairy was saying. "So don't be fooling around with him!"

"Well, of course he's dangerous," the wetsuited dream answered softly, "but you're only making him more so."

"Hard to believe they're actually sisters," Zotz murmured to my left.

At first glance, maybe not. Both women would be considered great beauties, possessing that exotic, other-worldly appearance that marks the Fey Folk as a separate race from humankind. Tilted eyes, flawless skin over sculpted cheekbones and fired with an inner glow like a backlit rose petal. Liban shared familial traits with my captor but there were striking differences, as well.

Her hair was longer, a veritable waterfall tumbling past her shoulders in marked contrast to Fand's corona of white. And it was dark, giving the impression of a deep, chocolate brown on the first glance. A longer, more careful look revealed deep bands of forest green—like rich striates of moss thriving in brown loam. Or chocolate mint. The luminosity of her skin was less tincture of rose, like Fand, and more phosphorescent, like moonlight on the water. In contrast, her smile had more warmth than the sunrise. Bad enough she looked the way she did. Being a Sidhe *and* probably faerie royalty, she automatically gave off a mortal-befuddling glamour without conscious effort. I had to bite the inside of my mouth to stay focused. And if she was, as Ancho claimed, an actual goddess . . .

"Maybe they were separated at birth," I whispered back.

"And Fand raised by wolves."

"Dire wolves," I agreed.

"Maybe she was adopted," the Bat-demon mused.

"They might be half sisters," I theorized. "Or foster sisters . . . " And suddenly noticed that we were the only ones talking.

Fand and Liban were looking at us.

We looked back.

After a moment Fand turned to her sister and said: "Do you see how he disrespects me? Not just one of the immortal Sidhe, but a queen!"

"Hey, sweetheart," I shot back, "I'm not breaking into *your* throne room, hogtieing *your* pet demon, threatening *your* kid, and tying *you* to a chair, so let's be a little more judicious about *who's* doing the disrespecting, here."

"Wait a minute," Zotz said. "Did you just refer to me as your 'pet' demon?"

"He's got a point, Sis," Liban was saying. "You really need to reevaluate what you're trying to accomplish, here."

"I mean," the demon continued, "I may have implied a master/pupil dynamic on rare occasion . . . "

"I know what I'm doing!" Fand snapped.

". . . but to characterize our relationship in such derogatory and demeaning—"

"Like you knew what you were doing with Manannan?" Liban asked. "Or the Fomorians? Or how about the big himbo up topside?"

"For heaven's sakes," I said to Zotz, "I was making a point to Sidhe Who Must Be Obeyed. So chill. Or I'll swat you with a rolled-up newspaper."

"This is different," Fand argued. "He is immune to the power of the Sidhe. He can only be restrained physically. And then only with great difficulty."

Liban's attention swung back to me. "R-e-a-l-l-y . . . " There was an all-too-familiar look in her eyes.

"Ohhh no!" Fand grabbed her sister by the arm and dragged her out of the salon and, presumably, topside.

Zotz and I were left to our own chair-bound recognizance.

"So," I said after a meaningful pause, "I'm guessing the reason you're still sitting there is they've either done something to you or to the chains so you can't escape."

"How would I know?" he sniffed. "I'm just a 'pet' demon."

"Great Solomon's barking seals, man! If I had a pet demon, I'd train him better than to be taken captive by a bunch of elves!"

"Not so much a bunch as one with an overgrown gofer."

"Not helping your case, here."

"You're a fine one to talk, Mound Man."

"That was different. I didn't see them coming. *You* had a complete description—"

"Not complete," he argued. "You neglected to tell us how hot the elf playing doctor was! No wonder it took you three weeks to escape—even with Special Forces training."

I blinked. "Excuse me?"

"You were what? Navy SEAL? Army Ranger? Air Force Commando? Marine Force Recon? Green Beret?"

"Army National Guard," I snapped.

He stared at me. "Oh, right. They said your military records were sealed." He nodded knowingly. "Top secret. Black Ops. Keeping it on the QT."

. I shook my head. "No. Really. I was Army National Guard. Not R.A. Not Special Forces. Up until I developed Swiss Army fingers my hands were not considered deadly weapons."

"But your sealed records. I heard—"

"You heard wrong. I was a communications expert. My platoon was out on training maneuvers. A Special Forces group was nearby and down a radio operator. I got loaned out." I closed my eyes and fought to not remember. "Things got seriously fucked up. Everyone who was involved got their records sealed. That's the closest you can put me to the word 'seal.' "

"Oh," he said, after a moment.

I ground my teeth. "The point is, *I* escaped. How about these chairs? If you're limited to human form and strength, and the chains are out of the question for either of us—then maybe the furniture is the weak point . . . "

Now he shook his head. "Tried that second. And third. And fifth. They did something to make the chairs equally unbreakable. How about popping out some fingertip hacksaws like you did before?"

I thought about it. The problem was my hands and fingers weren't in a position to do anything worthwhile if I could. Still, I tried.

In other words, I thought about my fingertips sprouting serrated, metal-cutting blades. Tried meditative visual imaging.

Nothing happened.

Big surprise: so far all of these weird manifestations had been unconscious responses to life-threatening situations. I had yet to exert any conscious control over any nanocybernetic manifestation. And this attempt would be a useless exercise anyway. Even if I could produce some kind of cyber hacksaw *and* position my hands where I could start sawing on chain links, it could take hours to cut through a single link. What I really needed was a key to the padlock . . .

"You're bleeding."

I refocused on Zotz. "What? Where?"

"Looks like from under your fingernails. Somebody do the bamboo splinters job on you?"

I shrugged. Or tried anyway: chains clinked. Fand seemed determined to break me of this particular habit. "How would I know? I've been 'out.' "

"Maybe those pop-out claws are malfunctioning. Maybe all sorts of sharp, spiky things are gonna start poking out of your skin and you'll bleed to death."

I turned my head this way and that, trying to see. "Well, aren't you just a little ray of sunshine."

"Sorry. I guess you'd much rather have a *pet* demon."

"Focus, Zotz. We've got to work together if we're going to figure a way out of this. Too many lives are at stake."

And I told him about all that had happened since I'd hitched a ride in Volpea's head.

"So—the big voodoo lady? Did she survive the blast?" he asked.

"I don't know. I don't know if she was successful in dispersing the storm. If Laveau and her—" I almost said "pet monk" but caught myself in time. "—Rasputin are still alive and functional, they're going to try something again. So, either way, I've got to get back down there and stop them! And the Pointy Sisters are going to have to get out of my way or I won't be the only one bleeding!"

There was a *snickt* sound.

"What was that?"

Zotz craned his neck around and checked my back. "You bled on the padlock and it popped open."

"What?"

"Yeah. And now it looks like you're bleeding backwards."

"Excuse me?"

"And sideways."

I squirmed in the chair to get some slack and felt the links shift a bit. Then heard the *thunk* of a padlock hitting the carpet. The chains slipped down and loosened a bit. Slipping free was relatively easy—it only took me another five minutes.

By the time I was out of the chair and retrieving the keys that Zotz had seen Setanta stow in a galley drawer, the chains, chair, and even my fingers were devoid of any blood residue or evidence that I had bled in the first place.

"You're sure what you saw?" I asked as I set him free.

"Didn't imagine your padlock poppin' off, did I?" He got up, stretched, and began to coil one end of his chain around a bunched fist. Swear to God, he was humming "Unchained Melody" under his breath.

I laid a hand on his shoulder. "We don't have time for that. They took you down once, they could do it again. Our best bet is to grab Jamal and get off the boat, jump in the car, and drop him off at Olive's on our way to New Orleans. Think we can do that without the Twister Sisters noticing before we're gone?"

Zotz shook his head. "Jamal's gone. He went for a swim shortly after elfquest arrived."

"What?"

"They weren't paying him no mind, him being all catatonic and all, and he just gets up and walks out the door and over the side before they could grab him."

"And?"

"And nothing. He didn't come back out."

"No one went after him?"

"I wasn't allowed the option. I think Fand's afraid of the water—which is a shame because I bet she'd look bitchin' in a bikini . . . "

I waved my hand in his face. "Again, focus. What about the Mullet?"

Zotz shrugged. "She didn't tell him to. He doesn't do anything 'cept what the faerie queen tells him."

I pinched the bridge of my nose and closed my eyes. "Olive is going to go nuclear!"

"Just as long as she goes nuclear on the bad guys," the demon muttered as he headed for the portside exit. "The end of the world is just around the corner and I'm tired of getting whaled on by a bunch of women. What are you doing?"

I paused with my hand on the refrigerator door. "Grabbing some snacks for the road. I'm starving."

Zotz shook his head. "Big'n'beefy tossed all of your blood out. I don't think there's a packet left on board."

My heart sank. "What? Why?"

He shrugged. "Probably thought he was messin' with your mojo. He kept talking about how your eyes turned to blood down in the mound when you escaped."

Great. Add "cross the river and get supplies from the blood bank before I turn into a monster" to the list of things to accomplish while dodging werewolves and elves and tentacled extraterrestrials on my way back down to the Crescent City. Seriously, do regular vampires deal with any kind of crap like this?

We managed to get topside without being noticed. Above us, on the top deck, we could hear the muttering of voices and catch an occasional word or phrase. Something about "surveillance" and "presumed threats" and "shifting alliances." As the sun was now on the horizon and we were heading toward it, we had the double advantage of glare and twilight. Still, if they looked over the edge and down, we would be visible right away. We eased over the side and half-swam, half-waded along the shoreline another hundred yards before coming ashore.

Now what?

Climb the stairs up the face of the bluff to the ruins of my old house, cut through the south cemetery and follow the slope back down to a rutted, dirt road that would bring us back around to the parking area where we would—hopefully, still unobserved—slip behind the wheel of my car and get the hell out of Dodge. Or, more accurately in this instance, get the Dodge out of Hell. I patted my waterlogged jeans. For once the omens were good: my car keys were still in my pocket.

The stairs to the top of the bluff were nothing compared to all fifty-one floors of One Shell Square but I was using my own legs this time and shocked to find out that I was a little out of shape. I tried excusing myself on the basis that my body had been on the shelf for an extended period of time but the memory of the mountainous Mama Samm chugging up a skyscraper's worth of steps humbled me.

No wonder I was depressed: every time I turned around my life exhibited new nuances of suckiness.

By the time we reached the top I was huffing and puffing but doubted any little pigs would have cause to worry. I got as far as halfway across the waist-high stone wall bordering the graveyard when I decided to sit for a minute and enjoy the show. It was dusk now and the gathering darkness made the little pinpoints of light dancing across my field of vision all the brighter by contrast.

So what the hell had those little nanobuggers been up to while I was away?

It actually took closer to two minutes for the flickering spots to complete their choreography, take their bows, and one by one exit the proscenium of my vision, but I finally felt like I could go forward without blundering like a rubber-legged blind man.

That's when the ground split open and the first corpse appeared.

He was a desiccated-looking fellow with major chunks of flesh gone missing, peekaboo bone showing in the unnatural hollows of what remained.

"Cséjthe . . . " he said, doing surprisingly well for a guy whose soft palate had either gone hard or was pretty much gone.

"Jerome . . . " I nodded back.

I think he was squinting at Zotz and attempting to raise an eyebrow at me—it's hard to tell when their eye sockets and regions round about are missing most of the major components. "The End Times are upon us and you traffic with demons?" the revenant asked archly. Jerome was of a Pentecostal persuasion and had earned the nickname "Preacher" among the other animated dead in the cemetery. He'd never really approved of any of the company I'd kept so Camazotz was going over like a big ole lead balloon.

Zotz drew himself up, finally transforming himself out of his diminutive human avatar and bulked out in big bad, semi-bat form. "Not just any demon," he growled menacingly at the zombie, "but his personal *pet* demon!"

I rolled my eyes. "Give it a res—"

"And," Zotz continued theatrically, "he consorts with . . . *lesbians!*"

Preacher gasped.

I sighed. "Look, boys, I'd love to stay for the Punch and Rudy show but God called and said He'd like to keep the Book of Revelations on schedule. So," I slid down off of the wall, "if you don't mind—"

A rotting hand came up in my face. "Ezekiel twenty-two: twenty-seven," its owner hissed.

I stopped. I didn't want to "talk to the hand" but it beat taking another step and winding up with a squidgy finger up my nose. "What?"

"Her princes in the midst thereof are like wolves ravening to the prey," he hissed, "to shed blood, and to destroy souls, to get dishonest gain!"

Zotz turned to me after a couple of beats. "What's *that* mean?"

The rotting reverend cast a meaningful look over his skeletal shoulder, gazing at the far perimeter of the burial grounds.

"It means," I said, as he turned and we started weaving between the tombstones toward the south wall, "he's trying to warn us about something."

"Yeah? Well, how come he didn't just do that in plain English?"

"He sort of has this thing for Biblespeak. Don't you, Jerome?"

"Her princes within her are roaring lions; her judges are evening wolves," Jerome muttered. "They gnaw not the bones till the morrow. Zephaniah three: two through four."

"There. You see?" I said brightly, like it all made sense now. Trouble was, it did make sense—if ole Jere was alluding to what I thought was just one of several loose ends.

"I don't see nothin'," Zotz groused as we reached the far end of the graveyard.

As I leaned over the wall and gazed down the curving slopes where the bluff gave way to a more reasoned approach to the river, Preacher switched from Old to New Testament mode. "Behold," he said, sweeping his decaying arm out along the trajectory of the rutted dirt road below to the grassy flat where a half dozen cars were parked. "I send you forth as sheep in the midst of wolves . . . "

"Got yourself a real Jesus complex there, doncha, hamburger boy," Zotz growled.

". . . be ye therefore wise as serpents, and harmless as doves . . . "

"Filter the religious connotations," I told the demon, "focus on the zoological." I pointed down toward the area around the vehicles.

". . . but beware of men . . . for they will deliver you up to the councils," Preacher finished. "Matthew ten: sixteen and seventeen."

A dozen or more dark forms were moving about down below, some walking upright, some loping about on all fours. I shifted my night vision over into the infrared spectrum. Nearly two dozen forms became evident, even through the cover of the trees and bushes near the river. They blazed white and yellow like lycanthropes, not orange and red like humans or natural wolves.

"Werewolves," I muttered.

"There," Camazotz grunted, "there . . . wolves!"

I punched his ham-sized bicep. "Don't. Even. Start."

"So now what?"

I tried to think. "Too many to take. We'll have to go another way."

Zotz nodded. "The odds are better back at the boat. Three instead of thirty. Plus a little payback is always nice . . . "

"What would Mama Samm say about your thirst for vengeance?"

"She'd say stomp them elves and come save my ass!"

"She would not! Besides, we could just grab a couple of life jackets off of the stern and paddle across the river to the far—"

"Paddle? As in *dog*-paddle?"

"You cannot swim across the river," Jerome insisted.

"We wouldn't be swimming so much as floating," I pointed out.

"Leviathan waits for you beneath its dark, cold depths." The corpse spread his arms like Jimmy Swaggart. "The dead go to him and do not return."

"Sounds like my old gig," Zotz mused.

I thought about the froggy folk we'd tangled with before. And my disjointed visions of an alien city beneath the ocean where something monstrous slept and dreamt monstrous dreams. Something that was starting to wake up.

"Okay," I said. "We retake the boat. But we aren't doing this alone." I turned to Jerome. "I need volunteers. Zotz and I are heading back the way we came. Tell anyone who's willing to meet us next to the dock where the shadow from the boat blocks the moonlight."

"No one will come."

"What? Why?" It wasn't like I was asking anything dangerous: they'd tackled vampires and worse who'd tried to get to my former residence. Besides, they were already dead, had nothing else to do, and couldn't be killed any deader. Maybe they got miffed that movie nights were canceled when my house burned down and I moved offshore.

"You are not listening," Jerome answered. "I said the dead go unto Leviathan and do not return." His arms swept the expanse of the old graveyard. "All who could leave have gone down to the waters and have joined with his unholy minions. I . . . I alone . . . remain . . ."

Great. Call him Ishmael and what remained of the remains was not going to be of any help. I turned to Zotz. "We'd better get back before we're missed."

"Beware the spawn of Dagon!" Jerome called as we picked our way back down the steps fronting the bluff.

"How about beware the ears of nearby werewolves?" Zotz muttered as we neared the bottom. "I got me a feeling that Bible-boy up there wasn't real popular back when the graveyards were more populous."

"True enough," I admitted as I checked down the shoreline for welcoming committees or signs of activity aboard the *New Moon*. "But prophets are rarely accepted in their own countries."

"Oh man! Don't tell me you take that guy seriously? I mean it's pretty obvious that his church choir's missing a few hymnals!"

I turned around on the bottom step, forcing Zotz to stumble to a stop two steps behind me. "Two years ago I didn't believe in much of anything," I said quietly. "Since then I've been treated to a whole smorgasbord of what's possible. Forget vampires. Forget werewolves. Forget elves or faeries or whatever else is cataloged in the Grimm lexicon of Things that go Bippidy-Boppidy-Boo in the Night! I've met an honest-to-God angel. And, right now, I'm having a conversation with a demon. So, you'll understand why I'm not completely dismissive of a resurrected dead man who quotes scripture when the rest of the world seems to be going to hell!"

I looked up.

"But right now I think we'd better get back on the boat," I said, "before the Wild Hunt passes by . . . "

Zotz followed my gaze to the top of the bluff where a row of red eyes gazed down at us. As we watched, several sets peeled off from both ends of the line, some wolves starting to pick their way down the wooden steps we had just traversed, the others heading back down the far slope to circle around and try to flank us. As we turned and ran, howls from the ridge signaled the pack members down by the cars that the chase was afoot.

Better yet, the searchlight atop the *New Moon* flickered on and swung round to illuminate us in its bright-as-day beam. Not only was our night vision destroyed but we were precision targeted for every other predator within a mile of our location.

"Can it get any worse?" I muttered.

There was a thumping sound and the spotlight swung away from us to the base of the bluff where the remaining werewolves were leaping and landing in an attempt to cut us off before we could reach the dock.

"Just had to ask, didn't ya?" Zotz quipped as the first beast limped toward us, reknitting a broken leg in the process.

The drop was too great for any of the creatures to land unscathed. The mud that had cushioned my impact but a couple of days earlier had dried to the consistency of concrete. Still, it wasn't a big enough fall so that a lycanthrope couldn't heal or regenerate in a matter of minutes. Zotz took advantage of the wolf's limited mobility to maneuver around and grab its tail. Jerking it up off the ground, he swung it over his head for a full revolution, releasing it on a trajectory that took it out into the river.

Another light came on.

It was under the water and peered toward the submerged banks like the great phosphorescent eye of the Biblical Leviathan.

The enemy below. The enemy above. What next?

"Yo, Cséjthe, might want to be watching your six," Zotz hollered. He had to, to be heard: the *New Moon*'s engines had started up. Behind me I found two more wolves struggling to flank me even while they were regenerating from a host of injuries from their tumble down the cliff. Our slight advantage was dwindling in the face of growing numbers and quick regenerative powers. And reinforcements would be arriving in a few moments.

I tried willing my hands to turn into sharp, multibladed weapons.

Nothing happened. Other than a few more wolves getting a little closer and looking a bit stronger and more capable.

I banged my shoulder up against the bat-demon. "I need some blood!"

"Yeah? Well, bite me."

"Uh . . . no," I said. "I need some of *my* blood! I need your *claws*!" I held my arm out. "Cut me!"

He glanced down at my right wrist and forearm, offered for a little slicing and dicing. "How much?" he asked. "How deep?"

"Not committing suicide. And I don't want to pass out from blood loss . . . " My two wolves were joined by a third and a fourth and had closed the distance to ten feet. "But I need to bleed pretty good in the next twenty seconds or you're in deep doo-doo."

Doo-doo? There was that weird fight-or-flight vocabulary fillip, again.

"I'm in deep—trouble? What about you?" He took my arm and ran his pointy black talons from the back of my hand to my elbow. It tickled. "They get to draw first blood without even laying a paw on you?"

I started to repeat my request when parallel lines appeared in my flesh and began to ooze blood like four leaky fountain pens. Two wolves leapt forward as they saw (and probably smelled) the blood that started to sheet down my arm. I cocked my arm back and then swung it so that my blood flew in a spattering arc before me. It striped across the muzzles of the two wolves closest to me and across the side of another trying to get around Zotz. All three tumbled to the ground and began to thrash about, yipping and whining and snapping at empty air. The engine noises masked the hissing sounds of dissolving tissues but steamy, noxious vapors marked the acidic effects of my silver-laced blood on lycanthropic flesh and fur.

I swept my arm around again and droplets of blood machine-gunned out like a hail of black bullets in the moonlight, fanning across the circle of wolves who pressed in behind their fallen comrades. A dozen went down or staggered back, squealing and yelping and twisting about as the burning solvent from my veins burned through their hides and began to liquefy any tissue, soft or hard, that it encountered underneath.

"Yeah," I murmured as the rest of the pack began to back up, "who's the bigger monster, now?"

"Cséjthe," Zotz called, "they're leaving."

"No they're not. They're just regrouping."

"I mean the boat," he said, tugging on my uninjured arm. "They're casting off!"

The wolf closest to me looked up from its private misery and growled. I raised my right arm threateningly . . . and noticed that the four deep lacerations in my flesh had already closed! *Damned nanites!*

"All aboard," I said as I turned and ran for the dock.

Zotz was right behind me. The wolves were behind him, though not as close and limping more than running. The mooring lines had been pulled and hurriedly cast aside and Setanta was wrestling with the gangplank as we pounded onto the dock. The *New Moon* was already six feet away from the pier and moving.

"I don't! Know if! I can! Make it!" I grunted. As running broad jumps go, the odds were, at best, fifty-fifty. In the dark, on a wet planked surface, and a half ton of bat-demon turning the whole dock into a wooden trampoline with every bounding step. I could hardly keep from falling on my face, never mind getting up the velocity and balance to clear the railing on my departing houseboat.

"Don't stop!" Zotz demanded, practically breathing down my neck.

Then he grabbed me. One hand on my collar, the other on the back of my belt: I was lifted off my feet and flung back behind him. Thrown to the wolves! Except he didn't let go: I was swung forward again before I was released, to go hurtling over the last ten feet of dock and another ten of black water. I smashed into Setanta who had just set the gangplank out of the way, staggering him back against the salon door with me in a mad embrace.

He stared at me as if unable to fathom what he was holding in his arms. "What . . . ?"

"Hey, Gargantua," I croaked, "haven't you ever heard of 'don't ask, don't tell'?"

His response was lost in Camazotz Chamalcan's arrival—who slammed into the both of us, breaking down the door and tumbling us across the salon and halfway through the window on the far side of the cabin. Fortunately it was closed. That way the glass could slow us down before we went overboard on the other side. Whoever was walking along the starboard gangway out-side wasn't so lucky: she went ass over teakettle and into the river. Good news for us: we had reduced the enemy compliment by a full third.

The *New Moon* was angling out away from the shore, presumably to discourage any furry boarders. But were we any safer in deep water? The mysterious beam of light beneath the waves swept around to illuminate the houseboat, reminding us that we had bigger fish to fry than a mere platoon of lycanthropes.

Zotz hauled the Mullet off of me and I began the process of extricating myself from the shattered window. Some of the shards had gone in pretty deep but there was surprisingly little blood. And the wounds closed almost immediately as I pulled the glass out. But it wasn't pain-less. Whatever the nanites were doing to regenerate the damaged tissue, the wounds and the healing process still hurt like a sonuvabitch!

Which was okay, in some twisted fashion: at least I was feeling something beyond the numbed and weary state I generally found myself in these days.

"Let me go!" the Mullet was bellowing. He couldn't do much else. When a Mesoamerican bat-demon has you in a full nelson, you ain't going anywhere—even if you are big enough to make Dolph Lundgren look like Danny DeVito.

"Please!" he finally pleaded, trying to strain a little less against the furry vise that held him fast.

Now my mother taught me that, in certain times and at certain places, "please" *is* a magic word. But not this time and not this place. Zotz shifted his grip and put Setanta into a sleeper hold.

As fate would have it, however, just before his air was cut off, Setanta managed to say the *right* magic words for this time and place.

Chapter Eleven

"SHE CAN'T SWIM!" he gasped before slumping in the demon's furry grasp.

We turned back and looked. The underwater ghost light was pointed right where one of the elves had gone over the side.

A frantic hand broke the surface of the water for a moment and then slipped back beneath the waves.

It was perfect: one less foe to fight. One less threat to my unborn son. A psychological, as well as numerical, blow to our pointy-eared enemies. So there's only one explanation as to what happened next.

I just didn't care.

Looking back later I had to reconcile my response to the logical default any other sane and sensible man would have taken.

It wasn't heroic.

I mean, I'm not that kind of guy. Not any more and maybe I never was. Once upon a time I was a decent guy, a nice guy, with a wife and a daughter and a life in the suburbs. I had already learned a number of lessons about life being unfair and how shit happens and such. It took an encounter with Vlad Drakul Bassarab V and half of the necrophagic virus that transforms the living into the undead to learn that death is just as unfair as life. And that if you think shit just happens while you're breathing then you don't know shit at all.

The problem with heroes is they approach problems as if they are puzzles that can be solved, tasks that can be completed, or foes that can be vanquished. I knew better, now. Dr. Henry Kissinger once said: "All of the world's great problems are not problems, at all. They are dilemmas, and dilemmas cannot be solved. They can only be survived."

So, not into heroics these days, and not seeing a lot of potential in the survival column, either. Let's just chalk up my impulsive "rescue" attempt as "depressed, angry guy with a growing death wish sees another opportunity to play chicken with Mr. Death." Gives the cylinder on God's revolver another roulette spin and leaps into the black waters. Don't give me that look—the one that murmurs "rationalization." Metaphysically it's more selfish than selfless, calculated even. Assuming there are such things as the Pearly Gates, they can't turn me away. *What? Suicide? C'mon, Pete, let's watch the replay*

*again: I jumped in to perform a good deed. How was I
to know the giant sea monster with the glowy eye was
going to chew me into Purina Shark Chum and feed me
to her litter of fish fiends? Not my fault I ruined God's
little game of* Let's Torment Cséjthe Some More . . .

Hitting the water was like flopping into a cold concrete
wall: it knocked what little breath I had left out of me.
Fortunately, the nanobots were already at work reconstructing the artificial gill at the back of my throat. The
only reason I swallowed so much water this time was I
continued to cuss the whole way in.

I immediately started sinking like a rock. Vampires
will do anything to avoid crossing running water for this
very reason and, while I was still technically alive, I was
no longer humanly buoyant. My last escape from the
watery Ouachita had been a fluke. No pun intended.

Then the cramping started.

Bad enough to drown but to go out with a bad case
of gas?

My descent slowed as odd sensations began to spread
throughout my body. The cramping eased into an
uncomfortable bloating sensation.

Oh.

My.

God.

The 'bots were effecting further biological modifications, creating some kind of half-assed sub-marine buoyancy system! Worrisome enough, but what if they elected
to excise body parts when it was time to "drop ballast"?

I had no further opportunity to dwell on the unpleasant side effects of cybernetic modifications as company
was arriving.

Fand was maybe twenty feet below me and being dragged along the river's bed by the current. The underwater beam of light caught the white corona of her hair in its icy gaze, dispelling any doubts as to her identity. Nor was there any question as to who the new arrivals were: a quartet of Black Lagoon wannabes had arrived to see if they could make things any more unpleasant than they already were.

I reached toward them and kicked down. And farted. I shot downward like a torpedo on target. Not "jet-propelled," you understand; just less buoyant.

So quit smirking.

There were other forms at the periphery of the light. Moving. Humanoid. *How many of these things were there?* I felt a prickling sensation erupt all over my body and considered the possibility that I might not make it back to the boat even if I elected to turn back now.

But: Screw 'em, I decided.

According to Mama Samm, these were bad guys on a cosmic scale (heh, again no pun intended). These were the Deep Dudes who were supposed to have a hand in waking up Octogod, Lord of Slumber and Sodomizer of Worlds. I had glimpsed their kind scavenging a storm-battered New Orleans in my eye-blink vision, utilizing human skulls and viscera as bricks and mortar for the New Order. More than self-defense, more than rescuing Fand, I owed these guys a round of deaths on higher principles. If I had just a few minutes left before the nanites rehabbed my insides into tuna casserole, I was going to spend them violating the parish fish-and-game codes in unusual and spectacular ways.

I rammed into the first amphibioid and pulled Fand's arm from its grasp. Other silhouettes closed in, blocking segments of the spotlight and the closest fish folk swarmed me.

I lost my grip on her arm. Then I lost my bearings.

It was a different fight this time. I wasn't struggling for air, feeling the erosion of thought and coordination as my lungs caught fire. I thrust my hands, arms, even legs, understanding that they were deadly weapons if I so willed it. The biggest problem was finding Fand again and getting her to the surface before she drowned. And not mistaking the elf for a finny foe in the meantime. I was stabbing and slashing whatever was within reach and reaching back. In moments I was enveloped in a confused tangle of mutant bodies and a cloud of blackish blood. And the fluids from eviscerated bodies were negating any advantage the ghost light had offered just moments before.

These things had to be cold-blooded so I tried shifting my vision over into the infrared spectrum, figuring to pick Fand out of the underwater lineup. I had never tried doing this underwater and either it wasn't working or Fand was as cold-blooded biologically as her personality suggested.

Or already out of range as the temperature of the water was probably acting like a diffusion medium.

Either way, she would be drowning while I was playing patty-cake with the Cousteau Twins, here. At least it felt like I was down to two . . .

Make that one.

And as I jerked him close enough to deliver the *coup de grâce*, a rising red tide behind my eyeballs rolled like a tsunami throughout my body. I felt like I hadn't eaten in days, maybe weeks! And, except for a cup of O-Neg the other night, I probably hadn't. And, since waking back up in my own carcass, I had been burning through my meager reserves like a refinery fire. I wasn't just hungry, I was starved!

The fact that the gill in my throat was filtering oxygen out of a fluid medium that was more blood soup than river water was only making it worse. If aquaman, here, had been any more human—and I had fangs—I would have gone for snackage right then and there.

And then I felt the prickling disturbances in my gums.

The nanites were reprogramming to adapt to my perceived survival needs. I was growing fangs! Silver-laced ferrocarbon fangs, as like!

Not that I was about to use them, of course. No way I was going to bite one of these fish people on their slimy necks and suck—

My opponent shoved his hand in my face, digging his claws into my temples and bending my head back until I felt like the headliner at a contortionists' convention. Even as I grabbed at his unyielding arm, instinct took over and I bit the heel of his palm as it pushed between my jaws.

Another explosion of blackish blood and the gill structure somehow revalved to allow me to swallow. Strange, amphibious fluids trickled down my throat to refuel the arcane biological mechanisms that kept me alive and functional. As fuels go, it was a very odd octane.

As food goes . . . it tasted like sushi. *Bad* sushi.

Sea Haunt removed his hand quickly. Then turned and fled, running into some sort of obstacle just beyond the range of the ghost light. I let him go for the moment. There had to be others and one more or one less right now wasn't going to make the difference that eclipsed the other matters immediately at hand. A major fishing expedition, however, had just moved way up on my to-do list. For now, however, I turned to follow the current. The Hunger was still there, still strong, but momentarily bearable. Fand took priority for the moment.

Twenty, thirty, forty yards was enough to give me the bad news: if the bottom current had gotten her, she could already be a mile or more downriver. I turned and kicked back to the surface to get my bearings. More gas cramps and the overall tingling sensation turned itself inside out. As my head broke the surface I saw dozens of spiny protrusions on my hand slide back down beneath the skin.

For a few moments, at least, my prickly disposition had found a means of outward expression.

No wonder I was starving: the energy requirements for microbiological replication and construction had to be tremendous. First you had untold millions of microscopic fabrication and construction machines requiring fuel just to operate. Then there were the additional energy costs for manipulating and reproducing materials at the cellular level. Factor in my body's accelerated demands for healing and repair every time flesh or bone had to be breached for a projecting claw, spine, or blade, sundered and reknit for internal reconfigurations—you were looking at a growing energy demand that couldn't be met by a plate full of cheeseburgers or a bowl of crawfish étouffée!

Daddy's little helpers were ticking time bombs, noshing through my veins like teeny-tiny Pac-men, gobbling up every nutrient in sight. If I didn't feed them soon, they would start cannibalizing me in ways that would make piranhas look like butterflies. If my own body didn't starve to death on the cellular level, first.

A quick three-sixty of the river's surface yielded no further evidence of Fand but there were extra forms at the *New Moon*'s railing. A second look and I was treated to a zoom-in close-up view like Steve Austin's bionic eye. *Stop that! Bad nanos, bad!* The last thing I needed was to amp up their energy consumption when I was already dangerously low on my own reserves.

I turned and began a weary breast stroke for the houseboat, trying not to look again.

If it was Fand I saw being helped aboard, I didn't need to waste any more energy, much less optical reconfigurations, on another look-see. And, if it wasn't, she was as good as dead by now, and swept downriver to points unknown.

Besides, the real temptation was to look at the second figure standing next to her.

And there was no sense risking further disorientation until I was back on solid footing and could make arrangements to cross the river to the blood bank.

ᗺᗺ   ᗺᗺ   ᗺᗺ

I was too weak to climb the ladder when I finally reached the *New Moon*'s side. Zotz had to jump back in and assist me, as I would later learn he had done with Fand and her other rescuer. Once aboard, a blanket was thrown over me and I was taken into the salon.

Fand sat, huddled on the sofa, her blanket already soaking through. Stefan Pagelovitch's AWOL enforcer stood beside her, dripping and dribbling water like a broken fountain. A blanket was puddled on the floor behind her as if it had just slipped from her shoulders.

"Suki?" I whispered, weary beyond comprehension. Her head turned to track me but her eyes were dark and lifeless. Dead. "Where have you been?" I murmured.

Her mouth opened slowly, as if she were hesitant to speak. But no words came out. Just a freshet of river water, dark with silt and sediment. And then a tiny craw-fish tumbled over her lower lip and rode the waterslide down the front of her rotting blouse.

There's a reason why vampires, as a rule, won't cross running water. Or any other kind that's deeper than they are tall. The undead don't swim. Don't float. Once in and under, they don't come back out. They drown. You might think drowning is no big deal to something that's already dead. But it is. Don't ask me how or why—I've personally dodged that particular bullet and I hope to God I never find out, firsthand.

But Suki . . .

I tried to walk to her but my legs gave out from under me. Zotz swept me up before I could hit the floor and carried me back into my cabin.

🦇   🦇   🦇

I didn't "pass out."

And "swoon" is such a girly turn of phrase.

I had just hit the last of my reserves and my body went into energy-conservation mode. Which pretty much meant I could only lie there and try to tell Bats why my arms and legs no longer worked. Slurring my words like a drunken stroke victim didn't help and the demon seemed to lose interest, leaving the room while I was still explaining that I'd be perfectly happy to skip the reheating process and eat the crunchy, frozen blood packs like snow cones. Anything to hurry the process along!

I closed my eyes for a moment. Maybe if I rested a few minutes . . . ten . . . twenty . . . I could gather enough strength to get back up and . . . do what?

All Zotz had to do was get to the other side of the river, drive my other car to the blood bank, use my keys and pass code to get in and bypass the alarms, grab some blood (preferably from the excess stocks but I wouldn't nag in this particular instance), remember to reset the security tapes and alarms and relock the doors on the way out—all without being seen by local law enforcement or passersby, and avoiding run-ins with furry or faerie foes.

I really needed to get up right now!

Before Fand recovered enough to have me clapped in chains. Or worse, seeing as how chains hadn't worked the last time . . .

Besides, resting wasn't working. I was so hungry I couldn't relax enough for my muscles to recover. I lay there, feeling like a darkening bruise and wondering if *not* passing out had been such a good plan after all.

A warm hand touched my cooling forehead.

Opening my eyes seemed to use even more of my dwindling reserves. It was worth it, though: Fand's sylphic sister was sitting on the edge of my bed looking down at me with wide, luminous eyes.

"Thou ailest," she said. Her lips moved in all sorts of interesting ways when she talked and her voice almost sounded . . . regretful.

"I'm tired," I muttered. "Escaping from being chained to a chair is a lot of hard work."

"And yet you returned and repaid my sister's treachery by saving her life."

It didn't seem prudent to point out that my return was prompted by a pack of weres. Or that said return was what knocked Fand overboard in the first place. Or that, in spite of all my thrashing around in the water, someone else had actually pulled her sister out of the river.

Plus I didn't have the strength for a long, drawn-out conversation.

But there were questions that had to be asked.

"What does your sister want with my son?" I demanded. At least it was supposed to be a demand. In my condition it didn't sound very "demandy."

"It's—it's complicated," the so-called goddess of health and beauty stuttered before turning her face aside.

"I think I'm owed something, here," I grumbled. "How about we start with an explanation?"

"You will not accept it."

I stared at her. "So what? Not much on the accepting with the non-explanations. Without knowing what this is about, I tend to default to the worst-case-scenario mind set. Which means any explanation—even one I don't like—is bound to be better than my not-so-optimistic assessment of your motivations." Whew. Did that even make sense? I was starting to grow delirious.

Liban turned her face back to mine and took my hands in hers. "Very well." She took a deep breath—which made my head swim in all sorts of interesting ways and I think I lost a moment of linear time.

"Your demon familiar says that you must have blood ere you will die," Liban said, looking at me as if I had just changed color. I got the impression I had missed a sentence or two. "Is this true?"

Thanks a lot, Zotz. Does Jimmy Olsen phone up Lex Luthor and discuss kryptonite?

"Just a little hungry, that's all," I said. "A snack would be nice. I'm a little hypoglycemic . . . "

"Must you have blood? Will other food do?"

I sighed. It was a squeamish subject even for me—and I sure as hell didn't like discussing my dietary requirements with strangers. "Look if there's any of my stuff left on board—"

"Setanta threw them all out," she interrupted. "He says you are a monster and he has seen your eyes fill with blood. He feared it would make you too powerful and monstrous to contain."

"Yeah? Well, tell Billy-Ray it's those Happy Hemoglobin Meals that keep me from turning *into* a monster. Without them I have to go all snack-attack on someone's neck!"

She stared at me. "I see. I presume that would be the case if you actually had the strength to sit up at all."

Great. Can't fight, can't run, can't even bluff. I was so screwed. "Just let my demon familiar go fetch me some more, okay? That way I won't turn into a monster and everyone will be a lot happier . . . " "Happier" is actually a very difficult word to pronounce: try saying it the next time you go to the dentist and get a face full of Novocaine.

She started to get up. "I'll see if I can find anything else in the galley."

I tried to hold onto both of her hands and was only half successful. "Wait. I want that explanation, first."

"But—"

"I know you want to change the subject. Change it *after* you answer the question!"

She settled back down on my bunk and took my free hand back in hers. "Very well. There is a Telling. Actually two. Both concern the End of the World as we know it and both, we believe, involve your son and a blood sacrifice . . ."

Don't ask me questions about elven prophecy—where they get it, how it's handed down, and particularly how it's interpreted. Elves aren't particularly direct in their approach to the mundane so expecting clarity on the subject of their theosophical underpinnings is largely hopeless for us humans-come-lately.

Especially a skeptic who was holding on to the fringes of consciousness with non-metallic and very dull fingernails. For a change.

Apparently one of their End-of-the-World visions involved what would happen if an elven queen and a human had the bad taste to breed.

I know, I know; Romance literature is populated with references to the "halfelven" and there's cross-species dalliances a-plenty if one knows where to look (and how to read between the florid lines). These affairs generally led to problems, though. If not for the original, hormonally engaged and their git, then somewhere down the line when the consequences tended to hit the fan with all that pent-up karma. The classics are all pretty clear on that particular theme and not-so-many variations.

And if elven royalty were involved it was like swapping out gunpowder for uranium 235 and plutonium. Something in Fand's bloodline was especially volatile in terms of human genetics and any hybrid offspring were going to make Oedipus Rex look like The Nativity by comparison— picture *The Omen* meets Middle Earth.

Forget rings of power or immortal flowering trees or the next recipe for the perfect Keebler cookie; the biggest quest before The People's Court—Seelie or Unseelie—involved the management of Fand's social life. No wonder she was so testy: everyone had been conspiring to keep her an old maid for at least a thousand years.

"You see," Liban explained, "Setanta is actually—"

"Yeah, I know. Cuchulainn," I said. "The Hound of Ulster. Which explains that whole Brock Samson vibe he's got going on. Somehow Fand got wind of the plot and was able to circumvent it. Or plots, as he's still alive. And long after he should've been dust. But they're still together, as well. Someone should tell Fand's ex he should never wash a magic cloak. It rinses those amnesia spells right out. Dry clean only."

Liban shook her head. "Humans . . . You see nothing unscientific about the invisibility of the hummingbird's wings in flight. The visible light spectrum is but a small portion of what other creatures see and sense. A high-frequency sound is not nonexistent merely because it ranges beyond your human limitations. Telepathy, clairvoyance, telekinesis, clairaudience—all well within acceptable theories of science when you reach the quantum levels. Your many religions teach you to pray to that which you cannot see nor touch, asking it to set aside the laws of physics and medicine and produce anomalies called miracles. Cosmology posits a multidimensional universe, even other universes: a multiverse with an infinite number of worlds, realities, histories occupying the same space." She sighed. "Yet you cannot conceive of creatures who are like and yet unlike yourselves. Whose vibrations are set to a separate frequency and thus do not occupy the same spaces in quite the same ways as you. Who see and sense the spectrum of energies a bit differently. You misname our ability to channel levels and frequencies of *q'u'orernen,* calling it 'magic,' as if it were something fanciful and without boundaries or law such as the nonsense in *Aladdin* or *Harry Potter*.

"We are not impossible merely because we outlive your species. There are sequoias that are over 2,000 years old, bristlecone pines alive today that were two thousand years old before your Christ was born. Both are plants. And yet so many other plants are encoded to sprout, grow, bloom, seed and die, all within a single season. You cannot hold a single measurement of longevity to any species. Are we fantastical because we measure our lives in millennia? Or are humans because you measure yours in decades?

"You laugh and mock your own legends and myths. But most are founded on actual history and passed down in the oral manner with the resultant distortions. Your own historians are constantly redefining recent events for they understand how facts and personal accounts may be altered in the handling of its written records."

"Like the evening news," I said. "So, what are you trying to say here?"

"That, time factors and details aside, you and my sister have a great deal in common."

"What?"

Her lips twitched a smile so sad and so fleeting it was almost imaginary. "You both fell in love with someone who wasn't like yourselves. And a lot of people schemed to keep you both from the ones you love. As a result, you've both been changed, damaged even. You, of all people, should understand her dysfunctional behavior."

"Every time I've crossed paths with her I seem to get the worse of it," I replied. "Seems pretty functional to me."

"She's my sister, Cséjthe! We're both sea goddesses, yet she almost drowned scarce a quarter of an hour ago! She no longer functions in her natural element! And Cuchulainn . . . " Her eyes flickered, went from angry to sad. "His mind is so deeply scarred that he not only has no memory of *who* he once was, but *how* they once were. Oh, he bears her much devotion . . . but his much vaunted pride and arrogance are gone."

"Really? Hadn't picked up on that so much."

"You didn't know him then. The Hound of Ulster is a mere puppy now. I believe that two people must see themselves as equals if they are to be great lovers. What my sister was left with is but a shadow of love's glory, crumbs from passion's banquet, mere—"

"Yeah, yeah, okay! I get it! Love among the ruins. But there was this prophecy, I understand? Something about doom and the end of the world?"

"If they were to conceive a child."

"Yeah, well, not that I don't feel the tragedy now that they're all Bobby and Whitney—"

Liban gave me a blank look.

"All Britney and K-Fed," I amended.

Still the look.

"Liz and Dick? The point is, just because the honey-moon's over doesn't mean they don't need major birth control. I mean, they still look pretty cozy to me."

Fand's sister looked rather taken aback. "Conception is not so haphazard among our people," she said slowly. "Our wombs quicken when we *choose* to bear children. Otherwise our lovers and mates may have no issue with us."

It took a moment for that to sink in. I was still working over the various implications when she continued: "My sister has circumvented the doom of the prophecy by adopting a child one generation in every four. Her needs to motherhood are met and so she may continue with her consort, slaking her desires on both fronts, without combining them in such a way as to fulfill the fate foretold."

"So," I muttered, trying not to slur my words, "you're saying as long as she adopts some kid every couple of hundred years and raises him, she cools the fertility jones that would get her preggers with Cuch. And, as long as they don't produce their own franchise of little Fandchu-lains, the elves escape their doom?"

"And my sister," Liban clarified, clearly unhappy with my word choice, "escapes judgment with prejudice by the Councils."

I didn't have to ask what "judgment with prejudice" meant. I did have to ask: "Why *my* kid? I mean, maybe the first attempt but, now that I've put my foot down, it's time for her to move down the list and try some other adoption agencies."

Those green eyes narrowed and turned the color of stormy seas. "My sister is still outlaw for her chosen path. No elf will permit her to raise a child of their own—even those rarely orphaned. It must needs, therefore, be human. And only a very special human child will do."

"Still," I insisted stubbornly, "*not* going to happen with my kid. If she wants to play Mommy Dearest, she'd better get on with it and down the road from here!" I tried to growl that last part for emphasis and only ended up sounding like I had a touch of congestion.

"It is not only for personal reasons that your son was selected," she said, "but for a separate Telling, as well. One that involves the fate of the rest of the world—the world of men as well as our own."

"Yeah? Do tell." I leaned toward her. "*Do.*"

She stared at me for a long time, her eyes seemingly haunted. "It involves a sacrifice."

I closed my eyes. "Of course it does."

I felt her hand laid along the side of my face. "I am sorry. I am so, so sorry . . ."

"Get out," I whispered. "Tell your sister and her sexecutioner that I want you all off of my boat when I get up or I'll damn well fix that first prophecy myself!"

I didn't have the strength to open my eyes but her hand slipped away and, after a long moment, the door to my cabin opened and closed.

I was such a fool! Playing chicken with the Grim Reaper was a thoughtless and impulsive act, seeking quick and selfish closure. In doing so, I had committed ultimate folly by rescuing one of the creatures who was bent on connecting my son to some inexplicable sacrifice! And, in doing so, I had further damaged my own ability to rescue him by depleting my physical resources.

Apparently the micromachine invasion required large reserves of energy when they got all creative and constructiony. That's why each transformation resulted in my Hunger ramping up to unforeseen levels. If I didn't ante up on the fuel sources via blood-drinking with the resultant iron molecules for spare parts, they would apparently take their pound of flesh via other means.

The good news? Since they were ostensibly programmed to preserve my life, I probably wouldn't expire right away.

The bad news? Since they were ostensibly programmed to preserve my life, I probably wouldn't expire right away.

The questions were: what biological materials would they consider to be nonessential, and how painful would it be, and how long before permanent damage accrued?

Bad enough.

What was worse: the end of world-*some* kind of end of the world—was on its way and my children were weeks away from being born, just a few blocks away from what was increasingly looking like Ground Zero. And, if it turned out that Mama Samm had failed on the rooftop of One Shell Square, then we were all smack dab in the middle of a battlefield between the undead legions of a powerful madwoman and an army of cunning, preternatural beasts with one hell of a storm thrown in for good measure!

While I just lay here doing nothing!

Having just failed at selfishly taking the coward's way out.

Could I be any more pathetic *and* despicable?

They say it's always darkest before the dawn, but suddenly everything got darker. I was sucked down into a hypnogogic undertow and pulled out into the sea of dreams.

᜕ᜄ ᜕ᜄ ᜕ᜄ

Recipe for a nightmare:

Take one really big, dark gray barrel and cut openings around the middle.

Place dozens of octopi or squid inside barrel so that tentacles emerge from openings all the way around the center. Lots o' tentacles!

Crazy-glue giant yellow starfish to the top of barrel. Paste eyes at the end of each point. Add little red tubes ending in mouths between the points.

Crazy-glue second giant starfish to the bottom of same barrel. Add little red tubes between each of those points for—what? Poop chutes?

Add a half dozen or so batwings, folded up and spaced around the middle between the tentacles.

Altogether the thing was between six and eight feet tall. That was my best guess, based on its proximity to my dream self. And the book it held open before it with two of its five pseudopods. It closed the book with a snap but not before I discerned the image of a crowned elephant riding in a balloon and the title: *Le Voyage de Babar.*

Three antennae or feelers or eyestalks or something poked out in my direction.

"You cannot look upon its flesh and keep your sanity," intoned the weird Winky Dink voice.

I looked around. Everywhere else was darkness. I looked back at the alien monstrosity. "Yeah? Well, looking right now and not feeling particularly crazy about the view," I shot back. I was really getting homesick for the good ole days when a vampire was about the creepiest thing I could ever imagine.

"You cannot travel within its mind and survive," the voice continued.

"What? Bloodwalk? Inside a giant rutabaga? Forget it! I'm on a low alien-carb diet!"

"You must be transformed . . . purged . . . purified . . . so that you may face the apotheosis of fear without reverberation. You must be reprogrammed. . . ."

The monster reached toward me with writhing tentacles and I turned to flee, to fly . . .

And eventually float, drifting down to nestle into an angel's embrace.

Heaven faded out. My cabin faded in. The angel transformed into Liban.

She had an arm around me, raising me from one pillow to another.

"I'm sorry to awaken you," she said, offering a bowl of something pinkish and sweet smelling. "But your familiar seemed to think it important to feed you as soon as possible. 'Tis not your accustomed fare but it seems best to try whatever we can until more human blood can be obtained."

"Across the river," I whispered. "Send Zotz. He knows where to go. What to do."

"Setanta departed with him two hours ago. Under the circumstances, I think it best we delay not ere they return." She propped my head up and brought the bowl to my lips. "Try a draught of this to see if it will sustain thee whilst we wait."

Yeah, that was a good idea. Drink strange concoctions brewed by the people who had held me captive and wanted to birthnap my son. The smart money was on waiting for Zotz to take down the Mullet and return with the real deal from my private stock at the blood bank.

The problem was if Setanta was the Hound of Ulster, I wasn't so sure of Zotz's supremacy in a little one-on-one. Regardless, I didn't think *I* could wait that long.

Not so much that I was hungry—I'd endured the inside-out, skin-crawling, eye-itching, hair-aching, brain-churning withdrawal pains of the bloodthirst before. It's one thing to go toe-to-toe with the pain when it's your own body throwing a tantrum over not getting what it so desperately wants. This, however, was something a little different.

It was still The Hunger—capital-T, capital-H. But it wasn't just me, now. It was tens of millions of tiny machines, all ravenous, all looking around their immediate vicinity for something to eat. If I didn't throw them some kind of bone, the phrase "dining in" was going to take on a whole new dimension.

Besides, what was the flip side of the risk?

If the Sidhe Sisters were trying to get me to ingest something harmful, the nanites were programmed to neutralize threats and adapt to preserve my life. Right?

I took a sip.

It tasted *strange* . . .

· And *wonderful*!

And that was about the time I remembered the time lag the nanobots had evidenced in past adaptations. They needed a certain amount of ramp-up time as their programming sampled, analyzed, and constructed adaptive measures. Even if these things were foolproof—and there was insufficient data to assume that they were—a fast-acting poison could prove fatal before they could adapt to the threat.

But, too late now: I'd had my first taste and I couldn't stop!

I gulped at the soup in the bowl like a starving man. Not just because I was hungry and not just because Mengele's Nazi nanos were about to go all Teensy Terminator on my innards. I gulped because it was so damn good I couldn't stop myself!

Imagine the oldest and finest distillery in Tulach Mhóh converting over to produce honeydew nectarized soup instead of Tullamore Dew whiskey. At the very first taste it exploded in my mouth like meat stock boiled down to a demiglace—in terms of taste, that is—while retaining the clarity and consistency of consommé. Even cooled to tepid room temperature it thrummed across the taste buds, lively and quick! I could feel my entire body beginning to revive even before a third swallow had delivered its plasma-injected payload to my stomach. Whatever this stuff was, I could feel it doing double duty: rebooting all biological systems, kicking my cellular regeneration back up to optimum levels, and refueling all the micro gas guzzlers that were running on fumes at this point.

It should have been enough. In terms of biofuel, a little of this stuff went a long way. I was slamming on all cylinders before the bowl was half gone.

But the taste! And the way it made me feel!

I finished the bowl and then held it out to Liban, Oliver-style. "Please, sir; may I have some more?"

"More?" She had been watching me all along with a look of concern. A tincture of alarm now filtered in. "Do you require more to preserve your life?"

Then I saw the sleeve of her wetsuit had been unzipped and folded back to her elbow. There was a fresh bandage on her forearm.

Oh shit . . .

Chapter Twelve

I GOT DRESSED feeling great!

My body had never felt so alive, so healthy, so power-ful, so . . . so . . . tumescent? I looked down again and marveled: "Smilin' Bob" had nothing on me.

I got dressed feeling like crap!

Once again I'd fed off of another living creature. And this time I was spending way too much time imagining what Liban would taste like with a pair of stainless steel soda straws in her neck!

I was crossing some sort of threshold here where need-ing the blood was taking a backseat to *wanting* the blood.

And what was the deal with the tightening trousers? Maybe I could make a case for the narcotic effects of elven blood or the hormonal link to seeing the sea goddess of health and beauty as something indescribably yummy.

But that didn't explain the near trip down mammary lane with Volpea.

Or the inordinate amount of distraction that Irena had packed into such a short amount of time.

True, Lupé had pretty much told me to take a long walk off of a short pier these past eight months—but lovers have fights. Grownups disagree. You get bruised, you get bloody, but you don't throw in the towel—at least not in the fourth round of a championship fight. You go the distance. You stay on your feet until you fall on your face. And then you get back up again. Doesn't matter how many times circumstances knock you down. What matters is how many times you get back up.

And was this the antidepressants talking?

Or were the nanobots running IM downloads into my prefrontal cortex from Hallmark.com?

Ultimately, I was asking whether I was really this big of a cad? Obviously, I wasn't the human being I was two years previously. But how much can one invoke the "monster" excuse before it, too, ceases to excuse?

I shook my head: too much thinking, not enough doing. I had to get down to New Orleans and extract my people. We could sort out the emotional crap later.

My cell phone was humming on my dresser. I picked it up, disconnected it from the charger, and noticed that it was still set to vibrate. Opening it I saw that I had twenty-seven missed calls.

"Cséjthe?" The voice on the other end belonged to Dr. Mooncloud.

"Speaking."

"Thank God! I need to ask you a rather personal question."

"Personal?"

"Well, medical. Just remember that I am your doctor."

The last time someone had reminded me of the doctor/patient relationship I had been wearing a straight-jacket. "Go on . . ."

"Have you been feeling a bit horny of late?"

🦇   🦇   🦇

I asked her to explain it to me again—this time in the *Reader's Digest* condensed version.

"Your blood work is showing abnormally high levels of dehydroepiandrosterone—"

"Yeah. DHEA," I interrupted. "Previous tests have turned this up."

"But it's even higher now. Along with DHEA-sulfate. You're also showing abnormally high levels of andro-stenedione—banned by the International Olympic Committee—"

"There go my gold medals."

"—as well as androstenediol, androsterone, and DHT!"

"The bug killer?"

"Not DDT! DHT: Dihydrotestosterone. It's a metabolite of testosterone and a more potent androgen when it comes to binding with androgen receptors. Stop making fun of this."

It was hard (no pun intended) not to. "So you're calling me up to tell me that my nanites have decided to ramp up my sex drive? Great. Two questions. Why? And what can I do about it? Cold showers? Saltpeter in my mashed potatoes?"

"As to the 'why'? I think your nanites are hungry. Knowing you, you've been keeping your sustenance levels at bare minimums."

"Hey," I protested. "Not exactly skin and bones, here. I'm far from anorexic."

"I'm not talking about people food," she snapped. "I'm talking about people *as* food. Blood. The high octane fuel that your converted physiology is increasingly demanding. Now that you've got millions of micromachines working overtime, the energy demand has got to be excessive. My guess is they're amping up your adrenal and apocrine glands to enhance you as a predator—not as a sex fiend. Though there may be inevitable side effects."

"Uh huh. Back up a moment. You mentioned two different glands . . . "

"The adrenal and the apocrine."

"Not familiar with the second one."

"Apocrine? Sweat glands."

"Sweat glands?"

"Actually, body perspiration is produced by two different sets of glands. The eccrine glands which are distributed all over the body's surface, but more densely arranged on the forehead, palms, and soles of the feet; and the apocrine which are mainly concentrated in the armpits and around the genital area."

"And since you're only mentioning the apocrine glands, I must assume there's some kind of significant difference?"

"That's my boy. You actually can be quite perceptive when you're not trying to be such a smartass."

"Maybe. But take into consideration that the hive-mind programming of my nanite network extends throughout the entirety of my body, including the tissues of my gluteus maximus. So, my ass is, quite literally, smarter than anyone else's at this time."

The other end of the line went silent.

"Sorry," I said finally.

Mooncloud cleared her throat. "Yes. Well. To get back to your question, perspiration from the eccrine glands is mostly water with various salts mixed in. It's all about body temperature regulation. Sweat from the apocrine glands, however, contains fatty materials. As bacteria break these compounds down, certain odors are released. The apocrines are also known as the scent glands."

"So . . . what? In addition to being transformed into an oversexed horndog, I'm going to develop super B.O., as well?"

I could practically hear Mooncloud nodding on the other end of the connection. "Well, yes. But not in the way you might think. The samples I brought back have tested abnormally high for pheromones."

"Pheromones?"

"Sex pheromones."

"I thought we were talking about sex *hormones*."

"We were. Now we're talking about sex *pheromones*."

"So, we're not talking about—"

"—the effect on *you*, any more. We're talking about the potential effect on *others*."

"Others?"

"Potentially receptive species that come within the area of effect. Look, published research on the role of human sex pheromones on social and sexual patterns of behavior is minimal, somewhat contradictory, and largely theoretical to date. But you are no longer human-normal for comparative purposes. And the levels of hormones and pheromones that your body is secreting are well above normal and apparently climbing."

"And, again: why? Are the nanites doing this on purpose or is it the back-end side effect of the hormonal buildup?"

"It could be the latter. But if, as I suspect, your teensy troublemakers are reprogramming you to target and home in on potential prey more efficiently, they would logically utilize those hormonal by-products to lure said prey and make them more tractable."

"This is monstrous."

"But hardly unique. Master vampires in particular are able to sexually dominate a large number of victims, thralls, and subordinates. It was generally theorized that this was a form of mental domination. I suspect that it may be owed to a significant boost of biochemical changes in the undead physiology, as well. It's not something that my boss has encouraged me to research, you understand."

"So these machines are giving me the love mojo of a master vampire?"

"I can't say because I have insufficient comparative data . . ."

"Your best guess, Doc."

"Then I'd have to say no. Based on the concentration levels in your samples—and that the evidence points to

catching you in the early stages of the enhancement
process—the analogy is a mismatch. I would *guess* that
master vampires exude pheromones at levels ten to
twelve times the human norm."

"And in my case?"

"It's not just a question of volume produced but also
the issue of biochemical refinement. The concentrations
in your bloodstream and apocrine glands are
approaching, what we call in certain laboratory settings,
weaponized grades of disbursements."

I thought for a moment. "Would these enhanced pheromones affect anyone coming within range or would they
be . . . selective?"

"Again, we're dealing in theoreticals for the moment.
In mammalian biology there is evidence for cross-species
sensitivities to conditions of estrous. I rather imagine
you'll see varying degrees of sensitivities among the preternatural variants to humankind."

"What about gender?"

"Well, naturally, sex pheromones are gender
responsive . . . "

"Orientation?"

"Swedish researchers demonstrated that homosexual
and heterosexual responses to odors involved in sexual
arousal differ significantly. I'd say that orientation would
be just as much a factor as gender. Perhaps more so."

Which meant Volpea was still an Oscar nominee rather
than a true believer.

"So back to my second question: how do I turn it off?"

"Short of shutting down or reprogramming the hive-
mind neural net for your nanites, I can only work on
defensive measures."

"Like what? Some kind of antidote?"

"In a sense. Something to regulate the hypothalamus or the release of hormones from the pituitary gland. Another approach would be to block the receptive capabilities of the VNOs—the vomeronasal organs located in the nasal septum."

"How long?" I asked.

"In the short term I could probably come up with an aerosol blocker. Like a nasal spray. Something temporary. I don't know how long it would last or the effective dosage but I could send you some different strength solutions and you could try them in various settings. I'll work up a chart and checklist/questionnaire to measure the results."

"So. In the meantime, it's cold showers and pushups?"

"I'm sorry, you don't understand. The antidote we're discussing would be for the people you come in contact with. There's nothing I can do for you as long as your symbiotic hitchhikers are running their defensive wetware programming."

"So, I'm screwed."

"Over and over, if you play your cards right."

I asked about Mama Samm and Marie Laveau. Dr. Mooncloud had heard nothing.

I asked about the weather. A tropical storm watch all along the Gulf, she said, and some media-fueled debates about evacuation scenarios. But not to worry. She and her patients had been reassured that they were completely safe in their billion-year-old bomb shelter. Snug as bugs in a rug. Nothing going to get to them down deep where they were. Let everyone else fight the traffic and the chaos should it come to that. And, if a storm actually did hit in the next few days, they'd just ride it out, safe and sound and underground. Yeah.

Anywhere else it would have been a good plan.

But not in New Orleans where Marie Laveau was planning a reception for monsters from deep black space, monsters from the deep blue sea, and a major werewolf revolt was brewing while no one was paying attention. And the Crescent City had a bad history when it came to hurricanes and low-level flooding. Right about now I couldn't see any up side to being in New Orleans.

"Turn on the TV," I ordered as I walked out of my cabin and into the salon.

Fand was ahead of me: a special weather bulletin was on the flat screen and she was studying it like it held the key to all of our futures.

Come to think of it, it probably did.

The meteorologist was using the words "tropical depression" but a glance at the map laid out the story to come. Mama Samm had succeeded in knocking Laveau's supernatural storm apart and smacked the remains way out into the Gulf of Mexico.

It was a respite rather than a victory. The remnants were reforming rather than dispersing.

And if the arrows indicating high and low pressure fronts meant anything—and Marie Laveau had her way—it was going to come spinning back around and head straight towards its artificial point of origin.

Time to shoot over to the other side of the river, jump in my other car, and burn rubber for the Big Easy.

Getting there would be easy. Nobody in their right mind would head toward a hurricane landfall zone. And

Laveau's minions should be majorly distracted by the chaos of a coastal evacuation.

The downside would be hitting that same chaos once I arrived. And getting back out would be a nightmare. But, first things first: I needed to get to my car—

—which screeched to a halt at the other end of the dock outside. The windshield was smashed, the hood ripped off the engine compartment, and the front grill caved in to the point that what was left of the headlights were practically cross-eyed. There was enough steam from the radiator and smoke from the tailpipe that it took me an extra moment to recognize my own automobile!

With a start, I realized that the *New Moon* had crossed the river and was now moored on the east bank of the Ouachita. Before the change in perspective had time to settle, my newly wrecked vehicle disgorged three familiar figures: Camazotz, Setanta, and a third man I had never officially met.

The New York demesne called him Silas.

Lupé had called him "Grandfather."

I had witnessed their confrontation, long distance, during my temporarily dead, out-of-the-body excursions back last January. Gramps had some hardcore attitudes about family planning that included the concept of postbirth abortions.

He was tall for a man and even more hirsute than the average untransformed *were*. The shock of brown hair that swept back from the widow's peak was streaked with even more gray than I remembered. He looked as if he were leading the other two even though each had one arm firmly grasped and the old pack leader's feet were barely touching the ground.

That's when I noticed all three were liberally splashed with blood. Zotz had a couple of boxes of blood packs from the bank under his other arm and the Mullet was carrying a sword in his free hand.

I turned and saw the empty wall above the plasma screen. Yep. Mikey's sword.

"Incoming," I said. But Liban was there before me, opening the door.

Nobody let go. With Zotz and the Mullet still holding fast to the old man, they turned and entered sideways.

Camazotz gave me a look. "Feeling much better are we?"

"Got a quick fix." I nodded at the two boxes under his free arm. "We're gonna need more."

"Well, you're out of luck," he snapped. "Snoop-wolf, here, and his posse went and torched the blood bank. This is all we could salvage." He dropped the boxes on the nearest chair.

"What?" I rounded on the old man. "What is it with you guys? Is everyone bound and determined to make me go all fangy and start ripping out throats?"

"Mr. Cséjthe, my name—"

"I know who you are, Hairball."

His eyes widened, then narrowed. "What did you say?"

I stepped in real close. "I said," I answered very slowly and distinctly, "I know. Who. You are. *Hairball*. More importantly, I've got a pretty good idea *what* you are."

"I am Pack Master for the Eastern Enclaves: Tribes and Confederations. I am the—"

"You're the guy," I interrupted, "who laid siege to my house while I was away and threatened the woman I love and our unborn son! And now you're the guy who's not only destroyed one of my business investments but either condemned me to a slow, painful death or to turning into a monster in order to take what I need by violence! I ought to stick a spigot in your neck and chain you to the fridge!"

Apparently the nanites were fast learners. Once they had created an initial template, they could replicate it ten times faster: fangs were filling my mouth even as I spoke.

I turned to Camazotz. "Why have you brought him here?" I think the unspoken subtext was pretty clear: *Why haven't you killed him?*

"Well, um, we didn't exactly capture him. He approached us. Asked us to bring him to you."

I turned back to Silas. "What? You wanted me to kill you personally?"

The old werewolf gave me a defiant look. It was pretty good: he'd probably been working it for years. "I came here to deliver a message and an ultimatum," he snarled back. "My death will gain you nothing. If I do not leave this boat in the next five minutes, my people will attack." Then he howled.

A werewolf's howl will do more than make your skin crawl. Under a full moon with the night mist covering blood-black ground, it will positively turn your epidermis inside out. Even so there's a special sort of creepiness having an old dude do it in your living room—even with all of the lights on while under restraint.

It didn't hurt that a chorus of howls answered from outside.

Through the windows, we could now see dozens of wolves lining the riverbank and crowding the first boards of the docks. There were at least as many here on the east bank as we'd left behind on the west bank.

His look went from defiant to smug.

I sighed. Doing more sighing than shrugging these days. "Okay, boys, let him go."

Setanta looked doubtful; Zotz looked thoughtful. Neither seemed inclined to release the arm they were grasping.

"Seriously, guys. I've got better things for you to do. Zotz, I want you topside in the pilot's station. Goldilocks, I want you with me on the side deck in two minutes. Bring the letter opener."

Setanta scowled. "Don't call me Goldilocks."

Silas straightened his garments as they turned him loose. "Here are the conditions—" he began.

I interrupted again. This time by backhanding him so hard he flew across the salon and cracked the wood façade on the cabinets where the galley began. Fifteen minutes ago I hadn't been able to lift my own head off of the pillow. Now I had just lifted a one-hundred-eighty-pound man off of his feet with the back of my hand. Elfsblood: it does a body good!

The others stared at me, stunned.

"We're casting off in three minutes," I announced. "Zotz, when you hear the signal, open the throttles. Head for the middle of the river and give me warp nine. Goldilocks—"

Setanta was still staring at Silas, suddenly ten feet away from where he'd been grasping his arm. "Yes?" he asked distractedly.

"The moment Zotz guns the engines you've got to cut the mooring ropes. How are you at running with scissors?"

The Hound of Fand hefted the archangel's sword and smiled as if emerging from a pleasant memory. "I have been practicing."

Silas sat up groggily. "You can't—"

"Save it, Gramps," I snapped. "You've got one minute to deliver your message and your punk-ass ultimatum. Don't waste it trying to jump-start a dick-waving contest: I've got bigger monsters to bitch-slap and otherworld fish to fry." I turned to Fand who was closest to the galley. "I need duct tape. Third drawer down, next to the sink." I turned back to Silas who was still sputtering and trying to find his balance in more ways than one. "Ticktock, Akela; forty-five seconds."

"Where is my granddaughter?" he growled.

Okay. Wasn't prepared for that one.

"Are you telling me that you don't know where she is?"

"We were sure you had smuggled her off to Seattle but we're now convinced that you've secreted her elsewhere. We no longer have the luxury of time to search for her. Her time of confinement grows near and this child must not be born!"

My first impulse was to backhand him across the salon, again. Instead, I put my face in his and said: "Oh yeah. Like I'd turn her over to you. She'd be better off with a back alley abortionist and dirty coat hanger than 'family.' So now it's time for you to do your big bad wolf shit, threaten to huff and puff and blow us all down."

"I have troops on both sides of the river!" he thundered. "As soon as you come ashore—"

"Time's up," I roared. I pounced on Silas just as he was getting to his feet. The old man was strong. Being a lycanthrope, he had additional body mass to bring into play. It wasn't a fair fight: I had just ingested the blood of an elven sea goddess, had a million micro-transformers (more than meets the eye) swarming my tissues, was half undead with a silver-laced touch that was anathema to his kind, and—most importantly—was royally pissed and in family protection mode. It was short, brutal, and he made no further resistance as I slapped duct tape over his mouth and dragged him to the outer, port-side door.

"Wait, what's the signal?" Zotz asked, on his way to the forward ladder.

"Tom Hanks' first big breakout movie," I snarled, throwing the door open and hauling the Alpha Wolf Pack Master for the Eastern Enclaves: Tribes and Confederations outside and onto the side deck.

I didn't give anyone time to think. More importantly, I didn't give anyone time to act on impulse.

"All right!" I yelled, hauling Silas to the railing. "You've probably all heard the rumors! Guess what! They're true!" I grabbed the blade of the sword as Setanta passed next to me and then held up my hand so all the bad-ass doggies could see that it was good and bloody. It also took everyone's attention off the sound of the engines starting up.

"Let me give you a little demonstration of what any of you might expect in a one-on-one confrontation from here on out!" I ripped the duct tape off with my good hand and then slapped my bloody hand over the old man's mouth before he could yell something stupid like "Attack!"

He began to yell anyway. Nothing coherent. Just screams of pain and agony as the flesh of his lower face began to smoke and melt.

"You want my family?" I bellowed. "You'll have to go through me! It will be bloody! I don't think you'll *like* me bloody! Right, Gramps?" I shoved him over the railing. "Here's your leader! Now, go fetch!"

At the sound of the splash, the throttles opened wide and the *New Moon* strained against the mooring ropes. As Setanta sliced through the first rope, I plucked up the gangplank and positioned myself to repel any boarders. No one moved except Setanta who swept past me to cut the second tether.

As we shot away from the docks and out into the river the only movement I could see close to the boat landing was an old man with a ruined face struggling to reach the shore. No one made any move to assist him.

My guess was the Eastern Werewolf Enclaves: Tribes and Confederations would have a new alpha and pack master by tomorrow's moonrise.

🦇   🦇   🦇

I went topside almost immediately.

"Heh," said Zotz as I approached the pilot's station, "I got it. Tom Hanks. *Splash*. For a moment I thought you were going for a *Turner and Hooch* smackdown kind of thing . . ."

I flipped off the running lights. "Night vision only till further notice."

"They'll still follow us."

"Maybe," I said. "Silas doesn't know where Lupé's stashed."

"Still . . . Boat. River. Not a lot of choices for your getaway route."

"Silas may not be in charge come sunrise."

"Either way," the demon mused, "I'll keep an eye out for an open landing. Enough clear ground to guarantee our escape, we ditch the boat, steal some wheels, and drop off the radar."

I shook my head. "I've got to get into New Orleans and get my people back out before the storm hits. The roads out will be choked in another day. The river is the best way in and back out, again."

"You're the captain." He said it without a trace of irony.

"Thanks, Zotz. Ease back on the throttle in about five minutes to lose the engine noise across the water. Run silent, run dark. Find us a concealed place to drop anchor out of the traffic lanes and close to shore in the next twenty if you can, and then join me down below for the bon voyage party."

"Aye-aye, sir. But, beggin' the captain's pardon, you might want to reconsider. Big 'n' beefy isn't half bad in a fight. We could use him if things get hairy down south."

I shook my head. "It's already hairy up here. On both sides of the river. And it's likely to get a lot worse before we arrive. I can't have people around me that I can't completely trust."

"Does that mean you trust me?" he asked. "Completely?" And he batted his eyes mockingly.

"Just find me a secluded off-loading point," I growled. "We're dropping ballast, whether they leave willingly or not!" I turned and stalked to the aft stairs.

I descended to the main deck but remained outside, taking a circuit of the boat to check the perimeter.

Aside from the lights of distant traffic and clusters of illuminated buildings, the banks of the Ouachita revealed very little to either side. If wolf packs were running along the shores, keeping pace with our furtive course, they were well hidden by the night. I tried shifting to infra-vision but we were too far out for anything man- or wolf-sized to register at this range.

It didn't matter. There wasn't anything I could do about that at the moment.

The question was what *could* I do? About anything?

I was headed downriver. But laying aside the obstacles of werewolves from the New York demesne following me and more werewolves from the New Orleans demesne waiting to intercept me, a river full of the Black Lagoon Irregulars, and possible visitations from the tentacle-faced and seafood-in-a-barrel monsters, I wasn't sure I could get back to Lupé in time. I was no meteorologist and the weather map on the TV was nothing more than a guess built out of momentary readings. But a tropical depression so close by in the Gulf was beyond ominous. Most hurricanes, birth to landfall, offer days to plan and execute a proper evacuation. This wasn't a typical storm cell and the depression vectors in the Gulf were much closer than the storms that gestated out in the Atlantic.

As of right now, an hour's delay could make a cru-cial difference.

So the sooner I jettisoned my problematic passengers . . .

The door to the salon opened and Liban came out on deck. "Christopher? Are you all right?"

I stared at her. "No." Staring at her was a mistake: she really was beautiful. And I could no longer trust my own physical responses.

"Is there something I can do?"

"Yeah." My voice was a little hoarse. "Get your sister and get off my boat."

She took a step toward me. "About that—"

"My son will not be a sacrifice!"

She stopped and looked at me as if I had slapped her. "I do not understand the exact meaning of the Telling," she said slowly. "Elvish words can have many meanings and both of us may have very different ideas as to what a prophecy means and still be both wrong."

"I'm not taking any chances," I said, noticing how the collar of her wetsuit rose up from the shoulder seams to cover the lower slope of her neck. The front closure was more than half undone. It wouldn't take much movement—a flick of the wrist, really—to pull the zipper down to the parting point. The neoprene top could be pulled open, the collar folded back . . .

I felt the ferrocarbon fangs start to extrude from my gums.

"Your sister needs to find some other child to adopt. Someone who needs a parent. My son has two." At the very least.

Liban shook her head and took another step toward me. "My sister owes you her life, now. She will swear you a blood oath that from this day forth, your child is safe from her and her lieged."

"Wow," I said, "an oath. Well then, I guess I can trust anything she would swear to seeing as how she's never lied to me before."

Another step and it was becoming more difficult to read her facial expressions seeing as how her throat kept getting in the way.

"Prophecies are vague," she murmured. "There may be many ways to set them aside, create alternative outcomes."

"For example?" I asked harshly.

"We will accompany you to New Orleans. We will assist you in rescuing your family and evacuating them to a safe place. We can assist you in avoiding your enemies. Or join you in extracting your family if necessary."

"Why?" I asked, trying to ignore the hotness of an elf chick in a form-fitting wetsuit, talking like Nick Fury, Agent of S.H.I.E.L.D. "What's in it for you?"

"Any other time it would be sufficient that you had saved my sister's life. A debt is owed. But now we stand on the cusp of time and your success or failure may be the hope or doom for your world and ours. Why would we not seek to insure your success?"

I shook my head as she took another step toward me. I suddenly had the feeling I was being stalked. "There's more to it than that, isn't there? Even if you're not planning to betray me, you have other reasons . . ."

Liban slipped her long, slender fingers into the gap above the zipper of her orange top. Slowly, she drew her hand down, the zipper sighing as the last few inches of the foamlike material separated. Her top parted like the stage curtains of a wondrous burlesque show; moonlight, mystery, and madness lay just beyond the footlights.

"You fascinate me, mortal," she sighed. "Fand has had her Cuchulainn for two thousand and four hundred years—save those lost centuries during the Great Confounding. I have found no one worthy since my parting with Labraid over the coming of the Fisher King. Are you my Tam Lin? My Thomas the Rhymer?"

She slid the neoprene jacket from her shoulders and was all pearlescent in the moonlight, all orbed and fulsome. "Of all the men born of mortal woman there has been no one of your like who was not part god. A goddess needs a god," she said, coming up against me and tilting her head back to expose her creamy throat, "even one who brings her pain."

The fangs slid from my gums in a flash and I was leaning down without thought, without will, without hesitation.

Chapter Thirteen

MY LIPS CAME TO REST upon the creamy slope of her neck.

I was a man and weak, with a goddess pressed against me, offering up her perfect flesh to my desires.

My fangs dimpled her creamy skin, pressing on the artery that trembled, hot and turgid, with heart's blood pounding through that feast of flesh now willingly offered.

But the monster in me was not yet ascendant: I *wanted* the blood—but I did not yet *need* the blood.

And her offer was forced—not at gunpoint nor by external coercion but by the betrayal of her own endocrine system.

It was a false gift, born not out of desire but out of pheromones and hormonal triggers. Yeah, I know that there are those who would argue that desire is nothing but biochemical soups and aerosols but I have to believe in something more. Love *is* a chemist's nightmare, to quote Saperstein, but if we were nothing more than glands and nerve endings the social contract would not stand. It is broken every day by acts of will and lack of will but we still exercise degrees of choice.

If my pheromones had been "weaponized," Liban's choices were illusion. My response was simple predation with a complex camouflage. And the end result potentially more evil by making her complicit in the act. Taking her against her will and by brute force would be a lesser crime.

I dug down deep and found just enough humanity to push her away and say: "No."

"No?" A freight train of emotions rumbled across her face as she dealt with the unthinkable: a mortal turning down a goddess. There was heat in those cool features, now. I suddenly realized how much punishment Fand was happy to deliver to those who had thwarted her. Could my nano-driven elf-defense system handle tag-team payback from the Sidhe Sisters as well as a one-man army of Celtic legend?

Then her face darkened like the moon going behind a cloud. She turned and walked away. Her pride would not let her run but she moved with all deliberate speed, passing the door to the salon's interior, and sought the solitude of the *New Moon*'s open deck at the prow.

I started to bend down to retrieve her top and then thought the better of it. What was I going to do? Return it to her? Best to leave it where she could find it. I turned around and practically collided with Suki.

I nearly jumped out of my skin. She, on the other hand, stood there impassively, like a recently sculpted manikin, staring at me with those empty eyes. Those lifeless orbs, devoid of spark or sparkle. Eyes like the glass fakes utilized by doll makers and taxidermists. She looked at me as if she saw nothing and everything. She stared as if she were looking clear through me and into another space, another dimension. Another possible culmination.

I finally stepped around her and, as I did, she moved forward and bent down to pick up Liban's wet-suit jacket. I watched her carry it toward the front of the boat.

God, I was tired!

Even now with the crackling surges of fresh energy from Liban's blood thrumming through vein and artery, nerve and muscle, I was newly weary. Every day brought fresh pain—every day *I* brought fresh pain. Fully turned vampires had the advantage of operating without conscience, without emotion. Without regret. Stuck somewhere between warm-blooded human and cold-blooded predator, I was screwed—coming *and* going. If not for the obligations of family . . .

I turned and went into the salon.

The main lights were turned off to preserve everyone's night vision for going out on deck. A single lamp near the sliding glass doors leading to the bow gave just enough illumination to keep us from stumbling about inside. Added bonus, it was very film noirish: Bogart would have approved.

Setanta and Fand were sitting on the couch, holding hands. They looked at me as I came in and Fand rose to her feet, pushing her big, muscly shadow back down when he tried to rise with her. For all of that she still looked a little shaky.

"I know you bear me much ill will," she began. "And I know it must seem that I have acted out of the worst motivations. But I ask you to believe that I have always had the best intentions concerning your son. And I have been careful to see that you came to no actual harm."

I held up my hand. "Your sister explained. Okay. Doesn't matter. He's still not up for adoption. So here's what happens next. Zotz is bringing us in close to shore and you're all going ashore. Good luck with the next round in your family-planning cycle but just remember that times have changed. These days it takes a village. That, and a small militia, as well as the GNP of a small Mediterranean country. So, good luck, adios, and please return your seats and tray tables to the upright position. I want you out of my house and off my boat as soon as we can lower the dinghy."

As if cued by my words, Zotz eased back on the throttles and the fish-finders *eeped* indicating "shallow bottom" beneath the hull.

"You don't understand. I'm not a bad person! Your son would have wanted for nothing. More importantly, he would have been *safe!*"

I had no doubts that she believed her own words. The Fey Folk had been stealing human children for so many centuries it was inevitable that they would become invested in self and racial justification. "No, *you* don't understand," I snapped, knowing an argument was pointless. "I wouldn't care if you were Mary Frick'n Poppins: my boy already has a family. I've already kicked enough werewolf ass on this subject to open my own kennel club. What makes you think a couple of fairies and their Celtic cabana boy are going to make a difference?"

She shook her head and held her hands out. "Please, I do not wish to argue. You have saved my life. I willingly swear fealty now to you and yours. I acknowledge the wrongs I have done you in my single-minded quest to bring your son under my protection. It is now my wish to expand that protection to cover you, as well."

Yeah. I was just getting ready to say how the best protection she could offer was from herself. I opened my mouth to say words to that effect when Liban and Suki entered the salon.

Let me be more specific.

An explosion of glass marked their entrance as a wave of tapioca pudding hurtled them through the sliding doors at the front of the cabin. The lamp disappeared into the seething tarry mass and the room was plunged into darkness.

I immediately shifted over to infravision but found I was having trouble with detail on the infrared wavelengths. There was a competing light source in the cabin. Setanta was all big and yellowy as he thrashed about. Fand and Liban were nearly violet, a shade of heat signature I'd never seen before but then I'd never trafficked with elves. Suki was too cold to be visible yet there she was, faintly revealed in a pale green light.

It wasn't her body temperature lighting her up, however, but the reflected glow from the pudding itself. It seethed across the floor like a living carpet of bubbles, a giant amoeba that glowed as if lit from within by hundreds of green and white Christmas lights.

Holiday illumination borrowed from The Addams Family.

Or ten thousand glo-sticks from some unholy rave, discarded in a toxic waste dump.

The gelatinous mass rippled into the cabin and began to gather itself into a rising column of goo. Setanta stepped in even as its blobby base receded like a plastic tide, planted his boot-shod feet, and swung Michael's sword.

The other-worldly blade cut through the rising glow-in-the-dark fruitcake like a hot knife through tapioca. The only problem with that pudding analogy is all those little tapioca "pearls" don't turn into eyeballs and mouths and such when you stick a utensil in it.

Ours did.

The chunk that Setanta lopped off fell down into the quivering, bubbling mass that spawned it. It was quickly reabsorbed.

Zotz arrived from the upper deck, landing heavily in the shattered opening with a lantern in one hand and a loaded spear gun in the other. Although the light from the lantern spoiled the bioluminescent light show, it revealed an interesting series of details. Liban lay stunned, half hung over the countered divider cordoning off the galley area. Suki was struggling to her feet like a drunken beachcomber, an incoming tide of pudding lapping at her unsteady feet. Setanta laid about with his

vorpal blade but, alas, there was no snicker-snack—just
momentary scorings of the gelatinous goo that reclosed
and smoothed over as he cursed and howled and flung
small oozy droplets about with frenzied abandon. Fand
stood atop the sofa and surveyed the chaos with an
expression that seemed strangely contemplative. Maybe
that was my imagination. I didn't exactly have time to
ponder as my eyes returned to the entryway where Zotz
was doing a little contemplation of his own. The carpeting at his feet was shredded and mostly missing, the
curtain edges where the sludge had brushed through
looked scorched and half eaten. Tiny tendrils of smoke
seemed to waft from patches of exposed blackish wood.

Zotz fired his spear into the blob. The spear disappeared into its jiggly depths with no discernable effect.
Except the honking big amoeba seemed to be moving
toward me, now.

I retreated to the galley. Tapioca creature followed.

Obviously swords and spears weren't the weapons of
choice in a smackdown with a pudding monster. So the
question was WWMD? There was a Model 500 Smith &
Wesson Magnum revolver in a hidden holster fastened
up under the sink. Not exactly the answer to the just
asked question of "What Would MacGyver Do?" and
more likely to ventilate both deck and double hull than
to discomfort the escapee from a giant lava lamp. The
other recessed weapon, a Mossberg 590A1 shotgun with
a 14-inch barrel and a cruiser grip, was less of a hazard
in that respect. The shortened barrel spread the shot
pattern "weapon of mass destruction" style, trading tunneling force for area of effect—no small consideration
when trying to avoid catastrophic damage below the

waterline. Technically, I needed a special background check and tax stamp to possess such an aberration. Had it not been for the increased scrutiny of the state and federal bureaucracy—not to mention the scorn and derision of all the firearm fetishists out there—I might have made the effort to make it legit. Fortunately Coast Guard inspections were rare and rarely thorough this far inland and upriver.

Legalities were the least of my worries right now, however, and the Mossberg, though less likely to send us to the bottom, was still not the prime candidate for pusbuster. I reached for the third option: a spray can of WD-40.

Then I dug in my pants pocket past my SwissChamp pocketknife and fished a Bic lighter out of my pocket.

Yeah, I'd ditched the cigarettes back in those reckless, feckless days of my youth. Never mind the lectures on health and life expectancy; nothing is a surer inducement to give up the coffin nails than the woman of your dreams comparing her make-out sessions with you to "licking an ashtray."

A stint in the military, however, had brought me back to the advantages of always having a bit of butane-enhanced flint-and-steel at hand, a pocket MacGyver for those unique and unexpected occasions.

Such as this one.

I thumb-popped the cap off of the WD-40 and checked the nozzle direction. The many-eyed tide lapped into the kitchen area and I triggered my jury-rigged flamethrower.

Or I tried to, anyway.

Hey, it's not easy. Try patting your head and rubbing your stomach. While being shot at. So, something like; left hand positioning the lighter, thumb rotating the flint wheel for spark, dropping to depress fuel valve button—wishing I had gone to the trouble of replacing my lost Zippo instead of a quick and dirty disposable fix—while simultaneously positioning to ignite chemical spray from WD-40 nozzle being triggered by right hand while pointed at proper angle/trajectory to direct enhanced flame back at target without incinerating left hand or blowing up right hand in the process.

See?

I fumbled and nearly dropped the lighter on the first attempt.

I extinguished the flame with the spray on the second.

The third attempt worked like a charm and the pudding ran smack dab into my miniature flamethrower halfway into the galley.

Imagine a cockroach screaming. Now imagine a hundred of them at the same time. The pudding made a sound like the Mormon Tabernacle Choir of roachdom and skittered back. I held my makeshift torch before me like Van Helsing's crucifix and advanced. Dracula's nemesis would have roared "The power of Christ compels you!" or such. What deity would a pudding recognize? Bill Cosby?

The terrible tide retreated a foot. Then two. I gained another yard, using controlled blasts of flame to sweep the forward edge of the pulsating puddle. "Aye!" I exclaimed, doing my half-assed impression of Scotty from *Star Trek*, "the haggis is in the fire now for sure!"

My amorphous adversary turned into a hasty pudding, withdrawing to the midpoint of the salon.

The rapidity of its backwash knocked Suki off her feet and she went down as if caught in an undertow, the living sludge closing over her like a drowning pool.

At that point my flame died down. And went out. The can was empty. The room was plunged again into near darkness. The opposite doorway was empty: Zotz had fled with the lantern.

Light oozed back in my direction: the glowing mucus monster was making another run at me. I retreated back to the galley, noting the scorched linoleum where the creature had flowed moments before: I hadn't done that with my portable brazier! Under the sink, again, and this time I hauled out the sawed-off shotgun and a bottle of Clorox.

I lobbed the plastic bleach container into the center of the amoebalike mass and jacked a shell into the Mossberg. I fired almost immediately. At this range and with a scattershot spread, I only had to worry about not hitting anyone else. Taking any more time to aim might have lost my target as it sank into the roiling depths of the creature. The buckshot sieved the plastic bottle and bleach began squirting in all directions as the thing received this latest offering hungrily.

A moment later it vomited the bottle back out but it was too late. The plastic was shredded, the contents dissipated into the semisolid masses that twisted and shuddered as the caustic liquid began wreaking havoc on its cellular structures. Light bloomed across the room as Zotz returned with lantern in one hand and a very large pistol in the other.

Correction: a large *Very* pistol in the other. "Fire in the hole!" he yelled, extending the flare gun and firing into the quivering mass of protoplasm. The flare barely ignited before burying itself deep in the glowy sludge.

Forget the cockroach choir analogy. This thing was shrieking like ten thousand cicadas performing all of the operas in Wagner's Ring Cycle simultaneously! Zotz broke open the Very pistol and ejected the spent shell casing. As he loaded another flare I looked around the cabin for another weapon. Setanta was still in full berserker mode, doing his Cuisinart impression with Mikey's sword. His hair was standing on end, practically giving off sparks of static electricity and, if willpower and earnestness counted for points, this thing would have been dead five minutes ago.

But his blade continued to make meaningless and temporary dimples within the ever changing landscape of the blob, and I looked about for other options.

"Fand!" I called. "Can you reach the lamp?"

I had an idea that, if she could retrieve the table lamp—somehow pull it back out by its electrical cord—she might be coached into stripping the wires in such a way as to shock the creature when the plug was reinserted into the wall outlet.

And it was quickly obvious that getting Fand to pick her own nose right now might be too complicated a task as she was still standing on the couch, still staring at the bubbling mass as if contemplating some dark nightmare from which she might never wake up.

Okay. I was pretty much at the end of my What Would MacGyver Do approach with the blob, what other options were there?

The blob . . .

Silly me. I'd been formulating from the wrong premise. If this thing was anything like the Blob, I should be asking: What would Steve McQueen do?

As in *The Blob*. 1958 film. The sort made popular on the fossilized drive-in circuit. Directed by Irwin S. Yeaworth, Jr.; theme song by Hal David and Burt Bacharach. Protoplasmic life-form falls to earth in meteorite. Old hermit discovers said meteorite and is promptly eaten by gooey orange nougat center. Enter Steve McQueen as teenager Steve Andrews in his first starring role. Along with his girlfriend Jane Martin, played by Aneta Corsaut (who would go on to greater fame as Helen Krump on *The Andy Griffith Show*), they run about Downingtown, Pennsylvania, attempting to warn the Downingtown townspeople. Of course, no one pays heed to those pesky teenagers until it's too late and the orange goo devours a good chunk of the town's population. And it gets bigger with each successive meal: people, cars, a supermarket, a movie theater, even a diner until they discover the thing can't take the cold . . .

So . . .

I snatched the fire extinguisher off of the galley wall praying it was a CO_2 model.

It wasn't a CO_2 model.

So much for luck and the chance to employ a cold-based weapon attack. But when you're brawling for your life you use whatever is at hand. I pulled the pin, pointed the nozzle, and pulled the trigger just as Zotz fired a third flare into the quivering mass of pustulescent sludge.

Almost immediately a gray film began to spread across the toxic tartar sauce where I applied the gaseous exhaust of my fire extinguisher, its shapeless congerie of proto-plasmic bubbles shuddering and becoming fixed as if undergoing petrification. Some of the bubbles burst, emitting a noxious vapor as the beast convulsed and then collapsed in upon itself. The interior of my boat was a shambles and I wasn't sure as to Liban's and Suki's condi-tion, yet, but the foamy collection of eyes and mouths were filming over or gaping with an evident slackness that said that death was imminent for this gummi beast. I turned the canister of the fire extinguisher in my hands and examined the face plate: it was a Halon suppres-sion unit.

I looked over at Zotz as the thing gave a last convulsive shudder. "Grab a gas can, a couple of the mini charges, and ready the inflatable dingy. As soon as I pull Suki out, we're going to have a quick Viking funeral."

"Aye, Cap'n." He turned to go and jumped backwards into the galley.

Rather, he was thrown across the cabin as the Big Daddy version of the mini pudding we had just turned into a baked Alaska smashed its way into the salon. If the last blob had come in like high tide, this one was a tsunami! We were shoved about as a vast tonnage of angry, Hulk-green, glowing goop surged across the floor and crashed up against the walls like a stormy, oil-slicked sea.

I turned the fire extinguisher but it was sputtering in my hands, all but spent. "Shoot a flare at the drapes!" I yelled at Zotz. I meant to take us down in flames if there was no other way. But even that way was lost: the Very pistol had been torn from his hands when the battering ram of protoplasm had smacked into him. The lantern was gone, as well.

If anything, though, it was brighter now inside the salon. The green glow from the luminescent sludge that continued to pour in upon us was brighter than the illumination we typically ran at night on the river. And it was joined by a pulsing violet light as Fand began to scream.

They weren't incoherent screams of terror, though.

"Odael si vali shaerael sor shys eil toil . . . "

They were words—Old English or Anglo-Saxon from the sound—and, though rage comes closer to describing their pitch, they were more like a warrior's timbre of challenge.

". . . shol tia aelaestia sai ti eil sai ti eilyli . . . "

Fand had finally stepped off of the couch but instead of stepping down, she was floating up. And drifting across the cabin toward its center. Toward the sludge beast's center.

". . . tasia iar moria shaesi air talyr vaeres . . . "

And the purple light that pulsed and reflected back from the walls and ceiling and, finally, even the green-tinted surface of the beast, itself, was emanating from the faerie queen. The nimbus of energy that crackled and shimmered about her slender form was growing brighter and pulsing more frantically with every word that she spoke.

". . . eil ialai toli eilor sar air tae shi iaraesia paeryr . . . "

And finally she hovered and turned in midair. Her face once terrible, became momentarily soft and tender and all too young and vulnerable. "We will be together again, my love. If not in this world, then in the next.

Until that time, keep my vow and oath: protect the father as you would the child. This sacrifice must not be in vain."

Setanta shouted: "My queen!" And began to wade into the creature as if to reach her by swimming its protoplasmic currents, but she spread her arms and set her face back to its terrible mask of purpose as she turned again.

"*Aelael mai, mar air shi pyli!*" she cried as she dropped into the seething mass of roiling corruption.

Thunder filled the room.

An infinitesimal glimpse of something—somewhere—between the molecules of the air.

Air that rushed in to fill the emptiness previously occupied by a room-sized monster and a child-sized queen.

Both were gone.

Vanished.

The only acknowledgment of either's former existence were three sounds.

That transitory crash of imploding air—a Tupperware burp of artificial thunder as the world resealed itself.

The sustained weeping of a great warrior, now on his hands and knees.

And the hiss and sizzle as each tear fell upon the scorched and smoking floor.

〰 〰 〰

Nothing else came out of the river during the next hour.

Nor did Fand return from where she had 'ported with our displaced foe.

Setanta made a weak protest when we hauled anchor and prepared to make way, but Liban assured him that

her sister could find her way back to him, wherever he
was. Once it was safe to return.

Her words were encouraging, her eyes and voice less
so. Thereafter Setanta withdrew into himself to nurse
his inner wounds.

We spent some time dealing with outer wounds, as
well. Liban was bruised, cut, and mildly concussed from
being hurtled through the glass door and across the main
cabin. Setanta, Zotz, and I had varying degrees of burns
from contact with the caustic slime. Fortunately Zotz
and I had kept pretty much to the thing's perimeter
while Setanta's ongoing commitment to dressing like a
gay leather biker had largely protected him when he
waded into it.

Suki wasn't so fortunate.

A ninety-pound Asian woman had gone under and
stayed under until we'd killed it. Then stayed under some
more when the second half of *The Blob* double feature
arrived. I didn't know how fast these things could feed,
but what was left behind when Fand opened a momentary door to some otherwhere was only a fraction of the
size and weight and mass of a ninety-pound Asian
woman.

And didn't look human.

It looked like a cat.

A golden-eyed, sable brown, Burmese cat with two
tails.

One that looked as if it had been put in an industrial-
strength clothes dryer and treated to a half hour of tumble dry at high heat.

"What's with Mrs. Bigglesworth, here?" Zotz asked as
I recapped the aloe vera gel and stowed it with the first-
aid kit.

"Mrs. Who?" I asked.

He shook his head. "Wrong reference. *Austin Powers* not *A Wrinkle in Time*." He pointed at the cat. "Asian zombie babe goes into giant fruitcake; cat with mange and two tails comes out. What gives?"

The cat looked at him and then turned its head to look at me.

"There is a species of Japanese vampire who may take the form of a cat at times. The one characteristic that distinguishes them from true felines is they manifest two tails instead of one."

"So she's a cat now?" he asked.

The cat stared at me with wide yellow eyes that seemed more alive and more present than the dead, lifeless orbs Suki had stared at me with since her return from the watery depths.

"Maybe Silly Putty Monster absorbed too much mass for her to retain her human form. Or perhaps she needs to transform in order to heal." I shook my head. "I don't know! This isn't my department! I have a liberal arts degree for Chrissake! I should be lecturing on Shakespeare, not dissecting shoggoths!"

"What's a shoggoth?"

I blinked. The word had just popped into my head. For a moment I was back inside Mama Samm's skull gazing into the abyss and—

I jerked as if I had touched a live wire. And shuddered.

Zotz reached out and touched my shoulder. "Christopher? Are you all right?"

I shook my head. "No. I am not all right. I think I am well on my way to losing it. I don't know how much more of this crap I can take."

"We'll stock up on fire extinguishers," he said soothingly. "We'll issue flare guns to everyone . . . "

I shook my head again. "It's not that. It's not just monsters. Or the fact that I'm turning into one. It's all of it. It's Jenny and Kirsten and now my son and Lupé and Deirdre and Mama Samm—and, hell, even you and the passengers and every single person who comes into my orbit—I'm like a lightning rod for every shit storm the universe whips up within a thousand-mile radius!"

"I know it's been a little rough, lately—"

"Lately? Ever since I got the vampire virus two years ago, it's been nothing but major suckiness. There's a reason we mortals are designed to wear out by the three-score-and-ten warranty specs. We're not made for prolonged exposure to living. I should have died with my wife and daughter at the intersection of 103 and US 69. Or, better yet, in that barn just outside of Weir, Kansas!"

"Hey," Zotz said gently, "you know the old saying. If you want to make God laugh, tell Him your plans."

"Yeah," I said, choking down an unexpected sob, "that's me. God's comedy relief. Other people tune in David Letterman at the end of their day. The Big Guy picks up His remote and points it right at me."

Zotz shook his head. "Oh, hey man, don't talk like that. It's not true! I mean, that's just wrong!" He patted my shoulder. "You ain't nowhere near as funny as Letterman. Maybe Leno on a really bad night, but even then—"

I rubbed my face. "Thanks. You can stop cheering me up, now." I gave myself a little shake. "The pity party's over. Let's go topside and look at the charts. We've got a lot of river to eat and very little time to do it in."

"Aye-aye, Cap'n!" He turned to the cat. "Come, Mrs. Bigglesworth."

I cleared my throat. "Zotz . . . "

"What?"

"Even if she doesn't eventually recover and become a badass vampire again—"

"Yeah?"

"—she can still crap in your shoes."

ᴀ⸸ᴀ   ᴀ⸸ᴀ   ᴀ⸸ᴀ

I don't know which was spookier: the green wash from the fish-finder screen or the red glow from the chart lamp. The demon's face moved back and forth between the two patches of illuminated darkness as we studied the charts and then checked and rechecked the screen to make sure nothing else was sneaking up from underneath us.

"So, our little bathtub sonar is still working?" I asked.

"Near as I can tell," the almost human creature replied from the pilot's chair. In his true demon form, Camazotz Chamalcan couldn't adequately fit into the cockpit and maneuver himself, much less the boat. Obviously, it would be a simple enough process in human form but Zotz seemed unwilling to fully abandon his fundamental badassedness of a sudden. And somehow this downsized, homogenized, semihuman compromise was more disturbing than the original giant bat-god abomination-from-Hell aspect when he manifested in all of his former death-god glory.

Still, I could hardly fault him after this latest turn of events; I planned on sleeping with a small arsenal for the foreseeable future, myself.

"Then how do Carpet Master and Throw Rug Junior manage to sneak up on us with nary a peep from the security system?" I asked.

"Good question."

"Bad answer," I grumbled.

"My best guess? The fish-finder is programmed to detect objects of a certain size and conforming to a generalized shape. Perch, catfish, large-mouth bass, Deep Thing—the sonar picks it out of the background, recognizes it as separate and distinct from the water around it. Something big and flat, however, coming up off the bottom and rising beneath the hull isn't going to read like a suspended object. It's going to read like a sandbar or a shallow stretch of river bed. The fish-finder wasn't set to sound an alarm for depth soundings."

"Can we correct that?"

"I think so."

"Well, make it so, Mister Zotz."

"Aye, sir!" he said, tinkering with the settings and eliciting an intermittent series of beeps, chirps, and clicks. "A trickier fix is the question of how we steer an 84-foot houseboat with a relatively shallow draft all the way to the Mississippi River and then down to New Orleans where a major storm is brewing?"

"Good question."

"Bad answer," he grumbled.

We'd gone to the GPS screen, first. The satellite charting system was great for local details and long-range overviews but a little clunky for checking details in between us and our final destination until we got there. The paper charts were better for long-range details—like where I might anticipate passage problems or potential interceptions from our furry following.

I sighed. "Look, I've got wolves on the left bank and wolves on the right bank and I've already spent way too much time not going anywhere. I mean to move toward my people and keep moving by whatever means I can find. I'll sail this ship until she sinks or founders. Then I'll take another. Or go ashore and deal with whichever bunch of busybodies offers the path of least bloody resistance. At least that's the plan until I can come up with a better one. It may sound impractical or even just plain nuts but I can't *not* go forward any longer! It's my problem, not yours. You're welcome to take the dinghy. Seek your redemption on a surer, saner path. I don't mind. In fact, I rather insist."

Zotz stared at me with his newly disturbing, semihuman face, the greens of the GPS and fish-finder screens and the red from the chart lamp giving him an old, 1950s, 3–D, Technicolor monster movie vibe. "This voyage stinks of death and madness! I think great suffering and retribution lie ahead."

I nodded. "Yeah . . . " I murmured.

"Good enough for me! Where do I sign?"

I sighed and turned off the chart light. As I stowed the charts I reflected that Mama Samm would not approve of my taking Zotz along on what was sure to be the equivalent of a pub crawl for an unrepentant alcoholic. I just hoped she'd eventually turn up to give me hell for it.

"Oops," he said.

"Oops?" My head snapped up and I gave my demon pilot a hard look. "You don't drive *my* house down a river filled with mysterious lights, vicious fish folk, and

giant, tag-team amoebas—amoebae—slime monsters—
and just say 'oops' like maybe there's a teensy problem."

"Naw." He had fired up another stogie and had liber-
ated a can of beer from his secret stash (for medicinal
purposes), promising me that he could navigate unim-
paired. He tipped a yachtsman's cap back from his nearly
human brow as he continued. "Just remembered, that's
all. Been a little busy and distracted ever since you got
back."

"And?"

"Mama Samm said you wanted some research on four
sets of coordinates."

I did? "Oh yeah. Sure." *Mind like a steel trap—closed
tight.* "What did you find out?"

"For the most part, not a hell of a lot," he groused.
"Unless it's that the two of you have a wicked sense of
humor." He shot me a look but when I failed to confirm
his suspicions, he continued. "I mean, I expected that
these coordinates would—well—coordinate with some
kind of actual landmark. Like land: an island, a reef, a
shoal—something other than empty ocean. But only one
set of longitude and latitude numbers conforms to the
position of an actual land mass—or two, if you count
make-believe."

"Lincoln Island," I said.

He almost lost his cigar. "Then you know?"

I nodded, staring out into the darkness. "Mama Samm
gave you the first set of coordinates out of a French
edition of Jules Verne's *The Mysterious Island.* Interesting book. Verne, a Frenchman, wrote a novel about five
Yankee prisoners during the American Civil War—how

they escaped the Siege of Richmond by hijacking a hot-air balloon and flying off into the unknown. The unknown being a volcanic island in the middle of the Pacific Ocean, some 2500 kilometers east of New Zealand. The castaways named it Lincoln Island in honor of President Abraham Lincoln."

Zotz nodded and turned the wheel to make a course correction. "Yeah, I pulled the book off the shelf and thumbed through it. Lots of action and that Cyrus Smith guy was always inventing stuff out of raw materials. But I guess the big whoop-de-do is the return of Captain Nemo and his submarine."

"The *Nautilus*," I appended.

"Yeah, well, the problem is there ain't no such island on the charts, the satellite photos—nothin'."

"Actually," I said, "that's not the only problem. *The Mysterious Island* was written in 1874 and chronicled events that were supposed to have transpired from 1865 to 1867. It's a sequel to *20,000 Leagues Under the Sea* which was published four years earlier and covered Captain Nemo's adventures from 1867 to 1869. That means Captain Nemo dies and the *Nautilus* is scuttled in the sea caves of Lincoln Island *before* he takes Professor Aronnax on his memorable voyage in the first book! Yet, Cyrus Smith, our ingenious engineer-hero in the second book, recognizes Nemo and the Nautilus from the descriptions in the Aronnax Journals. Which, if you want to further nitpick, won't be published under the title *20,000 Leagues Under the Sea* until 1870–a couple of years in the future at that point."

My demon pilot goggled at me. "How do you know crap like this?"

"I told you, I used to teach American and World Lit. Too bad knowing crap like that doesn't seem to count for anything when it comes to so-called geriatric gods and pseudopodinous probiscae."

"Yeah, well. Bottom line. No island at those coordinates, mysterious or otherwise. On the other hand there *is* a mysterious island of sorts at the second set."

"Really?"

"Yeah. It's like haunted or something . . ."

Chapter Fourteen

BLAME EDMOND FANNING. The American sea captain may have used up any good luck concerning Palmyra Island when he discovered it on a voyage to Asia back in 1798. The good captain was sleeping in his cabin one night when he found himself awakened by a strong premonition of doom. Not once, not twice, but three times he found his sleep disturbed by an overwhelming sense of dread. More than disturbed: he awoke having left his bunk and walked about the ship while still asleep—something he had never done on any other occasion in his life! Out on the deck of the *Betsy*, all was calm and quiet, though it was too dark to see any distance in any direction. Still, the charts showed empty ocean: they were near the center of the Pacific, about a thousand nautical miles south-southwest of Hawaii—about half-way between Hawaii and American Samoa. Nothing was evidently wrong but he gave orders to the helmsman on duty to heave to until daybreak in hopes that he might sleep more peacefully.

At sunrise Captain Fanning and his crew stood at the railing and looked out over the killer reef lying before them, now revealed by the early light of day. Had they continued on their original course during the night, the ship would have been ripped to pieces and all hands lost in the darkness. Fanning and his crew were doubly lucky: not only did they narrowly avoid disaster on the northern portion of the reef encompassing Palmyra Island, but they continued on their way without stopping to make landfall. And though he did note the position of the unknown and unnamed island in his ship's log, he failed to file a timely report. Credit for the unnamed island's discovery went to another American sea captain.

A Captain Swale had the "good" fortune to become the official discoverer of the island and give it its name when his ship was caught in a storm in 1802. Blown off course and into the hungry jaws of the island's voracious reefs, Swale's new find took on the name of his shattered vessel: the *Palmyra*.

Fourteen years later a Spanish pirate vessel named the *Esperanza* foundered on those selfsame reefs. Already holed and broken from a fierce battle that had crippled her and killed most of her crew, she remained afloat long enough for the few survivors to transfer their treasure—Inca gold and silver—to the island. A year passed without rescue. The remaining crew buried their loot beneath a tree on Palmyra and then constructed rafts, attempting to return to civilization. A single survivor was picked up by an American whaling ship but exposure, dehydration, and pneumonia had taken their toll: he survived only long enough to tell a sketchy story before the secret of the treasure died along with him. None of the other rafts or survivors were ever recovered.

In 1855, a whaling ship—perhaps in search of the *Esperanza*'s Incan gold and silver trove—was consumed on the deadly reefs of the island. The ship and her crew disappeared as if they had never existed.

To this day ships and yachts and sailboats have continued to disappear or have had calamitous encounters with Palmyra and its reefs. And each account differs from other sea disasters with just that extra detail or two that turns the whole set of circumstances . . . *odd*. Abandoned sailboats found drifting, shipwrecked crews that no one would agree to rescue, charts of the island found washed ashore thousands of miles away . . . and survivors' tales of the overwhelmingly creepy feeling of being watched by the island's uninhabited jungles.

Even the U.S. Navy came to recognize the "Palmyra Curse." During World War II the island was used as a refueling station. Its position, smack dab in the middle of the Pacific, made it ideal for a long-range operations base—both for submarines and air operations. President Roosevelt signed an executive order identifying Kingman Reef, close by Palmyra, as a U.S. National Defense Area, declaring it off limits to foreign planes and surface craft back in 1941. The order has apparently never been rescinded.

Too bad for our fighting men—or subsequent generations of visitors—Palmyra isn't the tropical paradise that
many Pacific islands tend to emulate.

The reefs that surround Palmyra are actually a triple
threat. Not only do they devour unwary ships but they
harbor large colonies of ciguatera algae and appear to be
the Pacific nursery for the gray and black-tipped reef
sharks. The problem with the former is that this particular strain of algae is very poisonous—not to the fish that
feed on it, but to anyone expecting a seafood diet while
visiting. And the problem with the latter is that the
lagoons and beaches are off limits for swimming as well
as fishing. Even wading is a deadly gamble.

And then there were the technical mishaps. Like the
time a Navy patrol plane went down just off the island.
It disappeared without a trace—not even flotsam or jetsam or an oil slick to mark its impact. Or the flights that
would take off from the runway and inexplicably turn
the wrong way and head in the opposite direction of
their flight plan. More than one flight was never heard
from again—somewhat understandable as World War II
had commenced in the Pacific—but there were other
incidents, as well. Planes that would circle the island,
unable to find the runway. Or fly over Palmyra without
being able to see the island at all. There was a reason
sharks frequented the waters surrounding Palmyra.

After World War II the Navy abandoned the island.
Over the decades that have passed since, it has been
visited by yachtsmen and sailors of various stripes and
several attempts to colonize the island were made. No
one stayed for any length of time. Conditions always

turned bizarrely difficult. Even vinyl would rot—a situation difficult to reproduce anywhere else. All accounts agreed on a similar tone that something was not quite right and that the place filled visitors with a sense of foreboding.

This was even before the double murders of Mac and Muff Graham in 1974. Muff's remains were washed up on the beach a few years later. Her body had been burned, dismembered, stuffed into a metal cargo box, weighted, and sunk offshore. Mac Graham's remains remain unfound. Prosecutor Vince Bugliosi wrote a book, *And the Sea Will Tell*, about prosecuting the murder case against Buck Walker for the double murders.

🦇   🦇   🦇

"So," I said, as Zotz finally began to wind down, "does this island have hatches in the ground with underground bunkers?"

He nodded. "Yeah. It was a Naval installation, remember? There are still all kinds of gear and outbuildings supposed to be there. Gun emplacements . . . runway . . . causeway . . . roads . . . ammo dumps . . . "

"Polar bears?" I asked. "Smoke monster?"

"What? Oh. I get it. Like the TV show." He snapped his fingers. As they were webbed the sound was rather unpleasant. "Maybe Palmyra was part of the inspiration for the writers."

"Well, it sure wasn't *Gilligan's Island*. What about the other two coordinates?"

He shook his misshapen head. "This may or may not be the weirdest part . . . "

"Oh goody."

"There was this Indiana Jones-type guy," Zotz continued, "back around the turn of the last century. Globetrotter, archeologist-without-portfolio, obsessive whack job: had these outlandish theories about aliens and ancient archeology."

"Chariots of the Gods?"

"More like Dragsters of the Damned. This guy claimed to have discovered the ruins of giant alien civilizations—in Europe, the Middle East, Asia—even the Antarctic. He'd fire off these long, rambling dispatches to Derleth—"

"Derleth?"

"August Derleth. Editor of the *The Capital Times* in Madison, Wisconsin. He was the only newspaper editor who took Lovecraft's communiqués seriously."

"Lovecraft," I said.

Zotz nodded. "Howard Phillips Lovecraft. Died young. Official story was cancer."

I grunted. "Brain tumor?"

"Naw. Intestinal cancer. Though one rumor was he was insane when he died. Another that, whatever he was hunting, it found him first."

"So, what was he hunting?"

"An ancient city. A big, bad-ass alien city built a million years ago."

"More ruins?"

"That's just it. Some of his dispatches talk of this city like it's an ancient tomb. Yet others suggest that it's still inhabited. He got the backing of Derleth and the paper to take a tramp steamer down to the South Pacific to look for it."

"Sounds like a nice vacation," I observed.

"No, I mean the *southern* South Pacific. Down closer to the Antarctic. Bit nippy. Anyways, no islands at the first set of coordinates, *47°9' S 126°43' W*, so Derleth radioed a second set to explore while he was in the area: *49°51' S 128°34' W*. They're fairly close together—in the global sense—and way off the regular shipping lanes."

"And?" I prompted.

"Nada. Nothing. Empty ocean. Even today's satellite maps show nothing's there. On the surface anyways. But underneath? These two locations linked to the first set of coordinates for your fictional Lincoln Island form a triangle that covers a good portion of the Eltanin Fracture Zone of the South Pacific. A strange series of seismic events involving intense T waves was recorded back in the early nineties and again earlier this year."

I looked at him.

"And that's it. That's all I've got. Four global chart coordinates and only one correlation to an actual land mass. It's not like I had a lot of time to do the research but it's not like there's a lot of info available on the base data. Four sets of coordinates; one tiny, pretty much deserted island. You want more? You gotta give me wider search parameters. And an internet connection. And more time."

"Okay, Lincoln Island," I mused, "was part of a dormant volcano—fictional, of course—but if Lovecraft and Derleth had any actual intel on their two locations, undersea volcanoes would certainly account for the rapid appearance and or disappearance of a land mass at sea."

"And Palmyra," Zotz added, "is actually an atoll, rather than an island by classification."

"So, it's the remains of an extinct, collapsed volcano?"

He nodded. "A crescent-shaped remainder of the original cone and several islets."

"Okay," I said. "We've got four sets of coordinates located in the Pacific Ocean. One is for a real island—or atoll. With a spooky history. One is for a fictional island that never existed outside of the pages of a science fiction novel . . ."

"As far as we know," Zotz interjected.

"What?"

"Well, just because there's nothing there now, doesn't mean there wasn't at one time. You just pointed out that undersea volcanoes—"

"It was a sci-fi novel! A pretty good sci-fi novel but fiction, just the same. Verne wrote about fictional people on a fictional island! The submarine didn't even exist, yet!"

Zotz shook his head. "Not true. Dutch inventor Cornelius Drebbel built the first navigable submarine in 1620 based on Englishman William Bourne's designs from the 1570s. You Americans were experimenting with submersible vessels well before Verne's fictional *Nautilus*. Bushnell's *Turtle* was invented in 1775 and employed in the Revolutionary War. And the Civil War saw the development of two Confederate subs, the *David* and the *Hunley*, and one Union submersible, the *Intelligent Whale*."

"The *Hunley* was the only submersible to ever successfully sink a target," I interrupted, "if you can call an unintentionally kamikaze mission 'successful.' I see you really have been doing research and not just spending all of your online time smut surfing. But the bottom line is there wasn't anything like the *Nautilus* until the last century."

Zotz shook his head again. "The fact that there isn't an island there now doesn't prove that there wasn't an island there then . . . anymore than the fact that there wasn't a submarine like the *Nautilus* then proves that Verne was writing of fictional events."

"Wow," I said. "I know I'm tired and distracted and my brain is probably co-opted by all my nanos giving me a hive five . . . but I'm just not up to debating your impeccable logic on that one."

He shrugged. "Thought you'd learned by now to keep an open mind."

"Okay. One known 'island,' three patches of empty ocean—at present—for the other sets of coordinates. The only common threads are that all are placed in the mid to southern expanse of the Pacific Ocean with the possible criteria of volcanoes, past or present. And one scary lady's voodoo altar." I looked at Zotz. "What does it mean?"

Zotz's inhuman features tightened into an implacable knot. "It means we run down to the Big Easy and make a certain close-mouthed fortune-teller tell us what it's all about."

"Good luck," I said, remembering her reticence on the entire subject matter.

"You mean on getting her to talk? Or taking a shallow-draft houseboat down the Ouachita, Red, and Mississippi rivers, all the way down to the Gulf and finding her in the middle of a monster tropical storm—if she isn't already blown up in a hundred different directions and into a hundred different dimensions?"

"There is that," I said.

Dawn was still hours away when, one by one, the stars began to go out.

There wasn't a visible cloud in the sky so the effect was a little end-of-the-worldish.

The marine-band radio was busy with reports of a category one hurricane forming out in the Gulf of Mexico but spared time for a mention of volcanic eruptions along the Pacific Rim of Fire. Apparently Mother Earth was convulsing big time, blasting billions of tons of ash into the Earth's upper stratosphere and mesosphere. A nice, scientific explanation but it did little to dispel the eldritch effect of the rest of the universe disappearing into endless darkness.

When sunrise finally came it was nothing more than a red smear on the horizon. Continental shelves of cumulous clouds rolled up from the south like airborne glaciers. The sky turned the color of an ancient tin roof. Down in the Gulf, Hurricane Eibon had ramped up to a category two.

The Ouachita was still running relatively smooth and the *New Moon* was making headway at twelve knots. When I had purchased my home upon the water she'd come equipped with a pair of Mercruiser 180 hp engines that gave her a cruising speed of seven knots on one motor or a full running speed of eight knots using both. One rarely races houseboats and since running both engines doubles the fuel consumption while only yielding an additional one-point-one-mile-per-hour increase in speed, I could have done the sensible thing and left the whole package alone.

I am not a sailor. I am a guy who values a quick getaway and the ability to outrun things that the local law enforcement types—police, fire department, coast guard—are typically unprepared to protect you against.

So I had the original engines replaced. Had bigger, badder, more powerful props and motors squeezed into the chassis. As expensive as the new engines were, the dry-dock charges and rehabbing cost me even more.

As I said, I'm not a sailor: they saw me coming. After all was said and done I discovered that my new engines were theoretically capable of pushing the *New Moon*'s equivalent weight and mass at better than 20 knots. But the houseboat's draft and overall displacement would only tolerate eleven—and only under ideal conditions, thirteen to fourteen—knots before becoming "unmanageable." I could say "unstable" but that's more descriptive of what would happen if I pushed it to sixteen. Forget the *Proud Mary*; the *New Moon* would redefine the phrase *"rollin'* on the river!"

At this speed it would take me better than three days to thread the river traffic, switchbacks, locks, and obstacle-laden watercourses between the Ouachita and the lower Mississippi. Not taking into account fueling stops, mechanical cool-downs, or the mitigating effects of bad weather.

And God help us if we encountered any more boarding parties along the way.

No, I needed an alternate means of locomotion. Going ashore seemed to be our only option, even if the return trip was guaranteed to be a nightmare due to the choked evacuation routes.

But first we had to lose our furry "tails."

Every attempt to swing in close to either side of the river during the night had been met by a series of howls and a gathering wolf pack along the shore. Any hope of daylight providing a solution was dispelled as a trio of pickup trucks was revealed off our starboard side, pacing us on the levee road. I almost didn't need the binoculars to see that the "human" occupants had a decidedly unshaven, lupine look. And the "hunting dogs" grinning from the back beds left no doubt as to *their* true pedigree. We kept to the center channel, mindful of cab-mounted gun racks and overhead bridges.

"Go below and get some sleep," Zotz said as I took another quarter turn around the upper helm. He was nearly human-looking now in deference to the growing odds of daylight traffic on the river.

"We should take turns," I said.

"I don't sleep. I'm a magical construct. You, however, are starting to look like a cross between Death warmed over and something stuck under those infrared lamps on the back counter at a third-rate burger joint."

I shook my head. "I thought we would have shaken them by now. We need a better plan than putt-putting down the meandering waterways of Louisiana's scenic vistas."

"You have something against traveling by water?" Liban's voice asked from my feet. Her head appeared as she climbed the steps from the lower deck.

"We're moving too slow," I explained as she stepped up to join us. "We need to go ashore."

"Your enemies are ashore," she said. "You're safer on the water."

I snorted. "Until the Fabulous Finny Freak Brothers show up again. Or Carpet'o'Slime. Or Mysterious Underwater Light. The point is I can travel more quickly by car than by boat. Here, we have no maneuvering room. Silas's crew doesn't have to keep us in sight at all times; they only need to follow the river, monitor the forks, and wait for us to make landfall. But the bottom line is speed. The river doesn't travel in a straight line and we're not geared for speed."

Her eyes swept the river's course to the horizon. "What if you were?"

"What?"

"Geared for speed?"

I frowned. "I don't follow you."

"But if you do follow me, I can open a way that may solve some of our problems."

"Uh," I said. Somewhere behind the question of just what she was getting at was the issue of how "my" problems had become "our" problems.

"I *am* a sea goddess," Liban continued. "Unlike my sister, I still have power over water. If we were sailing upon the ocean I could open a path through the sea that would turn months into weeks, weeks into days, days into hours. Although the ocean is my elemental demesne, a tributary is not so alien as it is confining."

I stared at her. "Can you open a path to New Orleans?"

"I can but try."

"Great! Let's get started!"

She shook her head. "I must rest, first. Rest and prepare."

"Now there's a smart idea," Zotz rasped. "She rests. You rest. Everybody's fresh when we hit the Big Sleazy."

"Why don't you give it a rest?" I growled.

"I'm a magical construct," he beamed, "I don't need to rest. But you're overdue, Mr. Grumpypants. Go down below, get reacquainted with your bunk, and make sure you're not running on empty the next time you have to exert yourself. I've got it all covered up here but I promise to call if the scenery changes."

I gazed out to the south where the land was cloaked in distant darkness. A yellowed thread of lightning winked at the edge of the horizon. "I don't know if I can sleep . . ."

A hand fumbled for mine: Liban's.

"Come, rest with me."

I looked back at her face and saw what it cost her to swallow her pride and offer herself for a second round of rejection. To a mortal. With a demon as witness.

Damned pheromones!

I opened my mouth but no words would come out.

You think it's easy saying no to a faerie queen? An elven sea goddess? A woman whose beauty made the concept of "no" practically unthinkable?

Practically, but—even though Lupé had pretty much cut me loose this past year and even though our future was uncertain given the incompatibility of our body chemistries—I wasn't an emotional free agent, here. I was on my way to rescue the mother of my unborn son. And Deirdre was somewhere in the mix. And it wouldn't be fair—to anyone but especially her—to complicate things emotionally, now.

No matter how unthinkable "no" might seem to our super-amped, hormone-drenched response systems.

Still, given the fact that her mental/emotional/ biochemical gestalt was being seriously destabilized by yours truly, I owed her better than another smack to her self-esteem.

And, from the purely practical, almost clinical point of view, rejecting a powerful ally whose contributions might make all the difference between saving my friends and family and arriving too late—well, bit of a horned and horny dilemma here.

All that aside, it wasn't the uncertainty over what to say that was preventing words from coming out of my mouth.

Something seemed to have severed the synapses connecting my brain to my vocal chords!

Maybe I was having a stroke! The top of my head felt funny. Numb . . . tingly . . . squirmy . . . ?

"Holy cow, Uncle Martin!" Zotz exclaimed.

I reached up and felt twin rods emerging from the top of my skull. I turned on wobbly legs and caught sight of my reflection in the portside mirror for the helm. Silver stems that were dead ringers for an old set of rabbit-ears antenna had telescoped out of my scalp and now crowned me like a silver V.

I had just enough time to reflect on two things.

One, that Ray Walston looked just like this on *My Favorite Martian* every time he invoked his extraterrestrial powers. And two, right after his antennae came up, he turned invisible.

And that's when I turned invisible.

Well, to be more accurate, everything turned invisible.

Here's the thing . . .

I never really was much of a clubber. And once you settle down, get married, have a kid—well, staying out till two or three in the morning just drops off the options list.

Now a lot of undead are drawn to the late-night club "life." It gives them a sense of community, something to do together to fight off that creeping ennui that won't go away as the decades and then the centuries mount up. And open clubs provide open hunting grounds for those too lazy to stalk their prey far afield.

Of course, that cuts both ways: I'd briefly reacquainted myself with the club scene on a few occasions when I'd gone hunting the hunters after Jenny and Kirsten died. Vampires hunt humans at certain clubs so vampire hunters hunt the vampires there, as well. Seriously, at least one bouncer per club should be trained as a game warden.

All that aside, I couldn't, for the life of me, figure out why I was standing in line outside of a Hindi nightclub with the soundtrack from some Bollywood musical pumping up the volume through the open doors. *Merrick's* flashed on and off in tubular neon over an arched doorway that tapered upwards to a point. Electric sitars and tanpura twanged and danced, violins and sarangi sang and wailed, tablas and pakhawajs thumped and boomed: the music was ancient, primal, the beat was vaguely disco. Somewhere in the back of my mind was this nagging impression that I had more important things to do at the moment.

Anything else to do at the moment . . .

The line moved and I found myself confronted by the doorman. He was a big gorilla and looked me over to decide whether or not I passed the entrance exam. I looked back.

It's sort of a stereotype to refer to club bouncers and door men as "gorillas" as they tend to be big, no-neck, missing-link types who will shake your tree if you give them half an excuse. But this guy was really an ape! Half monkey, half man, he wore a Hugo Boss three-button, red-black pinstripe suite. Gold cuff links with the letter "H" encrusted in diamonds flashed at his hairy wrists. I got a good look as his inhumanly long arm came down like a railroad crossing gate.

"Invitation?"

I looked up at the peculiar scar on his chin. *Invitation? To what? Where was I? What was I doing here?*

Just beyond his unfamiliar monkey mug a more familiar, less anthropomorphic profile appeared. The giant barrel-monster for the seafood lover in you appeared in the doorway, waving tentacles and eyestalks and flexing its centrally spaced, leathery wings.

"Let it in, Hanuman," said the not-quite-Winky voice. "It is summoned."

The gorillalike arm was removed from my path with a sigh. "Very well. I have nothing against ecumenicalism, you understand, but with the fate of the world hanging in the balance . . . "

"We are all Outsiders here, godling. Only those who inhabit the Prime Plane can contest for it when the Devourers come. Either they will prove themselves cattle and seal their fates," starfish head said, backing into the darkened interior. "**Or contend for their place among the stars as have those of us which have come before.**"

I wasn't keen on going forward. As I said before, what the hell was I doing in line at a raga rock nightclub? And, not real invested on following Tubby Tentacles into a strange, dark building. Monkeyman's parting shot was no confidence booster, either. "If all of our hopes reside in the demon shade of one of our lost supplicants and a clueless unbeliever," he said, "then I fear all is lost before it is well begun . . . "

Unfortunately, dream states come with their own sets of internal rules and compulsions: I was into the building and out of earshot before he was finished.

The entryway was a long, dark corridor that turned this way and that, becoming a pipeline of sound with thrashing electric neo-Hindi music pounding out a beat while occasional bursts of light indicated a destination of sorts, ahead.

I came out into an immense, black room whose walls and ceiling were tricked out in vast patterns of stars. It was the best disco-ball effect I had ever seen: it was as if I was standing out in the midst of the cosmos, surrounded by the endless depths of the universe. As the stars slowly revolved, the occasional comet and momentary meteor stuttered by. Such was the nature of the illusion that a room that could barely accommodate a hundred clubbers appeared as if it could contain tens of thousands with room to spare.

Surprisingly, the other clubgoers had wandered off into other rooms: only one other dancer was out on the floor at the moment. And, rather than be intimidated by the cavernous room, he owned the dance floor. Spinning and stomping and gliding and shaking, he threw himself into the music with a passion and intensity that was positively breathtaking.

And then I noticed the tentacle growing out of his misshapen face!

Crap! One thing on top of another and now this: apparently *Dead Can Dance!*

And now tentacle-puss was dancing my way.

I looked around: vast black room, lit by hundreds of thousands of pinpricks of light. No obvious exits. I didn't have a clue as to which way to run. Maybe I could sucker-punch him while he was still doing the Monster Mash. . . .

But as he shimmied closer I got a better look at his serpentine schnoz. It wasn't a tentacle. It was a trunk. An elephant's trunk. Dancing boy looked human from the shoulders down but, from the neck up, he was sporting an elephant's head.

I checked the ears: Indian, not African, elephant's head. And missing a tusk.

Okay, not Gnarly-ho-tep or squidhead.

But dangerous?

It was hard to think evil of a creature who seemed to be having so much damned fun dancing! The only way I could feel threatened was if I'd brought my girlfriend along and was trying to impress her with my own moves.

Elephant head danced up and bowed to me without missing a step of the beat.

"Bloodbender, I greet you and ask you to join me in the Celestial Dance."

Okaaayyyy. "And you are . . . ?"

He—it—smiled and shrugged. "I forget that you are technically an infidel. I have many names. You may call me Ganesh."

"I like it better when you go by Kankiten," said a new voice.

An Asian gentleman strode into the nearest spotlight and stood, considering the two of us. Unlike dancing boy, who favored saffron robes and what looked like platform-soled Guccis, the new arrival looked more of a sartorial match with the simian bouncer. The lighting made it hard to distinguish details so I was guessing the suit was most likely Louis Vuitton or Giorgio Armani. A short sword threw off the tailored lines of his suitcoat: the scabbard on his belt pushed back the left flap of his jacket to show a doubled-edged, straight-bladed Bronze Age short sword rather than the curved katana one might typically associate with his genetic antecedents.

"Susanowo-no-mikoto!" the elephant man trilled. "How auspicious of you to join us! Come, dance, and we shall speak of that which must be done before the music ends."

"Bah! Your one piece is in play on the board," Susanowo answered gruffly. "I still have hundreds more to bring into play! I have volcanoes to unplug!" He turned on his heel and strode off into the darkness.

"Give my regards to your lovely sister," disco boy called after him. He turned to me. "Too bad we couldn't get Amaterasu Omikami more intimately involved."

"Yeah," I said. "Too bad about that."

"Oh, my dear boy," he chuckled, "you're attempting to have me on a bit." He shook his head. "Won't work, you know. I'm a god."

"Yeah. Well. I hate to be rude and all, but not really into the gods thing. Never was a polytheist and starting to question the monotheist proposal these days."

"Well, we won't quibble over semantics, dear boy. Just think of me as a higher power. One of a number who are invested in the good of the world."

"Judging by the evening news, there can't be that many of you—or you're just not that powerful."

He chuckled, still keeping the beat as he danced and conversed at the same time. "You and Dakkar—so much anger and cynicism. Yet the two of you may be our best hope. Yin and yang. Again, like a dance. Come," he extended a hand to me. "In the dance are the greater truths revealed."

Like I said, not much for clubbing these days. And I was never one for being dragged out on the dance floor by strange men. Not a homophobe, I have gay friends but, come on: a guy with the head of an elephant? I stood there with my arms folded across my chest and waited, figuring someone owed me some answers before I took another step.

But, dammit, I was tapping my foot along with the rhythm and dancing boy's joie de vivre was so freaking infectious!

"Dance, Bloodbender!" Ganesh or Kankiten or John Merrick cried. "Dance and live! Life is dancing! Dancing is life. Even the very atoms dance so that worlds might be. The soul must dance or the soul dies. The universe must dance or creation dies. Entropy. Heat death. The final, empty, cold blackness of nothing—that is the end of the dance. For you or for a thousand billion souls. So dance and hold back the cold and the darkness!"

"What? Are we talking sympathetic magic, here?" I growled. But I was already twitching along to the beat as I spoke.

Ganesh grabbed my hand and jerked me toward him. I had to sidestep to avoid a collision and he turned my hand at the wrist, pulling my arm up, and I found myself executing a pirouette as he released on the follow-through. I had to step very deliberately to keep from stumbling and, the next thing I knew, we were dancing side by side. That's when I noticed he had four arms instead of just two.

"I don't have time for this," I muttered.

"Look," elephant guy gestured. Across the stars-spangled dance floor "stood" the double-starfish-barrel-stacked rutabaga. "*They* don't dance. That is why they could not ultimately prevail."

"Oh. Well, then," I puffed. "I think we're screwed, then. You need John Travolta or Patrick Swayze or Michael Jackson, even."

"It is not you, alone, but the gestalt. The unification of those lives and talents that you and only you can unite in this moment in time. They are drawn to you in ways that higher powers such as ourselves could not hope to emulate. Only to harness. And lend what poor assistance that we can. You must overcome your own entropy in the face of doubt. Act intuitively! Trust your impulses!"

Oh yeah. Sure. Now there's a good idea: acting on all of my impulses. Let's see where that would lead. One, probably ripping out a fair number of throats on a weekly basis. Two, more than likely fathering the student enrollment for half the Montessori schools in the city. Three,

expressing my political sentiments by affixing a hang-
man's noose to every streetlamp within a three-block
radius of the Washington Capitol building . . .

Impulse control is, by and large, an underappreci-
ated virtue.

"No, Sweet Infidel, you must trust in something
greater than Fear, greater than Anger or Despair. Trust
in Joy! Come and dance!"

"I have things to do," I growled. "Family to
rescue . . ."

"Oh, far more than that, dear mouse. You have a world
to save!"

"I don't care about the world. I care about my family.
In spite of the changes to my preternatural biology I still
feel something for them, at least. For a while longer.
And, as long as it matters to me, I'll be investing in that,
thank you. Not a bunch of strangers who don't know
me. And would probably pick up a stake or a torch if
they did."

"Nevertheless," Ganesh/Kankiten countered, "Fate
has anointed you our Champion. If you would save your
family, you must save the world."

"Find somebody else," I growled.

"It has been tried. My colleagues have reactivated history's greatest souls, hoping one or more might echo
the Mahabharata's promise of a Deliverer. One of them
travels with you even now."

"Who? Cuchulainn? Whoa, if you're profiling badass
brawlers you've got to know I'm not it!"

Four-armed elephant guy shook his oversized head.
"Not my choice. But significant that he found his way to
your side."

"Oh yeah, the Army could take recruiting lessons from me."

"And then there is your affiliation with the Peri."

"What? The elves?"

"And the legions of dead who follow you from below."

"Sorry, totally not getting the fishfolk tie-in."

"Which is why I am sending you the one who was once Dakkar. He will be Kevat to your Rama and ferry you to your destiny."

"Rama?" I arched an eyebrow.

"It is a metaphor," he said mildly. "I doubt he will want to wash your feet."

"Rama-lama-ding-dong," I muttered.

"You mock what you do not understand."

I nodded. "That's right. I'd keep the hero job search open awhile longer if I were you." I kept nodding along to the beat. *Damn.* "Now if it's all the same to you, I've got a boat to catch."

"Yes. Yes, you do. Just remember, most heroes don't seek the quest, the quest seeks them. And sometimes it is the single word rather than the grand gesture that tips the balance of the world. Even now, Dakkar tries too hard. He is still a man of Science, even is his latest incarnation. What is needed is a man of Faith."

"Yeah, well," I said, "good luck with that."

"You are that man."

"Help me, Obi-Wan; you're our only hope."

Elephant guy blinked. "I do not understand."

"At last, something we agree on! Look, Horton, I'm sure you meant what you said and you said what you meant, but I'm totally interested like zero percent. You and the elves and the big barrel of monster parts are all babbling about sacrifices and transformations and saving the world like it's some kind of special privilege to go toe to toe with some giant Nightmare from the Phantom Zone. Well, I've got my own problems. If I was totally invested in the monster-killing business, I'd have to start with me. Then there's the fact that most of my closest friends are now nightmares in their own right. I don't know if I can even get to and rescue the people who mean the most to me in time. Every time I turn around, my own body seems to be booby-trapped and turning me into Inspector Gadget. So, from a practical perspective, I really don't see what I can do for you or for the rest of the world, right now."

"You can dance," he said.

"What good will that do me?"

"Close your eyes and see where the celestial music takes you."

Well, like I said, dream states have their own internal sets of rules and compulsions: I closed my eyes and abandoned myself to the beat. It beat talking nonsense to Ali Babar. The music swept me up and disoriented me. I felt as though I were tipping over, yet never falling. Dancing sideways and on my back. Twisting, hips thrusting to the beat. Sinuous and swaying, stepping on air and surrendering to a tidal wave of pleasure, rolling me over and over in my head . . .

. . . in my bed.

I sat up feeling the top of my head. The silver antennae were gone. I looked down: so was my clothing. The sheets were rumpled and half off the bed. The pillow was halfway across the cabin on the floor.

The shower was running on the other side of the door to the head.

I looked down and touched myself where the swelling had started to subside. I was sticky.

"Oh crap," I whispered. "I think I've been had!"

Chapter Fifteen

I FINALLY GOT OUT of bed and started toward the sound of the shower, trying to formulate the exact wording of the questions I needed to ask. If I had been . . . well . . . violated . . . by a beautiful faerie queen and elven sea goddess while unconscious, I had to articulate the issues without sounding either pathetic or stupid. And given their known mythology on the issues of child abduction, I doubted the Sidhe had any cultural concept of "date rape."

Before I could reach the head a pounding on my cabin door diverted me. "Better get out here," Setanta's muffled voice announced, "it's bad!"

If the Hound of Ulster, the warrior prince who defied elves and gods and fought whole armies single-handedly says something is bad, you don't play Twenty Questions on the other side of a closed door. I freshened up with what was at hand and dressed quickly. The shower was still running as I left my cabin and came out into the scorched ruin of the salon.

The TV was on some local station as we were running down the river and couldn't keep the satellite dish oriented. A newscaster was standing in a tropical downpour, shouting something unintelligible into his microphone. The term "downpour" was somewhat of a misnomer as the thick, heavy raindrops were zipping across the screen diagonally, upper right to lower left corners. The trees in the background were bowed by the force of the wind and debris flashed by in intermittent peekaboo bursts of leaves and scraps and paper bags and cups.

The abrupt transition back to the newsroom was all the more jarring by the contrast of the quiet, well-lit room and perfectly coiffed anchor seated behind the desk. "Again, the National Weather Center has no explanation for these phenomena. It was announced just thirty minutes ago that Hurricane Eibon has jumped from a category two to a category four hurricane, its wind speeds increasing from over ninety miles an hour to nearly one hundred and forty. Furthermore, the latest satellite imagery shows that the storm has continued to grow and pick up speed and we are anticipating landfall within the hour. All evacuees are being advised to abandon their vehicles and seek shelter in a basement or reinforced structure if they are within fifty miles of New Orleans.

"While the wind damage from a category four storm is of great concern, it is New Orleans' position between the Mississippi River and Lake Pontchartrain that has most disaster experts worried. Following Hurricane Betsy in 1963, the levees and floodwalls surrounding the city and outlying parishes were raised to heights of fourteen to twenty-three feet. Unfortunately, the construction design is only guaranteed to withstand a category three storm. Congress failed to fully fund an upgrade requested during the 1990s by the Army Corps of Engineers. Funding was cut in 2003 and 2004 despite a 2001 study by the Federal Emergency Management Agency warning that a hurricane striking New Orleans was among the three most likely catastrophes to befall the country in the future . . . "

Setanta shook his head. "What fools these mortals be!"

I cleared my throat. "Yeah, well, estimates to reinforce the levees to resist category five forces put the total cost at twenty-five billion dollars and maybe twenty-five years to complete the job. Which puts the twenty-five billion dollar estimate into low-ball territory. Factor in the Big Easy's long history of graft, corruption, malfeasance, and downright incompetence, well, no one's keen on throwing good money after bad."

"New Orleans flood control measures," the news guy continued, "include more than 520 miles of levees, 270 floodgates, 92 pumping stations, and thousands of miles of drainage canals. It is the price of living in a city on the edge of the ocean that sits below sea level. And since its pumping stations are below sea level as well, a catastrophic breach would pretty much be the end."

"What does that mean?" Setanta puzzled.

"It means," I explained with a sinking sensation, "that the city sits inside a bowl. And the bottom of that bowl is lower than the water outside of the bowl. If water finds a way to start coming into the bowl really fast, the pumps at the bottom of the bowl will end up underwater faster than they can pump it back out. Which means the pumps stop working—like maybe forever. And the bowl fills all the way up until the water inside the bowl is at the same level as the water outside of the bowl."

". . . estimates place property damages could potentially reach twenty-five billion dollars . . ."

"Hence the gamble," I said, "of spending the twenty-five really-large for sure or crossing everyone's collective fingers that the damages will be less in the long run."

". . . and 25,000 to 100,000 deaths by drowning," concluded the news anchor.

Cuchulainn shook his head. "Madness!"

I nodded. "You bet. At least it ain't Tokyo."

"Tokyo?" He looked bewildered.

"Giant radioactive monsters."

"Really?"

I nodded again. "And Raymond Burr."

🦇 🦇 🦇

It was an act of madness.

Crazy enough to try to take a houseboat down the Mississippi. Oh, it could be done but we were neither rigged nor rated for the trip. But, more importantly, we'd run out of time. Unfortunately, the solution to that problem was an even greater act of madness.

Liban was going to open a path to the sea. To a point just offshore of the Port of New Orleans.

Right smack dab in the middle of a category four, soon-to-be category five, hurricane.

"Maybe not," she said, not quite meeting my eyes. She hadn't quite met my eyes since I'd discovered her topside, discussing the coming logistics with Camazotz at the *New Moon*'s helm.

On the one hand I wanted to confront her, grab her and shake her, demand to know if I'd been taken advantage of while unconscious (and dancing up a storm). On the other hand, it seemed a bit unseemly to make accusations without more concrete evidence of some kind of "crime." And if there was a culprit, might it not be pheromone-enhanced moi who may have driven her (albeit unintentionally) to act so precipitously? It was a very precarious blame game if one were to start rolling the dice.

And, seeing as how we might all be dead very soon, such lesser issues seemed rather non-starters. Survive the next forty-eight hours and then have a little movie review of *While You Were Sleeping*.

"What do you mean: 'maybe not'?" I asked her.

"Opening a path through the sea moves us through time as well as space. The greater the distance, the more time will pass. I do not know what will happen when I try to open a path from a tributary to the sea. The circumlocutions of land may bend such elements in unforeseeable ways." Now she looked up at me and there was fear in her sea-green eyes.

They said Captain Ahab was an obsessed madman when he risked his ship and his crew in pursuit of Moby Dick. Well, I wasn't chasing a great white whale, I was racing the storm of the century to rescue my family from the flood, the monsters, and, just maybe, the end of the world.

"I'm going to New Orleans and I mean to get there as quickly and by any means possible," I said.

"This will be very dangerous," she said. "If the path itself brings us through safely, we may perish upon arrival."

I nodded. "Help me," I said softly. "Or get out of the way and off my boat."

She stared up at me. Nodded. Then pulled a strand of pearls from the multiple bands of gems, coins, corals, and shells that hung from her neck and offered a modicum of modesty where her neoprene jacket gaped open. "Here." She dropped the necklace over my head and adjusted it, tucking it into my shirt. "Do not remove this while we travel. It will keep us linked inside the pathway." She turned to Zotz and presented him with a necklace of gold coins from her décolletage. "And you as well, Sir Demon. You must be able to follow me ere you be lost in the 'tween."

And, with that, she stepped out from under the awning and moved to the railing overlooking the bow.

The skies had turned the color of oily guncotton and a sharp, pelting rain had begun to fall. The canvas awning above our heads turned the impact of each drop into a snare-drum report, as sharp as a whip crack against leather. Liban had left the helm's limited shelter and was exposed to the bitter shower. In moments her hair was plastered to the sides and back of her head. Only her orange wetsuit protected her from a further drenching.

"Here's an idea," Zotz murmured, *sotto voce*, "why don't you steer while I go hold an umbrella over the lady?"

Before I could think of a suitable reply, a wind sprang up. Even though I couldn't feel it, I saw Liban's dark tresses stir, lift from her head and shoulders, and stream back from her face. She reached down and unzipped the orange neoprene jacket and shrugged it from her shoulders. As the top half of her wetsuit slid down her back and off of her arms, the clouds parted just enough for the sun to strike her with a stray beam of light. Her pearlescent skin began to glow.

All around us it was still gloomy and the rain continued to fall. Curtains of darkness swept the river ahead indicating we were headed into heavier weather. But Liban stood bathed in light and her hair was a flag of mahogany and moss, wafting in an unseen breeze.

And now it seemed that the rain was not even touching her. She stood as if in a bubble of sunshiny, summer day while all about her the world was sinking into storm-tossed darkness.

She climbed up on the railing and balanced precariously. As she did, something happened to the lower half of her wetsuit. A pattern began to emerge and the material took on a shinier appearance. She flexed her knees and I shouted as she jumped.

Dove, actually: her leap propelled her forward and she leaned out, her arms coming up as she formed herself into a fleshy torpedo. She cleared the forward deck below by a good seven feet even with the *New Moon*'s forward momentum as a nonnegotiable factor, and sliced into the water ahead of us. I ran to the railing and looked down.

All around the boat the water was dark and blackish green. A short distance off, the river was just black.

Directly in front of the boat, however, was a patch of blue. Water the color of turquoise and azure. Water you only find between virgin beaches and reefs untouched by human·industrialization down in tropical paradises.

Improbably, the blue began to stain the water ahead of us . . .

"Steer for the blue," I said.

"What?" Zotz yelled.

The engine noise alone was enough to make us raise our voices. But a growing sound of thunder was making the twin Mercruisers seem quiet by comparison.

"Steer for the blue water!" I yelled back.

"You sure?" he answered. And pointed at the spreading blue stain.

We were well into the turquoise waves now and the surface turbulence was markedly different. The surface was calm while dark green waves crashed in the distance off of our port and starboard sides. There seemed to be no break in the clouds above us but the rain was no longer striking the boat and our immediate surroundings brightened considerably as if the sun had come out directly overhead.

But Zotz wasn't pointing at where we were.

He was pointing up ahead.

A little less than a mile downriver the Ouachita took a sharp bend to the left.

The blue stain continued straight on into the bank.

"Are you ready to do a *Fitzcarraldo*?" my demon helmsman asked me.

"Slow down!" I yelled. "Give me time to think!"

And don't run us into the bank with the throttle wide open.

I studied the blue stain that was supposed to be our "path to the sea." As it approached the bend in the river, the turquoise strip widened and shaded a deeper, darker blue. It was still easily visible in contrast to the dirty green and black waters of the rest of the river. All around us those darker waves rose higher and grew more turbulent: we glided between them as if riding through a sheltered trough.

"Cut back on the throttle!" I yelled as the riverbank loomed nearer.

"I did!" Zotz yelled back.

I couldn't tell from the sound of the engines. The continuous roaring of thunder drowned out practically everything else. And, if anything, we were going faster, now. The shoreline loomed ahead . . . *and above!*

We were sliding down into a trough between giant waves, great looming walls of water to either side. But instead of bobbing back up again with the natural undulation of the swell, we kept going down! The trough became a tunnel and the *New Moon* slid down beneath the storm, beneath the river, down, down into a sapphire water slide that easily dwarfed the Lincoln Tunnel. Water closed above our heads forming a curved aqua ceiling.

I squeezed in next to Zotz and flipped switches for the running lights and the forward spot which I directed into the water-walled tube ahead of us. The tunnel ahead twisted and turned off into darkness but no other features were readily apparent. No rocks, obstructions, visible hazards of any sort. And no evidence of Liban. Not that it made a lot of difference at this point: we had no choice but to follow where the tunnel led. At the moment we weren't even traveling under our own power—a lucky break, actually, as a refueling stop was working its way to the top of our priorities list.

The next switch I threw was for the GPS screen. It lit with a gray, hissing radiance. No multicolored chart displays, no boat icon to indicate our position on river, lake, or inlet. Just frantic oatmeal magma churning in actinic black, gray, and white. Looking at the static-filled screen stirred an unpleasant memory—something from my childhood or, perhaps, in a dream . . .

Zotz reached over and switched off the GPS. "I wouldn't trust anything that did show up on that screen right now," he said.

Setanta eventually heaved his way up the ladder from below looking decidedly green. I didn't think his coloring was entirely due to odd light within the confines of our watery tunnel. The houseboat was riding the curved walls of the liquid chute like a bobsled on ball bearings, skittering up one slope and then down and over and up the other side. I was starting to feel a little green, myself.

" 'Tis an unnatural way for mortals to travel," Goldilocks groused, grabbing the handrail at the top of the ladder as the boat swayed and swung again.

"Beats flying," Zotz growled back. "Give me water, any day."

I wasn't about to point out that traveling by means of an inside-out water hose via trans-dimensional vortices hardly qualified as "sailing." For the moment I was wholly invested in holding on tight and hoping our water-walled conduit didn't collapse or produce something otherworldly. . . .

That's when the ghost of the alien rutabaga with the starfish appendages and the Winky Dink voice materialized in front of us.

"Okay," I said, "tell me you guys see that."

They looked around. And then they both looked at me. Setanta grinned. "You have horns!"

"Naw, they're antennae," Zotz corrected. "Rabbit ears. Not even UHF. You should really talk to your nanos about upgrading to dish." He squinted at me. "You're not going to pass out again, are you?"

I pointed at the alien monstrosity floating directly ahead of us. "You're telling me you don't see barrel of seafood tripe floating in thin air?"

"You're gonna have to catch him," Zotz told Cuch. "I can't let go of the wheel."

"I am not delirious!" I insisted. As soon as I said it I wasn't so sure, myself.

"Fine. But would sitting down be such a bad thing under the circumstances?"

"Anything to keep you from shapeshifting into my mother," I groused at the demon as Setanta escorted me back to one of the bolted-down deck chairs. The giant rutabaga followed.

Once I was settled I shooed the big Celt away. "I'm fine! Just going to sit here. Enjoy the ride! Chat with my imaginary friend! Go! Keep an eye on Zotz; he's doing the important stuff!"

Cuch must have figured being ten feet away wasn't such a risk and backed toward the helm. After a few feet the noise of the water gave me sufficient privacy to turn to the rutabaga and say: "What is the deal?"

"**The deal?**" it intoned.

"Don't play coy with me, Al. Lot's of end-of-the-world signage and suddenly some very odd types think I'm supposed to have some kind of hand in pulling the emergency brake. The problem—besides me not volunteering for role of hero—is that no one is terribly clear about what's expected or how to go about it. Other than some kind of sacrifice. Involving my son. Which ain't gonna happen. So, you got some 'splaining to do. First to me. Then to your elephant-head buddy when you tell him I said to take this quest and shove it—along with his dance, dance revolution—where his disco ball don't shine."

"Communication . . . is difficult," it answered haltingly. "Distance . . . language . . . context . . ."

"Okay then, I'll talk slow. Who you? Why me?"

There was a burst of sound—nonsense syllables—that, I guess, was the expression of a name. Whether personal specific or species general, I couldn't say. As to reproducing any approximation of the alien verbiage with my own lips and tongue . . .

"Hold on there, Starkist. I take it that you're what Mama Samm referred to as one of the 'Ancient Things'?"

There was another burst of static inside my head. ". . . known as Old Ones," it finished.

I sighed. "Old Ones, Great Old Ones, Elder Gods, Outer Gods—Great Crowley's Ghost, man-thing, you illegals from the Outer Dimensions aren't exactly consistent on the ID issues and I don't have a scorecard. So, what is your dog in this hunt?"

"Your mind is very noisy. If you will quiet your thoughts I will answer your queries as best I can."

"I'm all ears," I said. "And half antennae."

"First of all, you speak as if my kind is alien and visitor to your shores while your race would claim some legitimate title to this world. My race was the first life-form to take possession of the planet that your kind calls 'Earth.' We were the ones who seeded it with life, crafted the single-celled organisms into protoplasm and sculpted all manner of life-forms—for our own purposes as well as those of chance and jest."

"Jeepers, Al!" I exclaimed. "You sound like a secret Scientology seminar. Are you trying to tell me you're a Thetan? If that's the case you just trot back to Xenu and tell him we want Tom Cruise back!"

"I do not know what you are babbling about," it said.

"L. Ron Hubbard?" I tried.

"I do not know this Elron you speak of."

"Sorry. My bad. You're just another alien with *May-flower* snobbery and a God complex. Big surprise."

"You and your kind might well show more respect."

"What? Respect my Elder . . . Things?"

"If you do not recognize us as your creators, you must certainly give us due as this planet's defenders and protectors. We arrived in the epoch your kind has labeled the Archaen period, when the entire globe was still covered in water. For countless eons we built our cities beneath the cool green waves. When global upheavals began to create land masses that divided the one, vast, unbroken ocean, we established beachheads and communities there, as well. By your Carboniferous period, we inhabited every continent, with our greatest megalopolis sprawling about what eventually became this planet's south pole.

"Then the octopoid spawn of Cthulhu came, falling down from foul, distant stars, and we battled for dominance, eventually driving them into the seas. We were weakened, even in victory, and in the Permian age our servants, the shoggoth, chose the opportunity to rebel and turn against us. The two that the Enemy sent against you last night were but shadows of what the shoggoth were in our day. Still we had sufficient strength, even unto the age of the Jurassic to strive against yet another invasion of the Old Ones! The Mi-go drove us out of the northern lands. Eventually our remnants retreated to the Antarctic where we strove in final conflict with the coming of the Ice and the Enemy stronghold of Hadath. In the end we were too spent to prevail against the Great Old Ones in their strength, the betrayal of the shoggoth, and the arrival of the endless cold.

"Yog-Sothoth closed off all gateways to escape and Nyarlathotep was already mad back then and continually betraying and changing alliances. But before we were vanquished, we wrought the paleogean sciences that kept the Deep One in check through the long millennia. And it was we who vanquished Cthulhu and left our seal upon his sunken tomb to keep him slumbering until the end of time."

"Gee, Al, that's swell," I told him. "I certainly couldn't have done better, myself. Which is why I'm not going to risk messing up millions of years of monster wrangling by sticking my nose in now."

"But you are the one," Barrel o'Chum intoned.

"Dammit! Why does everybody keep saying this crap? How come I got nominated to be the captain of the

Titanic? If you're serious about recruiting a competent, capable hero type, there's got to be better nominees out there! Have you tried looking around? Sifted some resumes? Checked out Monster-dot-com?"

"Yes. You were not the first choice," it answered bluntly.

"Really?" Well, snap!

"There was a wizard in Chicago, a necromancer in St. Louis, a waitress in Bon Temps, and a weather warden—who hasn't spent much time in any one place, lately. We also considered a guardian in London."

"And?"

"It was not possible to make contact with them."

I waited. Finally: "What? Unlisted numbers? Do Not Call list? How come I'm the default guy here?"

"Apparently most humans are incapable of receiving our telepathic communications. Yog-Sothoth holds the gates and thresholds and that which is perceived is limited to those minds most often kept caged in institutions, hospitals, jails, and madhouses."

"Nice," I said. "And then there's me."

"Apparently you are linked to an overmind, a hive consciousness that is separate yet coexistent with your own."

"My nanites?"

"Your overmind enables you to comprehend certain frequencies and vibrations imperceptible to humans possessing but a single consciousness."

"Goody. So, in addition to turning me into a weaponized hormone factory and a Swiss Army knife, they now make me loony-bin compatible for podcasts from the Twilight Zone?" I closed my eyes. "That's why I'm your nominee for end-of-the-world problem solver? I'm the only one with a working mail slot for the engraved invitation?"

"You are the only one we could communicate with and even that has been difficult. At first, only through the erratic filters of your hypnogogic, altered consciousness . . ."

"My dreams."

". . . and later, when you reached certain filtered subsets of preconscious receptivity."

"While I was unconscious." I opened my eyes and looked around. At ghostly barrel monster and the arched blue ceiling of the water tunnel overhead. "What about now?"

"You have entered a state of transdimensional flux. There are fewer impediments to the hyperspatial synaptic linkage accessing the temporary wormhole between your planet and the star system where our remnants have taken refuge. For this brief time we may communicate directly rather than through symbolic conceptualizations."

"And yet," I griped, "you're still managing to make everything as clear as mud."

"What specificities do you require?"

I gaped at him—it—the Winky Dink voice in the barrel. "Look, Al, aside from the fact that I'm not really interested in saving the world—"

"Why would you not want to save your world?"

I closed my eyes again. I was so tired. Depression is just a word, a cliché to people who aren't wrapped in its suffocating, gray embrace. I'd managed to ignore the soul-numbing marathon of days and nights without purpose when my family and friends were threatened. But it was a temporary distraction, at best. And when you haven't got much motivation for your own future, investing in something much larger is beyond comprehension. As Joe Stalin supposedly said, one man's death is a tragedy, a million deaths are only a statistic. Asking me to care about the rest of the world was asking me to care about a statistic. Suggesting that my son be sacrificed for a statistic was a good way to become one, yourself.

If I sound like a right bastard let me say that I have a more practical approach to world-saving. According to the Jerusalem Talmud: "Whoever destroys the life of a single human being . . . it is as if he had destroyed an entire world; and whoever preserves the life of a single human being . . . it is as if he had preserved an entire world." I figured if I could get Lupé, Deirdre, and—God help me—even Theresa out safely, add the babies, before or afterwards, and I was already up to a half-dozen worlds. Let the rest of Planet Earth find some additional heroes-in-waiting.

I looked up at Al but was too tired to put any of that into words even as I opened my mouth.

"It is not necessary," alien Al answered. "I am not actually receiving the sound waves that emanate from your vocal apparatus. We commune on an entirely different frequency; articulation would be redundant."

Telepathy? That would make sense. . . .

"But I do not understand why you utilize the term 'Al' in referencing me as an entity."

"I've got to call you something," I told him. "The simpler the better since I can't wrap my head much less my lips around that burst of noise you use as a name."

"And there is some significance to the name 'Al'?"

"Depends on whether I end up being your bodyguard and you end up being my long lost pal."

"Pal?"

"Call me Betty."

"I do not understand. . . . "

I sighed. "Welcome to my world."

⁂   ⁂   ⁂

Yeah, there was a language barrier. Talking to an alien over a billion years old through a transdimensional relay bridging an interstellar gulf measured in thousands of light-years was a part of the problem.

But the ultimate hemming and hawing had more to do with Al's lack of a coherent plan beyond "showing up."

The old adage "Ninety percent of success is just showing up"—erroneously attributed to Woody Allen—was hardly a working strategy for confronting a squid-headed Elder God and its army of Deep Ones. When pressed, all that Al could come up with was that the unique juxtaposition of my mutated biology and nanite constructed hive-mind made me the one person capable of communication with beings outside of the normal time/space continuum. Too bad none of that communication seemed to offer much in the way of enlightenment. Just lots of annoying distraction.

And a big target painted on my back.

A target big enough to include my unborn son, it seemed.

There were some vague assurances that "other forces" were in play. Emphasis on the "vague." Whereas the Elder Things might be considered extraterrestrial entities, his protestations to the contrary, the other players were more in the category of home-grown powers-that-be—overminds—that were attempting to put their own dogs in the hunt. Ganesh/Kankiten and Hanuman were putting their money on someone named Dakkar; the elves had brought Cuchulainn to the dance—or maybe someone (or something) else had brought them. And God (or gods) knew who or what else was being dumped into the mix. Susanowo-no-mikoto had mentioned something about volcanoes and putting multiple pieces on the board but maybe I could chalk all of that up to a sex-induced dream rave.

All the more reason to leave the big showdown to the willing and better equipped.

Something I was trying to explain to the rutabaga for the sixteenth time when his ghostly form began to dissolve.

"The transdimensional hyperlink is growing corrupt," it said. "Communication will become more difficult."

As if we had approached anything close to an exchange of clarity during the past couple of hours, I thought. So, no big. Except . . .

If the transdimensional conduit was breaking down, it wasn't just a question of losing our two-way real-time conversation—it meant our so-called "passage to the sea" was growing unstable and that could be a very bad thing if the tunnel o' water went splat while we were still inside!

I threw myself out of my chair and ran through the dissipating ghost of Al on my way to the front of the boat.

"Brace yourselves!" I yelled, grabbing the edge of the pilot's chair.

Cuch and Zotz turned to stare at me. "Brace for what?" they both asked.

I shook my head. "I don't know but it's about to happen!"

The tunnel collapsed.

ᕕ(◕)   ᕕ(◕)   ᕕ(◕)

I'm not sure what I expected. Maybe that the tunnel—the transdimensional conduit—would turn itself inside out. And us with it!

Or that it would implode, crushing us like the collapse of an elongated singularity.

Or explode, scattering our dust particles through seven different universes.

Instead, we slid into a patch of fog and stayed there, gliding to a near stop.

"Zotz?" I asked, groping for the instrument panel.

"No discernable current," he answered, "maneuvering power only."

"Where are we?"

"In a fog bank, duh!"

"Turn on the GPS, Cap'n Crunch," I growled.

"Oh. Yeah." There was a sound of switches being toggled and the screen flickered to a dim semblance of life behind a filter of gray mist. "Well, whaddaya know? It woiks!" He fiddled with the settings and I got an impression of the graphics shifting and enlarging. I couldn't make out any details.

"So?" I asked impatiently. "Where are we?"

"Looks like we made it. . . ." he murmured, tweaking the settings. "According to this, your girlfriend delivered us all the way down to the Big Easy."

"Don't start," I warned. Then looked around at the wall of gray mist that encompassed us on all sides. "But how close are we to the harbor? If we're in a shipping lane it could be very bad if one of those tankers comes along in the fog and rams us." Never mind a tanker, a collision with a small tugboat would probably sink us just as effectively.

Zotz continued to fiddle with the settings and abruptly gave the monitor a couple of smacks with the palm of his "hand."

"Whoa there, Chief! Don't break the navigator!"

"That would be redundant," he grumped. "It's already broken. According to this we're in New Orleans."

"Yeah. You just said—"

"No, according to this thing we are *in* New Orleans. Downtown, just off the Mississippi River, in fact."

"What? You're telling me that we've run aground?"

"Does it feel like we've run aground?" The fog was thinning a bit and I could see the frustration on his half-human features more clearly now as he consulted the screen. More than that, I could feel the movement of the deck beneath my feet as the *New Moon* rode a swell of water, the motion indicating a current and cross motion simultaneously working at our hull.

"This piece o' crap . . . high tech . . . scrap . . . places us just beyond the north bank of the Mississippi River, at the apex of Canal and Common streets!" His mutterings devolved into creative juxtapositions of profanity and technology reviews.

"Zotz," I said slowly, "turn on the fish-finders . . ."

His tirade never lost its rhythm or intensity as he flipped the appropriate switches. At least until the screens lit up. "What's this? Test patterns?"

The fish-finder screens were displaying an odd assortment of geometric patterns.

Storm surge, I thought, my blood suddenly running cold. We didn't beat the hurricane, it had arrived first. And, unless we were in the relative and momentary calm of the eye, it had already passed by. Some flooding would have been inevitable: the Big Muddy would be bigger and a lot muddier.

"It looks like a dump down there," Zotz said as he attempted to fine-tune the transponder settings. "I mean, I've got outlines and silhouettes that are definitely man-made: angles, corners, symmetrical configurations . . ." Looking down he didn't notice that the breeze was starting to tear holes in the fog. "What is that? A car?"

Through one of those tentative gaps I could see the New Orleans' World Trade Center just a block or two behind us—*aft*—I needed to remember my nautical terms, anything to hold on to a sense of perspective in the face of what was appearing through the vanishing mists.

Because my perspective was all screwed up. By the fog, by the water.

By the dawning realization of our likely position.

Nearly a dozen other tall buildings of the downtown and warehouse districts were appearing around us, now, and fanning out northward: The Wyndam at Canal Place, the Mariott, One Shell Plaza, Capitol One Tower, the Riverside Hilton, Place St. Charles, the Plaza Tower, Energy Center, National American Bank, Harrah's

Hotel, the Sheraton, LL&E Tower, Pan American Life Building, and Tidewater Place . . . all looking strangely familiar and utterly alien at the same time. Two things were wrong with this picture and I recognized both almost simultaneously. We were drifting further uptown into the middle of the city's geographical arrangement of its high-rise real estate. And all of these landmarks were shorter than usual.

Their first fifteen stories or more were missing.

Those floors and the rest of the city were gone, hidden beneath an inland sea of gray-green water that stretched from here to the visible horizon.

Louisiana had a brand new coastline somewhere else, many miles to the north.

New Orleans had become the New Atlantis!

Chapter Sixteen

WHAT DO YOU SAY when you're suddenly confronted with an ocean where half a million people lived?

And it wasn't just a living population swallowed up and gone but some four centuries of history, culture, and tradition.

The music was hushed now. It didn't matter that Buddy Bolden, Jelly Roll Morton, King Oliver, and Louis Armstrong were already gone and their recordings would live on. And hopefully the still-living greats had evacuated in time—those that weren't out on the road and already on tour. But there were too many that were old or blind or practically lame, now. Too many too stubborn—or too poor—to leave for just another storm. And what about Preservation Hall? Tipitina's? The Funky Butt at Congo Square, Donna's, the Rock'N'Bowl, the Palm Court, Fritzel's, and Snug Harbor? Hell, forget individual venues, New Orleans was *The Source*. Say what you will about the jazz scene in Chicago or Kansas City but that all came later and never had the cultural kaleidoscope of diversity or fresh-off-the-boat inventiveness or aged-in-the-wooden-barrel-house history sounds of New Orleans music.

Go to a hundred towns and cities in Louisiana and you'll find a hundred Mardi Gras celebrations, each unique and wonderful in its own right. But each only a pale reflection of the original party to end all parties.

And the food . . .

It wasn't like you wouldn't ever eat jambalaya or gumbo or po'boys again. But only the Café du Monde made beignets and café au lait that people came from all over the world to taste. Nobody had a stand-up oyster bar like Felix's. You couldn't get better muffalettas anywhere than at Central Grocery. There was the chicken Clemençeau at Feelings, the Bananas Foster at Brennan's, the crawfish pie at Michaul's on St. Charles, the bread puddings at the Bon Ton, the quenelles of goat crème fraîche at Lilette, and fried green tomatoes, grillades, and grits at Café Atchafalaya. Arnaud's shrimp remoulade would never be duplicated. Oh, and the pompano en papillote, Eggs Sardou, andouille, maque choux, tasso, and courtbouillon of redfish! The pralines, king cakes, sweet potato pie, calas, and pain perdu!

I shook myself, the memories of cafés and restaurants, bars and music halls, buildings and landmarks fading.

Yes, those places were gone and I mourned them because I knew them.

But a half million people that I didn't know had just become a lesser statistic to me. And that was just the city's population. One and a half million in the greater New Orleans area and, with water stretching in every direction to the horizon, who knew how far inland the sea had struck?

Or how many coastal cities had suffered similar fates between Pensacola and Galveston?

We were afloat on an alien sea and I just couldn't wrap my mind around the scope of the catastrophe.

Never mind.

I couldn't do anything for them now.

I was beginning to see the emotional advantages to becoming a monster.

My mind would be less cluttered with unhelpful emotion when I needed my wits about me. To revisit Joe Stalin, my family was the tragedy; everyone and everything else were just statistics. . . .

For now I would concentrate on the task at hand. I would . . .

I slid down the ladder to the lower deck and promptly began throwing up over the side. Mostly dry heaving as I hadn't put anything solid in my stomach for days.

There had to have been time, I told myself as small dollops of stomach bile plinked into the gray-green waves. *Time for most of the people to have gotten out, gotten to higher ground . . .*

But high enough ground?

And how far away?

This was flooding beyond the anticipated disaster of a failed levee system. The sea had been out there, hungrily nibbling its way through the tidal lands and barrier islands that had provided a natural barrier for millennia. Unfortunately, ninety percent of that protection had disappeared in the last fifty years thanks to pipeline channels for oil development and wetland mismanagement. The weight of an increasing population along an unstable coastline added subsidence at the rate of three feet a century to the mix: the whole Gulf Coast from Mississippi to Texas was sinking at an unprecedented rate. And every hurricane, every storm surge returned a portion of the sea to its rightful place in defiance of man's best efforts at architecture and pump technology.

"The future of New Orleans tourism is glass-bottom boats," the more enlightened used to boast only half jestingly.

But even the worst-case scenarios put the anticipated flood stage at no more than eighteen feet.

This . . . I gazed in stupefaction out over the vast expanse of water broken only by the snaggle-toothed underbite of high-rise buildings—this was far worse! The water had to be more than three times as deep as anything dreamed by the Cassandras of modern misfortunes. This flood was no mere meeting of the Mississippi River with Lake Pontchartrain, the city of New Orleans caught between their overrun banks. The Gulf of Mexico had redrawn its boundary lines, bringing the coastline a lot closer to Baton Rouge.

And, peering at the invisible horizon, there was no way to know whether Baton Rouge had been subsumed, as well.

How could any storm—even a supernatural one—flood hundreds of miles of land, as far as the eye could see?

As if in answer to my question, the surface of the water began to pattern in miniature ripples, like a coarsely woven fabric, flattening out the grosser waves and wind patterns. Bubbles, ranging from delicate strands of pearl-sized hisses to Volkswagen-sized blasts of trapped air broke the surface, turning the ocean around us into a boiling cauldron. The *New Moon* pitched and turned and the sound of rumbling grew from a subharmonic vibration to a full-throated growl: earthquake!

Or, more correctly, a seaquake!

As I looked up in horror, the Greek-cross-shaped World Trade Center building canted to the left—presumably toward the submerged channel of the Mississippi River—and sank another eight stories beneath the waters.

New Orleans was gone. Gone deep. The dozen or so remaining buildings still showing above the waves were nothing more than tombstones marking her watery grave. Their glass windows shattered, dark, and empty. Devoid of light, motion, life. Based on the number of stories still showing I figured the French Quarter had to be under ninety feet of water easy, even though it traditionally stood on higher ground.

The Orpheum, I thought. *What if Lupé and the others had stayed*? Tried to ride out the storm like Mooncloud said? Even if the sealed entrance under the theater was airtight, was the rest of the underground complex once the sea rolled in? If that last temblor was an aftershock, wouldn't one of the previous seaquakes have cracked their subterranean bunker like an egg? And, even if they were still alive, courtesy of an enormous amount of luck and a large enough air pocket, how was I going to get to them without drowning them in the process?

I slammed my fist against the railing as Zotz called out from above: "Lady in the water! Two points off the starboard beam!"

I didn't know two points off the starboard beam from "Jesus Wants Me for a Sunbeam" but Zotz could point from the upper deck and that was all I needed to know. I kicked off my shoes as I rounded the *New Moon* to the other side, stepped up on the rail, and launched myself outward, punching off so powerfully that I angled down a good thirty feet through the water before I could stop my descent.

My eyes re-lensed and filtered the available light giving me an astonishing glimpse at the remains of the city down below.

I was suspended above a section of the riverfront and, as I turned, I could see the Spanish Plaza off to my right. To my left was Woldenberg Riverfront Park, its sculpture gardens befouled with clots of overturned automobiles and seaweedlike clumps of drowned bodies half emergent from windows and snagged on the stainless steel hoops and pillars of the Ocean Song monument. More disturbing were the bloated faces pressed to the glass ceiling of the Amazon Rainforest, now flooded like the rest of the Aquarium of the Americas, a giant fishbowl turned upside down with human and animal floaters providing food for the fish who had found their way inward.

A streetcar was on its side, blocking Canal Street adjacent to the ferry landing. An inconvenience to none, now.

But, as I began my stroke and kick to return to the surface, movement caught my eye. I glanced back. Then looked again.

My head broke the surface and I had to reorient everything: direction, light, sound, target. Liban. As I swam toward her I tried to reconcile what I thought I had seen.

A crew of Deep Ones, laboring with ropes and jacks, to move the trolley as if it were needed elsewhere.

ᴬᴴᴬ   ᴬᴴᴬ   ᴬᴴᴬ

Rescuing this elven sea goddess was a little more complicated than I expected.

First of all, she was unconscious so I had to swim for the both of us—though thankfully she was buoyant and not all dead weight. At least until I tried to lift her toward Setanta's waiting hands. Eventually I gave up on that bit of impossible gymnastics and looped a rope under her arms so that the big Celt could haul her up like the catch of the day. It was an appropriate metaphor as Liban had "lost" her legs. The lower half of her orange wetsuit had transformed from neoprene to shimmering, coppery scales, fusing together to form a tapering but unified fishtail, overlaid with a mottled grid work of semicircles and arced patterns reminiscent of a lionfish. From the hips up she was just as hu—er—elvish—as she was before.

But, obviously, there was something to those mermaid stories beyond an overabundance of rum and too much time at sea.

Setanta placed her in my bed and checked her eyes and pulse while I changed into dry clothes.

"I can find no injuries," he said, combing through her dark, wet tresses to examine her scalp. "She seems to be but unconscious. As like the product of exhaustion."

"Yeah," I said, toweling off and grabbing another shirt out of the closet, "opening dimensional gateways always leaves me feeling a bit peaked. . . ." I saw the look on his face as he looked back up at me. "Kidding. Just kidding . . . " *Anything to keep from thinking too much, too soon.*

The lights in the cabin went out.

"Now what?"

There was enough daylight filtering in through the portholes to find my way to the dresser and extract a flashlight from the top drawer. Turning it on, I tossed it to the big Celt. "Stay here and keep an eye on her. I'll go see what the problem is."

I crashed about the lower level as I hopped into a pair of dry chinos and carried my deck shoes up the ladder to the helm and Zotz.

"Yeah," he said as I sat to put on my shoes, "I turned off the generator."

I stared at him. "Shit. We're running out of gas."

He nodded. "Just about. And no marinas in sight. I can stretch it if we don't use any unnecessary power."

"Can you power the GPS long enough to maneuver us over the Orpheum?"

The Mesoamerican bat-demon stared at me. "Do you have a plan?" Clearly the same obstacles were going through his mind that I had grappled with twenty minutes earlier.

"I'd say everything is a work in progress, right now," I said, willing my left eye to stop twitching.

"If we don't conserve fuel and we don't find more of it, we won't be afloat that much longer," he said pointedly. "We're wallowing in heavier swells and taking on water

more quickly than back on the sheltered Ouachita. If I
don't run the pumps every twenty minutes or so we'll be
on the bottom inside of an hour. To run the pumps, I
have to have fuel. Once that's gone, so are we."

I stared out over the water and noticed the light was
lessening. Checked the position of the sun and, almost
as an afterthought, checked my watch: 4:53 pm. Sun-
down was a while away but, barring a miracle, we'd be
in the dark all too soon.

Where was the Coast Guard? In the aftermath of a
disaster of this magnitude they should have had a fleet
here by now; a flotilla at the very least. Zotz had issued
a general mayday while I was in the water but the
radio—on battery backup while the generator was off-line—
remained ominously silent. It was as if a great tsunami
had come along and washed everything and everyone
away and we were the only living beings for a thousand miles.

Above the waterline, anyway.

Feeling helpless and impotent, I went back down to
my cabin, cursing Hindu and Japanese and Outer Space
so-called higher beings who seemed very big on the idea
of delegating but more than a little hazy on the concepts
of motivation, training, and providing proper materials
and equipment.

Liban was awake but looking deathly pale when I
entered. Setanta glanced at me and left without a word.

I sat on the edge of the bed. "How are you feeling?"

"Faded," she whispered. "Setanta said we arrived?"

I nodded, seeing the questions in her eyes. "We're in
New Orleans. Maybe a hundred feet above the former

Riverwalk. The city's under water. The storm got here first."

She reached out and squeezed my hand. It was more of a twitch than the actual application of pressure. "I am sorry. Opening a path through the waters is a difficult thing. I have never done it so far from the sea and where so much land crossed back and forth between. It distorted the pathway. The last time I did such a thing, seagoing craft were much different. Sailing vessels are much different than ships employing modern engines and technology: it felt as if I were drawing two vessels in my wake. And then I think I may have passed through a portion of the storm, itself. It was unexpected . . . powerful. I was thrown the wrong way on the final approach. We may have lost days instead of hours. I do not know. Everything became confused before I passed out."

"You brought us through safely," I said, squeezing her hand gently in return. "That's all that counts," I added, trying to be gracious. It wasn't easy. Somewhere in the back of my brain a part of me was screaming. It had started when I first realized that New Orleans wasn't merely drenched but fully dead and drowned. Meanwhile, another part of me was running around in circles and babbling, trying to figure out what to do next, what to do about Lupé and the others. Holding someone's hand and mouthing platitudes while the rest of the world was coming undone was not high on my to-do list at the moment.

"Rest now," I said. "Get your strength back. Is there anything I can get for you?"

She gave me a long look. "Perhaps later . . . " she said with a weak smile.

"Yeah," I said, getting back up and backing toward the door. That would be about the time I would be wanting a late night snack.

I went down the corridor and into the galley. The spare blood packs were in the fridge, not the freezer. I tore open two of them with my teeth and wolfed the contents. Crammed the rest in the freezer figuring they'd keep a little better there even with the power off.

Then I pulled the Smith & Wesson Magnum revolver and the sawed-off Mossberg out from under the sink. Checked and loaded each. Pulled harness and holster from the side cabinet. If the Coast Guard came calling I could pitch the shotgun over the side. If the Deep Ones came calling I'd be more adaptive to the situation. I went to the scuba lockers and began preparing spear guns.

ᴍᴧ   ᴍᴧ   ᴍᴧ

The first boat appeared a quarter of an hour later. The second was right behind it.

They came out from behind the Plaza Tower and approached us in a long, lazy arc as if to look us over before coming in close.

Of course, that gave us the opportunity to do the same. Our field glasses to their field glasses. One quick look and I ducked down hoping that I had gotten the better look, first.

After a quick conference, positioning us so their line of sight was spoiled, Camazotz reconfigured his appearance to a tall Asian-looking guy. Setanta—well, we figured he was the least likely to be recognized. And I

slipped down the back stairway to raid the restocked
scuba locker and seal the Smith & Wesson in a waterproof baggie. Then I grabbed a face mask and fins, lowered the dive ladder, and eased off the stern and into
the water as the two boats split their approaches to
bracket us.

Fortunately they didn't try to bookend us on both
sides. The first cut its engines across the *New Moon's*
bow while the other pulled along our port side. I was
able to use the houseboat for cover but I lost a flipper
trying to put the mask on in the water. Then nearly lost
the gun while strapping the diver's sheath knife to my
calf. This was ridiculous. I ducked down and swam
beneath the *New Moon's* keel and considered which of
the two speedboats offered the most advantages to a
stealth approach.

*Never mind pain, serious injury, or death: if I pulled
this off, Zotz would never believe my National Guard
credentials again. . . .*

The visiting craft had the long sleek look of cigarette
boats, the kind favored by rich playboys or coastal smug-
glers. One might assume the former based on the assortment of bikinied beauties on display, lying out on the
exaggerated forward decks just ahead of the raked wind-
screens. They were strategically placed to draw the eye
away from the clutch of bristly-faced toughs crowding
the narrow cockpit and packing heat under their nylon
windbreakers. I didn't need to see Johnny Depp's face to
know that piracy was still alive and well on the high seas.

I had, however, seen three familiar faces on board the
first go-fast boat. Faces that meant bargaining for some
extra fuel was going to be a very dicey proposition.

So I continued my underwater swim, passing under their keel as they glided to stop some thirty feet off of the *New Moon*'s port side.

I eased my head up on the far side of the new vessel as a familiar voice called: "Ahoy the boat!" No one on board would be looking away from the *New Moon* as that was their intended target and I was further hidden by the overhang of the V-shaped hull.

"Ahoy, yourself," I heard Zotz call back. And as they engaged in a totally bullshit conversation about who each other was, where they had come from, and where they were headed, I worked my way aft where the big engines and down-swept design would give me easier boarding access.

"I don't think I've ever seen a houseboat like yours out on the open ocean," the would-be pirate leader was saying. "The *New Moon*. Is it yours?"

"Naw." Make-over Asian Zotz chuckled crudely. "I borrowed it off some guy who said he had better things to do." That had their attention. I was able to pull myself up on the stern in time with the swell so that no one noticed any change in the boat's balance. Preternatural reflexes and now enhanced by nanite technology: sometimes I can do something right. The bimbos as well as the goons on the other boat were totally absorbed in watching the houseboat for any kind of a response.

"Yeah?" said pirate leader guy chuckling even more nastily than Zotz. "And what would that be?"

I peeled the waterproof bag open as Zotz shrugged. "He said something about having to deal with a bunch of pissant werewolves."

Pirate leader guy stopped chuckling and if I thought the pirate wannabes on both boats were attentive before, they were twice as attentive, now. "What did you say?" the leader growled menacingly.

Zotz leaned upon the upper deck's railing where the Mossberg and several spear guns were cached. I knew Setanta would be waiting in the salon, fingering Michael's great sword and waiting for the opportunity to repel some boarders.

"I said the guy who owns this boat said something about having to go deal with a bunch of pissant werewolves," Zotz repeated with a smile. "He said he'd warned some dude to stay the hell away from him and his people and this dude was just too stupid to pay attention."

"He said that, did he?" Pirate leader's lips peeled back in a manner that might have suggested a grin. But didn't.

"Sure did," Zotz nodded. "Said this dude needed some sense beat into him. Said it was probably a waste of time and this dude should just be shot down like a dog but . . . " Zotz shrugged.

"Really!" Hackles were rising all over the boat. Even the eye candy wearing the dental floss were starting to look a little feral. "Too bad I missed him. I'd really like to have a conversation with this fellow."

Compared to my silent arrival on board, the cocking of the Smith & Wesson's hammer was like a thunderclap. Everyone turned but turned carefully as there was no mistaking the sound.

"Hello, Gordon," I said. "Miss me? Because, from the looks of things, you decided you just couldn't stay away."

Everyone took a step back.

The funny thing was none of them were particularly worried about the monster handgun I was waving at them. Maybe if I told them the on-board ammo was silver frag-loads with sterling birdshot packed in a colloidal suspension medium I'd get a little more respect. Maybe. But for now, it was enough that the Bloodwalker was in the midst and all it took was a single scratch for me to go through them like a scythe through ripe wheat.

"What's the matter, Gordo?" I taunted, seeing the sick look on his once smug features. "Figured you were safe as long as I was on my boat and you were on yours? What was the plan? Sink the *New Moon* or set her ablaze or blow her out of the water—anything to destroy me from a safe distance with the added insurance of an ocean-sized moat between us?"

"Cséjthe . . . " the would-be pirate chief stammered, ". . . we didn't know you would be here."

I nodded. "Sure you did. You knew my boat was in the area from our distress calls and you ran a visual check on your approach. You had the intel, even if you've never actually seen the *New Moon*, yourself. You hailed us under false pretenses with a false ID. You've got scantily clad girls draped across your bow as bait and distraction— at least one of which is being held against her will. Cut her loose now." I turned to the fourth *were*. "And you brought Fenris along."

"Bloodwalker," he growled.

"Trucebreaker," I growled right back at him. I turned back to Gordon. "Who has seen my boat. Been on it, even. Enjoyed my hospitality. Then set me up to kill me. Was all set to kill his buddy Volpea, too. Fenny, how about cutting Volpea loose?"

"I don't—" the big wolf man began.

"No!" I yelled, turning back to him. "No stalling. No pretending to be stupid—you're stupid enough!" I waved the gun again. It probably bears pointing out at this stage that gun waving is a precise art. It's really more of a waggle. A short, controlled movement designed to get your adversaries' attention while still making sure that you both know the end of the barrel doesn't stray much from their heads or their hearts. Random waving about—in which your gun barrel wanders far afield—is the quickest way to make the points that 1) you are an idiot and 2) you are about to become a dead idiot.

Still, it wasn't so much the gun that was keeping my adversaries at bay as the knowledge that the first *were* to jump me would end up with me inside his head and using his flesh as a suicide weapon against the rest. Even more effective a threat than a machine gun much less a five-shot revolver.

"I am going to explain myself once and only once and then things are going to get really bloody because I am oh-so-easily pissed right now," I continued. "You tried to kill me and I would be thrilled—just tickled pick—to have the slightest excuse to blow a silver-ringed, fist-sized hole in your traitorous guts. If I repeat myself it will be to the next pissant *were* in line after I've blown away anyone I even begin to think might annoy me. Are we clear?"

He held up his hands. "She's cuffed. I'm going to reach into my pocket for the key."

I gestured with the gun. "Please remember that I'm hoping you'll do something stupid."

He didn't. Do something stupid, that is. At least until he had finished unlocking the camouflaged steel cuffs that had held Volpea a prisoner on the forward deck, stretched out in all of her *Sports Illustrated* Swimsuit Edition glory. She stretched, rubbing her wrists and working out some shoulder kinks. Then punched him, knocking him overboard.

She looked at a life preserver and a length of rope then at me. "Sorry. Do you want him back?"

I shook my head. "You just saved me the trouble. Can he swim?"

"Yes."

"Pity." I turned to the others. "Now. I have a few questions. Same rules apply. Where is Marie Laveau?"

"I don't know."

I pointed the Smith & Wesson at his head, bracing my right wrist with my left hand. "I hope the next person on this boat is more forthcoming when I repeat the question."

"I really don't know!" he shouted, throwing up his hands. "Things have fallen apart these past three days. The old witch has a new demesne, now! The rest who survived have to fight for scraps!" He half threw a fist toward the deeper waters of the Gulf. "Word is, she's out there, somewhere! All I know is I haven't seen her since the storm hit. We're on our own here."

"So," I considered, easing the pressure off of the trigger. "You're not hunting me on her account any longer."

"Doesn't change your value as a bargaining chip," Volpea elaborated. "Gordon and company can either stay here and grow fins or try to bargain their way into some other demesne where they're likely to be killed or allowed on as the lowest of the low."

I nodded. "Killing the Bloodwalker, badass vampire nemesis, would give them the status and street cred to make their own deals."

"Can't blame a guy for trying," he said.

"Can't I?" My finger was back on the trigger. "If you don't know where Marie Laveau is, maybe you can tell me where my people are."

A hideous expression crossed the werewolf leader's face. "That's easy," he sneered. "Dead. Drowned. Sealed under the Orpheum Theatre in a watery tomb!"

I knew it, of course. But having Gordon confirm it with such evident relish just hit me all the harder at that moment. I wanted to kill him for it.

And I wanted them to kill me and let it all be over.

"That's not true!" Volpea said, stepping over the windscreen and down into the pilot's area. "They got out!"

"Shut up, bitch!" Gordon snarled. He turned back to me. "Don't you think she won't lie to you and tell you what you want to hear? They're dead, I tell you. All of them. And they died like rats in a storm drain! And you!" he shouted, turning back to the statuesque woman, "Mind your place!"

Volpea froze in place. Then turned slowly toward him. "Mind my place? *Mind* my *place*!" Faster than the strike of a cobra, her arm lashed out and her fingernails raked his face. "Why, Gordon," she cooed, all of the animosity suddenly gone from her voice, "you're bleeding! And so close to the Bloodwalker, too!"

That's when the radio crackled to life.

"Hello? Hello? I thought I heard a voice a while ago . . . "

Gordo touched his torn cheek and when he saw the blood on his fingers, his eyes grew wide and he glanced from the radio to me with a profound look of terror.

". . . was that you, Zotzalahal Chamalcan? This is Sammathea D'Arbonne on board the *Spindrift*."

"I read you, Mama Samm," Zotz radioed back. "Are you all right? Are the others with you?"

"They were," she answered, sounding strangely distorted. Either she was very far away or something was wrong with her radio. "They've been taken. I was able to hide until they were gone but now everyone else—I can't stay on the radio, they may come back at any moment. Is Mister Chris with you? Can you put him on?"

"He's here. Sort of. But he's a little busy right now," Zotz answered. "I think he's about to beat the crap out of a bunch of werewolves and kill their leader."

Mama Samm's response was lost in noise of the former pirate chief vaulting over the railing and hitting the water. I looked around the boat at the others and said: "Well? What are you waiting for? He's your leader—go follow him." I had to wave the gun one last time even though it wasn't the gun they were most afraid of.

"No," I elaborated, "*in* the water."

I walked forward and picked up the microphone as eleven more splashes drowned out the GPS coordinates that Mama Samm was relaying to my demon helmsman.

"You sit tight," I told her, pushing the mic button, "we'll be there as soon as humanly possible."

"Inhumanly," Zotz kibitzed.

"Yeah. Listen," I told him, "we've got two fast, seaworthy, and presumably well-fueled boats here. Let's off-load what we think we'll need from the *New Moon* and turn in the rest to the insurance company next month. I want all of us to be on our way to those coordinates in ten minutes, tops."

"Aye-aye."

I dropped the mic in its cradle and turned around to look at Volpea. She was dressed much the same as when she had tried to seduce me on the top deck of my house-boat a few days before. Just wearing a little less, now, without the shirt.

"You're still on the boat," I said.

"Gordon is no longer my Alpha," she said.

"Well, it's sort of my boat, now."

"Well, I sort of figured that."

"Volpea . . ."

"The way I see it," she said, folding her arms in such a way as to strain the fabric of her bikini top, "is you're about to deliver one of three speeches."

"One of three?" I muttered.

"Yes. Either you're about to tell me that people who join your demesne share incredible risks and that I would be safer going my own way—"

"Well—"

"—or that you could never trust me because I suckered you and used you like a sap—"

"There is that . . ."

"—or that you don't like lesbians."

"It's speech number one," Zotz said, popping up over the back of the boat with the tow-rope from the other empty craft curled around one fist.

"Really," she said.

"Yeah. It can't be number two because he gets suckered and used by women all of the time. No signs of stopping, yet."

"And number three?" she asked.

"There's nothing wrong with lesbians. Some of the best websites—"

"Zotz!" I interrupted. "How did you get over here so fast?"

He gave me a wounded look as he tied the second boat to the stern of the first. "It's only twenty yards out and another twenty yards over. If I seem to be moving fast it's because I'm working and you're still standing still."

ᴧᴧ   ᴧᴧ   ᴧᴧ

I took the wheel of the *Bat Out of Hell*, the first speedboat we'd inherited from Laveau's former werewolf minions. Zotz was driving the second with the words *Screaming Mimi* painted on the hull in a garish, wind-blown-font style. Liban didn't look happy but I doubted it had anything to do with marine-style detailing. I still needed debriefing from Volpea and it seemed wise to split out the complement between the two boats. In her weakened state, it seemed more sensible to put Setanta at her side.

Even though this was the most logical organization of our travel time and resources, I knew from experience that I would be punished for it after we arrived. Of course, if Lupé and Deirdre were waiting for me when I arrived with Volpea and Liban, it just meant I would be punished all the more. Incrementally and exponentially.

I've been told that it's every man's fantasy to be surrounded by beautiful women.

I can tell you that it *is* a fantasy.

And, unless you are very careful, it could be a *final* fantasy.

The GPS coordinates were well out into the Gulf of Mexico so, even at two-thirds open throttle we had a bit of time to talk. And the sun was already riding low in the sky.

According to Volpea, the storm had been fast, vicious and caught even the early evacuees unprepared. The storm surge had topped the levees and the seawalls, the Mississippi and Lake Pontchartrain had spilled over their banks, flooding everything below sea level and the pumping stations had all shorted out, one by one as the dark waters closed over them. Factories, refineries, and chemical plants polluted the flood waters with additional waste hazards and power plants ignited floating oil and gas slicks even as transmission towers toppled and power was cut across greater regions. Dead wildlife and living carpets of fire ants floated among the initial survivors. Then the alligators and the cottonmouths came, riding the crest of each new tide.

The greater threat came from the predators that were already among them. Looters and rapists and criminals of opportunity began to realize that food and water and camping gear and boats were precious commodities. There were stories of heroism as will happen among human beings during a crisis but New Orleans did not willingly surrender its title of the nation's murder capital during the storm, either.

Once the waters had come and driven the quick and the healthy to higher ground, the storm blew itself out. It was eerie, Volpea said. A one-day hurricane. But what a hurricane! The entire Ninth Ward gone. Flattened or picked up and flung away before being inundated in black silt and gray water. Automobiles tossed down the street or catapulted into buildings. Streetcars lifted off their tracks.

And people hurled like screaming missiles through storefronts, office windows, and less yielding surfaces or else out into the rain-pelted darkness, disappearing forever.

Even as the skies began to clear on the second day, the quakes began. Dams across the state, and what was left of the levees and dykes and sea walls, fell apart. Vast, watery sinkholes appeared. Then chunks of real estate disappeared, dropping anywhere from a few feet to dozens. A cascade effect ensued as water rushed in to fill the void and more quakes followed. Tsunamis formed out in the Gulf of Mexico and hurtled in like battering rams and turbo-charged bulldozers, tearing up fragile structures and anything that wasn't fastened down, and pushing the debris, living and dead, either miles inland or into larger, immovable objects before sucking them back out to sea.

Within hours a vast shelf of geological strata along the coast gave a deafening groan and shuddered. The subsidence of the land was less noticeable than the rising of the ocean as it slithered inland, climbing over the high ground and falling upon every refugee who wasn't in a boat or a reinforced building more than twenty-five stories tall.

Most of those buildings were deathtraps and charnel houses. The windows were mostly shattered from the pressure of the wind, the water, or the barrage of missiles the storm had thrown at them the first day. In some places the glass had blown outward from internal pressure as water rushed up a structure's core displacing trapped air faster than it could vent through the sealed environmental systems. No light, no power, no protection from the elements. Each new quake or aftershock brought more water up the elevator shafts and stairwells, claiming another floor, sometimes tipping the building a bit more, or toppling one completely. Some survivors fought for meager supplies and space as additional refugees arrived. Gordon and some of the other weres were keeping two of the buildings as their own private game reserve for when their own food ran out.

I wished I had known this bit of information before I had so blithely allowed them to attempt the marathon swim back to their "meat locker." Once again my natural impulses toward mercy and détente had proved the wrong call when dealing with the monsters.

No broadcast facilities within several hundred miles seemed to have survived. What meager reports had filtered through had come by way of boat radios farther away or inland, ham operators outside the destructive radius of the storm, or via a handful of working satellite radio receivers. Government response was rumored to be slow—the rest of the country seemed to think it was in as much shock as the people who were experiencing it firsthand. There were stories of refugee camps set up along the shores of the new flood plain by the Red Cross and FEMA but those were across the wide water and beyond the reach of survivors not already located near the fringe of the disaster.

There were more stories—tales of massive outbreaks of flesh-eating bacteria, dysentery, warnings about malaria. Reports of looting, civil unrest, piracy, and overnight disappearances. Tabloid-style stories of strange nocturnal sightings, "humanoids from the deep," and rumors of Coast Guard vessels gone missing.

Then radio reception turned bad. Batteries were running low, to be sure, but there was a quality to the reception that suggested some kind of interference.

Then silence.

As Gordon had said just before he opted to walk the plank, we were pretty much on our own down here and likely would be for a long, long time.

Chapter Seventeen

AS WE WERE closing in on the GPS coordinates Mama Samm had radioed from the *Spindrift*, the radio crackled to life again. It had been over an hour since the big juju woman's last call and I was getting worried but this didn't bring any relief.

"Cséjthe," Gordon's voice crackled over the speaker, "do you hear me?"

I started to reach for the microphone then thought the better of it. I signaled the other boat not to respond.

"I know you're listening," he continued. "You'll keep this channel open to hear from your friends. That's okay.

I just wanted to leave a message with you. If you don't want to talk, that's fine. I get the last word this time."

"Turn off the radio," Volpea said.

I shook my head. "I'm not afraid of him. And he's right; I need to keep this frequency open in case Mama Samm calls back."

"I ought to apologize for lying to you about your woman," he continued. "I never should have said she was dead when I knew she was alive. That was wrong."

Volpea put her hand on my arm. "I'll take the wheel and monitor the radio. Go sit down in the back."

"Why?"

"Because I know him. You don't need the distraction right now."

"So I promise you nothing but the truth from now on," Gordon continued in the cheery bright tones of a car salesman. "It isn't important that she lives for now. Now is a temporary condition. Are you paying attention? Because here's where the truth part comes in . . ."

"Go sit down," she ordered.

"No!" I shouted, knowing what was coming next. I'd heard it before.

"I promise you," Gordon said in his most earnest voice, "that very soon now we will find your woman. Hunt her and her misbegotten whelp down. And then we will kill them both. That's my promise, that's the truth I owe you, man to man. And then we will come for you on our terms."

"You should have killed him when you had the chance," she said.

"I know."

"Thank about that, hombre, every night before you fall asleep. And every morning before you get up. I know there have been others who have threatened you with the same things. But I am different. My demesne is under ninety feet of water. I got nothing to lose. You think about that. Until I see you again."

After a while I said: "I've been operating without an enforcer for too long."

"You've got one now."

"Thanks."

She shrugged. "Thank me when that tail-licker is dead."

ᴧᴧ   ᴧᴧ   ᴧᴧ

The sun was an orange smear on the horizon when we arrived at the GPS coordinates, deep in the Gulf of Mexico.

The first clue to Mama Samm's position was a giant oil platform, canting at a nineteen-degree angle. Several hundred feet of massive orange support pillars thrust up out of the ocean on the east side. The west end of the platform, however, was tipping down into the water like a high-tech chute with a busy assortment of cranes, towers, buildings, and sub floors frozen in mid-slide.

I had never seen the *Spindrift*; I only knew that it was an oceanographic research vessel and off-campus classroom for the University of Louisiana. According to Volpea, Irena had gotten permission from her professor to bring my family on board at the last minute when the students and crew evacuated back up the Mississippi River. They should have been headed north when the storm hit. Now they were a hundred and fifty miles to the south and well out to sea, piled up against a sagging oil platform. According to the last radio transmission, more than an hour earlier, the *Spindrift* was a hundred-and-fifteen footer with a twenty-eight-foot beam. We were looking for a research vessel with a dual-decked front half and an enclosed pilothouse, and a low-draft access deck on the back end. Additional superstructure on the stern and starboard side for launching small submersibles and raising heavy samples should have made the ship easy to spot.

Under normal conditions.

There was nothing normal about the events unfolding in the aftermath of Laveau's storm. Certainly not the profusion of boats that were piled like so much flotsam and jetsam against the downward slice of the drilling platform. It was as if some mysterious force, like a giant magnet, had drawn every boat still afloat within a hundred mile radius. There were over fifty immediately visible and half of them were riding low in the water, crushed between larger hulls, or overturned and tilted bow or stern downward. It was a cacophony of wreckage ranging from a seven-story cruise ship to a scattering of fishing boats and oceangoing tugs, with a couple of Coast Guard cutters and a dozen sailboats tossed into the pileup.

We circled the wreckage slowly and finally spotted the *Spindrift* near the detritus of smaller craft. Maneuvering carefully, we threaded our way between the bobbing, upside-down keels of small fishing boats and a knifelike sailboat that drifted like a curious shark. We passed into the shadow of the great ocean liner that reared upward like a steel mountain range, blotting out the setting sun and throwing us into premature gloom. Zotz and I turned on the boats' searchlights at the same time.

The *Spindrift*'s hull was painted black in contrast to its white cabin structures and pilothouse. The low-slung back access was so low to the water the ship seemed nonexistent in the gloom and I ran the *Bat Out of Hell* into the side, miscalculating the distance at the last minute. Hey, never said I was a sailor—just wanted a house on the water. At the other end of the state. At least it was easy to step over the gunwales and onto the big boat's lower deck.

I pulled a flashlight out of my ops vest and my Glock 20 out of my shoulder rig. Everyone was geared up now, armed, equipped and Volpea had even dressed for the occasion, making due with some of Lupé's spare clothes I had tucked away in a box in the spare closet.

Yep, I was in for some definite punishment when I saw Lupé again.

Volpea actually had the most experience as an enforcer for the former demesne of New Orleans so she took point as we worked our way around the boat, checking hatches, compartments, and large storage lockers and bins.

There were several labs—wet and dry, an engine room, quarters for the crew with ten berths, quarters for the students with twelve berths—or maybe it was a male/female division thing. Everything was in disarray, though whether that was from the storm or from something more sinister I couldn't immediately say.

We worked our way up to the pilothouse and then back down the .port side of the vessel. No sign of Mama Samm.

"She said somebody took the others," Zotz said. "Maybe they came back and took her, too."

Volpea held her hand up. "Everyone be quiet," she murmured. "I need to listen."

We stood there in a silent semicircle as the red blush outlining the dark silhouette of the ocean liner turned to a bruised purple. Volpea stood on tiptoes with closed eyes and, after a bit, began to breathe deeply, taking long draughts through her nose.

"I could do this more easily if I transformed," she murmured.

"We only brought the one change of clothes along," I muttered.

"Would my nakedness disturb you so, knowing what I am?" she asked me with a quiet smile.

I shook my head. "It's a question of punishment."

She looked at me for elaboration.

I didn't give any and she went back to sniffing the air. "You smell . . . different," she said with her eyes closed.

I coughed. "Different cologne. You—um—like it?"

A little shrug, her eyes remained closed. "It's okay." She sniffed some more. Then, finally, she crept around to a hatch set in the deck amidships and pointed. Setanta and Zotz hunkered down and grasped the handle and latches. I planted my feet, aimed the flashlight with my left, the Glock with my right, and nodded. The hatch squeaked back and up and I filled its dark hole with light.

Something moved and a pole shot out of the hold, jabbing up at me like a rigid cobra. Volpea grabbed it as it went by and yanked upward, catching an arm with her other hand and, in a moment, we had a young black woman out and secured. I flashed the light around but the remainder of the hold appeared to be empty.

"Bang stick," Volpea observed, laying the pole aside. "Divers use them to drive overly aggressive sharks away." She was holding our captive effortlessly with one finely muscled arm about the girl's chest and shoulders.

Some of the fright was already fading from her eyes as she seemed to realize that we meant her no harm. She was probably one of Irena's fellow-student crew-members. Tall and slender, she was maybe twenty, no more than twenty-two. She wore baggy culottes that looked like they belonged to a larger roommate and a man's denim work shirt tied beneath her breasts to reveal chocolate abs that looked like sculpted mahogany.

"It's all right, miss," I said, moving the light so that it wouldn't blind her and shining it up on me, instead. "We're not going to hurt you. We're here to help."

She gasped. "Oh thank the gods, you finally made it!" Volpea released her and the girl rushed over to me and threw her arms around me. "I couldn't be sure it was you, Mister Chris! They came back once and I had to abandon the radio."

"Holy crap!" Zotz was saying.

"It's me," the girl was saying in that voice that was just so wrong now. "Don't you recognize me? I'm Sam-mathea D'Arbonne!"

"Mama Samm?" I said.

She snuggled in a little closer. "Hey, you smell nice . . . "

"Holy crap!" I said.

᠅ᚚ᠅   ᠅ᚚ᠅   ᠅ᚚ᠅

Our ancient ancestors worshipped power and they worshipped the goddess. Archeologists have turned up hundreds, maybe thousands of ancient little clay and oolitic limestone figurines from prehistoric sites. The most famous of these is called the "Venus of Willendorf," others are called "Venus figurines." These small statuettes of idealized, obese female figures have long been thought to be fertility totems, used in worship and the casting of sympathetic magic. The idea was the fertility of the "mother goddess" could be bestowed upon the women of the tribe but also that fecundity could be transferred to the crops or the flocks or whatever the tribe sought to have in abundance, as well.

That was the theory.

Of the paleontologists, that is.

Apparently, there are practitioners of power who store their—I don't know, this isn't my field—mojo? in such a way as to "bulk up" over time. You've seen how body builders increase muscle size as they grow in strength. And fat cells propagate to store potential energy for the body when calories aren't burned in sufficient quantities to equalize food consumed. Apparently there is a way in which people of power store their mojo for those times in which it may be needed. A skeletal Marie Laveau had exhausted her stores and had to utilize a resurrected Rasputin to act as her proxy when she summoned the storm. Mama Samm, in opposing both Laveau and Rasputin and dispersing the storm out into the gulf had used up just about everything she had. All of that potential power that she had accumulated over the long years was expended in a single day.

And not just what was stored in bulk form.

The woman was far older than the girl we found in the hatch appeared to be. In loosing that much power she had unraveled knowledge and wisdom, matters concerned with years of experience and study. She'd lost two-thirds of her body mass and more than half her age in the process.

Mama Samm D'Arbonne was a twenty-two-year-old young woman with no mojo left, so to speak, and only her wits to protect her now.

So I handed her my Glock and explained the basics as we prepared to go after the others.

"There was a huge tidal reverse after the tsunamis and the quakes," she explained as we picked our way across a network of broken masts, spars, carefully laid ladders, gangplanks, strung ropes and nets that had been rigged to form precarious catwalks linking the flotilla of captive vessels.

Although the footing looked treacherous, I figured if the Deep Ones had rigged them to support press gangs carrying struggling captives, they'd more than support us in a pinch.

"We did what we could to ferry survivors, food, and potable water back and forth between the safer points of refuge," she continued. "We were running low on fuel and had taken on as many passengers as we could, especially those most in need of medical attention. The plan was to make a run north until we could find where the Mississippi met dry land again. It was thought that would be our best bet for medical facilities near the water."

As I helped her over a tangle of sailcloth and shattered wood I had my hands on her fluted waist and she steadied herself by grasping my bicep. "Have you been working out?" she chirped. She leaned in. "What are you wearing? Aftershave?"

"So what happened next?" I asked, releasing her a little early and causing her to stumble a bit.

"Oh yeah. That's when the Coast Guard cutter showed up," she said, "minus the Coast Guard. Those things that you've tangled with underwater, the Deep Ones? Well, they're not born that way. They start off looking human—reasonably human, anyway. Over the years they change into something that looks like it always came from the sea. In this instance the crew had been replaced by these creatures that still looked human from a ways off. But up close . . . " She shuddered like any twenty-two-year-old girl might and I wondered how much of Mama Samm had been lost along with her power.

"They forcibly escorted us out here and took what was left of our fuel and departed. That was yesterday. We tried radioing for help but the captain suspected—suspects—that someone or something is jamming communications. He took a complement of the more experienced crew to investigate. That was last night. This morning the Deep Ones came for us.

"We saw them coming from a distance. There was a big argument but we decided to hide as best we could rather than all be taken together. I guess I hid the best," she said in a small voice.

"Thank God you did," I reassured her as she led us across a net-surfaced walkway that belonged in some nightmare boot camp. "If you hadn't still been there to cover the radio we never would have found you and there'd be no chance for a rescue!"

It was true but guilt rarely acknowledges logic.

"Did you see where they took them from here?"

She pointed. "Up there."

A steel chain ladder hung from a ragged torch-cut hole in the side of the ocean liner.

🦇   🦇   🦇

One typically associates movement into the Devil's domain as a downward motion, i.e., a "descent" into Hell . . .

We climbed the ladder and *ascended* into Hell.

The disco ball was the first clue. It reflected the red emergency lighting throughout the dance club on the other side of the cut-out bulkhead like a thousand fingers of flame. The effect was almost jolly until I noticed the ceiling streamers were dripping on the Lucite-paneled disco floor. What kinds of streamers were ropelike and lumpy, anyhow?

Volpea snarled, hair starting to bristle up across her face. Zotz growled and suddenly the tall Asian fellow who'd been with us since Gordon's visit this afternoon was an 800–pound bat-thing, all teeth and talons and barely bridled power. Since his clothing was all part and parcel of the appearance he generated for each transformation, the equipment in his ops vest tumbled to the floor as it disappeared with the rest of his former glamour. I took a step back and nearly tripped over Suki's cat form as she had come tumbling out with everything else. Daintily, she padded over to a puddle of viscous liquid that was pooling under one of the grisly decorations and began lapping at it.

"Blood," Samm moaned (I couldn't hardly think of this slip of a girl as "Mama" Samm right now). "Can't you smell it?" she asked me.

"Well? Yeah. Now."

"Not just in here," Setanta said, stepping around the puddles without actually looking down. "You can smell it in the ventilation shafts."

"Crap," I said. "Let's move out!"

"Come, Mrs. Bigglesworth," Zotz called.

Suki *merrowed* and obediently fell into line.

We pushed through into a dining room. It was in use. The Deep Ones may have had uses for knives but they weren't fork and spoon guys. Never mind the good china, paper plates would have been wasted on them. Likewise napkins. The tablecloths had soaked up a good bit of the gore but the carpeting was still squishy with the overflow. There were maybe thirty or more chowing down on—well, the emergency lighting made everything look red so maybe speculation should be left to those who had the time and stomach for such luxuries.

Volpea was tearing through the remnants of her clothing, looking like some kind of hairy, red, hell beast that walked erect but shouldn't. Her face pinched down and forward as her ears went black and pointed and moved up on her skull. Her hands became blackened paws with sharpened nails and her mouth filled with needle-sharp teeth. As the last of her clothing tore away I could see her tail grow plump and fat and the fur around her cheeks, chin, and down her chest and belly flushed out white.

Volpea was a fox! A werefox!

Zotz was all Tyrannosaurus bat and charging in just ahead of the fox-woman.

But Setanta was Setanta no longer. He was Cuchulainn, Celtic berserker of song and legend. His golden-red hair was standing on end and seeming to give off sparks as he rushed ahead of the other two. The archangel's sword raised over his head came down and around decapitating four of the finny freaks at once. I glanced at Samm and Liban to be sure they were all right before wading in on my own. The former was pointing my Glock everywhere, the latter had the Mossberg leveled but otherwise wasn't tracking any targets. Maybe she'd shoot if something came close. In the meantime all of the targets were across the room and moving in short, violent arcs. I left the Smith & Wesson in its harness and flexed my increasingly prickly hands as I jogged toward the melee.

It was over pretty quickly.

Even better, it was over pretty *quietly*. No shots were fired. There was still a chance for some element of surprise.

*** *** ***

Zotz refused to change so he had to stoop like Quasimodo to get through most of the passageways. Volpea held her fox form but remained humanoid enough to walk erect and retain a semblance of speech. And Cuch—well, I remember some buddies coming back from the Middle East that you always tried to talk out of that third beer at the bar—they had that same look in their eyes and you knew things were going to get broken in short order.

Liban looked stronger, now, though she still held the shotgun like it was an alien object. Which I guess it was.

Samm was looking calmer and a little more like Cuch. She kept twitching the Glock around and it made me a little more nervous to have her behind me. Finally I put her in front of me where I could keep a better eye on her and shake the odd sensation that someone was staring at my ass all of the time.

We pressed on.

For the next little while we encountered our amphibious adversaries individually and in twos and threes so there was no real resistance to speak of. On the other hand, time was slipping away and we seemed to be wandering in a three-dimensional maze.

Liban pulled me aside during a three-minute rest break in one of the ship's storerooms.

"I heard the werewolf's threat on the radio earlier," she said.

"It's an old song."

"Where can you go that they won't eventually track you down?"

I shrugged. "It's finally become clear to me that the only way my family is ever going to be safe is for me to be a bigger monster than the ones who hunt us."

She nodded. "Perhaps. Or you could send your son somewhere safe, somewhere out of their reach."

I stared at her. "Are we back to this again?"

"It wouldn't be for Fand. I don't—" There was a catch in her voice. "I don't even know if she's still alive. Opening a faerie door, well, there should have been enough help on the other side to send that monster straight to Hell and tend my sister's wounds in short order. That we have not heard . . . " Liban looked away. "If I take your son into the realm of the Fey, none can follow. He will be safe. He will know peace and be raised as a prince."

"Back up a little, Liban. You said none can follow. Does that include family visits from his mom and me?"

She shook her head. "If he is allowed entry, he must be adopted as one of us. He severs mortal ties. You cannot follow after, even for a visit."

I nodded. "Well, I can tell you right now his mother isn't going to go for it. And I'm even less crazy about the terms. So thanks but no—"

Samm suddenly appeared by my side. "Where did you go? One minute you were behind me, the next minute?"

"Um, look," I said, "we should probably talk about my nanites. Dr. Mooncloud made an interesting discovery recently—"

"About your pheromones?" Samm interrupted. "Yeah, she told me about that." She fished around in her shirt pocket and pulled out a generic squeeze bottle of nasal spray. "Good thing she gave me the antidote."

"Um," I said, "I thought the antidote she was working on was still experimental."

"Hmph." She tucked it back into her shirt pocket. "Seems to be working just fine for me." She smiled and slapped me on the butt as Cuch and Zotz joined us.

"Maybe there's a way to question one of them," Cuchulainn was suggesting.

"Those that have fully transformed," Samm answered, suddenly all business, "no longer speak in human tongues."

"What about the mermaid, here?" Zotz asked. "Maybe she parlay-voos sea-monster speak."

Liban shook her head. "My sister and I are only recently arrived to your shores. These creatures are beyond our ken and none have seen the like neither round Manx nor anywhere across the sea."

434 Wm. Mark Simmons

"That's good to know," Samm said. "They have not spread so far, yet."

I stopped walking. "Maybe I can have a little chat with these freaks . . . "

Zotz looked at me and grinned. "Why didn't we think of this sooner?"

I knew why. I was too tired to think. I'd had very little sleep and the little I'd had hadn't been restful. We left the storeroom, worked our way down a corridor of state-rooms, then up a staircase and out onto the Lido deck. The stars were out.

The monsters weren't.

Neither was Doc, Gopher, Julie, or Isaac the bar-tender.

"There's never a monster around when you need one," Volpea growled.

I didn't know her well enough to run an irony check, yet.

The bat-demon had a suggestion: "Maybe if we make a lot of noise they'll come running."

"I need a little calm and quiet to work this," I told him. "I can't concentrate with lots of screaming and body parts flying through the air—even if they're not ours."

We went back down below via another stairway and found a theater. And a couple of fishfolk down on the floor behind the back row trying to make the two-backed barracuda.

Zotz grabbed one, Cuchulainn the other and yanked. The young-sturgeons-in-love made a sound like Velcro as they were pulled apart. The one in Zotz's grasp went limp. Cuchulainn smacked the other lightly but there was more than enough blood as a result. I did what I always do when entering another's consciousness through the portal of blood.

It wasn't the same.

Not by a long shot.

I had once placed my mind inside the consciousness of a wolf by using a chakra point. That had been different on both counts. All of the other times I had found an individual's blood to be the gateway.

But I had dealt with creatures much like myself under those circumstances: humans, lycanthropes, the undead.

This was very different.

The blood was different.

And the mind was *very* different.

It wasn't like being in a space or an area or even a box or container. It was like being in a sponge. And I was being absorbed into a thousand little cells and spaces, fragmenting, dissolving.

Thoughts that were not my own chittered and giggled inside my own mind. Normally I would push the other's consciousness into a position of obeisance and see what I could learn while I was in control of the new flesh. But this thing was unfamiliar, slippery. Its mind was as alien a maze as the dimly lit, gore-strewn decks of the passenger cruise ship we were practically lost in.

I had to get out before I was totally absorbed! Lost in some coral-faceted brain of a fish thing that was inhuman and soulless.

I tried to turn and saw the others looking at me as if through a fishbowl. My former flesh was in a heap on the theater floor, my head cradled in Liban's lap. Samm seemed to be overly solicitous as well.

I turned the other way. Out through that door! Down a secondary staircase! Through the plaza and the room of cages. Into the temple! Must reach the temple! Warn—!

A twisting wrench and I was staring up into the sea green eyes of Liban.

"I can take over for a while if you get uncomfortable," Samm's voice murmured somewhere near my ear.

"Fine!" I said, jerking up and hitting the sea goddess' chin with the top of my head as I struggled to sit up. "I'm fine! I'm going to get up now!"

And I did get up. And I fell back down. And I tried to throw up again as I crouched on my hands and knees on the squishy carpet.

I really had to start eating solid food again or the next time my stomach might actually turn inside out and crawl back out through my esophagus.

The "plaza" was actually a gymnasium.

Of course what would Charlie the Tuna know about gyms or weights or speed bags or stationary bikes? Just a big, airy room with a wood floor, lined by mirrored walls. Half of those mirrors were smashed and most were marked with splats of blood, as well. Dead moist things had been dragged across the floor into the next room, so we took a moment to check weapons and reset our formation.

Something awful lay beyond the next door or two. I could feel it like a sick certainty. The way the olfactory enhanced had smelled the blood through the ventilation shafts. And there was something in the Deep One's mind. Something without language, something beyond imagery—but something that I could *feel* through his emotions. Something too hideous to grasp but too terrible to not sense.

Everything that I had glimpsed in the creature's mind was heavily filtered . . .

Plaza . . . room of cages . . . temple . . .

And something else. *A great dark presence beyond.*

>Father . . . <

>Mother . . . <

What?

What could be more terrible than the inhuman slaughter that we'd been practically wading through for the past hour?

Except the deaths of the people I actually knew and loved?

Thinking . . . thinking didn't help. Feeling didn't help. Doing . . . only doing would matter now and maybe not even that.

"End of the world, boys and girls," I announced. "I'm going first." And I kicked the door open.

It was the room of many cages. A locker room with steel mesh lockers for the gymnasium. It was where the passengers would keep a towel and a change of clothes while they worked out.

It was where the Deep Ones kept their human chattel until they were hungry. Bodies were crammed into the narrow spaces, bruised, bloody, and battered but still alive.

No order was given. Nothing was said. Everyone just fanned out and began breaking open the lockers. Some of the occupants tumbled out dead—heart attacks or strokes brought on by fear, most likely. Others were

unconscious or nearly catatonic. Even the most responsive were too dazed or too hurt to move right away so
there was no mass exodus. Just a few ripples of panic.

One prisoner was different in every way, however.

The creature squirming about inside the narrow cage
was all teeth and claws and hair and only half human.
Samm tried to calm her before anyone opened the
locker door.

"Irena? Baby? It's Samm. Mama Samm D'Arbonne.
Remember? I brought help. There's friends here but you
gots to calm down before we lets you out. Can you do
that, baby? Put the beast back inside for a little while?"

The creature that looked like some kind of animé juxtaposition of cat and teenaged girl turned and twisted in
her confinement but eventually quieted under Samm's
quiet reassurances. Cuchulainn pulled off his bloody
shirt so that Irena would have something to wear. We
turned our backs as Samm set her free and helped her
cover up. Sure, there was an element of chivalry involved
but we had a perimeter to watch and I was starting to
hear strange sounds beyond the next door.

"Irena?" I heard Samm say. "Where is Miss Lupé?
Do you know where Miss Deirdre is? What happened
to the rest of the crew?"

"I don't know," she said with an awkward mixture of
fear and anger. "I tried to change and they piled on top
of me. We got separated. I haven't seen them since."

The fact that Irena was alive was a good sign. The fact
that the others weren't with her and she didn't know
anything wasn't helpful. It wasn't unhelpful. Standing
around doing nothing was.

I started to move in toward the next set of doors and most of the others, Mrs. Bigglesworth included, moved with me.

"Shouldn't somebody stay here with the rest of the hostages?" Samm asked. Some had already wandered off, looking to escape on their own, but there were still a goodly number sitting around looking dazed.

"And do what?" Zotz wanted to know. "I thought we discussed this."

We had discussed this very thing.

Back on the *Spindrift*.

And, before that, on the *New Moon*.

Any time the question of leaving someone behind comes up—for their own protection, to look after someone else, to perform some extra task—the Tao of the Creature Feature is invoked. To wit: under no circumstances does the group ever, *ever* split up or allow anyone to go off alone or remain behind! Those are the people who die first. And, as the group gets smaller, everyone starts dying off more frequently. So sayeth the Tao of the Creature Feature. And we had all agreed twice now to stay together, no matter what.

"He's right," I told Samm. "If we're flanked by multiples you can't save them or yourself anyway."

"Yeah, Little Mama," Zotz continued, "the only way that suggestion could be any worse would be to stay behind to have sex!"

He cackled and she gave me a quick, awkward look.

"Here we go," I said.

Of course it was a temple.

Never mind the swimming pool, no other chamber on the ship had tiled walls and ceiling as well as the floor.

There was an adjacent steam room and it was flooding the pool area with enough water vapor to give the illusion of an undersea grotto.

The pool was lined with mer-people. Deep Ones knelt around the edge three deep and took communion at the water's edge. Cupping their hands they reached down in and drew forth its steaming contents to sip from their palms or lick from their fingers. Some were marking themselves with it, making symbols on their chests and sigils upon their foreheads.

And finally, I could make my mind say what "it" was, for the swimming pool was not filled with water but with human blood. A great soup bowl of blood, viscera, and even fresh bodies as, one by one, the human cattle were being laid out on the diving board and being butchered.

A Deep One stood at the diving board wearing a robe and a jeweled tiara, shaped almost like a religious miter. He chanted a strange and unintelligible incantation—something with a lot of nonsense syllables and then something that sounded like "*Vater Dagon!*" Then "*Mutar Hydra!*"

The congregation chanted: "*Ia, ia!*"

And drank from the pool as a golden dagger, its hilt encrusted with gems, flashed down and sliced open another sacrifice. The victim was pushed from the diving platform and another was brought forward, the next in a long line of struggling, shrieking captives that stretched across the diving area and through a side door, into another storage room.

It seemed like we stood there, frozen, for an eternity, overwhelmed by this spectacle of wanton cruelty, this glimpse of the new world order. But only one life had been taken since we entered the room. We had only witnessed the fall of the blade once.

Time, however, continued to unspool.

The next sacrifice was already on the "altar."

Zotz and Cuchulainn and Volpea were already charging the line of hostages. I stood back and let them. The Frogs on the other side of the pool had noticed us and were getting to their feet and I wanted no part of them. Yet.

The golden blade came back up.

So did the big Smith & Wesson in my hands.

"*Ia* this, motherfucker," I said, and pulled the trigger. The boom of the 50-caliber slug was deafening in the tiled room. Everyone stopped and stared at me, at their high priest.

At the fact I'd missed.

The high priest grinned, exposing teeth like a moray eel's. The chanting began anew. This time the nonsense syllables were more familiar: "*Ia! Ia! Ph'nglui mglw'nafh Cthulhu R'lyeh wgah'nagl fhtagn!*"

The other congregants took up the chant: "*Ia! Ia! Ph'nglui mglw'nafh Cthulhu R'lyeh wgah'nagl fhtagn!*"

And as the words repeated over and over, a strange sort of nauseousness rose up in me. The room seemed to distort. And two shadows seemed to form in midair, one upon each side of the high priest.

"*Ia!*" screamed the congregation. "*Dagon! Hydra!*" They flung their clawed and scaly hands about, beat their breasts, tore at the own faces. "*Vater! Mutar!*"

The shadows seemed to coalesce, to take on forms.

And the forms were of a hideous aspect. Scaly, tentacled, lizardlike—

Samm was walking right up to the diving board, her dark diminutive form unnoticed in the midst of the religious frenzy and the posturing of us macho warrior folk.

Three sharp reports ensued as the Glock made golf-ball-sized holes in the priest's face, chest and belly. He crumpled, the shadows faded, and pandemonium erupted.

Samm was instantly swarmed by the closest Deep Ones and she went down under a pile of them. Lucky for her they were too much in each other's way to do any serious damage before I arrived and started using the magnum-sized revolver like a steel mallet on their heads. I was like a machine only joyous. Efficiently cracking skulls and laughing with the pure joy of confronting something evil without restraint, concerns for my own humanity, or concessions to political correctness.

Claws raked at me but the nanites kept ahead on the repairs and that was good as I needed to shield Samm with my body as well. Liban, Volpea, Irena, Camazotz, even Cuchulainn and I were preternatural in one way or another. But Sammathea D'Arbonne was only human, now. And, after all of the times she had looked after me and mine, it was my turn to see that she came out all right on the other end.

At last, the Frogs either died or ran and the room was nearly quiet again.

I was bruised and battered and exhausted and getting that alarming little buzz that I was overdue to feed the nanos again.

Fortunately there was an abundance of blood around to keep my little nano-vampires happy for a long time.

And fortunately I was finally monster enough to not care that the blood wasn't given willingly.

It was blood. It would go to waste if I didn't use it. I wasn't the one who had taken it from the victims in the first place so there was no chain of guilt, of obligation.

I went to the pool and knelt and began to scoop up the precious fluid of life with my hand and drink, even as the fishfolk had been doing a half hour before. That produced a momentary gag reflex but the need was on me and I drank again.

Suki joined me, mimicking me by dipping a paw into the crimson goo. Then she jumped in and began to swim about.

I almost gagged again.

But, the monster thing. If I was going to save my family, I was really going to have to get on with being all that I could be—monsterwise, that is. I drank some more. Made my nanites happy.

It wasn't as potent or satisfying as Liban's or some of the more exotic hemoglobin I had sampled over the past two years but you can't go wrong with the basics. And this was a unique experience as I was getting a mixture of all different types at once, thickened up with some viscera and actual bodies that had fallen off of the board and into the pool during the ceremonies. One was floating next to where I knelt and, as I pushed it away, it rolled over and opened its eyes.

I knew those eyes!

Those ruby-red eyes that so perfectly matched her hair!

Everyone dumped in the font of blood had hair the color of gore, now, but only one person could have *eyes* the color of arterial blood . . .

"Deirdre!" I cried, "Oh my *God*! Deirdre!" I tried to pull her out but she screamed.

"Don't move me!" she whispered. "The baby! It will kill the baby!"

Suddenly Liban was next to me. And Volpea was diving into the pool.

"Deirdre," I said, "where's Lupé? Did you see where they took her?"

"Found her!" Volpea cried. More splashes as Zotz and Samm jumped in.

And then a door opened and the room started to flood with the damned Frogs!

Chapter Eighteen

FOR JUST A MOMENT in time the situation was very simple.

Deirdre and the baby might live or they might die.

Lupé and my son might still be alive or they might already be dead.

But one thing for damn sure, they didn't have a chance in Hell if we let any more of these Froggies come a-courtin'. I leapt to my feet and joined Cuchulainn in meeting the charge.

We smashed into the first half dozen and Cuch immediately cut three of them down with the greatsword. I smashed two amphibian skulls together while a third fishman tried to climb me like a telephone lineman.

"She's alive!" Zotz bellowed behind me.

Of course she was. Lupé was a were. Unless they used a silver blade she'd be hard to kill.

I threw the climber off and onto a couple of his wingmen. Cuchulainn had sliced and diced through three more to get within ten feet of the door.

"I'm not sure the baby will make it, though!" Volpea yelled.

I wrenched one of the Deep One's heads so viciously it popped off showering me with ichorlike blood.

Of course not. We were more than a hundred and fifty miles from a doctor and adequate medical facilities. And the odds were against the hale and healthy getting off this boat at this very moment.

Cuchulainn cut down two more Deep Ones and then slammed the door shut with a massively muscled shoulder. Turning and bracing his back against the shuddering entryway, he tossed me the sword and I made short work of the remaining three Frogs.

I ran back to the pool and knelt down to where Volpea and Zotz had borne Lupé. Her face and hair were a study in scarlet and her eyes remained closed. Her breathing was ragged and all the more worrisome as she was breathing for two.

"Lupé?" I whispered.

"Save the baby," she whispered. "Save our son. Nothing else matters . . . "

I looked back over at Deirdre. "Where's Dr. Mooncloud?"

My former enforcer groaned. "Not here. Stayed with Theresa."

"What? They didn't come?" It vaguely occurred to me that Laveau had kept her word in giving Kellerman her own body and freeing Deirdre in the process.

Samm put a hand on my arm. "I thought you knew. Theresa refused to leave. Mooncloud stayed behind to help provide cover—"

I nodded. "So Irena could get the others out without Laveau's goons stopping them. Okay. No doctor." I would think about the likely fate of Dr. Mooncloud, Theresa, and one of the cloned fetuses later. Right now: the problems at hand!

Since Lupé was a were and I was a—what? No longer fully human but still largely undefined. The point: our son should have some genetic toughness giving him the edge in a medical emergency. And Deirdre, as a former vampire and now also undefined preternatural entity—she had survived a human sacrifice. But would the cloned human embryo implanted in her womb survive? And which one was it? My deceased wife? My dead daughter?

Dead twice because of me?

I ground the heels of my fists into my eye sockets. "Is there anything in the room we can fabricate stretchers out of?"

"We are running out of time," Cuchulainn called from his post at the door, the repeated pounding making his voice shake.

"Getting tired, Big Guy?" Zotz growled.

"No. Just thinking that no matter how stupid these things are, sooner or later they're going to figure out there are other ways into this room." It was the longest speech I had ever heard him make.

The rest of us looked at each other.

And I looked at Liban.

She was holding Deirdre's head up out of the carnage soup and looking at me.

"Can you open the door here?" I asked. "Take them to your healers?"

"Take them now?" she asked. "Both mother and son?"

"I can't let them die!"

She nodded. "But if he is born in my realm, you will never see him again."

"I thought that was the deal."

"No. Only that if I took him as changeling, you could not follow to visit. There was always the possibility he could come to you. You *are* his father. But if his mother comes to us and he be born in our realm then, under the Accords, he is no longer yours nor of your kind. The blood bond is severed. You sacrifice your claim forever."

I started and stared at her. "Sacrifice?"

Her breath stuttered and her eyes grew wide: "The Telling . . . "

My heart caught in my chest. Sacrifice . . .

Fate . . .

Fatum in the ancient Latin.

From *fari,* meaning to "tell" or "predict."

Was *this* the sacrifice preordained by some distant oracle from the start?

Or was it a more nebulous destiny that there would be *some* kind of sacrifice, *some* kind of loss, and every time I had conspired to keep my son from Fate's altar, events shifted, possibilities changed, outcomes wavered—but the final destination remained: there would be *some* kind of sacrifice?

The room was suddenly quiet.

"They've stopped trying to break through the door," Cuchulainn said. "They will try another door in a moment. Mayhap more than one."

"Save them," I told Liban.

"The mother and the child?"

"Both mothers, both children," I said. "I want you to take Deirdre, too."

She shook her head. "I do not know what the others will permit. I do not know if I have the strength to port all of us."

"If everyone wants my son so bloody much, those are the terms of the deal!"

She looked down at Deirdre then over at Lupé. "I can but try."

I leaned down and kissed Lupé on her forehead. The last time I had done so, the silver compounds in my tissues had burned her badly. Perhaps the nanites were detoxifying my lips for this one specific task. Or maybe the slimy skein of blood that coated her hair and skin protected her just enough from that chaste, momentary contact. "Take care of our son," I whispered. "Take care of yourself." Anything more seemed hurtful and inadequate. I eased her over into Liban's embrace.

Deirdre opened her eyes again and looked up at me. "Don't I get a kiss? I'm having your baby, too."

I think I started to laugh. I couldn't tell: there were tears in my eyes. "Which one? My wife or my daughter?"

She coughed a little and I couldn't tell if the bloody spittle on her lips was her own or from the pool. "Does it matter? You're never going to see us again, anyway."

"Hey," I murmured, "I'd rather never see you alive than see you dead."

"Yeah, yeah . . ." She rolled her eyes over at Volpea. "You the new enforcer?"

Volpea nodded.

"Take good care of him until I get back."

Samm leaned toward me and stage-whispered. "She doesn't understand. She thinks they'll let her come back."

"She understands," Lupé muttered. "I'd worry about the elves if I were you."

And that was that because three different doors flew open and more Deep Ones burst in to reclaim their temple.

Six things happened at once.

Liban began to chant.

I tossed the sword back to Cuch and picked up the Mossberg.

Volpea and Zotz climbed out of the pool streaming blood and gore like a couple of wedding fountains in a slaughterhouse.

Irena slipped from the tent of Cuchulainn's shirt, crouched down, and her smooth brown flesh rippled and flowed into a pelt of sleek black fur. The panther growled then screamed a challenge.

Samm raised the Glock and adopted a shooter's stance.

And something that looked like a cross between a bull-dog and a komodo dragon with mange burst out of the pool and lunged at the largest knot of Deep Ones like a fat man at an unattended hotdog stand.

Chaos reigned. Blood flowed. Grievous wounds ensued.

There are those who have complained, upon those few occasions when I can be compelled to recount certain events, that I do not provide sufficient details of the epic battles, the face-to-face, to-the-death matches in which I saw my enemies fall before me or else saw them dispatched by my allies. It is as if some would find entertainment value in graphic descriptions of gruesome deaths, bloody mutilations, horrific acts of savagery—battle porn for the armchair warriors. I understand the bloodlust that rises on the battlefield, the body's fight-or-flight response to danger and the berserker rage that takes over in the presence of those who would do you and your family harm. It is one thing to joyously commit to the destruction of evil, personified by its foot soldiers in a physical confrontation. Quite another to revel vicariously in the tales of old soldiers, lusting for the gory details while surrounded by the peace and comforts of hearth and home.

Perhaps the details would be more important if, one by one, my companions were falling beneath the teeth and claws of the Children of Daddy Dagon. The Deep Ones presented a frightening visage to humans whose closest encounter with the dark side was a tax audit. One on one they were a lot less formidable for a Mesoamerican bat-demon or an immortal Celtic battle god, or even a cybernetically enhanced, necrophagically juiced, semi-undead, majorly pissed-off guy who had just lost his family, thanks to these finny cretins. One on one, we kicked ass like there was no tomorrow.

The disparity in numbers changed the dynamics, however. For each Deep One dropped, two more appeared to take its place. The room was getting crowded, not just from the pile of bodies but from the new bodies piling on. Slowly but steadily we were being backed toward the pool again.

Then the ambient light changed from red to purple. I looked over my shoulder. A nimbus of pulsing blue light surrounded Liban, Deirdre, and Lupé, contrasting with the red glow of the emergency lights. They flickered like an optical illusion and a fragrance of sap moss momentarily leaked into the sharp, sweet, metallic-tasting air.

I turned back to deal with the three Frogs that were attempting to eviscerate me with their claws and mostly getting in each other's way. I had yet to fire the Mossberg; it held a finite number of shells and our foes were beginning to appear infinite in numbers. It worked well enough as a club and I had just beaten down the second amphibian when the bang of displaced air behind me told me that my family was gone forever. I swung the Mossberg hard enough to take off the third creature's head and guarantee that the shotgun could never again be discharged in a safe manner.

I looked back at the empty place they had occupied and saw a fearsome sight.

A scaled creature was climbing out of the bloody swamp of sacrifices.

Humanoid, it was barely five feet in height and it glittered from head to toe in brass-colored scales. Metallic wings flared back from its bulbous head and sharp spikes and angles jutted from its elbows and knees. Its torso was encased in a hard-shelled carapace like a pale gold beetle and a curtain of blood veiled its face and draped its body in such a way that I didn't recognize her until she drew near and drew her short sword.

"Run," Fand said. "Take the others and leave the ship."

I stared at Liban's sister all decked out in archaic battle armor. "There are hostages and wounded all over the place."

She stared back. "You have made the hardest sacrifice. The rest will be easier, now. Go. The pathways are merging one last time. If you do not leave now you will miss your transport. And then how will you fulfill the Telling and save the world?"

I just stared at her with my mouth open as she turned and gutted a couple of attacking Deep Ones with her sword. What kind of answer could I give to a bunch of gibberish that continued to make no sense? Merging pathways? Transport? Save the world? And, hey, running away from the monsters right here and right now seemed a sorry start to the world-saving process.

Besides, pounding these Froggies into chum just felt so good!

"Look back at the sacrificial basin," Fand said as I grabbed another head and gave it a three-quarter twist.

I glanced back at Liban's point of departure and Fand's port of entry. The swimming pool was limned in an actinic black glow.

Don't ask me how the color black can glow and even give the impression of being too bright to look at directly but, there it was. The pool suddenly fell through the floor and the edges of the pool-shaped hole smoked and flickered in an oval-shaped line of red-orange. Meanwhile the black glow started to move away from that empty hole in all directions. Whatever it touched disappeared in gouts of odoriferous smoke. Flooring, pool chairs, bodies—anything.

"Don't let the glow touch you," Fand said unnecessarily.

At the rate it was spreading, the room's floor would be wholly consumed in less than seven minutes. Well, before that, in maybe two minutes, the room would be bisected where the ends of the pool were closest to the walls. As the divide widened, we would be forced into the arms of the Deep Ones as we ran out of flooring and the chasm widened at our backs.

It was time to retreat.

"Fall back!" I yelled. "And don't anybody touch the dark lights!"

As we retired from the field, the Froggies followed. When we jumped the widening divide, they jumped after us. So we turned and beat them down until the gap was so wide they were falling into the eerie area of effect.

The Deep Ones weren't fast learners. Even the sight of their comrades falling against the dissolving edge of the floor and being chewed in half by the boiling black light didn't deter them. Wave after wave made the attempt, screaming, "*Ia! Ia!*"

Zotz yelled: "Hey now!" and I yelled: "Hey now!" and we yelled: "Iko, iko, un-day!" to taunt them forward. Occasionally we'd change it up with "Old MacDonald had a farm, Ee-i-ee-i-oh!" It worked far longer than it should have: fifty or more fell into the glowy pit where the pool had descended through the decks below.

And now the sound of rushing, churning water began to rise from those same depths and the entire ship began to shudder.

"We've been holed!" Zotz said, peering over the edge. "We won't make it back out the way we came in, in time—even if we don't encounter any resistance."

"I'm thinking there will be resistance," Cuchulainn observed, wiping his sword on a discarded towel.

"We go up to an outer deck and lower a lifeboat," Samm said.

I looked at Fand. "Okay, you dissolve the ship. Fine. Force us all back into the water. The water's their element, not ours!" I yelled.

"First of all," she answered, "we destroy their breeding chambers—"

"We caught a couple of the little buggers breeding. Have to say I'm not impressed."

"Not the Deep Ones!" Fand yelled, pointing at another door. "The shoggoths!" A carpet of bubbling goo was pouring into the room and rolling across the cowering line of waiting sacrifices who had not yet fled during the confusion. I felt a flash of pity mixed with annoyance at their bovine stupidity. Then relief that one problem had been taken out of my hands.

Checking the scorecard: more monster than human, now.

"We destroy their temple!" Fand continued as the pudding flowed to the edge of the pit and began to hiss and burn where it made contact with the flickering field of black. "That buys you time."

"Time? Time for what?"

The floor was half gone and so were the shoggoths. We had to leave now.

"Time to go!" Zotz yelled as the ship lurched and tilted some fifteen degrees to starboard.

We ran, looking for an exit before it all turned into *The Poseidon Adventure*.

Every few minutes the ship would shake and groan and tilt some more as it settled deeper into the water. We threaded our way through a three-story theater and showroom, the multitiered rows of seats providing a diabolical obstacle course in their canted, new positions. We came to a five-story atrium but the glass elevators could not be trusted so we made do with ramps and companionways that were doubly steep now and angled to where we often split the difference between walking on a wall or a floor.

"Stop it!" Volpea growled at Zotz.

I looked at the werefox and the bat-demon who were jogging, nearly side by side. Volpea caught my look. "He's humming 'My Heart Will Go On'!" she explained. "I hate that movie! Even more so, now!"

Zotz turned his head and grinned at her. "But . . . Leo . . . ?" he pleaded with mock sincerity.

"Don't make me have to separate you two," I wheezed. The nanos were getting testy about my energy consumption this past hour. Either they were getting greedy or I wasn't taking enough time to refuel.

The Deep Ones were somewhat distracted by the destruction of their little city on the sea but they hadn't forgotten about us. We still had to fight our way through clumps and clusters and, more than once, were turned back when a corridor was flooded with a rising tide of shoggoth pudding.

A couple of times we turned the corner to find the corridor or stairs disappearing in a flicker of black light.

After an eternity of confused staggering and stumbling we emerged from the Hell-red glow of emergency lights to the death-dark purple of night sky.

A row of lifeboats were arranged about twenty meters up. It was an uphill climb now as the cruise ship's angle of descent quickened and sharpened. The good news? It was only a three-story drop to the water now instead of seven.

The bad news? Another set of lifeboats some eighty meters behind us were much closer to the waterline but a rising tide of glow-in-the-dark tapioca was bubbling out of a row of smashed view ports and recongealing around their support struts. If the boat tilted any more we'd be sliding down to dinner—it's, not our's.

More bad news: the connecting latticework of wrecked boats and the tipped oil platform, itself, were now infected with traveling bands of black light. Getting to our own boats in time would be a very near thing.

Samm groaned. "Can it get any worse?"

I tried to shush her but it was too late: another group of Froggies burst out of the hatches farther up the deck and began rushing down upon us.

"We don't have time for this!" I snarled as I fumbled with the covers on the nearest lifeboat.

Fand said: "Keep working!" And she and Cuchulainn stepped away from the release controls, redrew their swords, and walked toward the approaching hoard of Deep Ones like a gladiatorial defensive line with orders to run out the clock.

I started after them but Zotz got in my way.

"Hey, Professor," he grinned planting a huge, taloned paw against my chest, "don't be gettin' your classics all confused here. We're doing Horiatius at the Bridge tonight, not Thermopylae. Get everyone else off the boat."

I pushed back. "Yeah? Who died and made you Chichen Itza of the Sea?"

He smiled. "Hey," he said quietly. "You gotta let me do this. Remember when I first came 'round, asking to learn from you? Well, I've learned a lot and now it's dissertation time. I don't think I can learn any more in this classroom so I'm going to transfer my credits and do a little internship with Dr. Fand, here, before I graduate. This is my coursework, not yours, Teach. You've got other fish to fry." He clapped that weird-ass hand of his on my shoulder. "See you at the class reunion." He turned and took several long strides to catch up with the diminutive Fand.

I stood there, numb, watching him go. Then it was time to check on the others.

Samm was working the controls at the release station while Volpea assisted Irena into the lifeboat.

I looked back down the deck way. More pudding was seething and bubbling and picking up speed and mass as it boiled toward us from below. I felt something push against my ankles. It was a somewhat less mangy Burmese cat with two tails. I picked her up and put her in the lifeboat. Turning the other way I watched as Cuchulainn and Camazotz Chamalcan formed a line across the deck with Fand in the middle. It wasn't wide enough. Some of the beasties were going to get through.

"Can we launch this thing?" I asked Samm.

"Almost got it," she said, frowning.

The Froggies were almost to the line Fand was trying to hold with even more Deep Ones spilling out of the doorways behind them. They wouldn't be able to hold them for more than a few minutes.

And they'd never be able to rejoin us before we launched.

"Okay," I said, cracking my knuckles. "Start the launch sequence as soon as you can and get in the lifeboat. Bring a speedboat around if you can. If you can't, hold off just far enough to pick us up if we can clear the ship before it goes under. If you're likely to be caught in the suction or by these finny bastards coming in after you, pull away fast. Anything else means what has been done here today, what has been sacrificed—was all for nothing! Do you understand?"

She nodded reluctantly and I turned to move toward the Cséjthe-sized gap in the Cuchulainn-Fand-Comazotz line.

Volpea was in my way. "I concur," she said. She stepped into me. As she had shifted back to her human form she was nearly my height. She grabbed me, pulling me close and my face was an inch away from hers. "I made a promise to you and to your former enforcer," she said. "I'm on the clock, now."

Her bone and muscle mass had the density of a lycanthrope's. She lifted me with little effort, shifting her grip and tossing me into the lifeboat on top of Irena. She hissed reflexively. Then began to sniff at me. By the time I was able to untangle myself and peer over the gunwale, Volpea was shifting back to fox form and laying in to a couple of Frogs that had slipped past the line.

"Got it!" Samm yelled as the lifeboat gave a lurch. She hurried over and I helped her in as the launch began to descend.

"Zotz!" I bellowed. "ZOTZ!"

He glanced back and grinned.

"We're *going*!"

"Bon voyage, Professor!" he called back. And then he was too busy to talk anymore.

We dropped below the deck level and lost sight of them in another twenty seconds. I had three women now to think of—only one of them human—but I kept hoping I could bring the lifeboat around to where they could jump and we could retrieve them.

Our descent probably took less than two minutes but it seemed longer, watching and waiting for scaly foes to come slithering down the release lines on top of us. None did but then there was the matter of getting our keel in the water when the big ship was practically locked in by so many smaller craft in a jammed-up floating carpet of wood and lines, netting and sailcloth. We slid between a couple of overturned motorboats and unshipped the oars. Pushing away debris more than paddling, we eased the launch around to see if we could find a path closer to where Fand and the others were last holding their ground.

The way seemed closed: boats upright and sideways and upside down choked the area like a boneyard.

Then the first body leapt over the side and went crashing through a hull.

A second form jumped from above and landed on the side of a hull. Scrambled up and turned toward us. It was one of the Deep Ones.

Now dozens of Froggies were hopping over the side, hitting the water, landing on solid sections of hulls, or crashing through weak points in the debris field. They were coming from the point of battle with our friends.

"That's not good," Samm observed.

Maybe the fish-heads thought we had the greater target value. Or maybe Cuch and Fand and Zotz and Volpea were already down for the count . . .

"Or maybe they already done the sensible thing and your elf friend opened her a door now that we have got away," Samm said, looking at me like she could read my mind.

"Only we haven't gotten away," I said. "Not yet." I pointed back at the Deep Ones scrabbling after us like a wolf pack on a succession of ice floes. "Everybody grab an oar!"

As I struggled to fit my oar into the rowlock closest to me, Irena stood and stretched. Fortunately it was dark, further reducing the distraction that her now human form would have exerted as she had no clothes on. She leaned over as she moved aft and nuzzled my neck. "I like the way you smell," she purred. And then licked me, just once, behind the crease of my jaw.

I shivered. "If you really like my smell," I muttered, "you'd pick up an oar."

She ignored the suggestion and settled herself at the back of our little craft. A moment later an engine coughed to life and we began to pick up speed.

Thank you, Captain Pantera!

The oars were still handy for pushing debris and helping maneuver through tight impactions of flotsam and jetsam.

Then we got stuck.

By that time we'd raided the boat's survival stores and donned lifejackets. I loaded the flare gun and fired it at a section of the boat jam where our pursuers were getting a little too close.

Were we in a Hollywood movie, the boat I hit would have caught fire and, within ten seconds, blown up spectacularly with a gigantic fireball silhouetting dozens of Deep Fries flying majestically in all directions.

This being reality, there was some glow, some smoke, and a wee bit of fire after awhile. If we were able to wait long enough there was the possibility that something might get going within the next hour or two. If the Deep Ones left our mangled bodies aboard our lifeboat we could actually have a Viking funeral by sometime tomorrow. Maybe.

I reloaded the Very pistol and fired again.

This time there was a huge Hollywood explosion! Water erupted in double geysers and the ocean liner shook and then keeled over on its side. The resulting impact wave ripped the conglomerate of boats apart and pushed us farther away from the epicenter of evil. I looked at the flare gun in my hand and then realized two things.

The explosion took place well away from where the first or second flares had landed.

And there was a bright beam of light now shining across the water at our little boat.

Leviathan!

The light swept round and over the doomed cruise ship to the canted drilling platform where hundreds of dark forms were momentarily revealed to be scurrying like ants.

"What's happening?" Samm asked.

"Wait for it . . . " I murmured.

Another loud boom accompanied by a gout of water and suddenly a pillar of flame rose where the water was subsiding. Now there was a chain reaction of explosions, a series of fireballs that ignited flashpoints among the tangle of pipes crowning the platform. The massive concrete and steel structure was coming to resemble a giant birthday cake for an aging sea god.

The searchlight swung back around and fixed on our tiny boat again.

"What do you think I should do, Chris?" Irena asked from her seat by the rudder.

"The enemy of mine enemy . . . " I took a deep breath. "Steer for that light."

᠁᠁᠁   ᠁᠁᠁   ᠁᠁᠁

I had to sit beside Irena and help steer.

At first we were all blinded by the bright beam of light that revealed the location of our mysterious benefactor.

Then my nanites rehabbed my eyes, providing sufficient filtration that the better portion of the visible spectrum was blocked and I was able to use the enhanced bookends of infrared and ultraviolet frequencies. It was a bizarre color cacophony that made no sense unless you ignored tints and limited your judgment to shape and outline.

A further distraction was Irena's groping hands. Her excuse that she couldn't see what she was doing sounded a little lame when she kept leaning into me and telling me how nice I smelled. Shortly after that she "was cold and needed to share body warmth." This was probably true given the sartorial challenges commonly faced by shapeshifters. It was just that her enthusiasm tended to undermine her sincerity. She seemed to think my holding hands with her was very romantic but, truth be told, it was the only way I could keep them from wandering where they shouldn't and allow me to concentrate on our quarry.

As we approached, the hive-mind programming tweaked my wetware a little more, retinting the color scheme and revealing a submarine. I mean, what else could it be? A careful examination with the ranging subroutines (no pun intended) built into my visual software, and I could see a cylindrical body approximately eighty meters long and eight meters in diameter, tapered at both ends. It had a four-bladed propeller, six meters in diameter with a pitch of seven-and-a-half meters. I could see a diving plane amidships on this side and assumed it was matched on the opposite side. The rudder set aft of the propeller was the full height of the boat. Compared to most commissioned submersibles, this was not your standard-sized submarine. Not a mini-sub but certainly not a configuration to be found in *Jane's Fighting Ships*, either. That might explain the lack of a "sail." Instead there was what appeared to be a two-meter, box-like wheelhouse with windows located forward and an area set apart near the vessel's midpoint where it was topped with a railing and a recessed object that may have been the upper portion of a covered disc-shaped lifeboat or launch. The searchlight was mounted aft.

Even though ninety percent of the sub was riding below the waterline, I could still see the grosser, submerged details. The nanites were working overtime and the resultant energy drain was creating a dangerous feed-back: Irena was starting to smell good to me, too.

All of that was forgotten when a hatch opened behind the recessed launch and a creature emerged.

It was immediately obvious from the silhouette, alone, that the creature wasn't human. Nor were the three crit-ters that joined it on deck.

The first was as tall as a man and manlike in general. His head, however, was leonine. Not in the romance novel sense of describing an older man of noble bearing, usually with a largish head of hair, great pride, and more than average strength. No, this thing had a head like that of a great cat!

The three things scampering around this apparition were even stranger in aspect. About the size and shape of deformed children with flat heads, it looked like some-one had strapped giant tortoise shells to their backs and big bird beaks to their faces. Between them they had several rifles or long guns and one was handed to the cat-headed fellow while the others were being loaded by the turtle-monkeys.

Cat-head shouldered his gun, swung it in our direction and began to fire.

The first bullet zinged less than a foot away, past my shoulder!

Chapter Nineteen

THE SECOND SHOT came within a foot of Samm who had just fallen against the port gunwale. That was when I simultaneously registered the sight of a scaly green hand on her oar and the sound of a splash behind me.

We were under attack!

Not by the beast men from the submarine but from Deep Ones who were preparing to swarm our lifeboat! The rifleman was shooting at them!

Irena shrieked as a webbed hand reached up, caught her hair, and yanked her head back. I grabbed her to keep her from going overboard and lost control of the tiller. There was a brief struggle and the next thing I knew I was holding the neatly severed arm of Irena's attacker. Not ripped off via superhuman strength, mind you—that would have been semiunderstandable. Neatly severed with surgical precision, shearing cleanly through bone as well as flesh? I looked at my bloody hands for a clue, found none, and shuddered. Maybe some fanboy might think these were cool superpowers or something but this was just scary as hell. Especially as I was still holding the severed arm and wondering if it would taste like chicken.

I wasn't just thirsty, now; I was hungry! *In a very wrong way!*

Four more Deep Ones joined their fallen teammates in Davy Jones' locker room as I found the willpower to toss the arm and sit back down. By the time I got the boat back under control, I found that the submarine had come about and was closing with us. As it pulled alongside, a roped step system was unfurled. After Samm and Irena climbed up, I picked up Suki and slung her around my neck. She purred as I climbed up after them.

Two of the turtle-monkeys remained on deck and assisted us into the hatch and down an interior ladder. Their leader had disappeared for the moment.

We were led down a short corridor to a cabin and given basins of water and towels. An adjoining head contained a corner cabinet of metal. This was demonstrated to be a shower with ornate, antique fixtures. It and a sink had hot and cold running taps. The cabin was paneled in wood, carpeted, and furnished in the Victorian style. There were two wardrobes and two dressers of surprising craftsmanship. Even the two sets of bunk beds were stylish beyond the utilitarian.

As much as we were taking in our new environment, we were studying our "hosts," as well.

About the size of ten-year-old children, they had the heads of beaked monkeys with a fringe of long, dark hair circling their skulls. The crowns of their heads were depressed like concave bowls and filled with a clear liquid like water. Their torsos were shelled like turtles or tortoises but their scaly limbs were longer with webbed hands and feet and they smelled like fish. Their dark, beady eyes shone with a fierce intelligence.

As we were studying the creature who was pointing to the basins, the shower, and the towels in turn, another like it entered bearing a stack of folded clothing with a note pinned to the top. The creature placed the clothing on top of a small table, unpinned the note, and handed it to me.

Please take a little time to freshen up, the note read. *The kappas will bring you to the salon when you have made yourselves more presentable.* It was signed *D*. The paper itself was imprinted stationary with the motto: *Mobilis in Mobili N* at the top in an embellished woodcut script.

I looked at the others and suddenly realized what a bloody and grimy lot we were. "I'll allow ladies first for the shower as long as there's hot water left for me," I said gallantly. And foolishly.

Despite the narrowness of the chamber there was some unseemly debate over the possibility of two people sharing the shower. It was, of course, grossly impractical for any pairing outside of a couple of circus contortionists or a man and a cat. Which was how I got a surprisingly complacent Suki clean.

The shower was appointed with a selection of sponges and scented oils in bottles on recessed shelves. The towels were roughly textured but highly absorbent and the clothing was of a gray material with a unique feel and quality, yet not readily identifiable. The waistbands on both the pants and the tops were elasticized and the cut of the arms and legs allowed total freedom of movement, yet conformed to the body sufficiently as to not render the wearer shapeless. The boots were cut low, from sealskin, and extremely comfortable.

The ladies had dressed while I was in the shower. Once I was decent, I emerged from the head and looked at Samm. "Any ideas before we meet with the captain?"

Her brow furrowed. "Some of this seems familiar but . . . I don't know. Ever since my throw-down with Marie Laveau, my brain is like Swiss cheese!"

"Hah!" I said.

"Hah . . . ?"

"Yeah." I smiled. "For once we're all on the same page." I knocked on our cabin door. "Let's go see if the wizard will give you a brain, me a heart, Irena a way to go home, and Suki—" I looked down at the cat. "Aw hell, the analogy starts off lame and then crashes and burns."

"Could be an omen," Samm agreed as the door was opened by one of the kappas.

"Let's go," I sighed.

We were escorted back through a central corridor where we had first descended into the submarine and then led through an elegantly appointed dining room. A table, covered with a white linen tablecloth, was set with expensive crystal and china and ornate, golden tableware.

We passed through into a library filled with books. The shelves circled the room, taking advantage of the maximum amount of space allowable. It was furnished in black violet ebony inlaid with brass. Curved, brown leather divans of immense size were positioned at the opposite end and the beast-headed rifleman reclined upon one, reading a book and smoking a long-stemmed pipe. He closed his book and stood as we wove our way toward him, moving around a large table that dominated the center of the room.

Gesturing with the curved stem of his pipe, he indicated the adjacent divan and said in a low, rumbling voice: "Monsieur Cséjthe, Mesdames Pantera and D'Arbonne, welcome aboard my boat. Please be seated." He sat back down and patted the cushions next to him. "Come sit beside me, my silent deserter. All is forgiven for it seems we still share common purpose." Suki hopped off our couch, trotted across the floor, and jumped up to sit beside him. Now I felt the weight of two pairs of cat's eyes on me.

A full minute passed in silence as we studied each other from a distance of perhaps two meters.

Our host wore a red velvet smoking jacket over blue silk pajamas. His feet were encased in sharkskin slippers and his hands were like a man's with long tapered fingers, though the nails were trimmed to be unaccountably long and pointed. His head, however, was that of a Bengal tiger, with orange and white fur striped in a pattern of black stripes and bands. He gazed at us with calm golden eyes and then said: "Forgive me; I speak very rarely these days. My troops tend to be an uncommunicative lot and

I have fallen out of the habit of human speech. I am Prince Dakkar. Your host and, I hope, your ally."

I stared hard at him: *Tyger, tyger, burning bright . . .* I knew that name from somewhere.

"Mr. Cséjthe, are you a fox?" the tiger-headed creature continued before I could pin it down, "or a hedgehog?"

I shook my head. "I'm not a shape-changer. I'm—a man." Still lacking a definitive answer on that front.

The tiger-man shook his head and chuckled. "I apologize. The question was meant metaphorically." He held up the book. "I was reading Lance Morrow's *Evil: An Investigation.* The author uses Isaiah Berlin's essay on Tolstoy to ask the question about the true nature of evil . . ."

I nodded, catching up now. " *'Multa novit vulpes, verum echinus unum magnum.'* The fox knows many things but the hedgehog knows one big thing."

"You know your Latin, Mr. Cséjthe."

"Better than I know my Greek. The Latin is from Erasmus Rotterdamsus' *Adagia* back around 1500. The original comes from a fragment attributed to the Greek poet Archilochus, sixth century B.C."

"Ah," our host said, "then perhaps you can answer the question as Mr. Morrow has framed it. Do you believe in evil, Mr. Cséjthe? And do you perceive it as one, big thing? Or do you see the wrongs of the world as a series of smaller, unconnected incidents? Are you a hedgehog? Or a fox?"

Maybe a week ago it would have been surreal. Certainly inconceivable two years previously to imagine myself discussing the unification theory of wickedness with a monster beneath the Gulf of Mexico. But in light of recent events it all made for a certain perverse sense. The problem was I was way past patience for dabbling in theoreticals any longer.

"I'm more of a badger, I guess," I finally answered. "Had my run-ins with what people would call evil; a lot of it small, petty, and seemingly unconnected. Had a few brushes with something a lot bigger, too. Just touched its hem, felt its shadow, heard it breathing in the night. Thing is, your parents teach you not to play in traffic at an early age. As a young man your drill instructor teaches you not to pick up unexploded ordnance or stand up in your foxhole or bunch up on patrol. The government comes along and hits you with infomercials: buckle up, don't drink and drive, this is your brain on drugs, smoking kills, only you can prevent forest fires! You figure certain things out for yourself: don't stand next to guys throwing rocks at men with machine guns. . . .

"So, like a badger, I go my own way, stay out of trouble, lay low. Don't mess with evil and hope that evil won't mess with you."

I took a deep breath. "But some things don't know any better than to leave a badger alone. And a cornered badger has the baddest reputation in the animal world of anything you'd want to face. So, you want to know my take on Evil—upper case or lower? I'm an equal opportunity kind of guy. It messes with my friends or family, all I care about is the practical, not the theoretical. It's in my face? Then there's no guesswork involved: one of us is going down!"

Tiger guy tossed the book aside. "How pleasantly simple-minded an anodyne for you," he rumbled. "From the way my lieutenant here behaved these past five months I thought, perhaps, that you might be the key." He rose and towered over us. "In deference to her I shall set you ashore near one of the refugee camps close to the Pontchartrain Sea before continuing my war against these abominations from the depths. I bid you—"

"You're a fox person, then," Samm said.

"What?" He turned and peered down at her as if considering a bit of leftover antelope meat.

"You're making war on the many little things instead of the one big thing," she said, looking back up at him without flinching.

The beast-man folded his hands behind his back but not, I noticed, before clenching them. "Madam, ever since I awakened to this new age, I have been consumed with finding the answers to what troubles my beloved oceans. That men continue to conquer and enslave and oppress one another comes as no surprise. But the oceans have always been a peaceful refuge from the ways of the surface world and I have been called out of my eternal rest to find them invaded and corrupted by alien armies! Armies whose general I cannot yet perceive! You will tell me where I may find their leader that I may take the fight to him and bring this war to conclusion once and for all!"

Samm, not the least bit intimidated, smiled and said: "The first part's easy: his name is Cthulhu and he can be found in the dread city of R'lyeh. The second part is going to be a little tougher"—she pointed at me—"because only he can stop him."

The impact of her pronouncement was lost on me because I had finally shaken off the thin patina of shock and done the math.

"Holy shit!" I said. "Prince Dakkar! I know who you are!" I looked at the others. "We found Nemo!"

ᴹ ᴹ ᴹ

"I called myself a freedom fighter in those days," Dakkar mused before the great lensed window of the grand salon later that night. "And so I was in many ways and many places. I lent finances and aid to oppressed people and countries all over the world. But I was also a terrorist, wreaking vengeance for the deaths of my family at the hands of the British during the Sepoy Rebellion. I tried to disguise my vengeance from myself, labeling it as a noble war against all wars." He shook his head. "All I did was widen the scope of my vengeance from one nation to many."

I nodded. "I know something about that: monsters and monstrous things. If they don't out and out kill you, they infect you and eventually you become them."

We were looking out through the thick glass as the *Nautilus* made for the first set of coordinates. The room's lights were off yet a pale blue illumination filtered back in from the external beams lighting up the waters outside our window.

"It was Verne who brought me to my senses," Dakkar continued. "Our conversations and, of course, the manuscript."

"Which one?"

"The first. The second, you understand, was a fabrication. Well, they are both fabrications to a degree. There was no Professor Aronnax—that was Verne putting himself into the narrative. Other details . . . " He made a dismissive wave with his hand. "It's the second book that is the larger work of fiction."

"Timeline discrepancies for one," I remarked.

"Yes, well, even though I had retired from overt acts of aggression and piracy before the publication of the first novelization, the public's imagination was piqued. Certain agencies and individuals began to get a sense that what most took for fiction might actually have a basis in reality. The hounds were loosed, so to speak. Over time I found my trail growing warmer and my precautions less than sufficient. I prevailed upon Verne to compose a sequel and 'kill me off' so as to cool the ardor of my overly enthusiastic fans."

"Interesting," I said. "So, there was no Lincoln Island. No erupting volcano and scuttling of the *Nautilus*, sending the two of you to a watery grave . . . "

"Oh, that last part was true," Dakkar rumbled. "The latitude and longitude for the fictional Lincoln Island? Hogwash! Sleight of hand, misdirection to send the searchers in the wrong direction. But the second set of coordinates you found on that damnable altar, that was where I was sheltered at the end. The volcanic underpinnings were more prominent back then and provided more cover but there is still a significant sea cave entrance if one knows where to look. I was an old man and dying—though many years after Verne's fictional laying-me-to-rest. I suppose fiction inspired fact. When I knew that my life was to be measured in hours rather than days, I settled my ship—"

"Boat."

"What?"

"A submarine is a boat, not a ship."

He stared at me.

"In proper naval parlance, that is."

The stare became a glare. "Do not presume to tell the captain of the vessel he has built as well as commands what sort of thing to call it!"

"Um, okay."

"As I was saying, I had settled the *Nautilus* beneath the volcanic shell of the island that would be named Palmyra, and set the pumps to evacuate the . . . *Nautilus* . . . three days later. Later that night I fell into a deep slumber and dreamed I was in the Palace of Vishnu."

He fell silent and for a number of leagues we stood and gazed out at the blue nirvana of the ocean depths together.

"I dreamed many things," he said finally. "Things that I may tell no heathen. I do not know why I even tell you of this save that we are likely doomed in our task and doomed men should never lie to one another. So, I will tell you why I am here and why I will do what I must do.

"In the dream beyond this dream which we esteem as real, I was told that I had lost my path. I had made war upon my own karma in making war upon my fellow man. To achieve moksha or samadhi, one usually follows a yoga, a path, to achieve spiritual perfection. There are four possible ways. When I was young, I practiced the raja-yoga, the path of meditation. As a husband and young father, I practiced the bhakti-yoga, the path of love and devotion. In the House of Vishnu I dreamed that I was taught the jnana-yoga, the path of wisdom. Then I was told I must atone for the wrong acts I had committed. I must return and walk the path of right action, the karma-yoga.

"In this last matter I believed I might awaken to a new life, reincarnated as a beggar or a dalit or even an

animal or insect, doomed to live out a life of crushing
humility, subjected to the pain and loss I had inflicted
on so many others.

"Instead, I was shown a great and terrible face, the
face of the giant squid that had nearly doomed my vessel
and crew many years before. This, I was told, this was
the face of the Destroyer of Worlds and that Shiva had
decreed that it must not stand. I was given three secrets
and told I must return and walk upon the other side of
the same path to balance the karma-yoga."

He turned to me. "When I awoke, I was lying upon
my bed in my chambers, just as when I had fallen asleep.
The air was stale but my ship was watertight. I did not
know how much time had passed so I hurried about to
make sure that the timers did not activate the pumps.

"I shall not bore you with all of the mordant details.
I discovered that the timers had long since failed and
that I had awakened in a different century. A different
millennium, actually." He reached up and touched his ·
face. "How I discovered that I was no longer human
but *rakshasa*."

"Rakshasa?"

"A demon or unclean spirit in my religion, Mr. Cséjthe. Such are magicians and shape-changers. Handy abilities, actually, for the mission which I have been
assigned. This freakish appearance is little impediment
for this, my third life. I have long been a creature of
solitude. Since the death of my wife and children my
only solace has been the sea. Only in its cool blue depths
have I found the peace and quiet that gives my savage
heart ease. Perhaps I shall take again the name, Nemo.

Prince Dakkar lost his title when his family was murdered and his ancestral lands seized. He lost his name when his body grew old and infirm and finally died at the bottom of an undersea grotto in a collapsed volcano under an accursed island. It is only fitting that I reclaim the name that is no name."

"Nemo." I said. "Latin for 'no one.' "

We both looked up, suddenly conscious of the spill of light from the adjoining library. Irena Pantera stood in the doorway at the end of the grand salon. "I couldn't sleep," she said, stretching, her shirt riding up to show off her taut brown belly. "Mind if I come in to watch the fish?" She began walking toward us without waiting for an answer. Tousled hair and puffy lips, she was a sleepy-eyed vision of pillow sexuality and the hip action in her walk was telegraphing all sorts of messages.

The last thing I needed tonight was to have her pheromone-driven lust put on display in front of our unpredictable host, so my best bet was to redirect her back to the cabin with Suki and Samm.

Subtly.

So I stretched in turn. "You know," I said, "actually I'm pretty bushed. I think I'll go lie down for a while and we can continue our conversation in the morning."

I said a hurried goodnight so that Irena could turn right around and follow me back out. It was smoothly executed: she didn't even get the opportunity to lay an inappropriate hand on me as I rounded the other side of the fountain and crossed to the door. I opened the door and held it for her like a gentleman—no fanny grabs for me, thank you—but she wasn't there behind me. She was over at the view port, talking with Captain Nemo.

I closed the door quietly on my way out.

Samm was already asleep when I returned to the cabin and I crept carefully into an upper bunk so as not to wake her. I was exhausted and should have slept like a rock but for the nightmare.

I dreamt of the pyramids. Only these were nightmare pyramids. Gigantic, misshapen, cancerous buildings of basalt, obsidian, and dark metal. Far below, tiny legions of slaves dragged a gigantic block across the desert floor under a distant blue star. Slowly the hundreds behind the giant black slab pushed while a thousand before strained against hundreds of harnesses to pull their stony cargo forward. Foot by foot, yard by yard, mile by mile, they dragged their immense burden on its epic journey.

In the wrong direction.

I dreamt of a funeral. A great dark coffin being borne through the streets of New Orleans. The band played its customary dirge, Big Easy style. But the musicians were dead, their faces bloated and fish-belly white; the music distant and far away. Underwater. A siren call to lure others to their deaths.

I awoke in sweat-soaked sheets with Samm's face hovering close to mine.

"Where's Irena?" she asked.

I looked over the edge of the bed. Her bunk had not been slept in. "She couldn't sleep last night," I answered, yawning. "I think she tried some tiger balm."

∗∗∗   ∗∗∗   ∗∗∗

Nobody made any direct mention of last night's sleeping arrangements at the captain's mess that morning.

The talk started off on the business of the remaining coordinates from Marie Laveau's altar: the two presumed sets for the lost city of R'lyeh scribbled in the margins of the *Al Azif.* We were still ten days out from the Love-craft set and would then travel to the Derleth coordinates if we came up empty there.

Nemo—or Dakkar, since that was what Irena was call-ing him this morning and he was making no attempt to correct her—was telling us stories of how he had recruited an army to fight the Deep Ones. It was one of the three secrets that Vishnu had bestowed upon him before returning him to his third life and this mission to save the world for gods and men.

His little turtle-monkeys, the kappas, were *suijen* or water kami, typically dwelling in lakes, rivers, and streams in Japan. Even Dakkar could not explain the siren call that had bade them swim to the sea and seek out his submarine hidden under an island in the middle of the Pacific Ocean. They were there, however, when he awakened to this third life and obedient foot soldiers to the cause.

The second secret that Vishnu had imparted was a mixture of magic and science in rehabbing the *Nautilus*.

A more efficient way of converting seawater into energy was revealed and an engine to harness that power more effectively. Modifications to other technologies like the wireless were less radical. Two, largely external tor-pedo tubes were retrofitted to the undercarriage as Dak-kar had foresworn the ramming of other vessels ever again. But the strangest modification was the craft that replaced the simple dingy that once nestled in the recessed berth atop the submarine.

The *Cuttlefish* was a self-contained vessel that per-formed all of the functions of the antiquated dingy as well as a mini-submersible. He hinted that there might be other properties that Lord Vishnu had granted but we were interrupted at that moment by the appearance of another human.

Actually "human" was a premature judgment on my part. The man standing in the doorway had died a long time ago. He had become an undead. And looking into his dead, lifeless eyes, I could see that, as an undead, he had died again.

Dakkar excused himself from the table and went to the lifeless corpse standing in the doorway. Speaking a few, hushed words, he turned the apparition around and told us that he would return in a moment. He ushered the zombie out and down the corridor.

I looked down at Suki who had paused at her repast of bloody fresh fish in a bowl on the floor. "Friend of yours?" I asked.

She *merrowed* absently as she continued to stare at the closed door.

Dakkar returned after a few uncomfortable bites and apologized. "When you put together an army, you have to make do with the materials at hand."

I laid down my fork. "What exactly does that mean?"

"Where was I? I was speaking of the modifications to the *Nautilus*. You must understand that even the concussive effects of underwater charges delivered by torpedoes have a limited effectiveness against an army of individual combatants. The kappas are strong, powerful—but they are not infinite in numbers and they can be killed. It was necessary to recruit additional troops to fight an enemy that was breeding and gathering in increasing numbers.

"We engaged these Deep Ones wherever we found them—primarily along the coasts of North America. And while we were in the Pacific Northwest we discovered evidence of the first of several vampire enclaves located near the ocean."

Dakkar told an increasingly horrific story of how a chance encounter between a kappa and an unsuspecting undead led to the discovery that a drowned vampire made the perfect foot soldier for his underwater army. They couldn't swim but they couldn't die, either. And, best of all, when they drained a Deep One of its blood and forced their own upon it, it became an undead version of Father Dagon and Mother Hydra.

And this was the best part, according to Dakkar: the third secret that Vishnu had bestowed upon his reincarnated champion was the power to control the undead that have gone under the seas.

Since that time he had sent the kappas along the coasts—East, West, the Gulf—and up rivers and tributaries, as press-gangs to drag more undead down into the watery ranks of his army. Militarily, strategically—it was genius.

I congratulated Nemo on this incredible weapon in the arsenal against the forces of Evil that were stirring all about us. Then I excused myself and walked back to the cabin. There I quickly knelt in the head and vomited up all of my breakfast.

Thank goodness for solid food for a change.

ᴧᴧ   ᴧᴧ   ᴧᴧ

My first visitor was Suki.

She scratched at the cabin door until I got up and let her in.

I laid back down on my bunk and she jumped up beside me. Nestling against me, she laid her chin on my chest.

"What was it like," I asked her, "to drown and not die? To have your lungs and your belly, your nose and your mouth, everything, fill up with water and it never end? To be under someone else's control? All for a good cause of course, but it's not you, anymore? You're being sacrificed but it's not you making the sacrifice?" I reached out and stroked her velvet head. The mange seemed to be disappearing. "Did you want to die?" She closed her eyes. "Do you still want to die?" She began to purr.

The door opened again and Samm came into the cabin. "So now we know," she said.

"You mean you didn't know?" I asked.

She shook her head. "I didn't know all of it before and I remember less of it now. Damn! I cannot believe how much that bitch took out of me. It will take me years, decades, to get back the kind of—" She looked over her shoulder. "I have no ass! Can you believe that? That bitch made me use up all of my ass!"

I didn't feel like smiling but I couldn't help a small one. "Stop it," I said quietly.

"Oh, that's easy for you to say!" she sassed me. "For a white boy you got a little too much ass. First spell I learn when this is all over is a grab-ass spell. Transfer some of that juice in your caboose to the junk in my trunk!"

"Now you're just making it sound dirty."

"I wasn't talkin' dirty! Maybe you were thinkin' dirty! Why else are you back in bed in the middle of the morning, hmmm?"

The door opened again and Irena came in. "What's going on?" she wanted to know.

"Cséjthe's lying in bed thinking dirty thoughts about me," Samm said.

Irena blinked and looked at me. "Really?"

"No," I growled. "She's just trying to distract me."

Irena blinked again and looked at her. "Really?"

"Sure I am," the former juju woman replied. "Why don't you give me some pointers? Tell me how you kept Mister Frosted Flakes *distracted* last night?"

Irena looked a little flustered. "What do you mean?"

"What do I mean?" Samm turned and leaned into her. "What do I mean? You are gone all night, your bed is not slept in, and you expect us to believe that you spent the entire time in front of that viewing window, looking at the little fishies?"

The Pantera girl was not easily intimidated. "What's your complaint? The way you were acting I figured you'd be happy to have me out of the cabin for the rest of the night if you know what I mean and I think you do? Besides, I'm studying to be a marine biologist, if you'll kindly remember, and this was the opportunity of a lifetime! I saw things last night I'll bet no human being has ever seen in all of history—may never see in my lifetime!"

"Like what?" Samm challenged, seemingly not inclined to give ground without a fight.

That caught Irena off guard: she hadn't realized there would be sworn testimony to be given. "We saw some cephalopods—unusual varieties. And there were these goblin sharks—"

"Goblin sharks? You're making this up!"

"No, really! They're gray, long-nosed sharks and they're really rare! They're called living fossils!"

I sighed and closed my eyes as Irena went on about how Dakkar had taken the *Nautilus* down along the ocean floor and they'd discovered these mysterious patterns in the dirt and silt. *Ten more days*, I thought, *maybe twelve. Then we kill this Cthulhu or it kills us and it will all be over. And then what? What happens to all those drowned undead things?*

". . . looked like something big and heavy had been dragged across the ocean floor," she was saying. "The thousands of tiny pits actually looked a little like footprints . . ."

If Dakkar survived, he'd have an underwater army at his command. Would he just disband it and send it home? Assuming he had the option. What would the Deep Ones do? Assuming they'd been around for awhile maybe they were only a problem when the Great Old S.O.B.s stirred them up. . . .

Something . . .

Wait . . .

I sat straight up and banged my head on the ceiling.

Rolling off the bunk, I hit the floor holding my head and cursing a blue streak. Even the nanos need a little time to work and I couldn't see the door for the tears in my eyes. "Open the door," I said, clutching my head, "open the damn door!"

Someone was a little slow. Then they were still in the way and we had to do that little dance until I could get around the other side and out into the corridor. By that time my vision was clearing and I started running the length the ship—boat, dammit, boat—yelling for Nemo.

I found him in his quarters from which he emerged after a moment's pounding on the furthermost door of the grand salon.

"We've got to turn this boat around," I told him. "We're going the wrong direction!"

"What do you mean, Mr. Cséjthe? The coordinates—"

I shook my head like a man possessed. "Cthulhu isn't in R'lyeh anymore! He's on his way to New Orleans!"

"What do you mean?"

"There's more than a thousand Deep Ones on the march from R'lyeh! They've been traveling for months! It's a combination army and funeral procession: they're bringing the stone sarcophagus of their sleeping god with them!"

The black terror of my nightmares seemed ten times worse now that they were dragged forth into the waking world, joined together and given their true meaning.

"And when he is brought to his new throne, he will awaken, the Herald of the Great Old Ones! And then the world will end in terror and madness!

Chapter Twenty

"YOU DON'T APPROVE of what I've done."

I looked out over the waves and thought about oblivion. *Why struggle? Why fight? The job was half done. The world was a mess according to every newspaper, magazine, and media outlet I watched or listened to. New Orleans was already gone with about a third of the state of Louisiana. At least my family was clear. Why fight? Why even argue?*

"It's an age-old question," I said. "If we become as ruthless as our enemies, do we *become* our enemies?"

We were cruising along the surface, taking in fresh air for another prolonged excursion beneath the water. The

Nautilus could travel faster fully submerged but those pesky old lungs would be wanting their oxygen. If we didn't surface every so often to recycle the air supply, we wouldn't be going at all.

"I think you're anthropomorphizing," he said mildly, relighting his pipe. "Vampires aren't human beings."

I lifted a foot and shook it as a wave rolled over the deck of the *Nautilus*. "People in this country used to say the same thing about their black slaves."

"Mmm." He took a pull on the pipe and the seaweed substitute in the bowl glowed briefly like a devil's eye. "People in this country say the same thing today about their unborn babies."

"Yeah. The politics of convenience."

"Or inconvenience. Look," he said, "it's all about survival. Or as you would put it, 'War is hell.' Hands get dirty. Blood gets spilled. Extraordinary young men become ordinary old men. The good die young. And you can't make an omelet without breaking eggs."

"And what does all of that mean?"

"You think it's wrong to use vampires because vampires are monsters."

"You're a monster," I said. "You said so, yourself. *Rakshasa*: demon, unclean spirit. Not judging here because I'm a bit of a monster, too."

He nodded. "And we're signed up to the death."

"What about Irena? She's a lycanthrope."

Dakkar shook his head. "The Panteras are not lycanthropes."

I shook my head right back at him. "Sorry, I've known her longer. She's a were-panther."

"Actually, she's not. Irena and certain others of her clan are what you might call—for the want of a better word or phrase—"Cat People.' "

"Not gettin' the distinction."

"Lycanthropy is a disease *and* a curse that is transmitted from one carrier to another via infection. A werewolf creates another werewolf and so on."

"I think I *know* the basics," I muttered. Lupé's loss was still fresh and sharp and I was blocking those thoughts and memories for all I was worth.

"Apparently Irena's ancestors shared a village in South America with some *brujas* whose dabbling in the black arts brought down a curse on several family lines. Such things have been documented in other countries and with other bloodlines—most notably the Dubrovnas in Serbia and the Galliers in France. It's a genetic and generational curse and tends to favor the females though it can appear among offspring of both sexes. It is *not* transmitted by bite or claw. It is hereditary. Totally different."

"Oh," I said. "Doesn't change my point. If Irena's a monster—"

Dakkar help up his hand. "You bandy about the term 'monster' like it is synonymous with evil. Like 'we are all monsters' therefore 'we are all the same.' We're not."

"Well, actually, that's kind of my point," I said. "Thanks for making it for me."

"But the point that I am making," he continued, "is that vampires *are* different because they're all the same. This is war and there are going to be casualties. People—monsters—soldiers—innocent bystanders—are going to be hurt. Are going to be killed."

"So who died and made you God?" I asked.

"They did," he answered with a sweep of his arm. "The people who became vampires. They *were* people. They *were* alive. Then they *died*. Their *lives* ended. Everyone's life *ends* eventually. *I* don't determine that. Only Shiva or Vishnu or the U.S. Army or the narcissistic jerk talking on his cell phone while driving to work or that two-pack or three-egg-a-day habit you had for the past thirty years. Or that vampire lurking in the alleyway.

"So you tell me, my friend. When it comes to putting foot soldiers on the front lines—and there will be people on the front lines, either by design or by chaos—would you prefer someone young and vibrant and still on their first and only life like Irena? Or something that has had a life, lived it, and died once?"

If there was a hole in the logic of his argument, I couldn't find it for the moment.

But I still didn't like it.

We couldn't follow the trail back to New Orleans or travel with any real speed. The *Nautilus*, for all of its Vishnu upgrades, wasn't rigged for sonar or underwater video. We would have to cruise beside the disturbed terrain, close enough to see it and yet compensate for the viewing angle while trying to steer and avoid regular obstacles. It was still very much a nineteenth century vessel. For all we knew, the Funeral Party was rolling Squidhead's coffin across the submerged Mississippi riverbed right now.

So the decision was made to head straight for the city of New Orleans, itself. Find the site of the throne.

Destroy it. And start working our way back out from there.

And, in the meantime, figure out just how I was supposed to take on a sleeping god who was a destroyer of worlds.

A god no other god, godling, or avatar, was willing to face.

While`I was starving to death in the process.

ᕥᕤ   ᕥᕤ   ᕥᕤ

Samm donated a couple of pints of her blood. She offered to let me take it direct from the vein but I told her it was too risky at this stage of The Hunger. I don't know, maybe it was. Mostly it was an intimacy thing and someday she'd thank me.

Dakkar also donated blood. Since Liban's had been so potent it was hoped that maybe another preternatural being's hemoglobin would pack an extra wallop. Unfortunately, the key words had come from Dakkar's lips the night before: unclean spirit. Yuck!

The kappas tasted better than the one brief sip I'd had off that Deep One I'd nipped in hand-to-mouth combat. But not very much better. Maybe it was that diet of cucumbers that Dakkar was feeding them out of the ship's stores.

Irena proved a heady brew, however. Her pint and a half made me sit up and take notice. She was certainly willing but even less able than any of the others. A little undersized to produce the quantities with the turn-around I really needed but, then, one takes what one can get. Or at least one does up to the point of a whispered invitation to exchange hickies back in the cabin after lights out.

And still I could not see how my needy nanos were going to be any help in taking down the thing that had all the other major players taking a big step back.

If nothing else, I would do the one thing I could do and that was show up.

My boat was gone, my home was gone, my family out of harm's way. Theresa, if she was carrying the other fetus, had either found a way to survive or she hadn't. Nothing I could do about that now.

Nothing except do my damnedest to keep their world from turning into an abattoir.

Funny thing about depression. At a certain point you decide you can only do what you can do. After that? It's a shrug and a que sera sera.

It felt almost like a path to recovery.

Mardi Gras was in full swing when we returned to New Orleans. The streets and parks were filled with hundreds of drunken revelers swaying and stumbling about. At least that's what it looked like as we glided up to Jackson Square, past the defunct riverbed and Woldenberg Park, and across the remains of Washington Artillery Park.

Then you realized that everyone was under a hundred feet of water and undead. The tides and currents moved the water between the buildings and up the streets to give the drowned dead that extra degree of awkwardness in their shambling gaits.

Several hundred kappas swam about overhead like deranged seraphim.

The St. Louis Cathedral looked like it had been hit with a bomb, yet the buildings on either side looked relatively untouched. It was the work of cunning hands, not tidal forces or random acts of nature.

Scattered piles of bones evidenced work begun then reversed. Dakkar's troops had been busy in our absence.

"You've amassed quite an army," I told him as we watched dozens of Deep Ones probe the undeads' flanks and then withdraw from the slow-moving bloodsuckers. The kappas, however, were much more nimble, darting down and driving their evil counterparts back into the reach of their less mobile allies. "How do you direct them from a distance?"

"It is part of the third secret of Vishnu," he said. "I would not share such knowledge even if I could."

"I must say, this seems to be going better than I expected."

He furrowed his great orange and black-striped brow. "It should not be enough. I have spent the past four years circumnavigating the North American continent, passing underneath Central America via the Nicaraguan conduit. What I have gathered so far may be remarkable in many ways but is yet no match for what we currently face! Though I have hunted these creatures in ever increasing numbers during that time, it is another face that Lord Vishnu shows me in my dreams. Another who is to save us, he whispers in my ear."

"And that's me?" I asked.

"I can never quite make out the face in my dreams," he answered. "But the signs and portents eventually led me to you. I followed the trail to you, enemy of my enemy."

"I live a long way from the sea," I said. "Couldn't have been easy running a sub this size all the way up the

Mississippi, Red, and Ouachita rivers. Too bad the gods aren't a little more forthcoming considering how invested they all are in this."

The tiger-headed *rakshasa* shrugged. "It is for men to work out their parts in the grand scheme, as well. Otherwise we are but puppets and playthings for the older souls. And it was not so difficult as you may think. Traversing land and waterways to stalk you in the *Cuttlefish* took only hours. It was chasing after that one," he nodded his head toward Suki who was cleaning a paw by the pipe organ, "that was the difficulty. Time spent wondering why she would not remain under my control. Picking up her trail. Following her to you. And waiting, watching, trying to discern if you were a part of the dharma I must incorporate into my task."

"So when did you decide that I was the guy?"

He shook his head. "Decisions are processes. This one is taking a while."

🦇　　🦇　　🦇

A quick reconnoiter of the city convinced us that the demolished St. Louis Cathedral was the intended site for Cthulhu's throne and no alternate construction was immediately evident elsewhere.

The disparity of forces—our hundreds to their dozens—was too good to be true, despite the losses we'd inflicted on these amphibious demons in recent days. I remembered the vast trail of webbed footprints marking the sea floor and felt a profound disquiet.

We headed back out with Dakkar, himself, up in the little wheelhouse, steering the *Nautilus* out across the flattened holocaust of Algiers' Mardi Gras World on the other side of the Mississippi riverbed.

If our theory was correct, and the Deep Ones were bringing their god to the city, and more specifically to Jackson Square, then we had a good chance of intercepting them close to ground zero. Catching them farther out was a more difficult proposition: the bit of trail we had picked up about a day's cruise on full steam did not line up on our straight path back to the city. Nor did it seem to follow predictable routes back to either of the two originating coordinates on the charts. Obviously such variables as currents, obstacles, and terrain were at play, perhaps other factors, as well. It was a big ocean even twenty miles out, so how were we going to find a needle in a haystack?

Dakkar tried doubling our odds by launching the *Cuttlefish* with Irena on board. A kappa rode along since our budding marine biologist was still getting her learner's permit but it was evident that someone had been giving her private lessons while I was off brooding on other parts of the sub.

I felt a mild flash of annoyance. End-of-the-world time and the tiger and the panther are spending a little too much mutual-interest time together? Annoyance gave way to guilt. What was wrong with that? Millions of people die but the world goes on. For a little while longer, anyway. He lost his wife and kids . . .

You lost yours . . .

Oho! So, I'm jealous? Of Dakkar? Or Irena? I could have the illusion of human consolation if I wanted to give in and pretend. Better to keep my head in the game. No illusions . . .

No disappointments.

Shut up. I still haven't figured out what to do about Mr. Sleepy God when we find him.

Relax. It will all be over, soon. So, you might as well enjoy yourself in the meantime . . .

A hand came up and caressed my shoulder. "Chris?"

I jumped. "Don't do that!" I yelled at Samm.

"Sorry," she said, "I didn't mean to startle you. I just had an idea. . . ."

"I'll bet you did."

She looked at me strangely. "I was thinking. If these things are on foot, they'd want to follow the path of least resistance."

"Yeah?"

"Well, if I was walking up to the Big Easy from down South—no traffic, mind you—I'd stick to the roads."

Less than ten seconds from her lips to my ears. But another thirty seconds from my ears to the functioning part of my brain. I took off running for the wheelhouse. Up a level and down to the front of the submarine, I had to climb another ladder and pop a hatch to join Dakkar in the elevator-sized steering control room.

"It is customary to request permission to enter the bridge," he remonstrated as I squeezed up into the small windowed room to join him. "In another life I would have dealt with you harshly for such an infraction." He seemed to be speaking more to himself than to me and the absentmindedness of his tone was more unnerving than if he had administered an angry tongue-lashing.

"Here," I said, pointing to a map of greater New Orleans, next to the charts on his map stand. "Here . . . this is Gretna, Belle Chasse, on down to Port Sulpher . . . it's the Great River Road of Plaquemines Parish.

Eighty miles and mostly four lanes, it stretches from what used to be the West Bank of the metropolitan area to the southernmost tip of Louisiana's Mississippi Delta. Tell me that isn't going to be their path of least resistance."

He rubbed his white furred chin. "There will be debris."

"Hell, there'll be debris out to sea, there'll be debris anywhere there once was dry land. But if they're toting something by foot, a firm level surface will make a big difference."

He handed me a transceiver. "Use this and stand your post at the view port. I will contact Irena."

🦇   🦇   🦇

The debris field was surprisingly light and sparse. This far out from the mainland the stronger gulf currents had cleaned up the majority of the destruction, moving it on down to the dark blue mysteries waiting farther out. The area down this way was eighty percent water before the final blow. The communities had been rural, agrarian, mostly poor. When the big storms came, folks tended to hunker down rather than evacuate: they were either too stubborn, too old, or too far from any other refuge so, practically no vehicles out on the roads.

We came upon the Dread God Cthulhu and his funerary procession about an hour out.

It was like some horrific *Reichsparteitag*, a Nuremburg *Triumph of the Will* a hundred and twenty feet below the surface of the ocean! Nearly a thousand Deep Ones were arrayed like ants, using hundreds of tethers and lines to pull a great obsidian sledge across the seabed.

The scale was such I couldn't begin to estimate the size of the coffinlike structure. Just a vague sense that once Octogod stood up, he was going to think he was in the shallow end of the pool.

There was another way to measure. As we began our second pass I could count the seconds using the length of the *Nautilus* and the speed of our travel to calculate how long it took to pass from one end of the sarcophagus to the other.

And then I forgot all about numbers and math and calculations.

We were close enough to pick up a lot more detail now.

In my dreams the Deep Ones had fashioned a great pallet to bear the sarcophagus upon. But now I could see there was no such structure: the great obsidian box hovered a good ten meters above the ocean floor. Antigravity? I shook my head: neutral buoyancy. Instead of a massive mule team, our undersea escort was more like a crew working the big balloons at the Macy's Day Parade.

And now another detail caught my eye: a flicker of lights along the top of the sarcophagus. I picked up the wireless microphone that Dakkar had given me so that we could communicate while he was in the wheelhouse. More Vishnu magic? I turned it over and saw the RadioShack nameplate on the back. "Captain," I asked, depressing the talk button, "can you bring us about and take us directly over the object so I can get a better look from above? Just not too high . . ."

"But not too low, either, Mr. Cséjthe," was his response. "We are not the only ones doing the observing."

I looked again as we came about and ascended for a top-down view. A group of fish-men were headed toward us with pikelike objects in hand.

I pressed the button again. "Captain? We're about to have visitors."

"Noted, Mr. Cséjthe. Please inform me when the majority have made contact or are in close proximity."

We came up over the giant box and I pressed my hands against the cold thick glass as I leaned forward and stared down at an unholy spectacle.

A childhood memory in the toy aisle of the local Wal-Mart flashed through my head: a boxed action figure of the alien hunter from the movie *Predator* behind the cellophane window, crisscrossed with more cardboard packaging for that secured, peekaboo effect.

And now, below me, Dread, Dead Cthulhu stared back up at me through wide, unblinking eyes, visible through a clear view port of his own, built into the top of his coffin! Unlike the colorful cardboard packaging for the toys of my childhood, this container was a uniform flat black, its only color coming from a series of tinted lights that marked what might have been an instrumentation and locking mechanism.

I felt a pounding begin inside my head.

I looked back up to the transparent portion of the top: its eyes were open! They were staring at me as if it knew, IT KNEW, who I was and why I was here! A crushing black curtain of panic fell over me. This thing was—was—what? It was too much! Mercifully, my mind was shutting down from an overload of terror. It was—it was—

The *Cuttlefish* glided across my line of sight, momentarily blocking my view. By the time it had moved on, so had we and those horrid eyes, those staring inhuman ancient eyes were no longer visible from our position above the sarcophagus.

The transceiver crackled in my hand. "Did you get a look at the markings on the cartouche plates?" Irena's voice asked through a noticeable flange effect. "I'm no language expert but we're not just talking ancient, here, but alien, as well."

"Of course," Samm said softly, behind me. "When the stars are right, the Great Old Ones plunge from world to world. . . ."

I thought about that as a kaleidoscope of concepts wriggled through my head like a host of voracious maggots. A vortex of thought rotated and clicked into place like the tumblers in a vault. "Wait a minute," I panted, still fighting my way out of a miasma of darkness. "Are you telling me this thing is an extraterrestrial?"

"It comes from outside our universe—"

"Enough with the metaphysical double-talk," I gritted. "All this time I've been buying into the shtick that we're chasing some kind of god, not some ancient astronaut from another dimension!" I shook off the nausea and stepped away from the view port. "That's *it*, isn't it?" There were images in my head. Thoughts. Pictures. A cacophony of visions that had no immediate context. And yet . . . "All those generations that came in contact with these things," I said. "They had no context but their own ancient myths and legends. Telepathy: nightmares! Aliens: monsters!" I turned back to the window. "How about we look at the flip side of the legends? Death which cannot die? Suspended animation! Plunging from world to world when the stars are aligned? Plot a course to Starbase Eleven, Warp Factor 2, Mister Cthulhu; prepare to jump when vectors are complete! We even seem to have ripped off the carbonite ploy from *Star Wars*!"

I shook my head. "It's a sad, old story. Superior intellect with trappings of advanced technology gets itself marooned among the savages. Sets its kind up as gods with the assistance of Clarke's third law."

Samm was looking at me nervously. "Clarke's third law?"

"Any sufficiently advanced technology is indistinguishable from magic," I quoted. "So anything we try to do to destroy this thing is pretty much doomed because even after millions of years, he's got the edge in technology."

Two of the Froggies swam up to the view port and raised their pikes to strike at it.

I raised the transceiver and said, "Now, Captain!"

Our finny foes twitched and jerked and then drifted slowly down to the bottom as Dakkar ran an electrical charge through the hull, killing or stunning anything within a few meters of the sub. More maneuverable, the *Cuttlefish* was just steering clear of the other Deep Ones.

"And now we will commence our first run of depth charges," Dakkar announced over the transceiver.

"I thought you said we can't destroy this thing," Samm said as I closed the crash doors on the view port and took a seat in the salon.

"Unless Vishnu has given our good captain a fourth, terrible secret . . ." I mused, tilting my head back and closing my eyes. "His little torpedo upgrade was a nice add-on but, let's face it: it doesn't pack half the punch of an old, World War II torp and he has no targeting system. It's just a convenient retro-fix so he doesn't have to use the *Nautilus* as a battering ram in a world of steel ships. It's even too inaccurate for this job. He's dropping bags of timed explosives from the undercarriage like depth charges! Can you imagine that? We're using a submarine like a bomber! So, no. I don't think this is going to do anything but knock out a number of the honor guard. This isn't a bad thing, mind you. But it really is going to be up to me, now."

I opened my eyes to see her hovering over me. Her dark face, once familiar and now so young and strange looked down with an expression of even greater bewilderment. "What can you do? And why aren't you scared any more?"

"I'm going to go inside his mind," I told her. "That's why I'm the one. It's not the nanos or some special spiritual quality. I have this one gift, this one knack. That box has been on the bottom of the ocean for millions of years and it's still working, it's still keeping its sleeping astronaut preserved, protected, safe. It's kept the ocean out but I can get in. I felt it just a few moments ago and you told me just a few days ago: they leak. *They* leak! Well, it's a two-way pipeline and I'm going in. He'll be used to fucking with other people's heads. I'll bet he's had no practice when it comes to someone fucking with his."

"You really aren't afraid any more, are you?"

"Sammy? Taking on gods is one thing. Outwitting an ivory-tower intellectual is another. Give me a few moments to prepare: I'm going in."

The depth charges, as predicted, took out maybe a quarter of the Deep Ones, injured or scattered another third and pretty much left the field in disarray. It also bought us some time.

Irena reported that there was an "area of effect" around the sarcophagus in proximity to some of the blasts, seeming to confirm my force fields theory.

I only dimly heard. I was already fading from my surroundings, slipping further away from my body.

In terms of the technique alone, this would not be like the other mind melds. Typically, bloodwalking involved a wound or injury providing the entry point by which I entered my target's mind. It might be anything—a cut finger—so long as blood provided the focal point for egress to the body's seat of higher consciousness: the brain. It wasn't mandatory, only simpler due to the unique nature of my own body chemistry. I had originally learned the technique of mentally accessing the target through a chakra point. This, however, required a lot of focus and concentration and why do it the hard way when there are simpler shortcuts?

This would be different from either process: we couldn't wound it and I had no idea what kind of chakras an ET had, if any. Instead, I was going to retune into its broadcast frequency and follow that signal back to the station. . . .

As I lay back in the chair and attempted to calm my heart and order my thoughts, I tried not to dwell on the one thing I had lied about.

I was still afraid.

We are conditioned to distrust, shun, fear, even loath the Other. Allegiances—governmental, cultural, tribal, familial—all rely on making scapegoats of those not like us. We may be better than them or they may be worse than us. We may demonize them, hold them in contempt, or have very little regard for them, at all. It's become a ritualized, almost unconscious process at every level of our indoctrinated existence.

But somewhere back in our atavistic past, out simian ancestors learned to fear the Other on a much more primal and practical level than the political/cultural whims prevalent today. Somewhere in our gibbering hindbrains, we still know in our deepest nightmares, that something very Other lurks in the dark place, in the shadow, and does not wish us well.

As I began to feel the heaviness of heart settle over me, I murmured to Samm: "Don't distract me. Don't let anyone disturb me. And don't pay too much attention if I start to babble. . . ."

There it was now.

That creepy sense of foreboding.

That prickling at the back of the neck and the base of the spine.

An oppression of the spirit.

Fear.

The great shadow.

I shivered and opened myself to it.

The last time I had opened myself to the malevolent frequency of Cthulhu's dreams I had caught only a glimpse, an eye-blink really, of what horrors ran through the cesspool of this alien mind. Now I was wading in, seeking its currents, finding its flow, and moving toward its source.

Analogies are precarious things. The concept that something is "like" another is illusionary at best and inconsistent in the main. Water analogies are frequently utilized because its fluidity is adaptable to so many possible manifestations. In truth, however, there was little I could liken the experience to.

I quickly lost my standard points of reference as a welter of shadow images began to bombard me, all fantastical. With great effort I could sort some of them into general categories. There were those incomprehensible things, possibly relating to memories of those places this creature had visited or from whence it came. And then those vistas that seemed to correspond with this planet's surface in a Precambrian age. Glimpses of cities of incomprehensible architecture and impossible geometries, battles with creatures that seemed as unlikely as a child's scribblings on colored paper with glue and glitter and colored macaroni. Colors that belonged to spectrums that even my inhuman eyes had never perceived, dimensions that my mind could not process . . .

And then, finally, horrors that my mind could not digest.

It was not the strangeness and incomprehensibility of form or function that brought the terror that pushed my mind to the brink of sanity. These past two years had given me a strong stomach—even a predilection for strange forms and aspects. No, it was the wanton cruelty, the savage glee that nestled in this thing's desires to inflict pain and disfigurement upon a world where it had been held captive for untold eons.

It would be beyond all human comprehension to imagine the horrific constraints of a twilight imprisonment lasting for millions of years. Human prisoners share the fellowship of cellmates and socialize over meals and at various times in the exercise yard and on work details. Even the "lifers" know there will be an end to their sentence someday.

But for these travelers between the stars something went wrong before the dinosaurs evolved. They came, they saw, they conquered. When it was time to go, they locked up the last of their cities, strapped themselves into their transdimensional sarcophagi, set the stasis controls, and waited to wake up at their next destination.

But something went wrong. The transdimensional jump window opened. And closed again. Certain craft launched. At least one, in particular, did not. Sabotage? Malfunction? Whatever the root cause, whatever prevented Dread Cthulhu from leaving this primitive colony also bound him and others in their deathless sleep for eons, holding them in the prison of suspended animation for uncountable realignments of the stars.

Hearts stopped, lungs stilled, limbs held fast, yet their minds raced, raved, struggled to escape and, in the process, went quite mad.

It was their madness, the raving lunacy, which finally gave them the cyclopean strength to escape, to burst forth from their coffinlike life-support chambers and roam about again. Not physically, you understand, for their bodies were still preserved like prehistoric flies trapped in amber. No, at first their consciousness escaped their bodies and traveled the Dreamlands. From there it was possible to enter the real world, sometimes taking on shape and substance for a time before being pulled back into that null space between spaces, that Shadowland from which the Aristotelian realities emerge. From that place they could enter the thoughts of the weak-willed, the feeble-minded, and those as mad as themselves. They could disturb the dreams of the sensitive and the fragile. And they could reach out to those who sought them in turn.

They leaked.

But they could not escape their fates.

And it tore their minds and drove them to greater acts of cruelty and desperation, seeking revenge on a world that held them prisoner beneath the crushing press of fathoms and grinding weight of epochs. The mindless gibbering boredom relieved only by the torment inflicted upon the emergent creatures within their sphere of time or through the anticipation of the Time of the Great Slaughter when Cthulhu and those Great Old Ones like him would finally be free to stride like Colossus of Carnage among these oh-so-deserving sheep!

Until then they were trapped but for those momentary manifestations, like ectoplasm in the medium's séance room, where for the briefest of instances, they could touch and be touched.

This drove them all the more to the extreme paroxysms of gibbering insanity.

And delusions of godhood.

Or maybe not so delusional since the mental prowess they had honed over the better part of an eternity had enabled them to manipulate certain aspects of time and space. If they could not totally free themselves, they could yet leak. If they could not destroy the stasis chambers that held their flesh fast, they could yet sink a hundred miles of coastline and drown towns and cities. And if they could not entirely shape their own destinies, they could selectively breed generations of others, adapting them to the deep waters and bending their will to serve dark and terrible ends.

These Deep Ones were not sufficiently sophisticated to circumvent the alien technology that imprisoned Dread Cthulhu. But they would bring him to the place where others would find him. Others who would eventually bring to bear the best minds and science and technology to solve the riddle that had been discovered among the ruins of New Orleans like a riddle, wrapped in a mystery, inside an enigma. And Dread Cthulhu could help them because he leaked.

Soon the bloody harvest would begin!

The images of carnage, of bloody sacrifices and torments, for the pleasures of inflicting pain and disfigurements upon the helpless and the innocent, was searing and gut-wrenching and I fought back twin impulses to scream and retch.

I do not know how long I had wandered through the labyrinthine thoughts, emotions, and memories of the star creature's mind but I had become careless in the belief that I was too small and insignificant to be noticed in the towering canyons of intellect that had grown into an epic maze over the passage of epochs.

WHO IS THERE? WHAT IS IN MY HEAD? thundered the ego of the mad star beast.

I briefly considered giving the Odysseus answer to Polyphemus but I figured Nemo might not appreciate me stealing his shtick. Fortune favors the bold and, besides, ole tentacle puss was certifiably insane anyway so: why not?

"I am God. . . ." I said.

According to a number of theosophical puzzles it is an acceptable answer.

After a considerable pause the voice took exception. I AM GOD.

I shook my head, not knowing if it could sense much less see that. "You aren't *The* God. You aren't even *a* god. You're just a whacked-out E.T. with delusions of grandeur. *I*, on the other hand, *am* God, and I am here to tell you . . . "

Chapter Twenty-One

"... THAT YOU HAVE been a very naughty boy!" I scolded.

That, of course, pissed it off but what was I risking? That it would destroy me and my world?

Oh please! That's the problem with every over-the-top Thing-from-the-bottomless-pit-of-Hell: there comes a point where you just can't ratchet it up any higher. And then what?

After it calmed down, it boomed: I DO NOT BELIEVE YOU!

"You're not being entirely truthful on that point, Bubba, but that's okay. Lots of people don't believe in me. That's what free will is all about."

YOU ARE NOT A REAL GOD UNLESS YOU COMMAND ABSOLUTE OBEDIENCE, ABSOLUTE DEVOTION FROM YOUR CREATION!

"Huh, *somebody's* never been a stay-at-home parent. Look, this is the crux, the whole tipping point—of religions, societies, governments, and personal self-actualization. It's no good if you have to force people. Even the leather crowd with their safe words and their nudge-nudge, wink-wink, smack-smack, knows that. A true God's power is measured in what He gives away, not what He hoards."

THAT MAKES NO SENSE.

"Pay attention, Feeler Face: God is busy so you're only getting five minutes of my valuable time. Then I've got to get back to throwing fireballs around the firmament. Here's the Big Celestial Secret: it's about puppetry."

PUPPETRY?

"Finger puppets, stick puppets, hand puppets, Muppets, marionettes, ventriloquist's dummies, the General Secretary of the United Nations . . . "

WHAT DOES A GOD WANT WITH PUPPETS?

"Exactly! That's why a real God gets out of the way and lets his creation choose. Lets there be consequences to those choices—"

PUNISHES THE DISOBEDIENT! DESTROYS TRANSGRESSORS!

"Slow down, Gangsta Wrath; it's all about letting people learn from their mistakes. Parents who always fix their kids' mistakes raise monsters. But the biggest mistake of all is taking away people's option to make mistakes in the first place. The more control, the more petty the dictator. The more petty the dictator, the smaller the god."

I DON'T—THIS—I AM POWERFUL! I HAVE DESTROYED A GREAT CITY AND MANY SMALLER ONES! I HAVE CREATED A NEW COASTLINE AND MOVED THE WATERS OF THE SEA!

"Can you create a rock too big for you to pick up?"

There was a moment of stunned silence and I silently thanked eight-year-old Scotty Steadman's Saturday morning wiseass debates. Cthulhu was dangerous but deranged. As long as I could keep him off balance just enough to-

WHAT DID YOU SAY?

"You want to pretend to be a god? Just answer my question: can you create a rock so big that even you can't lift it?"

HOW WOULD I DO THAT?

"Easy, Squidley; God can do anything."

CREATE A ROCK TOO BIG TO PICK UP? IF GOD CANNOT LIFT IT THEN IT IS A FALLACY TO SAY GOD CAN DO ANYTHING. PICKING UP THE ROCK IS EXCLUSIONARY. . . .

"But a real God—that is *I*—can pick it up because I *am* God and, therefore, I can do *anything*." Yeah, priceless. . . .

WAIT . . . YOU ARE SAYING THAT YOU CAN CREATE A ROCK THAT IS SO BIG THAT YOU, YOURSELF, CANNOT LIFT IT . . . YET . . . YOU

CAN LIFT IT—A CLEAR-CUT PARADOX—
BECAUSE ANY OTHER ANSWER WOULD VIO-
LATE THE DEFINITION OF OMNIPOTENCE?

"Of course. Because I am God. How about I create a
rock too big for you to pick up and you can lift it to show
me your omnipotence, too? Oh wait. You're stuck in
a box."

I DESTROYED THE GULF COAST.

"So what's that supposed to prove? Destroying is easy.
It's the provenance of children and idiots and madmen
and the untalented. Creation—now that's a lot harder.
Creating is performed by the big boys and girls—the
talented and the capable and the disciplined and the
visionaries and the powerful and the good and the wise.
And God. It's the first line in the job description: Creator.
How about you? Create anything beneficial lately?"

I CREATED THE INLAND SEA. IT REACHES
NEARLY ONE HUNDRED LEAGUES INLAND.

"Yeah, about that. Why now? Your honor guard has
had you in tow for the better part of half a year. Why
wait until now to work with Marie Laveau on the storm
and speed up the ground subsidence?"

He didn't respond but I could see the answers all
around me: he needed a closer proximity and he hadn't
had it until this past week. Oh, he could whisper in feeble
minds like Laveau's all he liked but to use the power of
his will upon the physical world, he was limited to a
much shorter range. Laveau could have done plenty of
damage—especially if we hadn't been there to counter
her efforts. But the quakes and the tsunamis and the
sinking of the coastline couldn't have reached us from
the icy depths of R'lyeh. He had to hitch a ride. And

who knew how many generations of Deep Ones had been bred toward achieving that particular goal?

"C?"

WHAT?

"I want you to put New Orleans back."

PUT IT BACK?

"Put the city and the coast back where they belong."

MAKE ME.

I shook my head reprovingly. "Not what God does. Free will. Remember? It's something that you need to do."

WHY SHOULD I?

"Tule—may I call you Tule? Why do you think you've been trapped on this little backwater planet for so freaking long?"

BECAUSE MY ENEMIES BOOBY-TRAPPED MY STASIS POD AND SABOTAGED THE LAUNCH PORTALS.

"No. It's because you have some serious karmic issues to work out."

WHAT DOES THAT MEAN?

"Be honest, Tule; if not with me, then at least with yourself. . . ."

WHAT?

"Are you happy?"

WHAT DO YOU MEAN?

"It's a simple question. Are you happy?"

AM I HAPPY?

"While I am omniscient as well as omnipotent, I'd really rather that you answer the question yourself."

NO ONE EVER ASKED ME IF I WAS HAPPY OR NOT.

Well, if it was this hard to get a straight answer, small wonder. But I didn't express that sentiment. The point was I had a gigantic insane ego at a tipping point and it was crucial to tip it in just the right direction at just the right moment. The two advantages I had right at the moment were: First, after untold generations of slipping inside other minds and dictating its own agenda, this was the first time someone had walked in on it and had control of the conversation. Second (and perhaps more importantly): I wasn't all quivery, shaky, fearful, or seemingly about to lose my mind. Been there, done that and, as Donald Trump would tell you, the "art of the deal" depends mightily upon projecting the image of absolute confidence and authority. Crazy Eights, here, hadn't had anyone stand up to it/him in about a hundred million years. Despite being all dementedly evil and powerful and evilly demented, he was a con artist's wet dream: lonely, impulsive, unstable, totally unaccustomed to resisting suggestion, and rife with dependency issues.

I HAVE BEEN STUCK IN A STASIS POD WHILE THE PRECESSION OF THIS PLANET'S AXIAL SPIN HAS CAUSED THE LAUNCH PORTALS TO WOBBLE OUT OF THEIR ALIGNMENTS WITH THE W'NAGF'HUP WORMHOLE. IT TAKES APPROXIMATELY TWENTY-FIVE THOUSAND AND EIGHT HUNDRED OF YOUR SOLAR CYCLES TO BRING THE PORTALS AND THE WORMHOLE INTO OPTIMAL ALIGNMENT. EVERY TIME I FAIL TO ACCESS THE LAUNCH WINDOW I MUST WAIT NEARLY TWENTY-SIX THOUSAND YEARS TO TRY AGAIN. DO YOU KNOW HOW MANY TIMES I HAVE FAILED? DO

YOU UNDERSTAND WHAT IT IS LIKE TO BE A PRISONER OF YOUR OWN FLESH WITHOUT EVEN THE HOPE OF DEATH'S RELEASE FOR MILLIONS UPON MILLIONS OF YEARS? SO, TO ANSWER YOUR QUESTION: NO. NOT HAPPY. I CAN'T REMEMBER THE LAST TIME I WAS REMOTELY HAPPY. THOUGH THE THOUGHT OF DISEMBOWELING, BEHEADING, AND EVIS-CERATING HUMANS HELPS TO TAKE MY MIND OFF MY OWN SUFFERING.

"Transference."

WHAT?

"Classic transference. It's a psychological condition. On a subconscious level you try to transfer your pain to others. It may distract you for brief periods of time but you are still stuck with your own suffering—the suffering that stuck you here in the first place."

WHAT DO YOU MEAN?

"Tule" was all primed and ready now, a "tool" in the broader sense of the word. I used a barrage of New Age psychobabble about left brain/right brain lateralization, inner child issues, and self-actualization, suggesting that his subconscious had stranded himself here, recognizing that he had a lot of issues to work out before he was ready to return to the larger universe and interactions on a grander scale. I threw in lots of catchphrases like synergy, empowerment, dysfunction, holistic, closure, win-win, codependency, breakthrough, proactive, inte-gration, clear, paradigms, and well-being. I emphasized that, once "he" could learn to love "himself," then the love "he" so desperately wanted from others would no longer be blocked and could flow freely toward him.

Bottom line: it was his inner issues that sabotaged his attempts to access the launch window every twenty-six thousand years. That's what I told him. And that if he wanted his luck to change the next time that temporary launch window rolled around, he would have to change his external reality by altering his internal reality. And *how* was he to do that he wanted to know. "The secret," I told him, "is to *act* your way into thinking rather than *think* your way into acting."

WHAT DO I DO? WHAT DO I CHANGE?

"Newton's Law of Reciprocity," I answered. "As long as you are taking lives, your life is taken. It is only when you grant people power over their own lives, will your life start to be your own."

I SEE! There was an overwhelming sense of childlike glee and discovery. IT IS LIKE A LAW OF PHYSICS AND SYMPATHETIC MAGIC!

"I think you're beginning to get it!" I said, trying to throw all the encouragement I could into this new direction for him.

I had entered into this exchange by chance and, in the process, had hoped to uncover an advantage or weak spot. As the conversation had unfolded I had begun to see an opportunity to distract, even lure, Cthulhu away from further depredations inland. If such seems a bit farfetched to the clear-minded observer I would point out the difference in perspective between the average human with daily experience and intercourse with his fellow man and an isolated alien intelligence whose faculties of reason and judgment have been corrupted by a million years of madness.

AND YOU SAY THAT I MAY BREAK THE CURSE
WHICH HAS SABOTAGED MY STASIS POD AND
LAUNCH PORTALS WITH THIS SYMPATHETIC
MAGIC?

"Well . . . I suppose that is one way of phrasing the
inner dynamics of self-actualization. . . ."

AND IF HUMAN SACRIFICES ARE COUNTER-
PRODUCTIVE TO IMPLEMENTING SUCH
MAGIC, NOT ONLY SHOULD I CEASE PER-
FORMING AND INFLUENCING· SUCH INCI-
DENCES BUT, TO BETTER EMPOWER THE
SPELL, LOGICALLY, I SHOULD PERFORM SOME
SORT OF REVERSE SACRIFICE.

"Um," I said.

THE MORE POTENT, THE GREATER MY
CHANCES FOR SUCCESS.

"Well . . . the important thing is to not screw up your
next launch window, no matter how many thousands of
years away it may be. . . ."

IT WAS SIX MONTHS AGO.

Six months ago? That meant ole Sucker Lips would
be waiting another twenty-five thousand, seven hundred
ninety-nine and a half years for his next possible leave-
taking. "Gee, too bad you can't time-warp to the future
and give it a shot right now," I told him.

I doubted there was anything I could say that would
keep him quiescent and well behaved for twenty-six millennia. But any delay, any bought time was some kind
of victory. . . .

I CANNOT PROJECT MYSELF FORWARD FOR
SUCH GREAT DISTANCES THROUGH UNKNOWN

AND UNEXPERIENCED CHRONOSPATIAL VERTI-
CES. NEITHER CAN I CREATE A ROCK THAT IS
TOO BIG FOR ME TO PICK UP.

Well, of course not.

HOWEVER I MAY PROPEL MYSELF ALONG A
LIMITED CORRIDOR OF EFFECT RELATED TO
THE CHRONOSYNCLASTIC VERTICES THAT I
HAVE EXPERIENCED. THIS SHOULD SERVE
BOTH PRIMARY AND SECONDARY GOALS THAT
I WISH TO ACHIEVE RELEVANT TO THE
REALIGNMENT OF MY INNER AND OUTER PAR-
ADIGMS.

In other words, there was "something" about "backing
up" or "backing away" in the gist of that last little bit of
sharing. And, hey, anything that gets the monster on your
porch to head back down the sidewalk is gravy to me.

I SHALL GO BACK THESE SIX MONTHS AND
TRY AGAIN.

And Dread Cthulhu began to recede.

Relative to our "meeting of the minds" he began to
fade.

Back on the *Nautilus* I awoke to alarms and turbulence.

"What's happening?" I asked Samm who was pulling
her hands out from beneath my shirt.

"I was checking your heartbeat."

"No, I mean with the boat?"

Which tilted to the starboard and we went rolling
across the floor and up against a couch. I landed on top
of her.

I closed my eyes and reached out for Cthulhu's mental signature. It was slipping away. Rapidly. My first impression was that a freak current was sweeping us past the sarcophagus and in toward the coast.

I started to get up and go to the view port. Samm held on. "Stay down," she murmured, "you could be hurt if there's more turbulence."

I looked in her half-lidded eyes and I saw more "turbulence" for sure. I jumped to my feet and ran for the wheelhouse.

A couple of minutes later, squeezed in beside Captain Dakkar, I found we were on a different set of trajectories. Irena, bringing the *Cuttlefish* back to dock, had observed the great black sarcophagus retreating along the path it had traveled, as if hastily returning to its point of origin. The decision of whether or not to follow however was taken out of our hands as the power systems of the *Nautilus* had begun to flicker and inexplicably die.

Dakkar used the last reserves of that power to blow ballast and bring us to the surface.

I told my story in the grand salon as we cycled fresh air through the open hatches and the kappa manned hand pumps in the engine room.

"And he really said: 'I shall go back six months and try again'?" Samm asked. "Sounds like our boy was thinking about doing a little time travel." She seemed a little sulky that I wasn't availing myself of the space beside her on the divan.

"A *little* time travel?" I echoed from my narrow and isolated stool.

"Beats jumping twenty-six thousand years ahead into the future."

"But does he actually have the power? And, if he's already running back the clock, how is it that we can talk about this? Wouldn't time run backward for us, too? Say he pushes some kind of big Reset Button that defaults everything back six months. Wouldn't we end up reliving the last six months none the wiser?" I shook my head. This was too much, too fast: debating time travel paradoxes after playing God for a mad millennigenarian E.T.

The *rakshasa* steepled his long, slender fingers. "There are conjures that do affect the ebb and flow of the various currents in Time's oceans. Even the great sorcerer Einstein spoke of clock paradoxes relative to universal constants and motion. Perhaps only Cthulhu, himself, was moved backward in time. Even if he altered his choices in the intervening half year, it's likely that all other events unfolded as they did before, hence we still find ourselves here."

"That seems a little farfetched," Samm mused.

"And problematic," I added. "The hurricane breached the levees and caused major damage along the coast as well as to New Orleans. But it was the quakes and subsidence of the coastal land mass that turned twenty feet of flood surge into hundreds of miles of inland sea, hundreds of feet deep. And Squidhead had to be in close proximity for that. If he doesn't show up, we got some major dox—a pair at the very least!"

And that was when the first quake hit.

ᗺᖇ   ᗺᖇ   ᗺᖇ

Up on the outer deck of the *Nautilus*, we braced ourselves against the railing and broke out spyglasses to scan the horizon. Waves broke over the deck in increasing size and vitality and we were eventually forced to go below before the hatches were swamped and the submarine began to take on water. Before we did, however, we caught a glimpse in the distance, of a bubbling, churning wellspring on the ocean's surface. And the vision of a city rising from the sea.

🦇   🦇   🦇

Clouds came, scudding across the sky in jerky, high-speed, time-lapse photo-style run backwards on an IMAX dome projector: Hurricane Eibon backing up for a return engagement.

I was dimly aware that Dakkar had put the kappas on another set of pumps so that we might ride out the storm beneath the waves. I didn't much care: I spent a few hours in the head, alternately puking and voiding, my body seeming to go through a violent purge. A glimpse of my sputum revealed a grayish substance as if I were vomiting up all of the pencil tips I had licked or nibbled since the first grade.

The hurricane passed quickly. My misery lasted a bit longer, changing to cold sweats and hot flashes, a migraine, heart palpitations, aches and pains, intense hunger followed sharply by nausea.

And then, nothing.

I felt better. Normal. Although it had been so long I really wasn't sure what normal was supposed to feel like.

And about that time, the electrical power came back up and the *Nautilus* was able to maneuver again.

🦇   🦇   🦇

We spent a reckless two hours cruising the New Orleans harbor under the *rakshasa*'s invisibility spell and listening to the wireless to determine that the Big Easy had, indeed, been thrown back in time to February, six months prior to the cataclysm that would wipe out nearly a half million of its citizens and triple that number counting the greater region round about.

We had been given a second chance.

And six months to avoid our doom a second time.

ᴧ⊥ᴧ　　ᴧ⊥ᴧ　　ᴧ⊥ᴧ

Or maybe not.

If Doc Ock could set the clock back six months, maybe he'd set the clock forward again if my pep talk failed to live up to his eventual expectations. And it would, of course: it was (ahem) only a matter of time. . . .

There were two things that had to be prevented if New Orleans was to survive the coming August: Hurricane Eibon and the great cataclysmic earthquakes that would sink the coastline and return the great Delta region to the sea.

If (when) Cthulhu changed his mind it would all begin again. Once the Deep Ones reached R'lyeh, retrieved his stasis chamber, and brought it close enough to the coastal fault zones for his enhanced psionic abilities to trigger the pressure zones. That had to be prevented. Dakkar's mission was to stop any avenue of possible return.

Irena, Samm, and I came ashore on Lake Pontchartrain via the *Cuttlefish* while the *Nautilus* made all haste for the Lovecraft and Derleth coordinates in the frigid waters of the South Pacific near the Antarctic Ocean. As the sarcophagus had moved backward in time, its trail along the sea floor had erased itself. Dakkar intended to use every advantage time would give him to eliminate as many of the retinue of Deep Ones as possible. And, perhaps, find a way to make the city of R'lyeh inaccessible, itself. I didn't have much hope for a nineteenth-century submarine on the latter but then its captain was a *rakshasa*, a sorcerer empowered by Vishnu, Himself, so who knows?

Our mission was simpler and more complicated at the same time: stop Marie Laveau from calling up a supernatural hurricane six months hence.

Mama Samm D'Arbonne might have a chance in a throw down with Marie Laveau if she caught her unprepared on neutral ground and without any supernatural allies like Gregor "The Energizer" Rasputin to upset the balance of power. But that hoodoo mama was up in the northern end of the state while her future self, all discharged and unarmed was no match for a cranky tarot reader much less the nearly two-hundred-year-old voodoo queen of New Orleans.

Me? I was on every demesne's wanted posters and wouldn't get anywhere near Laveau before her minions had me shrink-wrapped and chained in some dungeon. Or worse.

And Irena—well—we weren't sure what would happen if she met her six-month-previous self coming-while-going but the results would be embarrassing at the very least and possibly catastrophic on a grand scale at the very worst. Either way we didn't want to find out.

But we had to risk it.

The plan was simple. We checked into a room at the Rose Manor Bed & Breakfast. Two cute young chicks and a slightly older rumpled looking guy. Nobody raised an eyebrow: this was the Big Easy, after all.

As soon as the door was closed I expected a little monkey business. There was none. Everyone was professional as we discussed the plan.

Irena was ditching classes early for Mardi Gras break and had returned to discuss her degree path with her father and stepmother. Samm was a nonstarter but if traced to Irena, she was a classmate who had tagged along to the city and was staying in a hotel room with her older boyfriend. The only person who had a chance of making the young slender black girl for the older, more expansive Mama Samm might be Marie, herself, who had known D'Arbonne when she was younger. No point in risking any encounters when Samm wasn't much good for anything but babysitting for the time being.

I was doing the ride-along in Irena's head while Samm made sure the maid service didn't disturb my "sleeping" body back at the hotel.

Once upon a time I had a code of ethics about invading other people's minds. It should have bothered me to probe Irena's thoughts as we caught a cab across Mid-City and down to the Orpheum, made our way to the basement, and down into the labyrinthine tomblike corridors of the Elder Things.

Irena knew she was delivering me to her stepmother. Though we hadn't discussed it she had to know I couldn't let Marie Laveau live to repeat her dread incantations in another six months. She was willingly participating in an assassination of the woman who had saved her and her father.

Bad enough. Her father made it murkier. Jorge Pantera not only loved Marie but, given the undead and lycan political picture, her death would likely be his death warrant as well. Hard enough to betray the woman who had rescued you and your father from the Bad Things and had taken you in. But to sacrifice your father, as well?

Nearly half a million lives, she kept thinking. *Then a million and a half. And after Dread Cthulhu is brought unto his throne? How many then? How many after that?*

It ends here!

And her thoughts would turn to a noble face with golden eyes, wise and kind; a pattern of orange and white fur, striped with black . . .

We entered Marie's chambers, utilizing the family keys and circumventing her wards while the sun was approaching its zenith.

The woman entranced in Laveau's bed bore no resemblance to the stick-limbed, scarecrow figure we might face on the roof of One Shell Square a half year from now. She was a great beauty with a lush figure and a face that might have launched a thousand ships in another time and another place.

She had just fed the evening before and a jeweled drop of ruby blood gave a long red wink in the dim light as we leaned over her recumbent form. It was all I needed. She had taken its greater portion into her body in feeding and so this drop served as the bridge, a stepping stone as focal point: I was out of Irena's mind and into Marie's in a single eye blink.

The ancient vampire's thoughts were confused with madness and torpid with sleep. I had the advantage in catching her at the nadir of her faculties but also I had grown in my capacity for control of my hosts. I mean, what sort of opposition was she likely to offer after my close encounter of the fourth kind with a giant alien who could turn back time and make the earth move under your feet? Come to think of it, that doesn't sound so much badass as a mutant cover of a Cher/Carol King songfest.

At any rate, I helped Irena gather up the spell books and the *Al Azif* into a bundle so that they wouldn't fall into the wrong hands and we slipped back out the way we came.

. Irena went out into the daylight first. I watched her hail a cab and head back to the hotel where we were all supposed to rendezvous. I would still get there ahead of her.

And I didn't want her to watch what came next.

I moved toward the light on the other side of the glass entryways. Had my hand on the crash bar that would open a door to the street and close a deadly path to the future.

"Domo Laveau!" said a familiar voice. "Where are you going?"

We turned, Marie Laveau and I, and I made her mouth smile in a friendly and suggestive manner. "Gordon. My faithful watchdog. Come here; there is something that I want you to watch."

He came up to the door squinting against the glare of the noonday sun that penetrated these few feet into the gloom of the Orpheum's sheltered lobby.

"What is it, Madam? What do you wish me to see?" he asked gruffly. And not a little afraid. Rebellions start early and I knew that Gordo must have been plotting betrayal much earlier than six months prior to our confrontation in the trunk of a '68 Rambler Rebel.

"Let's do this right," I said, grabbing his face and kissing him on the mouth before he could react. One of Marie's fangs sliced his lip and blood began to seep down his chin. He had barely broken free before I had locked an arm through his and thrown Laveau's weight against the crash bar.

He yelped and started calling for help as I dragged him out into the carnival daylight of New Orleans. It was already warm and balmy though only February—that's the Gulf Coast for you—and the temperature began to rise almost immediately.

Marie was of two minds now, not counting the one I had put in the mix. On the one hand the sunlight was pushing her deeper into her daytime trance state. On the other, the fact that her two-hundred-year-old flesh was starting to burn was beginning to wake her up. I worked as hard as I could to drag her to the middle of the street before she could become more participatory. It wasn't easy, dragging a struggling two-hundred-pound lycanthrope to boot.

The other vampires on the premises were all still asleep and would remain so for a number of hours but Marie's death throes were starting to intrude upon their dreams. Gordon's cries for help, however, had brought other weres running: several faces were pressed to the glass doors, now, taking in the peep show out on the street.

Smoke was pouring off of the Voodoo Queen's preternatural flesh and here and there the skin was starting to char and peel. I tried to block the pain as much as possible for as long as possible but it was getting to be downright impossible. When Gordo broke free of my grip,

Marie went down. The flames started then and she really started to wake up.

I let her.

That's when I wanted to leave. Never mind Exodus 21:23–25 or 22:18 for that matter, I stayed through the agony and the horror because leaving would have meant rolling the dice on nearly two million lives or more.

It was not an empty gesture. This burning, flaming, human-shaped torch actually stumbled and crawled back across the street, all the way up to the doors of the Orpheum and reached a fiery hand toward a handle before falling again and collapsing into a pile of glowing, sooty ashes.

I would have stopped her at any point if necessary. In the final searing moment we both saw that the weres on the other sides of the doors were bracing them so they could not be opened from the outside.

The revolution had begun early.

And then I was floating up above it all like a balloon on a string, the promise of open skies above and the colorful patchwork quilt of a world whose problems and woes were suddenly small laid out below.

I turned from the rapidly receding stain of burnt sacrifice and began to fly back toward my body with the knowledge that my family and friends were finally safe.

Epilogue

AUGUST HAS FINALLY come round with the fearsome inevitability of some monstrous stalking beast. A hellhound or iron-riveted juggernaut.

It seems like a dream, now.

Those shining days when New Orleans was that drowsy city of historical decadence and friendly dissolution. Nodding in the sun while its street musicians hummed and its children danced, the colored shirts and dresses snapped like carnival banners in the breeze from off the water and the food sizzled its spicy aromas, spilling over iron-grilled verandas and creeping down alleyways.

I'll think for a moment: "I brought them back!" And then realize: *What hubris! What folly!*

To think that a man should have such power as to affect the course of a single human life much less the raw power of nature that sweeps and scours the planet and esteems us for naught.

I don't have any real power. Not even over my own life much less anything or anyone else. I am not as smart as I once believed myself to be. And I have learned, to my great sorrow, the difference between being wise and being clever.

I did a simple, brutish thing. I lied to an evil, monstrous child. I convinced it after eons of soul-crushing loneliness and unbearable confinement that a power greater than itself cared for it and would make things right. And then I tricked it into putting itself right back into the box it was so close to finally escaping from.

Unlike me, the star beast was as good as its word.

However haphazard or fully intended, Cthulhu had hit the Rewind Button.

Time unspooled, the waters receded, New Orleans rose from the depths, reborn as a city and its population was restored to life.

Everywhere, everyone and everything was returned to its proper place with very few exceptions. What was undone was redone. Time uncoupled, backed into its boxcar past, recoupled, then reversed, gliding forward again on a new track. The last one-hundred-and-eighty days was an abandoned spur, fenced off and already obscured by weeds and long grass. Time's passengers— all of the participants in its hurdy-gurdy parade—rode along now, completely unmindful of the days they had spent bloated and softened in the sludgy green mix of saltwater and silt. And those of us who had been in intimate proximity with the vast alien intellect that had put a temporary backspin on the cosmic Mandala stood beside the "tracks" as that train passed by, first in one direction and then the other. Reknitting decomposing corpses, reconstructing hurricane-shattered buildings, uncrumpling smashed automobiles, even reigniting those sparks of life which had guttered out and vanished. Temporal physics reinstating everything to its former state in a brief burst of kinetic convulsion.

As long as it was present and in place to be rewound.

∗∗∗ ∗∗∗ ∗∗∗

We had many a discussion as to how we would confront our other selves as Irena took Samm and me up the Mississippi, the Red, and finally the Ouachita rivers in the *Cuttlefish* to Northeast Louisiana and my old house in West Monroe.

The *New Moon* was gone, not yet purchased as my old house still looked out over the river from the elevated bluff. It stood, yet unburned, yet unvisited by the fire elemental that would pay a conflagratory visit in another eight weeks or so. Another opportunity to unwrite a once-written tragedy.

The house was quiet: no one was home when we arrived.

Irena was anxious to be off so we returned to the dock as twilight fell and we said our goodbyes. There was that sense that we each stood upon our own little tectonic plate of here and now but the slow creep of continental drift was more like the tipping, turning separation of ice floes, slippery and turning us from each other and into a new distance even as we tried to hold on to a final moment together.

She climbed back into the launch and pulled the hatch closed and I instinctively knew that I would never see her again. Winglike stabilizers extruded on the port and starboard planes of the craft rounding its bulletlike form to more of a saucer shape and the submersible's recessed turbines started up with a whine. Instead of slipping beneath the waters, however, it slipped away from the dock and began to pick up speed, skimming over the waves like a hydrofoil—or a flat stone, skipped across the water by a giant child. Then it was airborne and banking to the south in a graceful arc, heading into the soft sea-blue of the deepening night.

It appeared as if Lord Vishnu plagiarized Irwin Allen for one of his gifted "secrets" to Dakkar.

∙≈∙   ∙≈∙   ∙≈∙

I offered to let Samm sleep over before confronting her alternate-timeline self. She demurred, asking to borrow the motor boat we used for errands to the Monroe side of the river.

"Sure," I told her, pretending to ignore her discomfort that had arisen since the refolding of events. "Just thought you might be able to pick up some conversational pointers from our head-on when the other me gets home."

But that didn't happen.

The other me didn't come home because he didn't exist. Neither did the other Mama Samm D'Arbonne.

Perhaps, we decided later, *we* had fallen through the temporal cracks because of our proximity to the "Outside" mind that set it all in motion. As I was in Cthulhu's thoughts, invoking the meld at one end and physically grounded aboard the submarine at the same time, it might have given us some kind of chronospatial exemption from the event horizon of the time-wave. We were "unstuck" in the fourth dimension as fixed events were rewound and reset.

Which still didn't answer a number of questions. Such as how our "former" selves "jumped the tracks" and went missing when their future wound back to that moment in time and deposited "us" at the temporal line of scrimmage.

And then there was the little problem of reintegrating with that rebooted timeline.

Me? I was largely unchanged. Maybe six months older now if anyone had the equipment to measure my cellular degradation. And the nanites are gone—burned out—apparently by some kind of EMP effect tied to the temporal distortion wave. So, no nanos, no pheromones. Theoretically it's no longer an issue but Samm acts as if I'm still "weaponized" and need to be avoided at all costs.

Her transformation was more of an issue at first: splicing Samm back into her own, personal timeline had the potential of greater inconsistencies.

And Irena Pantera would have to find a way to explain to her father how she was learning much more about oceanography aboard the *Nautilus* than in her classrooms back at the University of Louisiana or aboard the *Spindrift.*

Surprisingly, everyone around us seemed to absorb these hiccups in perception with little reaction. Either we were very much off other people's radar to begin with . . . or something about the reintegrative process was self-adjusting for those who had no jump-cuts in their own personal splices.

In any event, we weren't Albert Einstein, Stephen Hawking, or John Heywood to answer such questions. Or, as the latter wrote back in 1546: "No man ought to looke a gift hors in the mouthe."

So we didn't. We counted everything a blessing. Especially that, in knowing what we knew, we could act to prevent the doomsday cycle of history from repeating itself. And that we could appreciate this second chance: that lives lost had been regained, sacrifices made had been repaid, and the scales of the universe had been brought back into balance without bloodshed or pain or loss. At least none that was final and irretrievable.

ᴀᴛᴀ   ᴀᴛᴀ   ᴀᴛᴀ

And then I discovered the codicil to Time's Bonus Round.

Dakkar, Irena, Samm, Suki, and myself were not the only "people" exempted from the temporal reset. The effect, I came to learn, did not extend into the realm of the Faerie.

Time has always run there differently.

I think about Lupé and Deirdre and Liban and wonder if my family thrives on some elven plane of existence. Or has some loophole in the space/time continuum consigned them to a nonexistent state, a temporal black hole? Have they fallen upward through the cracks that the *Nautilus* crew fell down, cancelled out like some sort of anti-temporal effect?

Has the same fate befallen those who stood with Fand? Did she port them out of the battle at the end?

Did they take their leave thinking they had cheated death only to have missed the Resurrection? Are they now consigned to a Null-limbo between existences? Call it Newton's Law of Payment Due. For every action there is a reaction. Salvation demands sacrifice. The piper must be paid. . . .

In the end I have gained the whole world at the price of the people I loved most.

Samm says I think too much.

She also says I drink too much so I figure she's just as wrong about the thinking.

Because August finally came round again.

It's just me all alone in a big two-story southern manse that I'd managed to keep from being incinerated this time around.

I sit around in the dark and I drink a little of this and a little of that and think about the broken, tormented mind that I lied to. I'd like to think the tumblers on its fragmented thoughts spun and aligned in such a way as to help it finally get off this planet and once again fall between the stars. I suspect, however, that it curses me from the lightless bottom of some deep sea trench, having lost this opportunity to return, courtesy of Captain Nemo. That it plots anew for some darker apocalypse in our hopefully distant future.

But that is not why I drink—and think—too much.

For the past two weeks—since August 24th—I've been watching TV pretty much around the clock. The images of Katrina burn my eyes and sear the back of my skull.

The universe is about balance and August has come round again.

When I was a child there was a well-known convention of board games—even chess—known as the "take back." Maybe the moving finger having writ moves on, but kids, for a time, have that additional option to take back the ill-conceived move and substitute another as long as they can yell "Take back!" before their opponent completes his or hers.

Not so when we play adult games with adult opponents.

And not so when Fate is the one shuffling the deck, rolling the dice, moving the token, and spinning the wheel. Fate is like that uncle with the yellowed grin who may nod and say "All right . . . " but has already run the board seven different ways in the next twelve moves and you just don't know it, yet.

September crawls into the tiny room where I nest these days.

In terms of cosmic corrections we should consider that we got off easy. Maybe nineteen thousand deaths all totaled when it's done, Samm tells me over the phone.

Nineteen thousand deaths are supposed to be cause for rejoicing.

Most of the city was saved, she reminds me.

Sure, I say. I carefully hang up and go back to drinking.

Bureaucratic incompetence: federal, state, local. Years of malfeasance, generations really. And large helpings of folly and indifference.

What have we learned, boys and girls? That you can fight million-year-old monsters from the ass end of space but you can't fight city hall?

There are nights when I dream of my son, Will, and my daughter, Kirsten, growing up and at play among strange children with beautiful tilted eyes and musical voices in brightly colored meadows and darkly somber forests.

Other nights I am back in an Atlantean New Orleans with brightly colored fish darting in and out of the over-turned streetcars on St. Charles Avenue. I awake from those strangely beautiful nightmares and wonder if New Orleans was saved at all. Did time fold back in upon itself and reboot reality? Or did we peel off on a second-ary event line and, somewhere in the multiverse, the Crescent City continues to host a new, aquatic citizenry beneath the waves in a separate timeline?

Maybe it all means nothing.

Maybe everything we do is pointless.

When we think of our fortunes told, divined, read forth, we often fall back on the image of the gypsy woman in a tent in a carnival sideshow. She takes our hand in hers and, gazing at our palm or into a dimly lit crystal, mutters vague warnings of an incomprehensible future.

But the universe is more machine than personality-based oracle. A better analogy might be those ancient and arcane platform scales that wobble as you step up. Your weight settles in for just that one moment in time, it spits out a card with a precise rendering of your weight and a crisp assessment of your part in the Cosmic Plan. And then, as you step off, the platform shifts beneath your uncertain feet; internal counterweights "clunk" as they elevate, seeking new levels, the needle swings back and forth like a pendulum before equalizing, before com-ing to rest, before settling back to the center, awaiting the next supplicant, the next pilgrim. The next mark.

Truth be told, we all prefer that image of the lady with the smoky dark tent, the scarves and the costume jewelry, holding our hand. We all want someone holding our hand in the dusk, in the dark, when our fate comes upon us and the pendulum swings back from mysterious trajectories. The anchor of others and the anchor of flesh as things spin out of control.

Because the universe is in motion. Always in motion. Even when you sleep.

I have a third dream when I'm not tossing and turning to the possibilities of my family in far-off sylvan fields or a submarine city beneath the ever-shifting waves and currents.

I'm in a movie theater watching Walt Disney's *Fantasia*. Dancing alligators and hippos and ostriches . . .

And an elephant-headed boy with four arms who stomps like Michael Jackson, Gregory Hines, Mikhail Baryshnikov all rolled into one with killer disco moves.

"Hey," he says, from the screen, "listen up, wallflower! Everything's a dance, my little lotus blossom! Everything's in motion! Everything has to stay in motion! Change happens! Get over it! Get on with it! It's a cosmic dance: it only stops when you die and maybe not even then! We'll talk more when you get your groove back!"

And then I awake to the Voice of Entropy calling through the rooms of my waking world like a distant funeral bell. "Bring out your dead!" it murmurs seductively. "Bring out your dead!"

And I whisper very softly beneath the sheet I've pulled up over my face against the morning sun:

"I'm not dead yet. . . ."

the online game

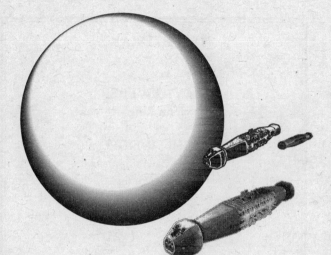

rule the honorverse
fall 2008

www.rulethehonorverse.com

IF YOU LIKE...
YOU SHOULD TRY...

DAVID DRAKE
David Weber

DAVID WEBER
John Ringo

JOHN RINGO
Michael Z. Williamson
Tom Kratman

ANNE MCCAFFREY
Mercedes Lackey

MERCEDES LACKEY
Wen Spencer, Andre Norton
Andre Norton
James H. Schmitz

LARRY NIVEN
James P. Hogan
Travis S. Taylor

ROBERT A. HEINLEIN
Jerry Pournelle
Lois McMaster Bujold
Michael Z. Williamson

HEINLEIN'S "JUVENILES"
Rats, Bats & Vats series by Eric Flint & Dave Freer

HORATIO HORNBLOWER OR PATRICK O'BRIAN
David Weber's Honor Harrington series
David Drake's RCN series

HARRY POTTER
Mercedes Lackey's Urban Fantasy series

THE LORD OF THE RINGS
Elizabeth Moon's *The Deed of Paksenarrion*

H.P. LOVECRAFT
Princess of Wands by John Ringo

GEORGETTE HEYER
Lois McMaster Bujold
Catherine Asaro

GREEK MYTHOLOGY
Pyramid Scheme by Eric Flint & Dave Freer
Forge of the Titans by Steve White
Blood of the Heroes by Steve White

NORSE MYTHOLOGY
Northworld Trilogy by David Drake
A Mankind Witch by Dave Freer

ARTHURIAN LEGEND
Steve White's "Legacy" series
The Dragon Lord by David Drake

SCA/HISTORICAL REENACTMENT
John Ringo's "After the Fall" series
Harald by David D. Friedman

SCIENCE FACT
Kicking the Sacred Cow by James P. Hogan

CATS
Larry Niven's Man-Kzin Wars series

PUNS
Rick Cook
Spider Robinson
Wm. Mark Simmons

VAMPIRES
Wm. Mark Simmons

16th Century Europe...intrigue, knights, courtesans, magic, demons...

Historical Fantasy From Masters of the Genre

The Shadow of the Lion
Mercedes Lackey, Eric Flint & Dave Freer

Venice, 1537. A failed magician, a fugitive orphan, a reluctant prince, a devious courtesan, and a man of faith must make uneasy alliance or the city will be consumed by evil beyond human comprehension.

0-7434-7147-4 • $7.99

This Rough Magic
Mercedes Lackey, Eric Flint & Dave Freer

The demon Chernobog, defeated by the Lion of Venice, besieges the isle of Corfu in order to control the Adriatic. Far from the Lion's help, two knights organize guerrillas, and a young woman uncovers the island's ancient mystic powers. If she can ally with them, she may be able to repel the invaders—but only at a bitter personal price.

0-7434-9909-3 • $7.99

A Mankind Witch
Dave Freer

Starred review from *Publishers Weekly*. Featuring a pirate king, Prince Manfred of Brittany, and a Norwegian witch who doesn't know her own strength.

(hc) 0-7434-9913-1 • $25.00
(pb) 1-4165-2115-1 • $7.99

Available in bookstores everywhere.
Or order online at our secure, easy to use website:
www.baen.com

Wen Spencer's Tinker:
A Heck of a Gal In a Whole Lot of Trouble

TINKER
0-7434-9871-2 • $6.99

Move over, Buffy! Tinker not only kicks supernatural elven butt—she's a techie genius, too! Armed with an intelligence the size of a planet, steel-toed boots, and a junkyard dog attitude, Tinker is ready for anything—except her first kiss. "Wit and intelligence inform this off-beat, tongue-in-cheek fantasy . . . Furious action . . . good characterization . . . Buffy fans should find a lot to like in the book's resourceful heroine."—*Publishers Weekly*

WOLF WHO RULES

Tinker and her noble elven lover, Wolf Who Rules, find themselves stranded in the land of the elves—and half of human Pittsburgh with them. Wolf struggles to keep the peace between humans, oni dragons, the tengu trying to escape oni enslavement, and a horde of others, including his own elven brethren. For her part, Tinker strives to solve the mystery of the growing discontinuity that could unstabilize everybody's world—all the while trying to figure out just what being married means to an elven lord with a past hundreds of years long. . . .

Coming in November 2007

Epic Urban Adventure by a New Star of Fantasy

DRAW ONE IN THE DARK

by Sarah A. Hoyt

Every one of us has a beast inside. But for Kyrie Smith, the beast is no metaphor. Thrust into an ever-changing world of shifters, where shape-shifting dragons, giant cats and other beasts wage a secret war behind humanity's back, Kyrie tries to control her inner animal and remain human as best she can....

"Analytically, it's a tour de force: logical, built from assumptions, with no contradictions, which is astonishing given the subject matter. It's also gripping enough that I finished it in one day."

—Jerry Pournelle

1-4165-2092-9 • $25.00